Suddenly he stepped back until he was behind her. His hold moved to her shoulders. Emma seemed unable to move. And then she felt his breath on the side of her face, the lightest kiss on her ear. His tongue darted into the tight shell, and his teeth gently nibbled on her earlobe.

And now Emma knew. That wicked tickling caress belonged to only one man. A man who knew exactly what squirming delight it gave her. She knew but she was frozen . . . frozen in this moment, in this enchanted garden. This was not happening in the real world. In the real world she would not want it. She didn't understand how it could be happening but she didn't need to understand it. Whatever was happening belonged on some other plane where all was paradox and paradox made sense.

His mouth moved from her ear to her neck. His tongue drew a moist, tantalizing line from the little knob at the top of her spine up the shallow groove to the hollow at the base of her skull.

Emma shivered with delight.

He slid his hands around her body. . . .

A Valentine Wedding

JANE FEATHER

Bantam Books

NEW YORK   TORONTO   LONDON   SYDNEY   AUCKLAND

A Valentine Wedding

A Bantam Book / January 1999

ISBN 0-553-57893-6

Published simultaneously in the United States and Canada

Bantam Books are published by Bantam Books, a division of Random House, Inc. Its trademark, consisting of the words "Bantam
Books" and the portrayal of a rooster, is Registered in U.S. Patent
and Trademark Office and in other countries. Marca Registrada.
Bantam Books, 1540 Broadway, New York, New York 10036.

PRINTED IN THE UNITED STATES OF AMERICA
OPM   10 9 8 7 6 5 4 3 2 1

A Valentine Wedding

Prologue

&

"They're gaining on us, Ned." The speaker swiveled in his saddle, one hand resting on his mount's crupper as he stared across the darkening landscape behind them. He could see faintly the rising dust of a headlong pursuit. He cast a despairing glance at his companion. Edward Beaumont, fifth earl of Grantley, was leaning heavily over his horse's withers, and his back was wet with blood.

"I know it." The words were a mere thread, tailing off in a gasp of pain as Ned dragged air into his shattered lungs. Blood bubbled from his lips. "I can't outrun them, Hugh. You must go on and leave me here."

"No, I will not." Hugh Melton leaned over and seized his companion's rein, urging the horse onward. "I'll not leave you to those Portuguese savages. We'll be in Lisbon by dawn. Come *on*, Ned!"

"No." The flat negative had more force than anything Ned had said since he'd taken the Portuguese sniper's bullet to his back an hour earlier. With his last strength, he hauled back on the reins. His horse whinnied and pranced, confused by the contradictory signals he was receiving. "Damn it, Hugh, you must go on . . . save yourself." He struggled for a minute, fingers scrabbling inside his jacket. "There's more at stake than you know."

Hugh was silent. He had guessed as much . . . had suspected for many months during this Portuguese campaign under Wellington's command, that his friend played a more devious role than his simple title of aide-de-camp to the duke would imply. And he'd guessed that this supposed jaunt to Lisbon from the lines before Torres Vedras had more than a few days of well-earned leave as its purpose.

"Here." Ned pulled out two thin packets. Blood smeared the protective covering of oiled parchment that enclosed their contents. He swayed violently in the saddle as he leaned over, pushing the packets at Hugh. "Get these on the first ship out of Lisbon."

"What are they?" But even as he asked the question, Hugh understood that Ned would not give him a straight answer.

"Send this one to Horseguards . . . Charles Lester." Ned struggled for the breath to speak as he indicated one of the packets. "I haven't written addresses . . . too risky. Do it when you get to Lisbon and make sure it goes on the first troopship!"

Hugh took the parchment and thrust it inside the breast of his tunic.

"This one is for my sister, Lady Emma Beaumont, at Grantley Manor in Hampshire," Ned gasped, holding out the second packet. "For God's sake, Hugh, *go*. The one for Horseguards cannot fall into their hands."

The wounded man slumped sideways in his saddle; the reins slid through his fingers. Only his feet in the stirrups seemed to hold him in place.

"God's grace!" Hugh reined in both horses before Ned could fall to the ground.

"Help me down," Ned gasped. "I can hold my seat no longer . . . for God's sake, man, quickly. They'll stop for me and give you a few moments' grace. You can outride them." A spark of desperation for a moment enlivened golden brown eyes that were growing dimmer by the minute.

Hugh swung off his horse. He caught his friend as he slipped from the saddle into Hugh's arms. Hugh laid him down on the hard, summer-parched ground that still held the day's heat. He stood looking helplessly down at the man whose blood was seeping inexorably into the earth. And then he heard the sound of hoofbeats, carrying on the still evening air, pounding the dirt.

Ned's eyelids flickered. "For pity's sake, Hugh. Don't let me die in vain."

Hugh hesitated no longer. He remounted with an agile spring and kicked his mount into a gallop. He would not, *could* not, think of his friend lying in the dirt waiting for the attentions of those who had been chasing them since early afternoon. If they were after what Hugh Melton now carried, they would not find it. By dawn it would be in Lisbon, on the first troopship bound for England.

The four horsemen reined in their plunging horses as they came up with the inert body on the ground, the patient steed cropping at a low bush. One of them, whose lavish silver braid and epaulets denoted his rank, flung himself from his horse with an oath. He bent over Ned.

"He lives yet," he said grimly, his hands searching roughly, tearing at the blood-soaked garments, rolling the man over onto his belly heedless of his wounds. He swore vigorously as his search turned up nothing. "He hasn't got it. Two of you go after the other one. Pedro and I will work on this one. For as long as he lives, he has a tongue."

Ned heard the words as from a great distance. A strange little smile quirked his lips as they yanked him over onto his back. He looked up at the swarthy face hanging over him. Hard black eyes, a cruel mouth beneath a thick waxed mustache.

"My apologies, Colonel," he murmured in Portuguese. "I may have a tongue, but it's not at your disposal." He closed his eyes, the smile still on his lips. He saw now a different face filling his internal vision. Eyes as golden as his own, a wide smiling mouth. "Em," he said, and died.

Chapter One

"It's outrageous! *Insufferable!* I absolutely will not tolerate it." Emma Beaumont tore at the lace-edged handkerchief between her hands as she paced the elegant salon. The flounced hem of her gown of dove gray crepe swung with every step.

"Oh, Emma, dearest, you cannot talk so," declared a middle-aged lady in a round gown of dark silk. The lappets of her cap trembled against her cheek as she shook her head decisively.

"Oh, can I not, Maria?" exclaimed the infuriated Lady Emma. "Mr. Critchley, something must be done about this. I *insist* upon it. I cannot imagine what Ned can have been thinking."

An embarrassed silence followed her declaration. Mr. Critchley coughed behind his hand and rustled his lawyer's papers. The middle-aged lady plied her fan vigorously. An elderly couple seated side by side on a sofa with guilded scroll ends stared into space.

The man thumped his cane on the Aubusson carpet with monotonous thuds, while his spouse pursed her lips and gave a sour little nod, as if vindicated in some way.

"Emma . . . Emma!" a voice drawled from the far side of the room. "You're putting everyone to the blush." Alasdair Chase was leaning against the wall of bookshelves, hands thrust deep into the pockets of his buckskin britches. His mud-splashed topboots gave evidence of a day's hunting. There was a wicked glimmer in his green eyes, a sardonic quirk to his mouth.

Emma spun around on the speaker. "All but you, Alasdair, I daresay," she said with the same bitter fury as before. "Just what arguments did you use with Ned to get him to agree to this . . . this intolerable *insult*?"

The tapping of the cane grew more pronounced; the elderly gentleman coughed vigorously against his hand.

"Emma!" moaned Maria from behind her fan. "Only think what you're saying."

"Yes, indeed, Lady Emma . . . only consider," murmured the distressed lawyer.

Emma flushed and pressed her palms to her cheeks. "I did not mean . . ."

"If you must rail at me, Emma, then do so in private." Alasdair pushed himself away from the wall and crossed the room toward her. He moved with a lithe step; his slender body was supple as a rapier, giving the impression of sinew and speed rather than muscular power. A hand cupped her elbow. "Come," he said in soft command, and drew her toward a door in the far wall.

Emma went with him without protest. Her color

was still high, her fingers still ripped at the now ragged handkerchief, but she was in control of herself
again, aware once more of her audience and the impropriety of her words.

Alasdair closed the door behind them. They were in
a small music room containing a handsome pianoforte and a gilded harp. He went to the piano, raised
the cover, and played a scale, a vibrant ripple of notes
that filled the small chamber.

Emma walked to the window. The winter afternoon
was drawing in, the stark leafless trees bending
against a sharp northeasterly wind coming off the Solent.

The notes faded and she heard the soft thud as the
lid of the piano was replaced. She turned around.
Alasdair stood with his back to the instrument, his
hands resting on the smooth cherrywood cover behind him.

"So . . ." he invited with a lifted eyebrow. "Between ourselves, you may say what you please. I shall
not take offence."

"It would ill become you to do so," Emma retorted.
"Your hand is in this, Alasdair. Do you think I don't
know how you could manipulate Ned when you
chose?"

A muscle twitched in Alasdair's lean cheek and his
eyes narrowed imperceptibly. "If you think that, you
didn't know your brother as well as we all believed,"
he said, without expression.

"If this was not your doing, then whose was it?"
she cried. "I cannot believe Ned, of his own free will,
would serve me such a trick."

Alasdair shrugged. "Why do you believe it to be a
trick, Emma? Isn't it possible Ned thought such an
arrangement would be in your best interests?"

"Oh, pah!" Emma exclaimed, and then was instantly furious that the childish exclamation had escaped her. She resumed her pacing and Alasdair watched her, the glimmer back in his eyes, as she stalked from one end of the small chamber to the other.

Lady Emma Beaumont stood five feet nine inches in her stockinged feet and was built on generous lines. Alasdair Chase, from intimate knowledge, knew that her height masked the rich curves of her body, and he was, as so often, distracted by the mental image of the figure beneath the elegant gown—the wonderful deep bosom, the long slope of her back, the flare of her hips, the taut swell of her backside.

Abruptly he turned back to the pianoforte and raised the cover. He played another cascade of notes.

Emma stopped dead.

Alasdair spoke almost casually over his shoulder as his fingers continued to ripple over the keys. "You know, my sweet, you had better accept it with a good grace. You'll only make yourself ridiculous otherwise."

He saw her wide mouth tauten, her eyes, more gold than brown, burn with another flash of anger. A needle of wind found its way between the glass and the frame of the window. The fire in the hearth spurted and a flame shot up; the wax candles in the branched candelabra flamed on the console table beneath the window. The light caught her hair. Amazing hair, Alasdair had always thought. Striped hair, where onyx mingled with tortoiseshell amid swaths of pale gold, like summer wheat. When she was a child, he remembered, the paler colors had dominated, but as she'd grown, the darker strands began to predominate.

"Don't call me that," she said with low-voiced intensity.

Alasdair turned once more from the pianoforte with a small shrug. "As you please."

Emma hesitated, then she walked to the door leading back to the salon. Her shoulders were unconsciously squared as she opened the door and reentered the room.

The scene hadn't changed since her abrupt departure ten minutes earlier. The room's four occupants still sat in the same postures, as if frozen in place by a wave of a wand. They stirred anxiously as she came in, with Alasdair on her heels.

"Mr. Critchley, would you go through my brother's will again," she asked, her tone moderate, although her body still thrummed with palpable tension. "Begin at the beginning if you please."

The lawyer cleared his throat, rustled his papers, and began to read the dusty lawyerly language that seemed to Emma to confirm Ned's death more decisively even than the formal notification from Horseguards, the personal letter from the duke of Wellington, the flood of messages from his friends and colleagues—more completely even than Hugh Melton's heart-wrenching account of Ned's wound and death in the barren landscape between Torres Vedras and Lisbon.

"As your brother was unmarried and had no direct heir, the title, Grantley Manor, and Grantley House in London are entailed upon your uncle, Lord Grantley." The lawyer raised his head and glanced toward the elderly man sitting upright on the chintz-covered sofa.

The sixth earl nodded solemnly and his countess

smoothed down her black silk skirts. "No hurry to leave, m'dear," the earl said bluffly. "No hurry at all."

"No, no, you mustn't think that we're in haste to dispossess you of your home, my dear Emma," the countess said. "But such a pity you haven't found a husband as yet. However, I daresay there'll be very few improvements that we'll be wanting to make, so you must feel free to remain as our guest until you've established yourself comfortably."

"You need have no fear, ma'am, that I shall drag on your coattails," Emma said dryly. "Pray continue, Mr. Critchley."

The lawyer looked uncomfortable. It was at this point in the earlier will reading that Lady Emma had lost her customary poise.

Alasdair had resumed his position against the bookshelves, hands thrust deep into his pockets. He had the air of one amused by if not indifferent to the proceedings, but the gaze that rested on Emma was sharp beneath half-lowered lids. There was no danger of another public display of fury, he judged.

"Lady Emma, you are your brother's heir and inherit all of his estate that is not entailed," Mr. Critchley intoned. "That is to say, the bulk of his fortune." He cast an apologetic glance toward the sixth earl and his countess.

"It does seem very odd of Edward, I must say," declared Lady Grantley. "To leave nothing to his uncle . . . particularly when Lord Grantley will have all the responsibilities of maintaining the estate."

"The estate revenues, if ploughed back, will take care of all maintenance," Emma pointed out through compressed lips.

"To be sure . . . to be sure." Lord Grantley, possessed of a much more conciliatory temperament than his lady, waved a hand in hasty acceptance.

"Lord Grantley will find that the estate will run itself if he leaves it in the capable hands of Dresden and his stewards." Alasdair idly flicked at a speck of mud on his coat cuff as he spoke.

"Lord Grantley will make his own arrangements. He will wish to put in his own bailiff and steward," said her ladyship in quelling accents.

"Then he's even more of a fool than I took him for," murmured Alasdair in a voice that only Emma heard. Their eyes met, and he offered her a languid, conspiratorial wink.

Laughter glowed for an instant in her gaze, banishing the tension, and her wide mouth curved in an approaching smile. Then she remembered her grievances and turned away abruptly. Alasdair had always had the ability to make her forget that she was angry with him. It was among his most infuriating characteristics. He'd been able to do it with Ned too. As boys, when they'd come home from school for the long vacations, Alasdair for some reason would suddenly get the devil in him and delight in provoking the easygoing Ned to a flash of temper. Then he would change in an instant, joke and cajole until Ned couldn't help but laugh.

"Could we get on, Mr. Critchley," she demanded, an edge to her voice again.

"The late earl appointed Lord Alasdair as executor of his will and trustee of your fortune, Lady Emma, until such time as you should marry."

Emma drew in her breath in a sharp hiss. "And what precisely would Lord Alasdair's responsibilities be as trustee of my fortune?"

Mr. Critchley took a large crisp white handkerchief

from his pocket, shook it out, and blew his nose vigorously. "Your brother has entrusted Lord Alasdair with the task of managing your fortune, Lady Emma. Lord Alasdair has sole control." He buried his face in his handkerchief again before saying diffidently, "Your brother, ma'am, made provision for Lord Alasdair to be compensated for his efforts on your behalf. His lordship is to receive a yearly stipend of . . ." he shuffled through his papers. "Five thousand pounds . . . yes, that was it. Five thousand pounds."

Emma took another turn around the salon, her step agitated, her color fluctuating. "It is *intolerable*," she said, but it was clear to her audience that she had herself well in hand.

"Oh, surely you don't begrudge me such a paltry sum, Emma!" Alasdair complained with a raised eyebrow. "You won't even notice it, dear girl. And I do assure you, I shall earn it."

She spun around on him. "And just how do you intend to earn it?"

He smiled. "By ensuring that your fortune grows apace. I have some small talent, as Ned knew very well."

"How could you possibly have any knowledge of investments, and the Exchange, and cent per cents, or whatever they're called?" Emma demanded. "You've never had a feather to fly with."

"True enough." He folded his arms and regarded her with a half smile. "My esteemed sire, as we all know, was not a thrifty gentleman."

"Bad blood," muttered Lord Grantley. "Came from his mother. Bad blood in all the Bellinghams. Hardened gamesters, the lot of 'em. Saw your grandmother lose six thousand guineas at one sitting. And your father was the same."

"The matter of my penury is thus explained," Alasdair agreed blandly. "The youngest son of a hardened gamester . . ." He shrugged. "However, I wonder if we're not wandering off course a little here."

Emma was silent. Alasdair's father, the earl of Chase, had been a vicious tyrant. A drunkard and a gamester who had fallen from his horse late one night on his way back from a card party and broken his neck, leaving an estate mortgaged to the hilt and more debts than a king's ransom could have settled. Alasdair, the youngest of three sons, had not a penny to his name. Not that you would ever guess that from looking at him, she thought. He lived like a wealthy man, but how she couldn't imagine.

"I wouldn't begrudge it if Ned left you twenty thousand pounds," she said impatiently. "You were his closest friend . . . closer than any brother could have been. But I absolutely *refuse* to accept your authority over my expenditures. Am I to ask you for my quarterly allowance? Ask permission if I wish to set up my stable? Have you approve all my household expenses?" She glared first at Alasdair and then at the lawyer.

"My dear Emma, I'm sure that Lord Alasdair will be everything that's accommodating," said Maria, rising from her armless chair. "And you don't want to be worrying about finances yourself. It's so . . . so unfeminine. Much better to leave such sordid details to a man. Men have much better minds for dealing with such matters. I'm sure dear Ned knew that he was taking care of your interests . . . just until you get married." She came over and laid a hand on

Emma's arm. "Maybe you should lie down on your bed and rest for a little before dinner."

"Since when have you known me to need to rest before dinner, Maria?"

"Well, to be sure, never," the lady said. "But this has been a very trying afternoon for you."

"An understatement," Emma said shortly. She addressed the lawyer. "Well, sir. Do you have answers to my questions? How much authority has my brother invested in Lord Alasdair?"

The lawyer rubbed his mouth with his fingertips. "By the very nature of the trust, ma'am, the trustee must review all expenses," he said hesitantly. "But there is no other area of jurisdiction."

"Oh, how fortunate. I am not obliged to gain his consent to my marriage, for instance?" she inquired sardonically. "Or to where I might choose to live?"

The lawyer shook his head and sounded quite shocked as he said, "No, indeed not, Lady Emma. You are of age."

Emma frowned down at the carpet at her feet. She traced the pattern with the toe of her blue satin slipper. "There is no way, I take it, that this will can be set aside?"

"None, Lady Emma."

Emma nodded almost absently. "If you'll excuse me," she said, her voice distant as she walked over to the door to the music room. She disappeared, the door clicking shut behind her.

"Well, I always said she had very odd manners," Lady Grantley announced, rising to her feet. She sniffed. "Of course, with such a fortune, she'll not be short of offers, regardless of her manners. We'll just have to pray she doesn't squander herself on a fortune hunter."

"Her fortune has always been large and she hasn't succumbed as yet, ma'am," Alasdair pointed out gently.

Lady Grantley gave him a look of supreme dislike. "She was seriously in danger of doing so once, as I recall." She sailed to the door. "I shall go to my apartments. Maria, would you send the housekeeper to me. I wish to review the menus for the week."

"I believe Emma has already done so, Lady Grantley," Maria said.

"Emma is no longer mistress of this house." Lady Grantley swept from the room. Her husband, with an apologetic look at Maria, muttered something about a glass of claret and followed her.

"Well," declared Maria, two bright spots of color on her cheekbones. "Well!"

"Well indeed, Maria." Alasdair pushed himself away from the bookshelves. "The sooner you and Emma are established elsewhere, the better for all, I would have said." He smiled at the woman, and the rather harsh cast of his features was immediately softened. His eyes lost their sardonic glitter and became warm; the thin line of his mouth took a less uncompromising turn. He patted her shoulder. "You have no need to take instructions from the countess. If she wishes to interview the housekeeper, let her summon her herself."

"Yes . . . yes, I think I shall do just that." Maria nodded decisively. "Mr. Critchley, I'm sure you'd care for a glass of wine before you leave. If you'd like to come with me . . ." She went to the door. The lawyer gathered his papers, bowed to Lord Alasdair, and followed his hostess with an eager step.

Alasdair flung himself down in a chair with earpieces and closed his eyes, waiting. He guessed

Beethoven. He didn't have long to wait. The first notes of the pianoforte were soft, tentative almost, as Emma found her mood. Then they grew and strengthened and he found himself listening to the *Kreutzer Sonata*.

He nodded his satisfaction. He still knew her as well as ever. He rose and entered the music room. If the player noticed him, she gave no sign. Alasdair took a violin from a lacquered marquetry cabinet and came to stand behind her. The sweet sounds of the violin joined with the pianoforte, but Emma didn't acknowledge him until the piece was over.

Her hands were still on the keys as the strains of the sonata slowly faded in the air. "Oh, how I *wish* we didn't play so well together." It was a cry from the heart.

Alasdair contemplated a response and decided against it. He placed his violin on a marble-topped table with gilded legs. "Do you have any idea how much you're worth, Emma?"

She turned on the thimble-footed stool. "Not exactly. A great deal, I know. Does it matter precisely how much?"

"I think so," he said dryly. "And if you don't think it matters, then I have to say that you're definitely not the best person to be managing such a fortune."

Emma flushed but was obliged to acknowledge the justice in this. However, she said, "That's not why Ned made this arrangement, and you know it."

"You are now worth something over two hundred thousand pounds," Alasdair said steadily, ignoring her statement. "You are an extremely wealthy woman."

"And you're going to make me even wealthier, I

gather." She rose from the stool. "But that isn't why Ned made this arrangement. Is it?"

"I don't know why Ned decided on this," he said dismissively. "All I know is that it's a fact. So let's get to points, shall we? Where do you intend living?"

"In London for the season. Where else?"

"Where else indeed?" he agreed. "Do you wish me to find you a suitable house for hire?"

"I would wish to buy," Emma snapped.

"I don't believe that would be sensible," he said evenly.

"And why not, pray?" Her chin lifted; her eyes threw their challenge.

"Because you will get married," he stated baldly.

"Not to you!" Emma flashed before she could stop herself.

"No . . . as I recall you made that painfully clear once before," Alasdair replied with a cool nod. "As it happens, I was not renewing my suit."

Emma controlled herself with difficulty. It was typical of Alasdair to turn the tables in that way . . . to put her at a disadvantage. She faced him directly. "I believe that was what Ned intended with this diabolical arrangement."

"Yes, so you implied. But Ned did not confide in me." He reached for the bellpull. "Sherry or madeira?"

Emma hesitated, then accepted that Alasdair was not going to admit what they both knew to be true. And what difference did it make anyway? The sharp spur of anger was gone now, and wisdom told her that somehow they had to find a way through their antagonism, through their shared past, to manage this situation. Whatever Ned's motives had been.

"Sherry," she replied and bent to warm her hands

at the fire while Alasdair gave instruction to the footman who appeared in answer to the bell. The silence
in the music room elongated. Emma remained at the
fire. Alasdair strolled to the window. The curtains had
not yet been drawn and they could hear faintly the
sound of the waves crashing on the beach below the
cliff on which the house stood.

The footman returned with a tray. He set it on the
marble-topped table and withdrew.

Alasdair poured wine and brought a glass to
Emma. "You'll have to preserve the proprieties of
mourning . . . or do you intend to flout convention?"

"Ned had no time for the conventions," she said.

"Very true." He sipped sherry, watching her
closely. "You'll dance?"

Emma suddenly smiled. "I'll not waltz," she said.
"Ned detested the waltz." Tears started in her eyes
and she brushed them away. "He also detested weeping." There was a catch in her voice and she put
down her glass. "Damn it, Alasdair. *Why* did he have
to die?"

He moved toward her, his arms sliding around her,
his breath rustling through her hair. And for a minute
it was as it had been so many times in the long-ago
past. He was comforting her . . . for a scraped knee,
a fall from her horse, a schoolroom punishment. But
Alasdair was grieving too, and in this moment of accord she comforted him in turn.

They clung together. And now it was not the long-
ago past, but the recent past. A past she had sworn
never to revisit. But she could feel the beat of his
heart, take the scent of his skin, his hair. The supple
length of his body was imprinted on her own. His
hands moved down her back, holding her to him.

The world swung on its axis. Her mind and senses whirled in confusion. She pulled out of his arms, her tears dried. "Take a lease on a house for me, then." Her voice was harsh and she picked up her glass again and drank. "I would be in town for the new year."

"As you command, ma'am." Alasdair bowed, irony in every line of his slender frame. "We will discuss the details of your financial arrangements when you're established in town." A smile flickered over his fine mouth. "I assure you I won't keep too tight a hold on the purse strings."

Emma held herself very still, then she turned and whisked herself from the room. The door closed quietly behind her.

Alasdair sat down at the piano and played a series of chords, each one more strident and discordant than the last.

Chapter Two

❧

"This is really a very superior house, Emma." Maria untied her bonnet strings and nodded her satisfaction as she looked around the large first-floor salon. "The rooms are such a good size and the furnishings quite above the general run. I was so afraid you might be melancholy, my dear, at finding yourself residing in meagre accommodations, after what you've been used to. Grantley House is such a distinguished mansion, and Grosvenor Square such a perfect address."

She gave a little sigh, and placed her bonnet on a chair. "But this is really a very pleasant house. And Mount Street is a most convenient location."

"I'd live in a chicken shed if it was the only means to get away from Aunt Hester." Emma drew off her York tan gloves. "The woman's pure poison."

"I must say I don't find her very good-natured," Maria agreed rather more moderately.

Emma smiled at her. "You on the other hand are a

saint, Maria. How you managed to bite your tongue when she sniped at you, I really don't know. I wish I could have done the same," she added a touch regretfully. "It would have been so much more dignified to have maintained a cool silence, instead of plucking crows with her all the time. And it does make it very unpeaceful for poor Uncle Grantley."

"Well, my dear, you always did have a quick temper," Maria said comfortably. "And dear Ned too. He would never stand quiet if he thought there was an injustice."

"No." Emma's smile was tinged with melancholy now. In search of distraction, she walked to the long windows overlooking the street below. "What a commotion! The post chaise is still blocking the street while they're unloading our baggage, and there's a dray behind it with a very irate driver." She went into a peal of laughter. "I don't know what he's yelling, but I'm sure it's far from polite. John-coachman looks ready to mill him down."

"Oh dear. What a vulgar scene." Maria shook her head. "London is such a noisy, dirty place."

Emma chuckled but said nothing. For all such protestations, Maria loved being in town for the season. She was a highly sociable creature for whom the endless round of callers and calling, of shopping and parties, even the insipidities of Almack's, were meat and drink.

She was a distant relative of Emma's father, whose husband had died and left her with a very small competency, not enough to maintain the lifestyle to which she'd been accustomed. Emma's own mother had died when her daughter was fourteen, and Emma's father had invited Maria Witherspoon to act as hostess and chaperone his daughter when she made her

London debut at eighteen. Maria had been delighted at such a generous offer and the prospect of returning once more to the vigorous social whirl of the wealthy and wellborn, and when Emma's father died, she had become Emma's permanent companion.

It was an arrangement that suited them both. While Maria was not clever, she knew everyone, had impeccable connections, and was ideally suited to the task of chaperoning a young and wealthy heiress in society. She was good-natured and easygoing, and since she would never dream of attempting to influence Emma's opinions or actions, they got on very well.

"I'll go and make sure the boxes and trunks are set in the right rooms," Maria said now. "You'll have that nice big bedchamber at the back, Emma dear, and I'll take the one at the front."

"Nonsense. You know you're a light sleeper. You won't sleep a wink if you're overlooking the street," Emma said. "I'd sleep like a log in a barn, so you take the back one."

Maria hesitated only a minute, then with a murmured, "So good of you, Emma dear. So thoughtful," she hurried out.

Emma remained at the window. The altercation between her own coachman and the driver of the dray was growing ever more heated, and quite a crowd was gathering. John-coachman was a burly man, but the driver of the dray looked like a prizefighter, and Emma was just beginning to think that she should send out Harris, the butler, to pour cold water on the smoldering flames before someone was hurt, when a curricle came bowling around the corner from Audley Street.

The driver pulled up his team of bays an inch before they could plunge into the obstruction. The maneuver looked almost leisurely, but Emma, who was no mean driver herself, knew the cool head, steady hands, and absolute precision that had been necessary. But then, she would not have expected anything less from Alasdair Chase, who now handed the reins to his tiger and sprang down from the curricle.

He wore the highly coveted blue-and-yellow-striped waistcoat of the Four Horse Club. A handful of spare whip points was tucked into the pocket of his many-caped driving coat. He addressed himself to the warring parties, and while Emma couldn't hear what he was saying, the results were instantaneous. John-coachman clambered back onto the box of the post chaise, the driver of the dray set to backing his horses up the road, and Alasdair, with a word to his tiger, turned to the front door.

He paused for a moment and looked up at the house. He saw Emma in the window and raised his curly-brimmed beaver hat in salute. Then he disappeared from her sight as he mounted the steps beneath her window.

Emma waited. She heard his quick light step on the stairs and told herself firmly that she would be neither provoked nor provoking in this interview.

Alasdair entered the salon, bringing the cold fresh air with him in the glow of his cheek, the brightness of his eye. "Good God, Emma, I can hardly credit the amount of baggage you have. How could two women need so much? There must be dozens of bandboxes and trunks. I nearly broke my neck tripping over a dressing case in the hall." He tossed his hat and whip onto a satinwood sofa table and drew off his gloves. His every gesture was smooth, supple, economical.

"So, how do you like the house? Will it do for you?"

"Maria is very pleased with it," Emma said. "I haven't as yet had time to look it over properly."

If Alasdair was disappointed by this noncommittal response, he gave no sign. "There's a music room," he said. "At the back of the house on the ground floor. I think you'll find the pianoforte to your liking. It's one of Pleyel's from Paris and it has a beautiful tone."

"Thank you," Emma said. If Alasdair had selected the instrument, she knew she would have no complaints, but she wasn't about to be effusive. "I'll try it later. When we've had time to settle in," she added pointedly, unable to help herself despite all resolutions. "At which time I daresay we shall be happy to receive visitors."

"If that was an attempt to snub me, my dear Emma, I have to tell you it went glaringly abroad," Alasdair stated pleasantly. He sat down in a deep chair before the fireplace and crossed his legs with the air of one prepared to make himself comfortable. "I am your trustee, if you recall. And as such have privileges not accorded an ordinary visitor." He smiled up at her as she still stood by the window. "Not to mention the privileges of an old . . . a very old . . . family friend."

"That was in the past," Emma said. "I've hardly said two words to you in private in the last three years. Which is why this is so damnable!" she added, impassioned even though she'd told herself she would be calm and polite and distant. She had struggled to resign herself, but it seemed impossible. Every time she thought she'd managed to accept Ned's diabolical will, just the thought of what it entailed would demolish her hard-won peace of mind.

"I don't find it damnable in the least," Alasdair

said cheerfully. "I'm more than happy to put our estrangement aside."

"How could you possibly expect me to forget . . ." She fell silent and turned back to the window, her shoulders stiff, back ramrod straight.

"I rather thought I was the injured party," Alasdair observed, in a voice now laced with acid. "I was the one left at the altar."

It was no good. She could not endure it. "If you will not leave, then I shall." Emma whirled to the door. "Harris will show you out."

Alasdair, with an almost leisurely movement, reached up and caught her wrist as she swept past his chair. Holding her, he rose from the chair. She was almost as tall as he, but Emma knew she couldn't match the wiry strength in his slender frame. The fingers braceleting her wrist were not to be pried apart, and she made no attempt to do so.

"I thought we had agreed that you were going to accept this situation with a good grace," Alasdair said. "You will simply make yourself ridiculous if you don't."

"It really pleases you to be able to taunt me with that, doesn't it?" she said bitterly.

"You forget, my dear Emma, that having once been made to appear ridiculous myself, I have an expert's knowledge of its discomforts. I merely wish to warn you of them, that is all." His eyes held hers, and they were bitter and angry, and a muscle twitched beside his thinned mouth.

"How dare you blame me for that!" Emma exclaimed. "After what you did . . . you would have expected me to endure . . . to pretend . . ." The words caught in her throat and now she pulled at her captive wrist.

Rather to her surprise, it was instantly released. Alasdair turned from her and picked up his hat, gloves, and whip. When he spoke, his voice was cool and even.

"Whatever you may think of the situation, it exists. I have certain responsibilities for your welfare, and you are going to have to accept that I am going to be a significant presence in your life. I came this afternoon to discover if the house suits you . . . if you're quite well after your journey . . . to ascertain that you had no nasty adventures with highwaymen and such like—the gentlemen of the road have been very busy over Finchley Common these days—and to see if you have any commissions for me to execute. I came, in short, to pay a visit of courtesy and friendship." He bowed with ironic formality and a sweeping flourish of his hat.

Emma stood unconsciously holding her wrist, where she could still feel the warm impress of his fingers. Alasdair was regarding her in silence, his green gaze narrowed but steady. Emma knew what he was doing. He was trying to put her out of countenance with his protestations of friendship and courtesy; trying to make her feel churlish and childish because she couldn't or wouldn't respond with maturity to an impossible situation.

"I have no interest in your friendship," she said coldly. "But I will answer courtesy with courtesy. Now, if you'll excuse me, I must go and help Maria supervise the unpacking." She offered him a bow as ironically formal as his had been.

Alasdair gave a half shrug as if the matter no longer interested him. "As you please." He drew on his gloves, smoothing the fine leather over his fingers. "Since you're clearly occupied now, I'll call upon you in the morning to discuss how you wish your allowance to be paid. Whether quarterly or monthly. It's up to you."

"We have not as yet discussed my needs," Emma said stiffly. "That should surely come first."

Alasdair paused on his way to the door. "I had reached a decision on that myself. I will impart it to you tomorrow. I give you good day, ma'am."

The door closed behind him. Emma, flushed with anger, went to the window. She watched him emerge from the house, climb into the curricle, and take the reins from his tiger. The street was now clear and he gave his horses the office to start, his hands dropping with a motion that was almost hasty and which set his team surging forward, too fast for the narrow street. He checked them immediately, but it was clear to Emma that Alasdair was as angry as she was.

They couldn't be in the same room together anymore without this bitter antagonism. They had hurt each other too deeply in the past ever to recover even a semblance of ease in each other's company. Ned had known that. So why had he made such a disposition? He had loved his sister, and he had loved his friend. Why would he choose to make them both miserable?

There was only one answer. Ned had believed that by throwing them together in this hideous fashion, the chemistry that had always been between them would reignite. He had been overjoyed at their engagement and devastated at its breaking. He had reproached neither of them openly, and had stayed close to them both, scrupulously refusing to take sides, but he hadn't been able to hide his sorrow and disappointment.

Emma left the salon and made her way to the front

bedchamber on the floor above. Her maid was in the midst of unpacking. Gowns lay on the bed, draped over chairbacks and the arms of the chaise longue standing beneath the window. Shoes, fans, scarves littered every surface.

"Lord love us, Lady Emma, but I never would have realized we'd brought so much with us," Mathilda said, laying an armful of linen into a drawer of the armoire. "And I'll lay any wager that you won't be wearin' a stitch of this stuff once you've been to the silk warehouses and the milliners and the bootmakers."

"You're probably right, Tilda," Emma said. "Everything must be hopelessly out of fashion." News of Ned's death had reached them only in November. Dispatches from Portugal took a long time a-coming. She had been in Hampshire throughout the summer and had stayed on through the beginning of the London season while lawyers had dealt with probate and the entail. In her grief, she'd had no interest in the fashion periodicals over which Maria pored, no interest in society gossip, had been content to live in riding dress and the light mourning she'd been obliged to adopt to receive condoling visitors.

But now she was tired of black and lavender and dove gray. It was time to return to the fashionable world. Eyebrows might be raised at such a swift putting off of mourning, but Emma, like her brother, had never cared a fig for public opinion, and she had a shrewd suspicion that public opinion would overlook any impropriety when it came with such a vast fortune. Flouting convention would be viewed as an interesting eccentricity.

She left Tilda to her unpacking and went into the next-door boudoir. Her writing case had been set out on the secretaire, and a footman was lighting the candles on the mantelpiece. A fire burned brightly in the hearth, and the room seemed a haven of quiet and order compared with the rest of the house.

She sat down at the desk and opened the case. Her fingers went, as they always did these days, to the fold of leather where she kept her private correspondence. She drew out the oiled parchment packet and sat with it in her hands, looking at the rusty stains of Ned's blood.

Then she slid the sheet of paper out of the parchment and opened it carefully. It was unlike any correspondence she'd ever received from Ned before. It was a poem of some kind, clearly one he'd written himself, and Ned was no poet, even the most partial sister had to admit that. It was really a very bad poem. Had he meant it as a joke? And why was there no covering letter?

Emma dashed a hand across her eyes. She refolded the sheet of paper, replaced it in the parchment, and slid it back into her writing case. Whatever he'd meant by it, she would never discover now. But this was all she had left of him—the last concrete thing she possessed of her brother. It had Ned's blood on it. And she would treasure it.

Maybe Alasdair would see the point of the poem. He understood Ned in ways different from Emma's ways. And Alasdair always had answers to everything. It was another of his infuriating characteristics. He wasn't always right, but he was always forcefully convinced that he was. So much so that people tended to go along with him. She and Ned had been rare exceptions. But then, they knew Alasdair Chase better than anyone.

Or at least, Emma amended, Ned might have done.

She had deceived herself into believing that she knew him . . . could trust him absolutely.

Emma rose from the secretaire and went to the fire. She rested a hand on the mantel and stood looking down at the flames, remembering the first time she'd met Alasdair Chase. She'd been eight years old that summer when Ned had brought his friend home from Eton for the long vacation. And she'd fallen instantly in love with the fourteen-year-old Alasdair, trailing after him the entire summer like a devoted puppy. He'd had his own style even then. The daredevil carelessness that still marked him, still made him so attractive . . . so dangerous.

He'd encouraged Ned to get up to all kinds of mischief. They'd roamed the forest at night, watching badgers and foxes; they'd taken sailing boats out onto the Solent in every kind of wild weather, under the moon and under the sun. They'd ridden the earl's unbroken hunters and taken guns from the gun room, disappearing for hours at a time on shooting excursions, sending the household into a frenzy of panic. But somehow Alasdair's charm had always averted the worst consequences. His charm and his undoubted competence. The unbroken hunter became as putty under his hands; he was a superb shot and never returned to the house without a full game bag; he swam like a fish and sailed like a mariner. And he seemed unafraid of anything.

The earl, like everyone else, had fallen under his spell. Alasdair's insouciant lawlessness had gone unpunished, and Ned had grown ever bolder in his friend's image. After that summer, Alasdair had become a permanent visitor to Grantley Manor. His own father was not interested in him. His brothers were all much older than he. His mother was a broken dab of a woman who probably didn't notice whether her youngest son came home for the school holidays or not. Quite who had decided that Alasdair would make his home with Ned's family, no one really knew. But Emma guessed it was Alasdair himself.

Emma had attached herself to her brother and his friend with limpetlike determination. And most times they'd accepted her with the lofty carelessness of youths basking in the hero worship of their juniors.

A log fell in the hearth, breaking Emma's reverie. She bent to poke it back, the heat warming her face. It was music that had wrought the change in their relationship. Music that had prompted Alasdair to treat her as an equal. Oh, he'd continued to tease her, continued to behave toward her with the casual ease of long friendship, but at some point, before she'd even begun to put up her hair, he had started to take her seriously.

He'd heard her playing one afternoon, at the point when she had discovered that music was no longer a drudgery of practice and scales but a source of delight. Until that moment, Alasdair had played only for himself, at night when the house was quiet. He had never revealed his gift. Only Ned knew of it, knew that his friend used music to ease his black moods, the waves of loneliness that came over him sometimes. And not even Ned understood how completely Alasdair used music to express all his emotions.

Emma had discovered that quickly enough. She and Alasdair shared both the passion and the need. And they were equally matched. Throughout the season of their engagement, they had played together, sometimes purely for their own pleasure, but often for the pleasure of others. They had become a regular entertainment at soirees and country house parties. Until everything went bad. . . .

Who was Alasdair's light-of-love this time?

The question reared its sickening head and Emma turned away from the fire. It was certain he had one. Alasdair always had a woman in his life. In fact, more than one, she reflected bitterly. The last she'd heard, it had been a Lady Melrose. A woman of a certain age and a most definite reputation. The affairs of Lord Alasdair were frequently the latest *on-dit*. He was supposed to be penniless, but he lived like a man blessed with a considerable fortune. He was a rake. An insouciant, enterprising, utterly charming and irredeemable rake. And society loved him for it.

ॐ

The house on Half Moon Street contained a twisted tangle of narrow corridors and small, low-pitched rooms. The fire in the small parlor abovestairs was smoking, the candles guttering as the January wind forced its way under the ill-fitting door and around the windowpanes.

The two men in the room stood huddled in greatcoats around the fire. One of them had a rasping cough that was not helped by the smoke.

"This is an infernal climate!" he said. "I don't know how you can live in it, Paolo." He spoke English but with a heavy accent and addressed a much younger man, dressed fashionably in pale gray pantaloons, a coat of blue superfine, a gray silk waistcoat. His goldtasseled hessians gleamed in the firelight.

"One becomes used to it, Luiz." The younger man shrugged, sounding almost bored. He had no trace of an accent, but there was something about his features, the olive skin and dark eyes, that lent an exotic cast to his appearance.

"To be sure, you were born here," Luiz said. "I suppose it makes a difference." He didn't sound convinced. He raised an eyeglass and examined his companion. "You certainly look the part. As fine as any of these London gentlemen. You think you can play it?"

"I can play it," Paolo said with the same slight air of boredom. "I can play the dandy as well as any of them." He laughed, his lip curling. "I can safely promise that no one will ever suspect the truth of my origins."

The door opened behind them and both men turned from the fire. A tall, imposing figure entered, kicking the door closed behind him. He drew his caped greatcoat around him. "It's cold enough in here to freeze the balls off a brass monkey," he stated crisply, with only the faintest trace of an accent. "Build up the fire, Luiz."

Luiz hastened to obey, throwing logs onto the flames. Unfortunately the wood was green and gusts of smoke billowed out, sending Luiz into a paroxysm of coughing.

The new arrival ignored this. He tossed his hat onto a stool and strode to the table where reposed a flagon of wine and glasses. He raised a glass and examined it in the light of the candle, then fastidiously wiped it with his kerchief before filling it from the bottle. As if his action granted general permission, his companions hastened to follow his example.

They drank in silence, then the new arrival raised his own eyeglass and subjected Paolo to close scrutiny. "Yes, you will do well," he said. He reached into the front of his greatcoat and drew out a sheaf of papers. "Here is your background. It should not be hard for you to memorize."

Paolo took the papers. "Easier, I trust, than the Italian diplomat," he said, riffling through the documents. "The intricacies of Italian politics were not easy to master, Governor."

The man thus addressed merely nodded and drank his wine. "The woman moves in the best circles. Your background as a French émigré of impeccable credentials will give you entrée into the upper echelons of this society. Princess Esterhazy will arrange for your vouchers for Almack's. She has been apprised of your arrival and believes you to be the scion of an old family with loose connections to her husband's. You will visit her as soon as you have mastered your background. It will be well if you produce a hint of a French accent. Your fluent English is, of course, explained by your émigré status. You have grown up in the English countryside but now wish to take your place in society."

The governor shrugged and set his glass on the table. "You will find yourself in good company. And hanging out for a rich wife—such a vulgar expression," he said with a grimace of distaste, "is considered a perfectly legitimate occupation, indeed a laudable one, for the young men whose ranks you will join."

"You have not as yet told me my mission," Paolo said, regarding his superior over the lip of his glass. "What am I to do with this rich young woman?"

The governor walked over to the fire. He bent to warm his hands at the sullen flame. "We have reason to believe she holds something that would be of interest to us. Wellington's spring campaign plans that were being sent to his masters in London. Her brother was one of Wellington's couriers. We knew he was carrying the details to Lisbon for shipment. When he fell into our hands, the document was not on his person and he died before he could give us anything useful. But we know certain things about him. We know he was very close to his sister. And we know that he died with her name on his lips."

He straightened from the fire and turned, warming his backside. "We know from our sources that the document never reached the military command in Horseguards. No one knows what became of it. If the woman has it, she may have destroyed it by now, not knowing what it was. We don't know if she was in her brother's confidence. We know very little, my dear Paolo, except that this is a matter of the most vital importance. It is for you to discover what Lady Emma knows, if she has what we are seeking, and if so, to get it from her. How you choose to do that is up to you."

He paused for a minute, his eyes staring into the middle distance. "If it is necessary to arrange an accident, or if some unfortunate mistake should be made, then you will, of course, ensure that it is discreet."

"Of course, Governor." Paolo bowed. He steepled his fingers against his mouth. "I have some small reputation, I believe."

"Which is why we are employing you on a matter of such delicacy," the governor said, his voice again crisp. "You will use Luiz as your conduit . . . and for reconnaisance or any other task." He nodded to the older man, who had remained silent throughout the discussion. "Luiz will stay in this house throughout the operation and will be available to you at all times."

Luiz coughed unhappily as another gust of smoke

billowed into the room. He shivered into his greatcoat and glanced toward the small window where a leafless branch scratched against the pane. It was not a cheerful sound.

"You will take up residence in lodgings on Albermarle Street." The governor withdrew another paper from his pocket. "Here is the lease. The lodgings are not grand, but adequate, and the rooms below you are taken by a nobleman of impeccable lineage if somewhat doubtful financial status. He also happens to be closely connected to the young lady in question, and was a dear friend and confidant of her brother. You will make of him a friend."

"I see." Paolo nodded, running an eye over the lease. "It seems I shall be more comfortable than poor Luiz here."

"Undoubtedly." It was an arid agreement. The governor picked up his hat again and looked ready to depart.

"It would perhaps be helpful if I knew what I was looking for?" Paolo said with a raised eyebrow.

"We don't know exactly. Edward Beaumont was an artful courier. He knew how to disguise his wares." He shrugged. "It is imperative that we lay hands on it if it's still in existence. The whole outcome of the Peninsula campaign depends upon it. You may be certain the emperor will reward such information . . . which reminds me." He dug deep into his pocket and drew out a leather pouch. He tossed it onto the table. It fell with a heavy clink. "Should you need further funds, they will be forthcoming."

With that the governor nodded to both men and departed.

Luiz shivered again. "And you know who'll get the

reward," he muttered. "Not the likes of you and I, my friend."

Paolo had picked up the pouch. He hefted it in the palm of his hand. "It seems this mission is an expensive one," he said grimly. "I shall certainly get my share, Luiz, have no fear."

His black eyes were hard as agate and he passed a hand over his mouth in a gesture that was somehow both sinister and predatory.

Luiz averted his gaze. He was not in the same league as Paolo, let alone the governor. And he wasn't certain that he wished to be. Cold, drafty lodgings and the role of go-between suited his talents and inclinations well enough. He was not comfortable with talk of accidents.

Chapter Three

"Emma dearest, Lord Alasdair is belowstairs." Maria entered Emma's bedchamber the following morning, her voice considerately low, her footstep soft.

Emma muttered something inaudible and burrowed deeper into her pillows. She was a night owl who viewed the hours before ten in the morning with something less than enthusiasm.

"Here's Mathilda with your hot chocolate," Maria coaxed, going to the window to draw back the curtains. Winter sunlight flooded the room and the sounds of the street below drifted faintly upward.

"Here you are, Lady Emma." Mathilda placed the tray on the bedside table and plumped the pillows as Emma sat up, blinking blearily. The maid set the tray on her knees, bobbed a curtsy, and left the room.

"What was it you said, Maria?" Emma took the silver jug and poured a dark, fragrant stream of chocolate into the shallow, wide-lipped Sevres cup.

"Alasdair has come to call," Maria said.

"At this ungodly hour!" Emma exclaimed. "You may tell him to—"

"You may tell him yourself." Alasdair spoke cheerfully from the door. He had opened it so silently neither of the women had heard him. "What should I do?"

"Go to the devil," Emma said, setting her cup down on the tray and glaring at her unwelcome visitor. He was looking disgustingly elegant for such an early hour, his cream pantaloons set off by a coat of emerald green superfine that made his eyes positively luminous. His cravat of starched muslin was tied in the elaborate folds of what she recognized as the Waterfall, and his glossy locks were brushed in a fashionably disordered style. Hat, coat, gloves, and cane he must have left belowstairs.

Maria gave a little shriek of dismay. "Goodness me, Lord Alasdair, you cannot be in here . . . in Emma's bedchamber . . . why, she's still in bed."

"So I'd noticed," Alasdair remarked coolly, coming into the room. "I should have expected it. You never were an early riser, Emma."

"But, Lord Alasdair . . . no . . . no . . . really this will not do." Maria flew around the room, gesticulating wildly as if she were shooing away a flock of geese.

"There's no need for such agitation, Maria," Alasdair said calmly. "I've been in and out of Emma's bedchamber since she was eight years old." He glanced across to the bed and there was an ironic glitter in his eyes, a slightly mocking curve to his mouth. "I've had all the privileges of a brother, have I not, Emma?"

And a great many more, Emma thought bitterly. But

she wasn't going to give him the satisfaction of seeing her react to the implicit reminder of all that they'd once shared. She merely shrugged and poured more chocolate into her cup.

"I know you must have many things to do, Maria," Alasdair said with a disarming smile. "And I need to discuss certain matters with Emma . . . trustee matters which I'm sure you'll understand are . . ." Here he paused significantly, raising an eyebrow.

Maria understood that such matters must be confidential. If Emma chose to tell her the details, that was one thing. But her trustee could not violate the confidence of his position. However, she made a valiant effort to honor her own position as chaperone. "Could it not wait, Alasdair, until Emma is up and dressed?"

Alasdair glanced at the little gilt clock on the mantelpiece. It showed half past nine. "Unfortunately I must leave for Lincolnshire immediately," he said with the same disarming smile. "And I cannot go without ensuring that Emma has sufficient funds in my absence."

"Why do you have to go to Lincolnshire so suddenly?" Emma asked, betrayed into curiosity. Alasdair had given no such impression the previous day.

Alasdair's expression lost its charm. The ironic gleam returned to his eye. "My esteemed brother has thought fit to summon a meeting of the clan," he said. "And as you know, when Francis beckons, we must all run to obey."

"Since when have you acknowledged your brother's summons?" Emma demanded in open incredulity. From the moment he had gained his majority, Alasdair, to all intents and purposes, had cut himself off from his family and in particular his overbearing brother, the present earl of Chase.

"It appears my mama is taken ill," Alasdair said gently. "I can hardly refuse a request to attend her sickbed."

Emma immediately felt as if she'd been put in the wrong, which, of course, had been Alasdair's intention. He had a tongue that could sting like an adder and few scruples how he used it when he considered someone had been overly inquisitive. However, she was a past master at dealing with Alasdair Chase's setdowns. She said blandly, "I'm sorry to hear it."

Maria still looked uncertain but she knew that not so long ago this informality between Emma and Alasdair had been customary. Ned had seen nothing wrong with it and she was not in the habit of pressing her own opinions on Emma, who she felt sure was perfectly capable of banishing an unwelcome visitor herself. So when Alasdair moved to the door and held it open for her, she said merely, "Oh dear," and went through it, murmuring as she passed Alasdair, "Give my regards to Lady Chase."

"With pleasure, ma'am." Alasdair bowed and closed the door firmly behind her. "Come, Emma, don't glower at me. I'm determined not to quarrel with you today." He caught up a straight-backed armless chair from beside the fireplace, swung it around, and straddled the seat, his arms folded along the back. He rested his chin on his arms and regarded Emma quizzically.

She was looking deliciously rumpled, her stripey hair tumbling down her back, her golden eyes beneath drooping lids still filled with sleep. Her complexion had a pink glow, her lips were moist and soft, her expression open and vulnerable, as if her face had not yet taken on the realities of the new day. Unbidden came the memory of how deeply she slept, how very still she lay all night, once she'd tossed and turned until she was in the right position.

Unbidden came the memory of her long, sprawling limbs tangled with his. Nothing would wake her. He used to amuse himself in the morning by touching her, stroking the lean length of her back, her belly, tiptoeing over the satiny inner skin of her thighs, trying to see if he could arouse the smallest reaction. But she would sleep on, her breathing deep and regular, but occasionally . . . just occasionally he would draw from her a faint murmur, a slight stirring of invitation. . . .

Emma's skin prickled. She felt her nipples harden under his steady gaze. She could read his thoughts as clearly as if they'd been written on vellum. Alasdair smiled slowly, a smile that started in his eyes before reaching his mouth. It was a smile that compelled a response—a smile to which she'd fallen victim more times than she cared to count. Deliberately Emma turned her head aside, picking up the tray that still rested on her knees and leaning sideways to place it on the bedside table.

"So," Alasdair said as if that charged moment had never taken place. "While I'm away, I imagine you'll be shopping . . . generally preparing yourself to burst upon the town in fine fig." He rose from his chair and strolled into Emma's dressing room as he talked. "Fashions have changed since your last visit to town. Hairstyles too."

Out of Emma's sight now, he continued to chat inconsequentially, his voice lightly ironical, but all the while his eyes darted around the dressing room, noting everything. He strode to the secretaire, where her writing case lay. His fingers ran lightly over the fine leather. There were drawers in the secretaire, twelve little ones for monthly bills and accounts, two deeper ones in the body of the piece.

"What are you doing in here?"

He turned around, seemingly casual, at Emma's voice from the doorway. She stood there in her nightgown, her hair tumbling down her back, fixing him with an indignant and questioning stare.

"Just looking around," he said easily. "I was interested to see how the rooms are arranged."

Emma frowned. "You haven't seen the house before?"

"No." He shook his head. "I saw no need. The specifications for the house seemed exactly right, so I simply signed the lease." He let his hand fall from the writing case and strolled to the armoire. "You're going to need a completely new wardrobe, I would imagine."

He changed the subject with an airy wave as he opened the armoire and began to riffle through the garments hanging there. "As I thought, all the necklines here are too low now for daytime. They're being worn higher with lace collarettes. Sleeves are longer too. Oh, and you can do without trains in most cases."

Emma was torn between annoyance at this insouciant riffling of her wardrobe and interest in his comments. Alasdair was an acknowledged arbiter of fashion, and his taste in dress, both male and female, was impeccable. Annoyance won the day, however. "When you've finished rummaging through my armoire, perhaps we could get on with discussing my finances?" she said frigidly.

Alasdair turned back to her. "Ah, yes." He raised

the eyeglass that hung on a black silk ribbon around his neck and regarded her through it for a minute. "You look cold, my sweet. Perhaps you should put on a wrapper or get back into bed."

Emma belatedly realized that her nightgown was of very fine lawn, fine enough to be almost transparent. She glanced down and saw that her nipples made dark splotches against the white material. Alasdair's gaze swept down her body and she knew he was recalling what was so barely concealed beneath the gown. The careless endearment, the pointed gaze, both infuriated her. She felt as if she were being appraised like a harlot in a whorehouse . . . as if he had mentally lined her up in the serried ranks of his innumerable liaisons.

The hurt was still as fresh and piercing as it had ever been.

Emma marched back to her bedchamber, snatching up a velvet wrapper from the chest at the end of the bed. Secure in its folds, she turned to the attack.

"I suppose all the ladies who bask in your favors benefit from your advice on matters of dress and fashion," she said with ringing sarcasm. "Maybe they pay for it too? I shouldn't wonder if Lady Melrose and her like are more than willing to keep you in funds in exchange for all those little favors you do them." Anger and pain were inextricable now and she continued in a devastating sweep of insult. "Indeed, I have often wondered how you manage to live so well with no visible means of support. Now, of course, I realize how it must be. Do you have a scale of charges, my dear Alasdair?"

Alasdair had crossed the room in three strides. She saw with grim satisfaction that she had broken through his shell of debonair insouciance. What price now his peaceful intentions? He was pale with fury, his eyes mere slits of green ice. There was a white shade around his mouth and the pulse in his temple throbbed.

"By God, Emma! You go too far." His hands circled her throat and she could feel her own pulse beating against his fingers. She met his furious gaze with a gleam of triumph.

"Under invincible propulsion," she declared. "But will you not satisfy my curiosity? I know for a fact that you have an income of five thousand pounds a year from my fortune. But that's hardly sufficient for a man of such expensive tastes."

Alasdair's thumbs pressed upward into the soft flesh below her chin. He wasn't hurting her but she could feel the force of will that kept him from doing so. "You really have a vicious tongue," he said.

"From a master, that's compliment indeed," she returned. Dimly she realized that they'd both now taken the high road of pure anger, and there was something almost heady about it. Almost a relief. It was as if finally she was free to give rein to the dreadful hurt he'd done her. She'd left him three years ago without a word of farewell, and they'd barely spoken to each other since. Now the red-hot surge of rage was like a cleansing fire.

There was a moment's silence, then suddenly Alasdair moved. One arm swept around her waist, clamping her tightly against him. His other hand clasped her head. He brought his mouth to hers, ignoring her struggles. There was passion in the kiss, but it was not of the soft and loving variety. It was hard and punishing and vengeful, and when at last he released her, she caught his cheek a ringing slap with her open palm.

"You bastard!" she declared, her voice choking with outrage.

"I thought you were asking for it," he responded with acid mockery, lightly touching his cheek where the marks of her fingers stood out. "It seemed clear that you were provoking me to some action. In my experience, when a woman picks a quarrel, she's usually seeking another, quite contradictory response." His smile was pure insult. "Have you been so long without passion, my sweet, that you must satisfy your need in such a perverse fashion? You have only to ask, and I shall be more than happy to oblige, you know."

This time Emma kept her hands at her side, her fists clenched against the folds of her wrapper. He would let her hit him again without physical retaliation, such crudity was not his way, but to lose control herself would be a kind of defeat. Alasdair was a past master at verbal fencing, and when he was as angry as he was now, he would put no check on his tongue. He might regret what he said later, but for now he would be as savage as he pleased. And so could she.

"I would not touch you if you were the last man on earth," she said softly. "You disgust me. You're a rake with all the instincts of a rutting stallion."

Alasdair's breath hissed through his teeth, but his voice was cold and deadly as snake's venom. "You must forgive the assumption then. There must be some reason why a passionate young woman would choose to spend three chaste years. I can't believe you've had no offers since our own ill-fated little venture. Could I be blamed for thinking that just maybe you might be finding it difficult . . . or even distasteful . . . to find an alternative mate?"

"You arrogant, conceited, overbearing, odious . . ."

Emma could find no words strong enough. "Get out of here. I never wish to see you again!"

"Ah, now there we have a problem." Alasdair perched on the corner of the dresser, crossing his long legs at the ankle. "For as long as I control your fortune, my dear Emma, you will have to put up with seeing me on a frequent and regular basis." A grim smile flickered across his tightly compressed lips.

"Oh, you may rest assured that your control will be very short-lived!" Emma cried. "Rather than endure it a minute longer than I must, I will take the first offer made to me, Alasdair Chase. And I will be betrothed by . . . by the middle of February." She flung her arms wide in an all-encompassing gesture.

Alasdair's laugh was scornful. "Don't be absurd, Emma. You're going to be besieged by fortune hunters—"

"Not for the first time," she interrupted. "And it wouldn't be the first time I succumbed to one, would it?" Even though she knew that her fortune had never been Alasdair's motive for proposing to her, she couldn't help flinging the accusation at him, and again she saw with satisfaction that she'd caught him on the raw.

"Believe me," he said grimly, "any man prepared to ignore your shrew's tongue for the sake of your fortune has to be in the most desperate straits. You'd better learn to sweeten your temper, Emma, if you intend to get a husband in your bed."

"By the middle of February," Emma reiterated, "I shall have a fiancé . . . and . . ." She paused, her eyes narrowing. It was high time someone taught Alasdair Chase not to make conceited and arrogant assumptions. She stated coolly, "A fiancé and, sir, a lover in my bed. By the fourteenth of February, the feast of Saint Valentine," she stated with a flash of inspiration. Saint Valentine, the patron saint of star-crossed lovers! She gave an angry little laugh. How very appropriate.

"One and the same? Or are you intending to cuck-old this mythical and unfortunate fiancé before the wedding?" He raised a sardonic eyebrow.

Emma stared him down. "I fail to see what busi-ness that is of yours."

The taut silence stretched between them. The fire in the grate popped and hissed. Then Alasdair shrugged as if the subject was of no further interest. He reached into his waistcoat pocket and drew out a bank draft. "This should tide you over as pin money until I re-turn." He held it out to her. "You may have your bills sent directly to me for settlement. Your household ac-counts also."

Emma took the bank draft in nerveless fingers. "I would prefer to settle my bills myself," she declared. "A quarterly payment into my own account will take care of that."

"I think I can best manage your fortune in this fash-ion." He uncrossed his ankles and pushed himself away from the dresser. His voice was now coldly matter-of-fact. "I need to be able to move your invest-ments around to ensure the best growth, and it doesn't make sense that a large sum should be tied up every quarter."

He walked to the door. "You need have no fear that I will question your expenditures . . . unless, of course, you start running up massive gambling debts. I give you good morning, ma'am." He bowed in the doorway and was gone.

Emma stared at the closed door in stupefaction. He was denying her even the independence of a quarterly allowance! It was insufferable that all her bills should be submitted to his inspection. Had he always intended this, or was it in response to that vile and bitter quarrel? It was worse than any they'd had before, and it had led her to issue that challenge . . . or threat . . . or whatever it was.

But she would do it. She would bring a rapid end to the powerful position Ned had given Alasdair in her life. It didn't matter whom she married. All that mattered was that Alasdair would be out of her life finally and forever.

However, honesty compelled her to admit that it mattered more whom she took as lover. That was a matter for both vanity and taste. It would have to be someone who appealed to her. She stared into the fire for a minute, wondering if she'd gone completely crazy. Did she really intend to go out and find herself a lover just to spite Alasdair?

Yes, she did. Ignoble, perhaps. Mad, perhaps. But he'd tried her too far.

She began to pace her bedchamber, tearing at a loose fingernail. How dared he assume that she'd remained single and unattached since their engagement was broken because she was pining for *him*? Of all the vain, conceited braggarts!

But was it the truth? Had she spurned all other suitors because none of them could match up to Alasdair, either as a lover or a companion or a sparring partner? Was it only Alasdair who could inspire every kind of passionate response in her? Only Alasdair who could make her laugh and rage and weep all at the same time?

Of course it wasn't that, she told herself with robust determination. And she would prove it to him . . . and, a little voice niggled at the back of her mind, also to herself.

Alasdair walked briskly back to his lodgings on Albermarle Street. No one looking at him would guess at the rage seething beneath his calm expression. A gentleman in a cherry-striped waistcoat pulled up his phaeton at the corner of Grosvenor Square and hailed him cheerily.

"Didn't know you was in town, Chase."

"I'm about to go out of town again, Darcy," Alasdair said with apparently unimpaired good humor. He rested a hand on the step of the phaeton. "But I shall return in a couple of days."

"I heard that Emma Beaumont is in town," Darcy said casually, looking somewhere off into the distance over Alasdair's head.

"Yes, she's lodged in Mount Street." Alasdair regarded his friend with a sharply assessing eye. He had little difficulty guessing the direction of Darcy's thoughts. "And yes, her already large fortune has been considerably augmented by her brother's will."

"So I'd heard," Darcy said. "You're her trustee, I gather."

"News travels fast," Alasdair replied coolly. "But if you're thinking of dangling after Emma, you need not apply to me for permission. She is her own mistress in everything but the management of her fortune."

"Ah." Darcy nodded and said hesitantly, "Not awkward for you, then?"

"Not in the least," Alasdair responded with a bland smile. "Why should it be?"

"No reason . . . no reason at all," Darcy said. "Three years, after all . . ." His voice tailed off.

"Three years is a very long time," Alasdair agreed. "A lot of water's flowed under the bridge since then. I assure you that Emma Beaumont and I are perfectly capable of moving in the same circles without tearing each other's throats out.'' He told the lie with perfect aplomb and stepped away from the phaeton, suggesting gently, ''Maybe you'd like to spread the word, Darcy. I'd hate society to be holding its breath for a reopened scandal.''

''Yes . . . yes, of course.'' Darcy looked awkward. ''No offense, I trust.''

''None whatsoever.'' Alasdair raised his hat in a jaunty gesture, and his friend drove off.

Alasdair's expression hardened. He could expect the old scandal to be chewed over with relish for a week or two. The situation would intrigue the gossips and provide speculation in the clubs of St. James's, where he knew that within days bets would be on as to who would bring the wealthy Lady Emma to the altar. There would be sly comments on his own situation as the once jilted suitor, and if he was to keep both pride and dignity intact he'd have to behave as if he were completely untroubled by the past. There must be no apparent tension between him and Emma—and that, after this morning's misery, would be no easy task.

His anger surged anew and his step quickened as he turned onto Brook Street. He despised the use of violence, but he'd come very close to it that morning, and even now he was sorely tempted to go back to Mount Street and box her ears—either that or wring her neck! Of all the absurdities! Threatening to marry the first man who offered for her! And then that nonsense about taking a lover! Emma had always been a headstrong, impetuous creature, but she was no one's fool. Surely she didn't expect him to believe she meant to do something so insane.

But even as he thought this, Alasdair could see again the look in her eye as she'd thrown her challenge. And it made him very uneasy. He hesitated for a moment, thinking that perhaps he would go back and try to put things right between them. They had both said things that should not have been said, and he should never have kissed her as he had done, even in the face of blatant provocation. But he knew he was still too angry to try to make peace. If he went back to Mount Street in his present frame of mind, it would only make matters worse. He would be out of town for a few days. It would give them both much-needed space and time to cool off.

And he needed a cool head to deal with this other business. A frown crossed his eyes. It was like looking for the proverbial needle in a haystack. Would Ned have sent such a sensitive document to Emma?

He climbed the steps to the house where he had his lodgings, and the door was opened before he could reach for the knocker. "Your portmanteau is packed, Lord Alasdair. The post chaise should be here any minute." His manservant stepped aside to allow his master entrance to the hallway.

"Good. Thank you, Cranham. I'll leave within the half hour." Alasdair's apartments were on the ground floor, and as he reached his own front door a step sounded on the stairs. He glanced over his shoulder and nodded courteously at the man descending the stairs. He didn't know him but guessed he must have taken the suite of rooms above his own, which had been empty for several weeks.

"Good morning. Am I addressing Lord Alasdair Chase?" The man spoke pleasantly and came forward with an open smile and hand outstretched. "I understand that we're to be neighbors. I have taken the apartments above yours." He shook hands. "Allow me to present myself. Paul Denis at your service." He pronounced the name in the French manner, not sounding the final *s.*

"Mr. Denis." Alasdair inclined his head in polite acknowledgment. "I bid you welcome. Are you newly come to town?"

"Yes, I have lived until now in the country. My family came from France in '91. I was a small boy at the time." He made a deprecating gesture. "We were able to bring nothing out of France, and my parents settled in Kent on the estate of an old friend of my father's."

"I see." It was a common enough story. The revolution had brought a flood of poverty-stricken émigrés from France to England. There were many aristocratic émigrés living in reduced circumstances in the country, and a good many of them in London, some on the fringes of society but many moving in the best circles. Monsieur Denis had the air of one who intended to move in the best circles.

"Unfortunately I have to go out of town for a few days," Alasdair said. "But on my return, I trust you'll dine with me one evening."

"I should be honored." The Frenchman bowed and Alasdair with another polite smile went into his own lodging. He was perfectly willing to introduce Monsieur Denis to his own circle of friends if he seemed agreeable. Judging by the impeccable cut of his coat and the elegant fall of his cravat, his neighbor had already mastered some of the necessities for cutting a dash in London. He certainly didn't give the impression of a country bumpkin.

Within the half hour, Alasdair was ensconced in a post chaise and four, driving out of London along the

Staines Road, which would have interested Emma considerably, since it took him in the opposite direction from his family home in Lincolnshire.

He arrived at his destination having changed horses three times on the road, just as Lord and Lady Grantley were preparing to go into dinner at the unfashionably early hour of five o'clock. Lady Grantley was not best pleased when their visitor was announced.

"What business could Alasdair have at Grantley Manor?" she demanded of her husband, whose eyes had lit up at the prospect of a male companion over the after-dinner port.

"A social call, my dear," suggested the earl.

He was rewarded with a snort of disgust. "Don't be a fool, Grantley. What are we to do with him?"

"We can't be keeping him standing about in the hall, my dear." Her husband was deeply shocked.

Her ladyship sighed. "Show Lord Alasdair into the library, Gossett. And you had better tell Cook to put dinner back half an hour."

"Yes, m'lady." The butler bowed and departed soundlessly.

"Go and see what he wants," instructed the countess with an irritable flap of her hands in her husband's direction, adding with a long-suffering sigh, "I suppose we must invite him to dine."

"Only polite, dear ma'am," the earl said, heaving himself to his feet and heading with some alacrity for the door.

Alasdair turned from the French doors and his contemplation of the winter-bare garden when his host entered the library. "My lord." He bowed. "Forgive this unheralded visit but I'm on a commission for Emma. It won't take me very long to execute."

"Oh, but you must dine with us, dear fellow," the earl said, making it sound more like an appeal than an invitation. "We're just about to sit down to dinner, and my lady begs that you'll join us."

Alasdair had a shrewd idea of how his arrival would have been greeted by the redoubtable Lady Grantley, and his sardonic smile flitted across his mouth. But he said, "That's very kind of you, sir. However, I have taken rooms at the Ship in Lymington and bespoken dinner there. I just need a few minutes in Emma's bedchamber and dressing room. She's convinced she's left behind a book of poetry that she says she cannot do without. I believe Ned gave it to her, and she's very distressed to have mislaid it."

"Oh, indeed we cannot allow you to dine at an inn," the earl declared with unaccustomed firmness. "Dreadful cooks in general . . . no . . . no . . . you'll do much better to take your meal with us, dear fellow. Lady Grantley's cook is quite tolerable—really quite tolerable. You shall dine first and then fetch Emma's book. Come, sir. Come along." He urged his guest to the door.

Alasdair yielded gracefully and steeled himself to greet his reluctant hostess.

"See here, ma'am, I've persuaded Lord Alasdair to dine with us," the earl said boisterously as he reentered the salon, where his wife sat with her embroidery. "He's come on a commission for Emma. She's mislaid some book that Ned gave her . . . thinks it may still be in her bedchamber here . . . sherry, Alasdair?"

"Thank you, sir." Alasdair bowed to Lady Grantley. "I'm on my way to friends in Dorset, ma'am, and

Emma asked me to stop here on my way. I trust it doesn't inconvenience you."

"Hardly," Lady Grantley said. "I'll have a small sherry, Grantley." She fixed Alasdair with a gimlet eye. "I fear you will be disappointed in your errand, Lord Alasdair. The housekeeper has turned out Emma's bedchamber thoroughly, and I don't believe she found any of Emma's possessions still there."

"Emma has slept in that bedchamber since she left the nursery, ma'am, and I believe she had certain private places that are perhaps unknown to the house-keeper." Alasdair took a glass from his host. "She gave me precise instructions where to look. Both there and in her dressing room." He sipped sherry and of-fered the lady a benign smile.

Lady Grantley huffed a little but could find no le-gitimate objection.

"I trust dear Emma's settling down in London," Lord Grantley said.

"I trust she's setting about finding herself a hus-band," Lady Grantley stated acidly. "A girl of two and twenty! She's almost on the shelf."

The return of the butler to announce dinner saved Alasdair from having to find a reply to this declara-tion. He gave his arm to his hostess and escorted her into the dining room.

Throughout the interminable and indifferent meal, he exerted himself to be charming, although he was plagued by memories of so many other meals he had eaten at this board, where for almost twelve years he had been as at home as Ned and Emma. Meals filled with laughter and wit. Meals where Emma had sat in her place across from him, her eyes sparkling, her hair taking on myriad colors beneath the candelabra. And Ned . . . Ned had sat to the right of his father until he had taken his father's place at the table's head. Ned had always had some story to tell, some witty joke. And the three of them had teased each other, and mocked each other . . . and loved each other. . . .

Twelve years carried a lot of memories . . . now all tinged with the sorrow of loss, with the bitterness of anger and betrayal.

He raised his glass and drank deeply. Despite Lord Grantley's promises, the food was indifferent, but the burgundy was fine. Ned's father had had a splendid cellar, and Ned had kept it up. The free-traders plied the Hampshire and Dorsetshire coast frequently, and there were few gentlemen's establishments that they didn't supply. Looking at Lord Grantley's rubicund countenance, Alasdair reckoned that the present earl would follow in his predecessors' footsteps at least as far as his cellar needs were concerned.

It was with great relief that he saw Lady Grantley make a move to rise from the table. He rose and bowed as she withdrew, leaving the gentlemen to their port with the firm injunction that Grantley was to consider his gout and not to take more than two glasses.

Alasdair spent half an hour with the earl and then excused himself to complete his errand. The earl was clearly disappointed that they weren't to sit long at the table, but his guest was adamant and with a heavy sigh his lordship set the stopper back into the decanter and rose.

"Well, you know your way, dear boy." He gestured to the stairs as they went into the hall. "I'll have Gossett light the lamps in Emma's bedchamber for you."

"There's no need, sir. I'll take a candle." Alasdair took up one of the small carrying candles from the hall table and lit it from the wax taper in a heavy silver candlestick. Shielding the flame with his free hand, he went up the horseshoe flight of stairs.

Sconces were lit along the corridors leading from the central hallway abovestairs, but when he entered Emma's old bedchamber it was dark and felt cold and very empty. He held the candle high and it threw its flickering light over the room that was so familiar and yet now so desolate and strange, deserted by the spirit of its former occupant. The furniture was the same; he could see the burn in the dresser top where Emma had once put down her hot curling tongs without due attention; the old stain was still visible on the carpet where she'd knocked over a cup of chocolate when he and Ned had surprised her, returning early one summer for the long vacation from Oxford.

He set the candle on the mantelpiece from where it would throw the most light and went immediately to the armoire. It was empty and he found the little concealed panel in the rear without difficulty. It sprang open to his touch and he ran his fingers around the small space thus revealed. There was only dust.

In truth he didn't expect to find anything, but before he began the much more complex task of searching Emma's possessions in her new abode, he had to rule out the possibility that she had left some of her private papers in one of her secret spots in her old home. He looked behind the pictures, remembering that on a treasure hunt she had once hidden a clue behind the backing of her mother's portrait. There was nothing there. He went through all the empty drawers in the dresser; he looked under the bed; he lifted the carpet. There was nothing. Not a single scrap of paper to be found.

And it had to be on a piece of paper. It would help

if he knew exactly what he was looking for, but his instructions had been vague; Charles Lester had had no more idea than he what medium Ned would have used to convey his information. When Ned's communication sent on by Hugh Melton had been opened at Horseguards, it had contained only a letter to Ned's sister. The letter had been scrutinized by the code breakers but had yielded nothing. The only conclusion they could come to was that there had been some confusion in that blood-soaked haste before his death, and the communication destined for Horseguards had gone instead to Lady Emma.

To Alasdair, the hole-in-the-corner secrecy of his search seemed ridiculous. He had said to Lester that surely the simplest thing would be to ask Emma if she'd kept her brother's last communication—the one sent on by Hugh Melton. But his suggestion had been vetoed absolutely. Lady Emma for her own safety must not know that she had in her possession something so dangerous, so vital to the course of the war with Bonaparte. If she knew its importance, she might pay it dangerous attention, and if she memorized it, for instance, that knowledge would make her a target for others seeking it.

And their methods of extracting information were both thorough and unpleasant, Mr. Lester had explained with steepled fingers and an almost apologetic manner. He did not address the issue that whether she'd remembered the document or not, she could still be subject to these unpleasant methods of interrogation. The enemy, if she fell into their hands, were unlikely to take her word for it if she protested ignorance. But it was clear to Alasdair that Emma's welfare was not of real interest to Charles Lester and his masters. The fewer people who knew of the importance of the document, the better. That was all they really cared about.

But did she have it? Alasdair asked himself as he carried the candle into the dressing room next door to continue his search there. She might have thrown it away. But he thought that an outside chance. Emma would not have thrown away anything that came from Ned, particularly after his death. He knew she kept all his letters. She was a hoarder, a highly secretive hoarder. She had always kept everything . . . every letter he and Ned had written her from school and Oxford . . . anything that had any personal relevance for her; hence her warren of secret hiding places.

His search of the dressing room drew another blank. Even the bookshelves were empty. Between the pages of books had been another of her favorite hiding places. But all her own volumes had been packed up and delivered to Mount Street. Alasdair supposed somewhat gloomily that he was going to have to go through them all. Through her books and through her writing case and all the drawers in her secretaire.

It was a hideous prospect. And in the present strained state of their relationship, well nigh impossible. He would have to find some excuse that would give him easy access to the house on Mount Street and the freedom to move around it at will. His position as trustee gave him access to Emma herself, but no right to roam her house.

But somehow it would have to be done. King and country demanded it. Or rather Ned demanded it. If Ned had died for this information, then his friend must do everything in his power to ensure that that death had not been in vain.

Chapter Four

❦

"Oh, do look at that enchanting gown, Emma. It will suit you to perfection." Maria leaned over and tapped the coachman's shoulder. "Pull up, John. Lady Emma and I will get down here."

John-coachman reined in his horses on Bond Street. He was accustomed to such frequent instructions from Mrs. Witherspoon, whose sharp eyes took in every shop window that they passed.

"Oh, Maria, must we?" Emma protested. "We have spent the entire day going from warehouse to warehouse, milliners to milliners, bootmakers to bootmakers. I don't think I could endure to look at another ell of material."

"This one, my dear, you will be glad to examine," Maria said with firm confidence as she took the footman's hand to descend from the barouche. "That particular shade of jonquil is so exactly suited to you, and you may wear it with the saffron kid slippers. So pretty it will look." She bustled eagerly into the shop.

"Walk the horses, John," Emma instructed with a little sigh, descending to the street. "We may be some minutes."

"So I would presume, Lady Emma." The coachman glanced rather pointedly at the mountain of band-boxes already filling the rear seat of the barouche.

Emma had forgotten how indefatigable Maria was when it came to shopping. Her own tolerance was much more limited, although she had no intention whatsoever of showing herself to London in out-moded gowns. It had taken her no more than a day's observation to recognize that Alasdair had as usual been quite correct on the unfashionable condition of her wardrobe.

"I think, my dear, that we should pay some calls tomorrow," Maria said when they were once more back in the barouche; the jonquil gown after some necessary alterations was to be delivered in Mount Street later that evening. "Now that you've done some shopping and are ready to face the world—that hairstyle by the by is all the rage—we should call upon Princess Esterhazy and Lady Jersey. Just to make sure about vouchers for Almack's. Once it's known that you're ready to receive callers, we shall be inundated," she added happily.

Emma didn't reply. It had been close to a week since Alasdair had left town after their hateful quarrel, and she had had ample time to question the impulse that had fueled her challenge. They'd been living reclusively these last days, but the time for that was now past. And once the doorknocker started banging, and the invitation cards poured in, as they would surely do, she was going to have to make good her challenge. Niggling doubts she resolutely quashed. She would free herself from Alasdair's control at the earliest opportunity. If only she hadn't also issued that impetuous challenge about taking a lover. A husband would be easy, but a lover . . . ?

However, she'd sworn to do it and she wasn't going to give Alasdair the chance to gloat. What he could do, she could do. Her mouth took a wry turn as she reflected how competitive they had always been with each other. Or maybe, to be brutally honest, it was she who had always felt the need to compete with Alasdair . . . and to a lesser extent with Ned. It was presumably a holdover from her early girlhood when she had always been afraid that if she couldn't keep up with them, they would leave her out of their activities. Maturity, of course, should have lessened the compulsion to compete, but it hadn't happened.

A flicker of derision, as much self-directed as otherwise, crossed her eyes. Alasdair had hurt her badly, so she had hurt him back. The wounds they had inflicted upon each other three years ago had been too severe to heal over. And they were still hurting each other in a pride-fueled, spiraling competition to inflict the deepest injury.

She had given herself until February 14 to achieve both an offer of marriage and a liaison. If the same man could fill both roles, it would make things easier, but she'd sworn to take as husband the first man who offered for her, and maybe he wouldn't fit the bill as lover. The possible inconvenience of being wed to a man whose bed you couldn't imagine occupying was one Emma chose to ignore.

"My love, Horace Poole is bowing to you." Maria nudged her arm.

Emma glanced up. The gentleman in question was

beaming and bowing from the side of the street. "Odious man," Emma murmured as she offered a frosty bow in return. "There hasn't been an heiress in the last ten years for whom he hasn't made a beeline."

"Well, my dear, you know it's only to be expected. They'll all be around you like wasps at the jam," Maria said. "It will be very tiresome, I'm sure. But you mustn't despair of finding a man who is not influenced by your wealth." She patted Emma's knee comfortingly.

That, Emma thought, would be truly wishing for the moon, but she silently amended the conditions of her challenge: she would take the first offer made her by a man who was not a gazetted fortune hunter.

Maria glanced at her companion's set profile and swallowed a little sigh. Emma had never before had to suffer the discomforts of being courted only for her fortune. She had been but three weeks into her debutante season when she and Alasdair had become engaged, and after their scandalous breakup, she had retired to the country, ostensibly only until the scandal had died down, but somehow she hadn't fixed a date to return to town and Maria had soon stopped asking her.

While Maria was relieved that those years of Emma's melancholy rustication seemed to be over, she was conscious of some anxiety about how Emma was going to deal with the social consequences of her wealth. She did not tolerate fools gladly, and she had an impetuous temperament, impatient of restraint. Her fortune and lineage should give her some leeway with the highest sticklers, if she transgressed the rigid rules of society again, but her high spirits had led her into trouble in her first season, even before the scandal.

There had been the incident of the carriage race with Lady Armstrong . . . Maria shuddered at the memory. That had nearly ruined Emma's reputation. And then there'd been the ridotto at Ranelagh, when she'd gone dressed in britches and pretended to be a footpad. Ned and Alasdair had been largely responsible for that escapade, and had taken part in it themselves. And as for her other adventures, if they hadn't directly participated in them, they'd certainly encouraged them. It was to be hoped that the intervening years had taught Emma some prudence. At least she wouldn't have the encouragement of Ned and Alasdair this season.

Had Maria been able to read Emma's mind at that moment, she would probably have succumbed to strong hysterics. Emma was contemplating the difficulties involved in taking a lover to order. The arrangement would have to be kept secret . . . from everyone except Alasdair, of course. So long as lovers were discreet, society would turn a blind eye to a liaison if, by some miracle, it could be arranged that the love affair was a prelude to marriage. She and Alasdair had managed to conduct their own liaison without a breath of scandal until its abrupt ending.

But could this putative lover also be husband material?

As she went up to her bedroom to take off her pelisse and gloves, Emma was conscious of a stirring of excitement. A faint twitch of exuberance. The first she had felt in the months since the news of Ned's death. She was twenty-two, too young to settle into a spinster's passionless retirement. Alasdair, damn his eyes, had been right. She had found it very difficult to live without the lovemaking that had gradually become indispensable to her happiness, her bodily well-being.

Alasdair had taught her the joys of passion, and once taught they were not easily forgotten. But they could be enjoyed with others. And she *would* enjoy them again.

❦

Alasdair arrived in Albermarle Street as the evening was drawing in. He jumped down from the post chaise and walked briskly up the steps. Cranham had been on the lookout for his return and had the door open when his master's foot was on the first step.

"A pleasant visit, I trust, sir." He took Alasdair's curly-brimmed beaver and his caped driving coat, reverently smoothing the folds. His eyes darted to Lord Alasdair's boots and he nodded grimly. Whoever had been responsible for their care during my lord's travels had not known the finer points of champagne blacking.

"Tedious for the most part, Cranham," Alasdair said, entering his own front door. He picked up the pile of missives on the table, flicking through them. Invitations, bills, a couple of sealed letters on scented writing paper. One sealed sheet of plain vellum he tucked into his waistcoat pocket. He went into the salon, where a fire burned brightly in the polished grate and a decanter of claret reposed on a silver tray on a marble-topped console table.

He tossed his mail on a sofa table and poured himself a glass of claret. "I'll dine at White's tonight, Cranham."

"Yes, sir. I'll unpack your portmanteau, sir. I daresay I'll find your clothes in a sad case."

"Doubtless," Alasdair said with a slight grin. "Although I considered I managed quite well for myself."

Cranham didn't dignify this impossibility with a response. He bowed and withdrew.

Alasdair's grin faded. He'd spent the last four days racketing around the Hampshire countryside, staying in damnably uncomfortable inns, because he couldn't return to London without having been away a sufficient length of time to justify a trip to Lincolnshire. Emma would have made some comment. It was possible, of course, that she would hear from the Grantleys of his visit, but he considered it unlikely. There was so little love lost between Hester Grantley and her niece that communication would probably extend no further than yuletide greetings. However, if it did come out, by that time this business should be settled once and for all.

He took the sheet of vellum out of his pocket and opened the wafer with his fingernail. It was from his contact at Horseguards. He scanned the vigorously penned lines. Charles Lester was a man of unsoldierly bearing, but his stick-thin frame, hunched shoulders, and concave chest belied a mind as sharp as a razor. He spoke in short, concise sentences and he wrote as he spoke.

> *It has come to our attention that others are interested in the document in question. We are making further inquiries, but you should be on your guard. I will keep you informed. CL.*

Alasdair scrunched the missive in his fist and threw it into the fire. Very informative it had been, he thought aridly, refilling his wineglass. Telling him to be on his guard without the slightest clue against whom.

He glanced at the clock. It was close to seven. Was

Emma dining at home? he wondered. Once he would have thought nothing of dropping in and inviting himself to dinner, claiming the privilege first of an old friend and then of a fiancé. He shook his head impatiently and went into his bedchamber next door, where Cranham was laying out his evening clothes.

Half an hour later, he was walking across the hall when his upstairs neighbor came down the stairs almost as if on cue. "Lord Alasdair, you are returned," said Paul Denis with his charming smile.

"As you see." Alasdair nodded politely, taking the other's outstretched hand. "I am going to dine at White's. Are you a member?"

"Oh, yes, indeed. Prince Esterhazy put up my name. He is an old acquaintance of my father's. I was on my way to dine there myself, as it happens. Perhaps I could . . ." He waited politely.

"By all means," Alasdair said. He was not averse to company after four days of his own, and it was always useful to maintain good relations with one's neighbors.

The evening was convivial, and when the company moved to the card tables, Paul Denis was quick to take his place at the first invitation to join them. Alasdair brought to the gambling table the same clearheaded skills he brought to investing. In fact, the two activities were inextricably combined. What he won at the card tables, he augmented at the Exchange in stocks and shares. It would have explained to Emma his apparent ability to live on air, had he chosen to enlighten her. Ned had known of his uncanny skill at making much of little. It had presumably been one reason why he had entrusted his old friend with Emma's fortune.

But not the only reason. Although Alasdair hadn't

admitted it to Emma, he agreed with her that Ned had hoped to achieve a reconciliation between his sister and his friend by throwing them together in such intimate conjunction. It would have grieved him to see how far off the mark he'd been. Alasdair took up his cards, a tiny sigh escaping him.

The subject, as he'd expected, came up within a very short time.

"I hear Emma Beaumont's back in town," Lord Alveston commented, pushing a rouleau of guineas across the table.

"Yes, and, as no doubt you've also heard, under her brother's will I am her trustee," Alasdair said coolly, making his own bet.

"Deuced awkward, that," remarked a gentleman with a startlingly painted face.

"Oh, and why is that, Sketchley?" Alasdair inquired with a raised eyebrow and a voice with an edge that would cut steel.

Viscount Sketchley blushed beneath his paint. It produced a rather interesting color scheme, Alasdair thought. "Oh, no reason . . . no reason at all."

Alasdair inclined his head in mocking acceptance and continued with his play. There was a short awkward silence, then the duke of Bedford, who held the bank, declared, "Rich as Croesus she is now, I hear."

Alasdair again acknowledged this with an indifferent nod.

"If she still has her looks—" continued the duke.

"Oh, believe me, she has," Alasdair interrupted, laying his cards upon the table. "My hand, gentlemen."

"I keep promising myself I'll not play at your table, Alasdair, and then I forget how damned lucky you are," Lord Alveston complained, throwing down his own cards in disgust.

"Oh, it's not luck, George," Alasdair said with a laugh. "Can you not recognize pure skill when you see it?"

"So, is she hangin' out for a husband?" the duke persisted.

"What unattached woman is not, Duke?" asked Lord Sketchley with a little titter.

"You're not still in the lists, Alasdair?" Alveston asked bluntly.

Alasdair was relieved to have the question at last brought into the open. Once it was dealt with, categorically denied, he hoped the past would be allowed to die. "No, I am not. Emma and I agreed that we would not suit. Nothing has changed. Do you deal, Duke?"

The duke picked up the fresh pack placed at his elbow by a groom-porter and shuffled deftly. "So the field's wide open, then?"

"As far as I know," Alasdair agreed.

"And you've no say in the matter?" Sketchley inquired closely.

"None whatsoever." Alasdair made his bet and changed the subject, wondering uneasily just how far Emma was prepared to go with her challenge. Surely not far enough to take such a painted fop as Sketchley for a husband. *Or lover?* He glanced across the table with a violent surge of revulsion at the image of that simpering fool's hands on Emma's glorious body. No, it was not possible that she would be so lost to sanity.

His eyes swept the salon, brightly lit by chandeliers whose crystal drops threw back the light of their myriad candles. Was there a man in this room whom he could tolerate in Emma's bed? The answer was immediately apparent. It seemed he was suffering from a virulent case of dog in the manger.

"But I daresay your opinion would weigh with Lady Emma?" the duke suggested. "Being her trustee and such a good friend of her brother's. If you spoke up for a man . . ."

"Lady Emma has a mind of her own," Alasdair stated flatly.

Paul Denis played carefully, as befitted a man who was not too plump in the pocket. His émigré status was well understood, and a wealthy émigré was a rarity. He offered no comment on the subject of Emma Beaumont, and his silence went unremarked. He could not after all be expected to contribute to a conversation concerning people he didn't know. And no one would guess the rapid calculations clicking behind his smooth olive-skinned forehead. If Lady Emma Beaumont was to be besieged by suitors, he could join their ranks without comment.

"Do you return to Albermarle Street, Lord Alasdair?" he inquired as the table broke up in the early hours. "May I walk home with you?"

"By all means." Alasdair took a glass of iced champagne from the tray of a passing waiter. "Give me half an hour. There are some people I haven't spoken to this evening." Glass in hand, he circled the room, making certain that everyone there understood that Alasdair Chase was not holding a candle for Emma Beaumont. That the mortification of three years ago was forgotten. Then he went in search of Paul Denis, who was sitting in the bow window that looked out on darkened St. James's Street, perusing a periodical.

"I hope you won't consider it impertinent if I ask for your help in making myself known in society,"

Monsieur Denis asked tentatively as they strolled along Piccadilly.

Alasdair gave him a shrewd glance. "Hanging out for a rich wife too, Denis?" he inquired.

Paul managed to look a trifle self-conscious. "Not exactly . . . but my situation is a little . . . well, a little constrained, shall we say?"

Alasdair shrugged. "No more than many, I daresay."

"Perhaps not. But this Lady Emma, I wonder . . ." He coughed delicately. "I was wondering if perhaps you could effect an introduction. If you have no objections, of course."

Alasdair felt a sharp stab of pain somewhere in the region of his breastbone. First Bedford and now this émigré. It seemed that he was to act as pander, procuring potential suitors and lovers for a woman whom he'd just discovered he couldn't contemplate belonging to anyone but himself.

"I suggest you ask Princess Esterhazy for an introduction," he said. "I'm not expecting to call upon Lady Emma in the near future."

Paul Denis accepted this in silence, but his thoughts raced. He had noticed the sudden tension in Lord Alasdair at the card table during the discussion of Lady Emma's possible marriage. It was well concealed, but not for an eye and an ear trained to notice any shift of emotion, any telltale flicker or hesitancy. It would seem that the governor had been misinformed. Whatever the close connection between Lady Emma Beaumont and Lord Alasdair Chase, it didn't appear to be a particularly easy one. Lord Alasdair was her trustee; was that perhaps a bone of contention? Whatever the reason for the constraint, it wasn't going to help his own plans any. He would have to find an alternative route to his quarry.

❧

"You're very preoccupied this morning, my love," Maria observed, dipping a finger of toast in her teacup and carrying the sopping morsel to her mouth.

Emma nibbled the end of her quill and then scratched out the lines she'd written. She pushed paper and pen aside and returned to her breakfast. "I have a very vexing issue to deal with," she explained vaguely.

"Oh, perhaps I can help?" Maria took another finger of toast and bathed it in tea.

Emma shook her head and said with a touch of mischief, "No, I don't think so. You're no judge of horseflesh." She regarded Maria's steady consumption of tea and toast with customary amazement, while sipping her own coffee and making inroads into a dish of bacon and mushrooms.

"We should visit Princess Esterhazy first this morning, I believe," Maria said, following her own train of thought. "The next subscription ball at Almack's is to be on the fifteenth, and we must be sure to have vouchers in time. I think the ball dress of ivory gauze over the turquoise satin would be perfect, don't you, my love?"

"Mmmm," Emma murmured, once more engrossed in her letter writing.

"Of course, the bronze crepe becomes you so well," Maria continued, untroubled by her companion's lack of concentration on such an important topic. "I wonder if perhaps the gold embroidered scarf would look particularly elegant with it. You should ask Mathilda to look it out, my love, and we'll decide later."

"Mmmm," said Emma, bringing the last line of her missive to a period with a decisive jab of her quill. "That's the best I can do." She waved the sheet in the air to dry the ink, then folded it carefully. "I must just get this sent off, Maria. Shall I order the carriage to be at the door in half an hour?"

"Yes, if you can be ready in that time," Maria agreed somewhat doubtfully. Emma, as was her invariable custom unless she was breakfasting early before a hunt meet, had come downstairs in a wrapper over her nightgown.

Emma laughed at this. "I shall be ready in twenty minutes." She whisked herself from the breakfast parlor, leaving Maria to finish her tea and toast.

She was as good as her word and was downstairs again well within the half hour, drawing on a pair of lavender kid gloves. "Did you send the message, Harris?"

"Yes, ma'am. Bodley took it straightaway. The barouche is at the door."

"Here I am . . . here I am," Maria trilled as she came down the stairs. "Dear me, I made sure I'd be ahead of you, Emma. I had only to put on my bonnet and pick up my gloves, and you had not even begun to dress." She ran an appraising glance over Emma's close-fitting driving habit as she chattered, hurrying all the while to the door. "That dark blue was a very good choice," she declared as the footman handed her up into the barouche.

Emma climbed in after her, allowing Maria's stream of inconsequential chatter to flow over her. Maria rarely required a concrete response to her remarks, and Emma had long perfected the art of appearing to listen politely while thinking her own thoughts. At the moment, those thoughts were entirely concerned with horses.

The Austrian ambassador and his wife lived in a stately double-fronted stucco mansion in Berkeley Square. Princess Esterhazy received her visitors in the upstairs drawing room overlooking the square gardens.

"Maria Witherspoon," she said with her vivacious laugh. "I haven't see you in town for months. Are you come up for the entire season?" She didn't wait for an answer but turned immediately to Emma. A dark eyebrow lifted slightly. "Lady Emma, my condolences on your brother's death."

"Thank you, ma'am." Emma bowed. She was aware that her hostess's scrutiny was somewhat speculative.

"You decided not to go into full mourning, I take it," the princess stated.

"My brother would not have wished it," Emma replied.

"Ah. Young people these days . . . so little respect for convention," the lady pronounced.

"Oh, that's a little harsh, Princess," Maria said, bustling forward. "Emma has been grief stricken for many months. But it was dear Ned's expressed desire . . . in his will," she added fallaciously but with great firmness, "that she set up her own establishment as soon as Lord and Lady Grantley moved into Grantley Manor."

The princess nodded. Her speculative gaze still rested on Emma's countenance, and Emma could almost hear her thoughts running along the lines of: *Two hundred thousand pounds! Not to be sneezed at, oh, dear me, no. Much can be overlooked for such a fortune.*

"Well," Princess Esterhazy said at last, "I must send

you vouchers for Almack's, mustn't I? I'll send them around this afternoon. Mount Street, I understand?"

"Yes, a most delightful house," Maria said. "Lord Alasdair Chase, Emma's trustee, hired it for her."

"Ah, yes," their hostess said. "Lord Alasdair." Her gaze became rather more intense and it was clear to her visitors that she was recollecting the old scandal.

"Lord Alasdair is a very old and steadfast friend," Maria stated confidently, looking the princess in the eye.

Any comment the princess might have made remained unsaid as the butler announced Lady Sefton and her son Lord Molyneux. They were followed by Lady Drummond and her three daughters, and the salon quickly became a buzz of conversation. Maria was immediately in her element and there was no further awkwardness on the subject of past scandals. Emma's return to society drew no comment, although she overheard Lady Drummond murmuring to Lady Sefton, "Is it true? Two hundred thousand pounds?"

"So I believe," the other replied. "How can it be that she's still unmarried? She's well enough looking . . . although too tall and lanky for many tastes. But with a fortune of that size, a man can overlook a few imperfections."

"Perhaps she's difficult to please," suggested Lady Drummond. "She has a definite air of consequence, wouldn't you say . . . and after the scandal . . ."

Emma moved away, her ears burning. It was most unpleasant to be talked of in such fashion, although she had known it to be inevitable.

"Mr. Paul Denis, ma'am," the butler announced from the door, and Emma glanced over at the new arrival. He was a man of medium height, black hair curled crisply over a well-shaped skull, very dark eyes gleaming in an olive-hued complexion. He bowed to his hostess with a flourish that seemed entirely in tune with his rather exotic appearance and spoke with a faint but noticeable accent.

"Princess, I am come to pay my respects. My father, I believe, wrote to your husband." He raised the princess's hand to his lips and kissed it elegantly.

"Oh, yes, I remember. Some family connection . . . a great-aunt, wasn't it?" She smiled benignly at this most presentable young man.

Paul agreed that it was indeed a great-aunt who connected them, and kissed her hand yet again. Princess Esterhazy drew him aside and began to question him in her lively manner as to his childhood and present circumstances.

Emma accepted a cup of coffee from a footman's tray and moved imperceptibly closer to the princess and her new visitor. There was something about the man that caught her attention. Something almost intriguing about his dark looks, about the way he held himself, as if poised on the brink of some dramatic action. She caught herself noticing that he was stockier than Alasdair, but his clothes didn't sit as well on his frame. Perhaps they were not so well cut as Alasdair's, she thought. Alasdair, of course, would know at a glance whether the man had had his coat made by Weston, or Shultz, or Schweitzer and Davidson . . . or some other, lesser tailor. But then, perhaps it was the frame that was at fault . . . the shoulders didn't fill the coat with quite the perfection of Alasdair's; the leg was not quite as long or well formed, so there was the faintest wrinkle to the pantaloons; the hips were perhaps a trifle foreshortened. . . .

"Lady Emma, permit me to make Mr. Denis known to you." Princess Esterhazy became aware of Emma standing close by. "He, too, has but newly arrived in town. Mr. Denis, may I present Lady Emma Beaumont."

"Mr. Denis." Emma was not sorry to have her comparative assessment interrupted. She moved forward with her hand outstretched. He bowed over it and raised it to his lips. The gesture struck Emma as slightly affected with its courtly flourish, and she reclaimed her hand at the earliest opportunity. "You are French?"

"An émigré family, ma'am." He smiled, showing very white, slightly crooked teeth. "I was a boy when we fled France in '91. Some kind friends of my parents living in Kent took us in when we first arrived."

"Do you remember much of the revolution, sir?" Emma had always been fascinated by the bloody horror of the Terror.

"I have some memories. Do they interest you?" Paul's smile deepened, his eyes focused on her face, and Emma felt a strange and disturbing intimacy develop between them. He was looking at her as if she had become the only person in the room. It had been a long time since anyone but the lumpy sons of country squires had regarded her with such pointed masculine attention. It was pure flirtation, of course, but she was not averse to the game . . . no, not at all.

She smiled, her eyes narrowing a little. "I must own to something of an obsession with the events of that dreadful time, sir. If you could bear to satisfy my curiosity, you'd find me a most attentive listener."

"I should be delighted." He offered her his arm and

they moved away from the center of the room to a sofa set in a window embrasure.

Princess Esterhazy nodded to herself. She liked to do favors for her friends and relations, and although she couldn't for the life of her place this great-aunt connection, if her husband said it was so, she was happy to take his word for it. The young man seemed unexceptionable. His manner was well-bred, his dress, if lacking the extremes of dandyism, perfectly conformable. And if he managed to secure the heiress and her two hundred thousand pounds, then the princess considered that she would have performed a very good deed.

Maria Witherspoon, however, was not so complaisant. She had a very simple and pragmatic view of the world. Emma should not be wasting her time on an impoverished and insignificant newcomer. She had come to London to get a husband, and Maria saw no reason why that husband shouldn't bear the blood of kings.

She bore down on the couple, wreathed in smiles, saying, "Emma dear, we must be on our way. . . . Oh, how do you do, sir?" She raised an inquiring eyebrow at Emma's companion.

Emma was surprised. Maria was not usually haughty, but there was a definite loftiness in her manner, as if she were crushing the pretensions of some social mushroom. She made introductions and watched in amazement as Maria bowed coldly. Paul Denis seemed not to notice, and greeted Emma's chaperone with courtly attention. But as Emma bade him farewell, he gave her a comical look of dismay that brought ready laughter into her eyes.

"I fear your duenna thinks me unworthy," he murmured as he took Emma's hand. "Dare I call in Mount Street, or will she deny me?"

"Maria is not mistress in Mount Street," Emma said, and then instantly, as she heard her own faint hauteur, despised her arrogance. It was a besetting sin. One, of course, that she shared with Alasdair.

"Then may I call on you?"

"Please do." She smiled warmly, adding, "Maria is the very best of companions. She watches over me like a mother hen."

"That has its comforts," Paul said with a gravity belied by the expression in his eyes.

Emma laughed. "Yes, indeed it does, sir. I give you good day."

She made her farewells, conscious of a lighthearted and exuberant feeling of gaiety; a feeling that hitherto she had always associated with her music, with dancing until dawn, or after a particularly splendid run with the hounds . . . or after some mad prank with Ned and Alasdair.

"I wonder if Mr. Denis is quite the thing," Maria ventured, once they were back in the barouche.

"He's related to Princess Esterhazy, Maria. How can he not be?" Emma tucked her hands into her sable muff against a sharp gust of wind whipping around the corner of Curzon Street.

"I don't know, my love. But there was something about him that I couldn't quite like."

"Oh, stuff, Maria," Emma scoffed lightly. "He'll be seen everywhere. Do you imagine Princess Esterhazy is going to deny him a voucher for Almack's?"

"I daresay not." But Maria remained unconvinced and was uncharacteristically silent on the drive back to Mount Street.

Once inside, Emma cast aside her muff and her

gloves and strode energetically to the music room, unpinning her velvet hat as she went, handing it to an attentive footman. She was under a familiar compulsion. "I'm going to practice for a while, Maria."

Maria understood that to mean that she would probably not see Emma again until the evening.

Chapter Five

"Good afternoon, Harris. Is Lady Emma in?" Alasdair strolled up the shallow stairs into the hall. "Ah, yes, I hear that she is." He nodded in the direction of the music room, then cocked his head. "Must be in a good humor," he observed, tossing his driving whip on a pier table and turning to allow a footman to help him off with his driving cape.

"Yes, sir," Harris said. He had been butler in the Grantley household since Ned's birth and understood exactly what Lord Alasdair meant. Lady Emma was playing an aria from *The Magic Flute*. She tended to play Mozart when she was in particularly good spirits.

Alasdair grinned and strode across the hall to the door at the rear. He opened it very softly and slipped inside, closing it soundlessly behind him. He stood quietly listening with an ear that was both critical and appreciative. A branched candlestick threw light over the music stand, but it was a light that paled against the brilliant winter sunshine pouring through the French doors that opened onto a walled garden at the rear of the house.

Emma was wearing her hair in one of the new classical styles, a silver fillet banding her brow, her hair looped over her ears at the sides and swept up at the back and tucked into the fillet. Her exposed neck was slightly bent as she played, and Alasdair's gaze was riveted on the tender groove running from the base of her skull, disappearing into the high collar of the driving habit she still wore from the morning's visiting.

He moved forward under a compulsion he could not resist. She was absorbed in the music and heard nothing of his step on the thick Axminster carpet. He bent his head and lightly kissed the nape of her neck, his hands coming to rest where the graceful slope of her shoulders blended with her upper arms.

Emma's hands stilled on the keys, her head falling forward as if under some weight, although the kiss had been the merest brush of his lips.

"Forgive me," Alasdair said before she could speak. His hands dropped from her shoulders. "Outrageous, I know, but I couldn't resist." He made his voice light and jocular as if what had just occurred were a mere commonplace.

Emma raised her head, straightened her spine. The back of her neck was warm, still tingling. She looked over her shoulder at him in silence.

Alasdair gave her a rueful smile. "You know I've never been able to resist the back of your neck."

"*Don't!*" she said in a stifled voice. "For God's sake, Alasdair!"

He held up his hands in conciliation. "It didn't happen," he said. "Listen, I had an idea while you were playing. Let me sit down." He gestured that she should move up on the piano bench and make room for him. "A more exaggerated pause between these notes . . . here . . . and again here." He played several bars one-handed, his other beating the time. "See? And then when Papageno comes in . . . here . . . it lifts the tempo, makes the conversation even livelier."

Emma nodded. "I wonder why Mozart didn't think of that," she said with a grin.

Alasdair chuckled. "All art is open to individual interpretation. Sing it; let's hear how it sounds." He swept his hands over the keys in preparation, then began to play.

Emma hesitated for barely a second, then began to sing. She had a contralto voice, well trained with perfect pitch, but she'd be the first to admit that it lacked true power. But then, both she and Alasdair were perfectionists, as critical of their own performances as they were of others'. But the aria was pure delight to sing, filled with sunshine and laughter, and she let her voice run with it to Alasdair's accompaniment. And when he joined in with his own pleasant tenor in counterpoint, Emma closed her eyes and lost herself in the sheer joy of making these beautiful sounds with someone so perfectly matched and so filled with the same pleasure.

She held the last note, her voice soaring, after Alasdair's fingers on the keys had fallen still and his own voice was quiet. The note faded slowly, perfectly controlled, and in the silence the sweetness continued to ring in sonorous echo for seconds after the note itself had died.

Alasdair let his hands fall from the keys. "You have more power than when I last heard you sing."

"My voice is better trained now," she said, rising from the bench as with the end of the music she became aware of Alasdair's thigh pressing against her skirt.

"Did you continue with Rudolfo?"

"Through two summers. He came to the country and stayed in the house and drove the staff insane with his fussiness. He's such a valetudinarian. But an amazing voice teacher." She straightened a pair of candlesticks on the mantelpiece, tidied a pile of sheet music on the table, her eyes darting restlessly, her fingers unable to be still.

Alasdair swung around on the piano bench and watched her for a second. "So, what did you wish to see me about?"

Emma's restless fidgeting ceased. "Horses," she declared. "I intend to purchase a curricle and pair. Oh, and a riding horse," she added. "Aunt Hester decided that all my horses belonged to the estate." Her eyes sparked golden fire with remembered indignation.

"Of all the unmitigated old cats!" Alasdair exclaimed. "It's not as if she could ride them herself."

"No, indeed," Emma scoffed. "I should like to see her try. She'd be thrown before they left the stable-yard. But they are to remain as part of the estate." Her lips were tightly compressed and she stared for a minute unseeing at the garden through the window.

"You couldn't lay claim to them?"

"If you mean, were they clearly my own . . . gifts from Ned or whatever . . . no. Strictly speaking, the old cat was right. They belong to the estate." She fell silent, her hands clenched at her sides, then she continued briskly, "So, I intend to set up my stable." She turned to him, saying with a touch of belligerence, "You have no objection, I trust?"

"No, why should I?" Alasdair responded amiably, ignoring the belligerence, rightly assuming that for once it was not really directed at him. If Aunt Hester had been in the room, it would have found the right target.

Emma flushed slightly and said more moderately, "I need you to escort me to Tattersalls to buy my horses. I know I cannot go there alone."

"You cannot go to Tatts at all," Alasdair stated, taking a lacquered snuffbox from his pocket.

"Why ever not?"

Alasdair examined the snuffbox minutely. "Because, my dear Emma, women do not frequent Tattersalls."

Emma regarded him in bewilderment. "But I went there with you and Ned once."

"Good God!" he said solemnly. "Whatever can we have been thinking about? It's not at all the thing."

"Alasdair, you're funning," Emma accused. It was impossible to imagine Alasdair giving a tinker's damn for pointless conventions. Three years couldn't have changed him that much.

"No, indeed not," he denied vigorously, but Emma could read him like a book and the little glimmer in his eye did not go unnoticed.

"Don't be absurd," she said roundly. "You know perfectly well that while a woman buying her own horses might be unusual, it's not a fatal flying in the face of convention. As long as I have a suitable escort, of course. And who more appropriate than my trustee?"

"Ah, so I have some uses after all," he observed,

flicking open the snuffbox and taking a delicate pinch between finger and thumb. He looked at her from beneath lowered lids, his mouth curving in a wicked smile.

"Since I have to put up with you for the time being, I might as well put you to good use," Emma returned smartly. "Now, will you be serious for a minute? Do you have time this afternoon to escort me to Tatts?"

He appeared to give this question some consideration. Emma watched him in growing suspicion, guessing that he was still teasing her. Then he rose from the piano bench, dropped the snuffbox into the deep pocket of his coat, and said with a small bow, "I daresay I can put off my other plans for the afternoon. I am at your service, ma'am. Shall we go at once? My curricle is at the door and you appear to be in driving dress already."

Emma hesitated. "Do you really have other plans?"

"Would you really care?" he asked, his smile now quizzical.

Emma almost stamped her foot. "You are so perverse!" she declared. "I am trying to be polite."

Alasdair laughed. "I am entirely at your disposal, my sweet."

Emma bit her tongue on her automatic protest. If Alasdair was determined to use the endearment, there was nothing she could do about it. Better to ignore it. He wouldn't use it in public.

"We had best not tell Maria our destination," she said instead.

"My lips are sealed." Alasdair went to the door and opened it for her. "I heard a handsome pair of chestnuts is to go on the block at Tatts next week. Chesterton's breakdowns, I believe. You might be able to get them before they go for auction for around three hun-

dred pounds. Shall I go and make my bow to Maria
while you fetch what you need?" He followed her out
of the music room into the hall.

"I'll be just a minute." Emma hurried up the stairs
to fetch her hat and gloves. She knew she could trust
Alasdair to buy horses for her without her being
there, but she had always made her own decisions in
such matters and was not about to change the habits
of a lifetime to accommodate some ridiculous notion
about what a female should and should not do, or
where she should or should not go.

She surveyed herself in her mirror as she adjusted
the set of her little velvet hat with its single plume
curling on her shoulder. Her nose wrinkled slightly as
she took inventory of her reflection. Her nose was too
large, her mouth too wide, she had always thought.
And her eyebrows were too thick and had a distress-
ing tendency to fly away at the edges. Not that she
cared twopence for her physical imperfections, she
told herself firmly, grabbing up her gloves and heading for the door. It wasn't as if she was out to impress
anyone this afternoon. She was only running an errand with Alasdair.

Her hand brushed unconsciously over the back of
her neck as she ran down the stairs.

Alasdair was waiting in the hall, idly slapping his
gloves into the palm of one hand. He turned as she
came down. "Maria is taking a nap," he informed her.
"Harris will tell her that we've gone for a drive." His
eyes appraised her as if it were the first time he'd
noticed her appearance. "That is an entrancing hat,"
he observed. "But . . . allow me . . . there, perfect." He made a deft adjustment to the brim where it
turned up on one side, and smiled down at her.

It was his old smile, the one she'd first seen all

those years ago when an eight-year-old girl had fallen irreparably in love with her brother's best friend.

Emma felt the ground shift beneath her feet. It had been so long since she'd felt the pure warmth of that smile. The sardonic curl, the ironical glint, were gone, the once familiar understanding and invitation in their place.

His hand slipped down the length of her arm, his fingers closing lightly over her wrist. "Truce, Emma?" he said quietly. "We can deal better with each other than we have been doing."

It was the first reference to their dreadful last meeting, and it was a relief to have it in the open. "We both said things to regret," Emma said, her own voice as low as his. "I will engage to be civil, Alasdair."

His mouth took a wry quirk. "Civility? Well, I suppose I must be satisfied with that."

"It is perhaps a greater concession than you imagine," she said, but without heat.

He looked at her for a moment, his eyes unreadable, then his fingers dropped from her wrist and he cupped her elbow, escorting her to the door held open by a footman.

Alasdair's tiger, a wizened ex-jockey by the name of Jemmy, saluted Emma with a grin and touched his forelock. "You drivin', Lady Emma?"

"If I may?" Emma glanced inquiringly at Alasdair.

"By all means," he said without batting an eyelid. He handed her up into the curricle, adding almost apologetically, "But I should warn you that the right leader is inclined to take exception to stray dogs, pedestrians, and most other traffic on the streets. I'm trying to break him of such unsociable habits."

"Then of course I won't drive them," Emma declared. "It would be the very worst thing for him to have someone else's hands on the reins."

"That was rather what I thought myself," Alasdair agreed solemnly. "But I didn't wish to cast aspersions on your driving skills."

"You are absurd!" Emma couldn't help laughing. "You knew perfectly well I wouldn't take it like that."

He cast her a quick sideways glance as he took up the reins. "I'm a little uncertain of the ground these days. It has a habit of shifting."

Emma made no response. She sat back, folding her hands in her lap with the air of one determined not to rise to provocation. Alasdair grinned. "Let go their heads, Jemmy."

The tiger complied and scrambled in his ungainly fashion onto his perch as the curricle swept past him.

"How's the rheumatism, Jemmy?" Emma glanced over her shoulder.

"Oh, there's good days and bad, thankee, Lady Emma," Jemmy said. He'd broken so many limbs in his career as a jockey that his thin frame was a mass of misshapen, ill-set limbs and crooked joints. But what he lacked in agility was compensated by his unerring way with horses. Alasdair had found him begging outside Newmarket racecourse five years earlier and on impulse had offered him a job. Jemmy had rewarded the impulse with unswerving loyalty and blunt and unstinting advice on the handling of horses. Advice that the youthful Alasdair had been wise enough to accept, with the result that Alasdair now had the reputation of a nonpareil and his tiger's advice was eagerly sought by every young blood in town.

Alasdair's impulses had always been idiosyncratic, Emma reflected as she chatted with Jemmy, but they frequently had a humanitarian motive that surprised those who didn't know him well—those who mistook the sardonic smile, the sharp tongue, the insouciance for the true Alasdair, instead of the mask that they really were.

"Penny for them."

Emma realized that she'd been sitting in frowning silence for an uncivil length of time. "Oh, I was just daydreaming." She turned her attention to the team of bays. "Does that leader always pull to the right?"

"Oh, 'e's jest objectin' to the rubbish in the kennel," Jemmy told her. "Thinks 'e's passin' too close to it. Right cantankerous bugger, 'e is."

Alasdair turned his horses through the Stanhope Gate into Hyde Park. It was close to five o'clock, the fashionable hour when anyone who was anyone was driving, riding, or promenading, engaged in the delightful twin occupations of seeing and being seen.

It was immediately apparent that they were the object of much interest. Emma said curiously, "Why would you choose this route? It's hardly on the way to Tattersalls."

"I thought we might as well get it over with," Alasdair replied. "If we do the circuit twice, acknowledging our mutual acquaintances, showing off our amity, we should put some of the nastier tongues to rest. So smile, Emma, and look as if there's no one you'd rather be sitting beside." He glanced at her with a slightly malicious smile of his own.

Emma's responding smile was as artificial as it was broad. "Like this?"

"If that's the best you can do."

"I thought we had agreed not to provoke each other."

"I didn't realize that suggesting you smile could be

considered provocation," he disclaimed with an air of injured innocence.

"You are not going to succeed in making me uncivil to you, Alasdair," Emma stated, continuing to smile. "I'm not going to be the first to behave badly again."

He just laughed and Emma, despite herself, laughed too. But the laugh died abruptly. A woman driving a sporty-looking tilbury was coming toward them, waving a hand in greeting.

"I believe Lady Melrose is trying to attract your attention," Emma said distantly.

Alasdair's countenance was suddenly wiped clean of all expression. He bowed in the direction of the approaching tilbury and looked as if he intended to continue driving, but when the lady holding the reins pulled up her horses as she reached them, he drew rein alongside her.

"Alasdair, I haven't seen you in days," the lady exclaimed. "I expected you at my card party on Monday." She gave a little trilling laugh. "I daresay you're going to say you were out of town. And not a word of apology . . . not a note of excuse. I declare it is too bad of you."

"My apologies, Julia, but I was called out of town rather suddenly," he said evenly. "You're not acquainted with Lady Emma Beaumont, I believe."

"Only by repute," Lady Melrose said with a pointed stare in Emma's direction. Her gray eyes were less than friendly as she bowed, and she gave another of her trilling laughs, managing to make it sound like an insult. "So tedious an arrangement for you both . . . in the circumstances," she added, dropping her voice conspiratorially. "Not to mention how irksome for you, Lady Emma, to be burdened with a trustee. It must make you feel like a naive chit."

"Watch your horses, Julia!" Alasdair said sharply. Lady Melrose had inadvertently dropped her hands, and her horses plunged forward.

She dragged them back with a heavy hand. "Such ill-schooled nags!"

"A poor workman always blames his tools," Emma murmured, smiling sweetly.

Lady Melrose flushed and her mouth tightened. She turned deliberately to Alasdair and said in a honeyed, cajoling voice, "Alasdair, you will come to call soon, won't you? I do so miss you when I don't see you for a few days." She pouted soulfully. "Tonight . . . I shall expect you tonight. Don't fail me."

Alasdair merely bowed again, but there was something in his eyes that shook Lady Melrose a little. She caught a glimpse of steel, something she had not seen before. She had been very sure of Alasdair Chase, sure enough to enjoy teasing him about the awkwardness of his present situation, sure enough to enjoy needling the woman who had jilted him, the woman whom she had no doubt he now detested. He had been her own lover for the last six months, and Lady Melrose was firmly of the opinion that she could twist him around her little finger. But that glimpse of steel was unnerving.

She returned the bow, said with the assumption of great good humor, "Good day, Lady Emma. I daresay we shall meet again about town. Now, don't forget, Alasdair. I'm counting on you." She shook the reins, flicked her whip, and set her horses in motion.

"Those horses must have the hardest mouths," Emma declared, her horsewoman's outrage for the moment overcoming her other reactions to Alasdair's latest conquest. "The way she jabbed at them! Poor brutes."

"She is cowhanded," Alasdair agreed calmly, giving his own horses the office to start. "And she has the worst hands and seat imaginable on a horse. You'll take the shine out of her the minute you show yourself in the park, driving or riding."

"Take the shine out of her? I can't imagine why I should wish to do anything so vulgar," Emma said in frigid accents. "What could it possibly matter to me how Lady Melrose rides or drives . . . or indeed does anything else," she added, and immediately regretted the furious addendum.

Alasdair looked at her, his expression once more sardonic. "Anything else? Whatever could you mean, my sweet? You aren't by any chance suggesting . . ." He raised an eyebrow.

"Oh, if you think to put me out of countenance, Alasdair Chase, you will need to do better than that!" Emma said with asperity. "If you think I could possibly be snubbed by a philandering rake, you are very much mistaken, my friend."

"Eh, steady on, now. A bit near the knuckle, we're gettin'," Jemmy was heard to mutter sotto voce from his perch. He had sat behind these two on countless occasions in what he considered the good old days, and he was accustomed to their volatile banter. But the bitter tone of this exchange was something new.

The observation went unanswered. Alasdair sighed deeply and said in a tone of mingled patience and exasperation, "I don't know what you expected, Emma. Did you think I'd reached the age of twenty-four living like a monk?"

Emma struggled with the surge of angry disbelief. He still didn't understand! "I had not expected you to be emulating the duke of Clarence and Mrs. Jordan," she said, a slight tremor in her voice. "Devoted father, loving—"

"Emma, for God's sake!" he interrupted. "It's over. Why can't you put it behind you now?"

Emma gasped. "How could it possibly be over? How could I possibly put it behind me? How could I possibly forget such a betrayal . . . such a deception? If you had told me . . . if you'd just said something instead of leaving me to find out in that hideous humiliating fashion! *Why* didn't you tell me?"

Alasdair without replying turned his horses through the Apsley Gate. *Why hadn't he told her?* He should have done, of course, but hindsight was a futile teacher—her lessons came too late. He hadn't told Emma because he'd been afraid to. And instead of acknowledging that fear, he'd told himself it was none of her business. She didn't need to know. It didn't affect her and never would. He could divide his life into compartments and there was no reason why the business of one should affect the business of another.

Dear God, he'd been so callow . . . such an ignorant, arrogant fool. But he had not been the only one at fault. Emma had been every bit as responsible for the hideous debacle. She would not listen to reason.

"It was a mistake, I admit it," he said finally. "But in the light of your reaction, it strikes me as an understandable one."

Emma sat very still, holding her trembling hands tightly clasped in her lap. How could he so willfully refuse to see *why* she had reacted as she had? Even now he refused to see it. How could he not understand how betrayed she had felt? How deeply insulted. They were supposed to be friends as well as lovers. She had committed her whole being to him, and he had not thought her worthy of such a confidence . . . had not thought it necessary to tell her of such a vital side to his life.

"Then there's nothing more to say." Even as she made the flat declaration, she realized that she had been hoping that somehow they would at last be able to haul the murky past into the light. That maybe three years would have brought Alasdair some understanding of why she had done what she had done. Even perhaps that they could have been able to forgive each other. But castles in the air were founded on such hopes. Alasdair had no regrets. He still believed he had acted reasonably and her overreaction had been unforgivable.

Far from healing any wounds, the exchange had driven the wedge between them ever deeper. Their earlier accord was now banished, but instead of the pure fire of anger that had always bolstered her and in some way salved the hurt, Emma felt only a weary wash of depression at the return of the familiar pain.

She sat silently beside him, glad that in the noisy chaos of Piccadilly there was no opportunity for further talk. Alasdair was concentrating on holding his skittish leader steady in surroundings that would have made the most well-schooled animal edgy. Dogs were barking, costermongers bellowing, iron wheels rumbling over the paving. A large old-fashioned coach came lumbering toward them, the ill-sprung body swaying alarmingly over the wheels, its team sweating and puffing as if they'd been in the traces overlong without rest.

The coachman hauled back on the reins, yanking the team to a halt so that Alasdair could inch his sidling horses past. A carter's dray traveling behind the coach was caught unawares and the shires pulling it had run their noses into the rear of the coach before the carter could pull them up. One of the shires threw his head up with a loud whinny of protest, and Alasdair's temperamental leader showed the whites of his eyes and plunged sideways.

Jemmy jumped from his perch and raced for the animal's head. Alasdair, his mouth set with concentration, his elegantly gloved hands taut with the strain, wordlessly, steadily dominated the wild-eyed horse, bringing him back into line as they edged past the coach and the dray.

Emma, for all her angry unhappiness, couldn't help but applaud, although she kept her congratulations unvoiced. She would not have been able to pull them out of that imbroglio unscathed herself. She maintained her stony silence, where the only clear thought that emerged was the absolute conviction that she would have no peace of mind until Alasdair was once again out of her life. And she could still see only one logical way to achieve that.

Alasdair drove into the yard of Tattersall's horse dealership and jumped down, handing the reins to Jemmy. He held up a hand to assist Emma to the cobbles. She disdained the offer and jumped down herself, shaking out her skirts, looking around with interest.

It was settling day at Tattersalls and the yard was thronged with men who had come to settle their racing debts and auction accounts. Emma put up her chin a little when she saw how much attention her presence in this male preserve was causing. Heads were turned, voices lowered, and several cits ogled her through their glasses.

"Come," Alasdair directed, his voice neutral. He

placed a hand in the small of her back with his usual familiarity. "Chesterton's breakdowns are stabled in the next yard." He urged her toward an arched gateway at the rear of the yard.

They entered a large stableyard, with stables on three sides. A man in buckskins and a green waistcoat hurried out of a tack room at their approach. He cast Emma an incredulous glance, then turned with clear relief to her companion. "Lord Alasdair, how may I be of service?"

"Lady Emma is in the market for a pair of carriage horses and a riding horse," Alasdair said. "Are Lord Chesterton's match-geldings still unsold?"

"They're due to come up for auction tomorrow, sir." John Tattersall stroked his chin. "I doubt his lordship would take less than three hundred and fifty for them before auction."

"Mmm. Let's take a look at them." Alasdair moved his hand to cup Emma's elbow. "I'd have said two seventy-five myself. But we'll see."

Emma understood that she was to have no part in the negotiations and was not sorry to have it so. It was interesting, if a trifle galling, to recognize that three years ago she would have relished the stares and the disapproval at her presence here, whereas now she felt out of place.

The chestnut geldings were brought out, trotted around the yard, put through their paces. "They're a well-mannered pair, Lord Alasdair," John Tattersall said. "And handsome too."

"Oh, very," Emma agreed warmly, forgetting in her enthusiasm her intention to be reticent. "What do you think, Alasdair?"

"What else have you got, Tattersall?" Alasdair asked.

The dealer looked disappointed. "Nothing to compare with these, sir."

"Nevertheless, show me."

Emma was not interested in any of the dealer's other offerings, and she guessed that neither was Alasdair. If it was a ploy to get the price down, then it seemed shabby to her. It wasn't as if fifty pounds, or even a hundred, made that much difference to her. But she was obliged to hold her tongue and go through the motions since Alasdair was in control of the proceedings and, not incidentally, the purse strings.

"Why, it's Lady Emma, isn't it?"

She turned at the vaguely familiar voice. "Mr. Denis. Good afternoon." She smiled warmly, holding out her hand. "Are you acquainted with Lord Alasdair Chase?" She turned to Alasdair, explaining, "I met Mr. Denis at Princess Esterhazy's this morning."

"Lord Alasdair and I are neighbors," Paul said, nodding in friendly fashion to Alasdair. "How surprising to run into you here, Lady Emma."

"It is a little unusual," she said with an attempt at airiness. "But I am in the habit of buying my own horses, you should understand."

"Quite so," he agreed heartily. "What true horseman . . . or should I say, horsewoman . . . would not be? Such nonsense that women should be considered less good judges than men."

Emma beamed at him. "Such enlightened views are very refreshing. Don't you think, Alasdair?"

Alasdair, who was thinking that Paul Denis hadn't wasted any time in getting an introduction to Emma, made some noncommittal response and said, "Are you buying, Denis?"

"Yes, a riding horse. I have been using a hired hack,

but they have such hard mouths, I really think I must buy my own."

John Tattersall put two fingers to his mouth and issued a piercing whistle. A man in a baize apron came running from the tack room. "Show the gentleman the hacks in stalls six and ten," the dealer instructed. "If you'd care to go with Jed, here, sir, he can show you what we've got."

"Oh, I'll come with you," Emma said quickly. "I wish to look at riding horses too. Alasdair, the chestnuts will suit me perfectly. I know you don't need me around while you settle the business side of it." With a jaunty smile, she took Paul's instantly proffered arm and went off with him, following the groom.

Alasdair stared after her, for a moment speechless at such effrontery. She'd treated him like a steward or bailiff, leaving him to deal with her business as if he was paid well to do so, while she went off with her new friend.

"So, what d'you say, Lord Alasdair?"

Alasdair became aware that the dealer was looking at him in some hesitation, and he had a fair idea why. His expression just then would not have been a pleasant one. "I'll not go above three hundred," he said crisply. If Emma lost her horses, so be it.

John Tattersall pulled at his chin, made a great fuss of considering the offer, then said reluctantly, "You drive a hard bargain, sir."

Alasdair couldn't help a faint grin. "Now, John, you know damn well Lord Chesterton told you he'd accept three hundred pounds before auction."

"He told you so?" Tattersall sighed. "These gentlemen don't know to leave me to do my business."

"Lord Chesterton would rather see his breakdowns in good hands than going to some jobber on the block," Alasdair comforted him. "Let's go into the office and I'll give you a bank draft."

"Is the lady to buy a riding horse as well, sir?"

Alasdair's expression lost its affability at this reminder. "What do you have?"

"A pretty mare, a real sweet-goer." The dealer's eye lit with enthusiasm. "Spirited . . . but I'd guess the lady could handle her."

"Show her to me."

Alasdair examined the mare. A dainty roan with a lively eye and beautiful lines. "I'll take her," he said decisively. If Emma objected to his choice, it was her own fault. He had better things to do with his time than wait around for her to return her attention to the matter in hand. "Keep them here until I've arranged their stabling. I'll send word as to where to send them tomorrow."

He emerged from Tattersall's office ten minutes later, the business done, and strode toward the stable block where Emma had disappeared with Paul Denis. He was halfway across the yard when they reappeared, arm in arm. Emma was laughing, her face turned toward her companion's. They were much of a height and made an attractive couple, Alasdair thought caustically.

"We have found Mr. Denis a very handsome gelding," Emma said as they reached him. "But I saw nothing in there that would suit me."

"I have already bought you a mare," Alasdair said smoothly. "You will like her."

Emma bit back an angry retort. She might have a quick temper, but she knew when to keep her sword sheathed. Objections would be on very slippery ground. She knew she could trust Alasdair's judgment. And by walking off and leaving him, it could be said that she'd abrogated her right to participate in the selection.

He was regarding her with unbenevolent amusement, correctly interpreting her chagrin. "Don't let me hurry you, ma'am, but if you're quite ready to leave, I do have some engagements of my own." He gestured to the curricle.

Emma had thought they would go on to Longacre to purchase her curricle. But Alasdair had clearly given her as much of his time as he was willing to spare for one afternoon. And in the present acrimonious atmosphere, she would not be sorry to part company at the earliest opportunity. She could go to Longacre herself without drawing remark. She turned to make her farewells to Mr. Denis.

Paul Denis was intrigued at the angry tension thrumming between Lord Alasdair and the lady. But he was quick to take advantage of it. "If Lady Emma would accept my escort . . ." he suggested with a smile.

Emma's responding smile was brilliant. "Why, thank you, Mr. Denis. I should be delighted." She turned to Alasdair, her chin at a somewhat challenging angle, flecks of golden fire in the tawny brown eyes. "There, Alasdair, now you may go about your business. I do beg your pardon for being such a nuisance. I didn't realize you had other pressing engagements."

Alasdair bowed. He wasn't going to pander to Emma's vanity by appearing to compete with the Frenchman. "I leave you in good hands, I'm sure."

Emma turned back to Mr. Denis. His eyes, very dark and brilliant, were fixed upon her face, creating the disturbing sense of intimacy she'd experienced at their previous meeting. She became aware of the controlled tension in his frame, an alertness that reminded her of an animal prepared to move against an impending threat. And she realized with a shock of recognition that she found him undeniably attractive.

A rush of excitement coursed through her. She felt color flood her cheeks and she swiftly lowered her eyelids, afraid of what her eyes would reveal. She had found the man she'd been looking for. A potential husband who appeared to have all the signs of one who would make a most satisfactory lover.

But above all, the man who would break the chains of her dependency on Alasdair.

"I'm sure Mr. Denis will take very good care of me," she said to Alasdair with quiet deliberation.

She cast a parting glance over her shoulder at Alasdair as she took the Frenchman's arm. Alasdair had a most satisfactorily arrested expression. He had taken her point.

Paul Denis would do very well.

Chapter Six

❦

Alasdair drove away from Tattersalls, his face dark, his eyes bleak. He had persuaded himself that it had been just an impetuous challenge that she'd thrown at him in the heat of the battle. He understood that. They were both inclined to rashness, and on that wretched afternoon he had provoked her beyond the bounds of reason.

But she had meant it. And this afternoon, he had felt the connection between Emma and Denis like a jab to the heart. He knew when Emma had a sexual response to someone. Emma was the most sensual and sensuous woman he had ever known. She reveled in her own sexuality, the passionate extremes of her nature. She brought the current of her sensuality to every physical activity, whether it be music or riding or dancing. And it added the spark, the liveliness, to all her encounters. It was contained in her eyes, in her smile, in the way she stood, sat, walked.

Men were drawn to her as if to some lodestone for lust, he thought savagely. He had watched it happen since she'd first put up her hair. From the sons of country squires and county gentry to the young puppies who'd hung around her during her debutante season. Even after their own engagement had been announced, she had moved always in a buzzing circle of panting swains. It would be the same again this time. And with two hundred thousand pounds added to the equation!

Alasdair knew that Emma's liveliness of manner, the flirtatious edge to her conversation, came naturally to her. She was too bright, too articulate, too independent-minded to hide her wit. It discomfited some and delighted others. Their own banter had always had that edge to it. A competitive, provocative edge that sparked the sexual nature of their encounters. It was intimately connected to the lustful passion that had been so vital to their adult relationship.

Had been so vital? Or *was still*? The question brought him up short. Were they quarreling so violently because it was the only outlet for a sexual current that continued to flow as strong as ever between them?

Lord of hell! Alasdair swore under his breath. It was true of himself. He saw it now with all the clarity of a newly sighted man. It wasn't simply a case of dog in the manger. He still wanted her for himself. He had not recovered from his passion . . . his love . . . for this impossible woman. Was Emma still confused? Did her attacks arise from confusion? And if so, how to get her to acknowledge it?

She couldn't seriously intend to take Paul Denis

into her bed. It had to be an empty threat . . . or promise . . . or whatever it was.

That smooth-talking émigré, hanging out for a rich wife! He was plausible; his breeding was good; he was not unhandsome; he had a certain address; and he would be very willing. If Emma was determined to get herself a husband quickly, Paul Denis had plopped into her lap like an overripe peach.

And as for a lover! Alasdair caught himself grinding his teeth. A hackneyed reaction that infuriated him as much as having to acknowledge that the roaring green-eyed dragon of jealousy had him in its talons.

If Emma wanted a fight on her hands, he would give her one with pleasure, he decided with grim satisfaction. He was going to stick some serious spokes in that particular wheel. Emma and Paul Denis were in for a few surprises.

He was driving through the village of Chiswick. It was dark and the streets in this backwater were unlit except by the lamplight glowing from cottage windows. He turned his horses onto a narrow lane lined with small whitewashed cottages that all had an air of respectable prosperity, and drew rein outside the small gate of the dwelling at the far end, where the lane gave way to green fields and a cluster of outbuildings that denoted a small farm.

"I'll be taking the 'orses to the Red Lion, then? Bait them there," Jemmy said, in half question, half statement. When his master paid one of his infrequent visits to Chiswick, he tended to stay several hours.

"Yes, and take supper yourself." Alasdair sprang down. "I'll find you there when I'm ready to return."

Jemmy tugged his forelock, took the reins and

whip, and scrambled into the driver's seat, turning the horses expertly in the narrow lane.

Alasdair opened the small gate and trod up the narrow path to the front door. Curtains were drawn over the front windows, but he could distinguish a crack of light where they didn't quite meet. He raised his hand to the knocker.

The door was opened before he could knock. A tall, gangly lad of about nine stood there, regarding him gravely from a pair of green eyes. "Good evening, sir," he said politely. "I heard the gate creak. It needs oil."

"Who is it, Timmy?" a voice called from the parlor.

"Lord Alasdair." The boy stood aside to let the visitor into the small hallway.

"How are you, Tim?" Alasdair drew off his gloves, smiling at the lad. "How's school?"

Tim seemed to consider the question, then opted for the unvarnished truth. "I don't like Latin and Greek." He took Alasdair's caped driving coat and laid it over a chair just as a plump, pretty woman came into the hall, holding a baby on her hip.

"Alasdair!" she cried, reaching up to fling her free arm around his neck. "Why didn't you send warning? I would have had a special dinner for you."

"I have no need of special dinners, Lucy," he said, bending to kiss her cheek. "Sally's dinners are always excellent." He stepped back and regarded her, smiling. "You're looking well."

"Oh, I'm getting fat." She wrinkled a snub nose, then laughed merrily. "It's living a life of idleness."

Alasdair laughed with her, following her into the parlor. It was hard now to see in the placid matronly housewife the opera dancer who had inflamed him as an eighteen-year-old youth. Driven him into the

wildest flights of joy and youthful excitement. He had
adored her, with a madness that had brought him to
the gates of debtor's prison. It was difficult to imagine
now.

His son set a chair for him by the fire and then
pulled up a stool and sat at his knee, clearly ready for
the paternal inquiries that always accompanied his father's visits.

The parlor was, as always, bright and neat as a new
pin. The fire crackled in the hearth, where the brass
fender and andirons gleamed. Alasdair felt himself
relaxing in the cozy, homely comfort. He stretched his
legs to the blaze, resting his gleaming hessians on the
fender.

"So, what's the problem with the Latin and Greek,
Tim?"

"I'm not at all good at them," the boy said. "Were
you?"

"I wasn't too bad at Greek." Alasdair took a tankard of ale from a rosy-cheeked serving maid. "Thank
you, Sally. Is this your homebrewed?"

"Aye, the master's right partial to it," Sally said.
"Will I get you some supper?"

"Where is Mike?" Alasdair took a deep draft of ale.

It was Tim who answered him. "There's a cow in
calf. I wanted to help, but Mike said I couldn't. He
said it wasn't work for me." There was a distinct note
of grievance in his voice.

"Now, Timmy, you know Mike wants what's best
for you," Lucy said briskly. "You're to learn your lessons and go to a proper school and grow up to be a
gentleman like your father."

Tim's expression was one of pure disgust. "I don't
see why," he said, his eyes on his father now. "I don't
want to be a gentleman, I want to be like Mike."

"Now, Timmy, don't you be talking like that!" Lucy advanced on him, her bright blue eyes flashing. "Such ingratitude! With all your advantages."

Tim subsided with a mutinous mouth. Alasdair sipped his ale without comment. He wondered why he hadn't noticed when his son had lost the tractability of early childhood. Alasdair's parenting role had been very simple hitherto, but it had been directed toward supporting Lucy. It hadn't so far taken into account the child's emerging character.

"Here's your supper, Alasdair," Lucy said with relief as Sally returned. "Timmy, fetch the table to the fire."

Tim dragged over a gate-legged table, and Sally spread a checkered cloth before setting out dishes and bone-handled cutlery.

"Will you take Ellen to bed, Sally." Lucy kissed the baby and handed her over, then she refilled Alasdair's tankard, helped him to game pie and a dish of roasted onions and another of baked cabbage and bacon. She was cutting bread for him when a door banged from the kitchen regions.

"That's Mike." Tim sprang to his feet and charged for the door, yelling, "Did she calve, Mike? Is everything all right?"

"So much for Latin and Greek," Alasdair observed.

"Oh, you mustn't take any notice of his fancies." Lucy laid an urgent hand on his arm. "Indeed, you mustn't, Alasdair."

"Evenin', Lord Alasdair." A burly figure appeared in the doorway from the kitchen. He was wiping his hands on a cloth. Mud clung to his boots.

"Evening, Mike. Was it a heifer or a bull?" Alasdair inquired.

"A fine little bull calf." Mike beamed and took the

tankard of ale his wife handed him. "Sired by Red Demon. The calf'll be a grand stud in a year, I'll be bound." He sat down and bent to unlace his boots, saying apologetically, "Eh, I'm sorry for the mud, Lucy."

Tim with an air of importance hurried over with the bootjack, and Mike ruffled his hair as the lad bent to help him. "We're tryin' to keep him at his books, Lord Alasdair, but I doubt he'd rather be out in the fields."

"Yes, that I would," Tim said firmly.

"You may think differently when you go away to school," Alasdair suggested, forking a piece of pie into his mouth.

Tim glanced at his mother and said nothing. Her usually sweet expression was for once very forbidding.

The conversation roamed pleasantly around farming issues, horseflesh, and the hopes for a good harvest, and when, after an hour or so, Alasdair rose to leave, Mike rose with him. "Your horses're at the Red Lion as usual?" he asked. "I'll walk you round."

Alasdair nodded his acquiescence. He sensed that the other man had something on his mind. Alasdair kissed Lucy, passed a caressing hand over his son's tousled hair, refrained from offering any paternal instructions as to sticking with his books, and went out with Tim's stepfather.

"Out with it, Mike," he said when they'd turned into the lane and his companion had still said nothing.

"Well, it's difficult, like. I know the lad's not my own." Mike drove his hands into the pockets of his britches. His long stride slowed a little. He took a deep breath. "But it's like this, see. He's got a right fine touch with the horses and cattle. He'd rather be learning about crops, and harvesting, and what to look for in the weather, and consulting almanacs, than he would reading Latin and Greek."

Alasdair wasn't at all sure what to say, so he said nothing.

Mike continued. "Lucy has it in her head to make a gentleman of the boy. And with his father, like . . . I can see why. But living as he does . . . with us . . . well, I don't see it working. No offense, Lord Alasdair."

"None taken," Alasdair said. "But he's my son."

"Not in my house, he's not."

Alasdair drew breath sharply. If anyone but Mike had said such a thing, it would have been a hostile challenge. But Alasdair knew and valued Mike Hodgkins. And he knew, an unpalatable fact perhaps, that the man spoke only the truth. Alasdair paid for his son's schooling and for his upkeep. His contributions to the Hodgkins household were considerable, but they were financial, not emotional.

As if reading his thoughts, Mike continued bluntly, "We're right grateful for your help, Lord Alasdair. I won't say it's not made all the difference in a lean year, but the lad's happiness is all that really matters. The lad's and Lucy's. I think they'd both be happier if we made a clean break, as it were." He gave a little sigh as if ridding himself of a massive burden.

"You're asking me to drop out of my son's life?" Alasdair demanded. "Not to see him again?"

"God's blessing, no, sir!" Mike sounded horrified. "You're the lad's natural father and he knows it. He'd not know what to think if you disappeared. I'm only saying that maybe it's confusing for him to think he has to live up to expectations that're so different from what he knows. The lads he plays with . . .

even . . ." Mike paused. He pushed back his cap, running a gnarled hand through his hair. "His sister," he said finally.

It sounded like an afterthought but Alasdair guessed that it was probably the central point of Mike's argument. The difference between his own child's future and his stepson's.

"It's not that I begrudge the boy his opportunities," Mike said diffidently into Alasdair's silence.

"I know that. And I know what a good father you are to Tim," Alasdair said warmly. They had reached the door of the Red Lion and he paused. "But I'll not have him thinking that I disowned him."

"He'll never think that, sir." With an impulsive gesture, Mike took Alasdair's hand between both of his own. "I just think he would be happier if he felt he wasn't different from the rest of us."

"You want me to bring the 'orses round, sir?" Jemmy's voice spoke out of the darkness. He had been on the watch for Lord Alasdair and now appeared from the inn's stableyard. He nodded to Mike, who nodded back.

Alasdair gestured his acknowledgment to Jemmy, who disappeared again. "I don't ever want it said that I reneged on my responsibilities." A deep frown corrugated Alasdair's brow. For the first time he could see clearly what Tim's life would be at Eton or Harrow. He would have no friends. He wouldn't fit in anywhere. The family circumstances of his peers would be a galaxy apart from his own.

Alasdair realized that while he'd been congratulating himself on doing more for his natural child than anyone would expect, his plans for the boy's future would do Tim a grave disservice. Unless . . .

"Should I take the boy in myself?" he said almost to himself.

"Only if you want to kill his mother," Mike responded instantly and with some ferocity. "And I'll not stand for that, Lord Alasdair, I tell you straight."

"No, of course not. Give me some time to think. I'll come back in a week or so. I'll talk to Tim about it then."

The clatter of hooves heralded the return of Jemmy leading Alasdair's horses.

"Good blood there," Mike approved. "You're a fine judge of horseflesh, Lord Alasdair."

"Maybe my son has inherited that at least," Alasdair said. It was an attempt at a jest, but he had the feeling that it had sounded more sour than jovial. He held out his hand to Mike, making up for that discordant note with the warmth of his handshake and his smile. "I'll return soon. Don't ever believe I'm not grateful for what you've done for Tim."

Mike looked satisfied. He shook Alasdair's hand briskly. "We'll be looking forward to seeing you then. I'll be having a word with Lucy in the meantime. Prepare her, like."

Alasdair took the reins and whip from Jemmy and climbed into the curricle. It seemed that Mike now considered the whole matter settled. He gave his horses the office to start.

Jemmy, who was accustomed to chat with his master when they were driving alone, kept silent during the drive back to London. Lord Alasdair was clearly preoccupied.

Alasdair was thinking of life's supreme ironies. That cozy domestic scene had been the ruin of his

relationship with Emma. And yet how truly un-
threatening it was.

Now.

Honesty forced him to admit that three years ago,
before Mike Hodgkins had appeared on the scene, the
situation had a different construction. Then Lucy had
been living under his protection with her child. He
had visited Chiswick several times a week, and while
their sexual relationship was on the wane, there was
still great intimacy between them. He hadn't wanted
to expose that intimacy to Emma. It had seemed
something very private, very special. And therefore,
of course, very threatening to the woman about to
become his wife. But in the arrogance of his own self-
absorption, he hadn't recognized that.

He would always be fond of Lucy, always take re-
sponsibility for his son's welfare. Emma had thrown
the example of the duke of Clarence at him that afternoon, and while Alasdair could hardly be said to be
the devoted father of ten children by a woman with
whom he'd lived as husband for some twelve years,
there were perhaps parallels. The duke was always
proposing to rich eligible ladies, but none had yet succumbed, even for the title of royal duchess. Mrs. Jordan and ten Fitzclarences would always be a factor in
whatever marriage the duke contracted.

But would Emma now be threatened by Alasdair's
past with Lucy, by his gangly son who wanted to be a
farmer? Would that cozy little cottage in Chiswick fill
her with revulsion?

She was no prude. Far from it. But when Henry
Ossington had dripped his malice into her ear, she
had reacted as violently as if she'd been told her fiancé was a depraved and murderous Bluebeard. She
hadn't given Alasdair the opportunity to explain, had

merely left London and gone to Italy the night before the wedding, leaving him almost literally at the altar. It had been left to Ned to tell him why—and left to the jilted bridegroom to offer an explanation to wedding guests and a world agog.

His lips were set as he drew up in the mews at the back of his lodgings. However much it could be said that he had wronged Emma, Emma had certainly had her revenge. His humiliation had been profound.

"Look into stabling for Lady Emma's horses, Jemmy."

"Aye, sir." Jemmy was untroubled by the curtness of the instruction and went to unharness the team.

"Oh, and there's something else I want you to do first thing in the morning," Alasdair said, and told the intrigued tiger what he wanted done.

Alasdair walked around to his front door. He glanced up at the windows of the floor above his own. They were dark. Where was Paul Denis? Paying court to Emma at some soiree?

He would have to develop a plan of campaign, but he was feeling too dispirited tonight for intelligent thought.

❧

He awoke in a much clearer frame of mind and was at breakfast when Jemmy was shown in. "Lady Emma and Mrs. Witherspoon's gone out in the barouche, sir. I watched 'em go."

Early for Emma, Alasdair reflected. It was barely ten o'clock. He rose from the table. "I'll not need you again this morning."

"I'll be about arranging stables for Lady Emma's cattle, then." Jemmy tugged a forelock and disappeared.

Alasdair called for his valet as he went into his bed-chamber, throwing off his brocade dressing gown. Ten minutes later, he was walking quickly to Mount Street. The street was quiet; a nursemaid shepherded a trio of children, one of whom was bowling a hoop that narrowly missed running up against Alasdair's immaculate beige pantaloons. He brushed aside the nursemaid's apologies. The careless child, an unprepossessing boy with a runny nose, was staring at him rudely. Alasdair regarded him through his eyeglass until the child dropped his eyes.

Alasdair walked on. As he turned up the steps of Emma's house, he noticed a rather hunched, elderly looking man in a heavy greatcoat on the far side of the street. He appeared to be looking up at the house, but when Alasdair caught his eye, he turned and shuffled off, coughing into a handkerchief, the rasping hack sounding painful.

Harris answered his knock with the expected information that Lady Emma was from home.

"I'll leave her a note, Harris." Alasdair walked into the hall. "I'll write it in the salon. I know my way . . . no need to show me up." He gave a pleasant nod and strode up the stairs.

The salon was deserted, although a small fire burned in the grate. Alasdair stood in the middle of the room and examined the bookshelves set into two alcoves on either side of the fireplace. Emma's library was extensive, augmented now by Ned's books.

Would she perhaps have kept a posthumous memento of her brother in one of his own books? It would be very like Emma. Either that or she might have put it in a book that her brother had given her. There had never been anything random about her many and varied hiding places.

He had known brother and sister so well that he recognized the volumes that came into both categories and began a systematic search through them. If he was disturbed by one of the servants, they wouldn't think it particularly strange of him to be looking at the books. His place in the Grantley family was too well established for anything he did to cause particular comment.

But no one disturbed him for a while, and he had opened, leafed through, and shaken out two dozen books before Harris opened the door and brought in a decanter of madeira.

"I thought you might like some refreshment, sir. Seeing as how we don't know when Lady Emma will be returning."

"Thank you, Harris." Still holding the book he'd been examining, Alasdair accepted a glass of wine. Harris had drawn the conclusion that the visitor had decided to await Lady Emma's return. There could be no other explanation for his protracted stay in the house.

He sipped his wine and glanced idly out of the window. The man in the greatcoat had returned and was still standing on the opposite side of the street, looking up at the house.

"Have you noticed that man there before, Harris?"

Harris looked out of the window. "No, sir. Should I run him off?"

"Unless he has legitimate business outside the house."

Harris went off and Alasdair watched curiously as a footman ran across the street and accosted the man. The exchange was a short one and the greatcoated individual turned and wandered off down the street.

Alasdair ran his fingertips over his mouth, deep in

thought. Why would someone be watching Emma's house? Some protective guard set by Charles Lester? Or was it more sinister? The mysterious someone else who was looking for the missing paper, for instance?

But then again, it could have been a totally innocent passerby with an interest in Georgian architecture, of which the house was a fine specimen. Alasdair returned to the bookshelves.

Half an hour later, he had turned nothing up and he had examined all the volumes he recognized as having some connection with Ned. Where else to look, apart from Emma's bedchamber and dressing room? To enter those rooms, he would need a much more elaborate strategy. But for now, there was the music room. Ned had not been a musician himself, but he had given Emma many gifts related to music. She could well have hidden something among her sheet music, or in the pianoforte bench, or in her music case.

He hurried from the salon and down the stairs. A footman emerged from a door at the end of the hall leading to the servants' quarters. He hurried toward the front door, thinking that Lord Alasdair was taking his leave.

Alasdair waved him away, saying that he had left something in the music room on his previous visit, and entered the room at the rear of the house. There he stood and took stock, trying to think where to look first. Emma was not the tidiest of mortals, and since she would allow no one to touch anything to do with her music, the room was littered with piled sheet music, books, score sheets, notebooks filled with her own notations and compositions.

He went through the piles of music, her music case, the contents of the piano bench, careful to leave ev-

erything just as he'd found it. The porcelain candlesticks had been a present from Ned, he remembered.
Graceful, delicate delftware, exquisitely painted. He
took out the candles and ran his finger around the
socket. It was just the sort of place Emma would
choose; but not on this occasion.

He set the candles back into their holders. His eye
drifted to the French doors into the walled garden. He
stiffened, moved swiftly to the door. There had been a
flicker of movement to the side of the garden, human
movement, he would lay odds. And yet there was no
one there, nothing to see but winter-bare trees and
sad looking shrubs.

Alasdair raised the latch and pushed the door open.
He stepped out onto the paved terrace that ran the
width of the music room. He stood still, gazing
around, ears cocked for the slightest sound. All he
heard was the chatter of a squirrel in the beech tree
that stood against the wall at the side of the garden
facing the service passageway that ran between this
house and its neighbor. His eye roved the garden, and
then he saw it. The indentation of a footprint in the
flowerbed against the wall by the beech tree.

He strode across the grass and stared down at the
print. It was a man's foot. Just one. Alasdair glanced
up into the tree. One foot in the ground while the
other reached up for that large knothole a quarter of
the way up the trunk. A hand on the branch above,
and an agile man would be up the tree and over the
wall in a flash.

Just who was snooping around the garden? And
did it have any connection with the man at the front?
He certainly hadn't looked agile enough for wall
vaulting and tree climbing. But he'd been huddled in

a greatcoat. There was no telling what had been beneath the voluminous garment.

There was a gate set into the rear wall. Examination showed it to be bolted and padlocked, with no evidence of tampering.

Disturbed and thoughtful, Alasdair returned to the music room, latching the door carefully behind him and shooting the bolt at the top. Interest in Ned's document was heating up. But speed was of the essence. The paper had to be stolen before Wellington began his spring campaign in Portugal if its contents were to be any good to Napoleon.

He glanced once more around the room, then went to the door. "Harris, tell Lady Emma I was here," he said casually as he crossed the hall. "I thought I'd left a glove behind in the music room, but it seems not. I'll be sending Lady Emma information about stabling for her horses . . . if you could just tell her."

Harris seemed perfectly satisfied with this and bowed Lord Alasdair from the house.

Alasdair ran lightly down the steps to the street. His expression was still troubled as he walked toward Audley Street. He was about to turn the corner when he caught sight of a tilbury bowling down Mount Street from the direction of Park Street. It drew up outside Emma's house.

Alasdair paused out of sight at the corner and watched. Emma and Paul Denis appeared to be having a lively conversation. She was laughing, animated, her face, framed in a black sable hood, aglow with the cold air. Her companion had a hand resting on her arm. He too was laughing, pointing up at the house.

Alasdair's mouth took a grim turn. They seemed to be on the best of terms in a dangerously short time.

And just where were Maria and the barouche? Abandoned for more lively companionship presumably.

"Oh, no, my friends, this really will not do," he murmured. He continued grimly on his way.

Neither Emma nor Paul had been aware of the watcher. Emma was in the best of spirits. She and Maria had come upon Paul Denis driving his tilbury down Bond Street, and Emma had instantly accepted his offer to drive his horses. Maria had been left in the barouche to continue alone on their errand to Colburn's Lending Library, and Emma had taken advantage of her new escort to go to the carriage makers in Longacre and purchase her curricle.

"I don't know whether I would have had the courage to purchase a racing curricle without some serious encouragement," she said with a chuckle. "There are bound to be some raised eyebrows. It's so very dashing."

"Your trustee will have no objections?" Paul raised a thin black eyebrow.

"Good God, no," Emma said. "Alasdair is never one to abide by convention himself. Besides," she added, "it doesn't concern him. He has control of my fortune, but of nothing else."

Paul heard the underlying note beneath this seemingly airy speech. Lady Emma was still not in charity with her trustee. Whatever the estrangement, it suited him very well. He wanted no interference from her friends and relations in his present scheme. The Witherspoon chaperone could be easily dealt with. She seemed under Emma's thumb anyway. But Lord Alasdair struck him as a man of very definite opinions and somewhat dominant character. To have such a man as an overinvolved trustee would prove meddlesome.

He laid a hand on her arm, smiling down at her. "Permit me to say, madame, that I find you entrancing."

Emma was used to compliments, and generally mistrustful of them. Alasdair never flattered her. He never needed to. However, Paul Denis's admiration was a promising sign. She returned his smile, saying, "You put me to the blush, sir."

"And how prettily too."

Emma had an absurd desire to laugh. She was quite certain she wasn't blushing in the least. She squashed incipient mirth vigorously.

"Tell me, where is your chamber?" Paul said, looking up at the house. "Is it in the front?"

"Up there." She pointed to the windows above the door. "The three central windows. Why do you wish to know?"

He looked a little flustered and self-conscious. "Forgive my foolishness. But if I walk down the street at night, I shall be able to look up and imagine you there."

This time Emma did laugh. It was irresistible. She went into a peal of merriment. "Mr. Denis, you must know that it's no good paying me compliments, particularly absurd ones. I have the most inconvenient sense of the ridiculous."

"Was it ridiculous?" Paul asked mournfully.

"Utterly," she said. "But don't look so cast down, sir. You weren't to know how hopelessly practical and unsuited I am to the gentler arts of courtship." Then she bit her lip. "Forgive me, that was very forward of me."

"Not in the least," he said earnestly. "To pay court to you would make me the happiest man in the world."

And a very rich one too, Emma thought. Why did she find this haste unseemly when it so exactly suited her own purposes? The feast of Saint Valentine was not many weeks away, after all. And of course he was interested in her money. How could he fail to be? And she found him attractive. He would make as good a husband as many and a better one than most. But there was something predatory about him. She had thought she found it appealing, but now she wasn't so sure.

But that was nonsense. She was set on this course, and it was going very smoothly to plan. "I must go in," she said. "Do you go Lady Devizes's masked ball this evening? Shall I see you there?"

"Without doubt. Wild beasts couldn't keep me away." He descended to the pavement and handed her down. His fingers closed over her hand for much longer than necessary. "Tell me what color domino you'll be wearing?" He added with a rueful smile, "And pray don't laugh at me this time. My pride is a fragile thing."

"Oh, indeed I won't," she said warmly, liking him again with this show of amused self-awareness. "I didn't mean to hurt you before."

"Your domino?" He raised a mobile eyebrow again.

Emma shook her head. "No, sir, you must find me yourself." She raised a hand in farewell and went up the steps, turning for a minute before she entered the house, to wave and smile again.

Paul climbed back into his tilbury, and his expression was now set, his black eyes once more hard and calculating. He looked up at the house. It was the devil's own doing that her bedchamber should be at the front. Direct access from the street would be impossible.

Unless of course she invited him into her chamber. Emma Beaumont was no naive chit. She was handling him with the sure touch of one who was not inexperienced in the games of flirtation and seduction. And that experience, Paul knew, was going to play right into his hands.

Chapter Seven

"Do you think anyone will know me, Maria?" Emma tied the gold silk loo mask behind her head and examined herself in the long mirror. The domino of silver gauze floated gracefully over her ball gown of ivory crepe adorned with knots of silver velvet. Her hair was bound in smooth plaits around her head, with side ringlets clustering around her face. A pair of very fine diamond drops complemented the diamond pendant at her throat and the bracelets at her wrist.

"Oh, my love, I'm sure they will," Maria said. "You have such a distinctive figure, and your hair . . . the color is so unusual. Is there a reason you don't wish to be recognized?"

Emma considered. "In truth, it would be amusing to be truly incognito. But I suppose masked balls aren't really intended to hide identities. . . . Thank you, Tilda." She smiled at her maid, who draped over

her shoulders a cloak of midnight blue velvet
trimmed with ermine.

There would be something both dangerous and exciting about a real masked ball, Emma thought. If
people genuinely were unable to recognize each
other. It would give the participants incredible license. Liaisons, flirtations, seductions, all conducted
in near invisibility. What a wonderful prospect for
some entrancing mischief.

"Emma love, you have a very wicked look in your
eye," Maria said uneasily. It was just like the look she
had had before going off to play highwayman at
Ranelagh, and Maria shuddered anew at the recollection. "The duchess of Devizes is very straitlaced, my
dear."

"I had a wicked thought, but I won't put it into
practice," Emma reassured, bending to kiss Maria. "I
doubt I'm too old and wise now to have such fun."

"Oh, what nonsense. You're but two and twenty,"
Maria declared. "But you do look quite enchanting,
my love. Right out of a fairy tale."

"Oh, pah!" Emma scoffed. "I'm far too tall and my
mouth is too big." She moved to the door, saying over
her shoulder, "Don't wait up for me, Tilda. I'll put
myself to bed."

As the carriage bowled toward Connaught Square,
Emma gazed out of the window, her chin resting in
her elbow-propped palm. Alasdair and Ned would
have seen the possibilities in a real masked ball. A
tiny sigh escaped her. Life seemed so very melancholy these days. She knew she was still grieving for
her brother, but it wasn't just that. So often these days
she felt such a sense of futility about everything . . .
about making plans . . . about contemplating the future.

If it weren't for Ned's damnable will, she could buy herself a house in the country and retire with her music and her horses, to live the life of a cheerful, reclusive spinster. But then Alasdair would control the purse strings, and she couldn't bear that. It was an insufferable prospect. Utterly unendurable.

And anyway, the little voice of honesty niggled, how cheerful a spinster would she be? Better, surely, a marriage of convenience with a personable and agreeable man. At least she'd not spend the rest of her life in an empty and passionless bed. And surely she'd have children. They would give purpose to her life.

The carriage drew up outside the imposing stucco mansion. An awning covered the flagway from the road to the front door, and linkboys ran up with flaming torches to light the ladies into the house.

At the strains of music from the vast ballroom at the back of the house, Emma's depression dropped away. She loved to dance. She'd promised herself that she wouldn't waltz this season, because Ned had detested the dance. She could hear his deep, amused tones even now, saying it had no life to it and he couldn't see why anyone would want to hold a woman that close just to moon around a dance floor. But the other dances, the quadrille, the cotillion, the boulanger, not to mention the country dances, had all found favor in Ned's eye, and Emma knew she could enjoy herself there with her brother's blessing.

She gave up her cloak to an attendant footman and with Maria ascended the stairs to greet their hostess. The ballroom was already thronged. They paused in the doorway, Emma's eyes darting around. She couldn't see Alasdair in the crowd. Although why his absence should have been the first thing she noticed was a mystery.

"My lady. May I have the honor of this dance?"

She turned at the familiar, delicately accented voice. Paul Denis wore a black domino and mask that covered more than half of his face. It accentuated his prominent, narrow nose and the thinness of his lips while giving him an air of mystery, but Emma felt a strange little shiver of apprehension. It seemed as if that predatory quality she'd noticed in him before was deepened, become truly sinister, as he stood bowing, all black, from the top of his dark, dark head to the toes of his black-shod feet.

But perhaps it wasn't a shiver of apprehension so much as a thrill of anticipation. There was something undeniably unsettling about Mr. Denis. And Emma was very ready to stir up the flat pond of her present existence.

"So, you found me, Mr. Denis. It wasn't difficult, I gather." She regarded him with a smile and candid invitation in her eyes.

"I sensed your arrival before I saw you," he murmured, bowing over her hand. "And once seen, permit me to tell you, madame, you are unmistakable and unforgettable."

"How prettily you do talk, Mr. Denis," Emma said approvingly. "But I did warn you that I'm a hopeless accepter of compliments."

"I am duly warned." He smiled into her eyes and maintained his hold on her hand. "But you must believe I don't flatter you. I speak only the truth."

Emma went into a peal of laughter. "*Very* prettily said, sir."

"Ah, madame, I am crushed," he said, placing a

hand on his heart and regarding her soulfully. "Is there nothing I can say that you would believe?"

"That you find this conversation as absurd as I do," she said. "You're an expert at the game of flirtation, sir, but don't ever think I can't distinguish the game from the real thing." Her foot was tapping; her eyes looking longingly to where sets were being formed for the next dance.

"Ah, but would you agree to embark upon the real thing with me, madame?" His voice now was utterly serious, his eyes fixed upon her face as if he would look into her skull.

This man was in a serious hurry. Was he so deeply in debt, then? Once again, Emma felt that flicker of distaste. But she told herself firmly that she had to get over it. She was under no illusions. Paul Denis might find her attractive, but he was in love with her money. She found him attractive, but she could never love him. This was not about love. It was about convenience. And convenience before the feast of Saint Valentine.

"Perhaps," she said in a low voice. "But for the moment, let us play the game."

"As you command," he said with a smooth smile. "I will follow your lead, my lady."

"Then let us dance." She gestured to the floor.

Paul gave her his arm and led her onto the floor. He had sensed her withdrawal, read it in her eyes. He would have to go more carefully, but he had so little time. If he couldn't achieve his object by seduction, he would have to use force, and that would be messy and dangerous, and altogether unsatisfactory. He was a man who liked to work smoothly, to come and go without leaving a trace of his passing.

Maria watched them dance for a minute or two,

trying to put a finger on the source of her unease. She hadn't cared for that Mr. Denis from the very first. There was something about him that disturbed her. Perhaps he was too smooth, too suave, with his dainty French manners and handsome if saturnine countenance. He was an excellent dancer too, which would further endear him to Emma.

But Emma was a levelheaded young woman, as strong willed as she was independent. There was no need to fear that she would make a foolish choice when she would have every young buck in the Upper Ten Thousand at her feet. Marry she must, of that Maria was convinced. But she would make a wise choice . . . of course she would. Maria, thus heartened by her own strictures, went off to join her cronies in the card room.

For propriety's sake, Emma danced with everyone who solicited her hand, although she was not alone in noticing that while she was dancing with someone else, Mr. Paul Denis was standing against a wall, arms folded, his black eyes following her every move through the slit in his mask.

Emma knew that such devotion would be generally remarked and bets on the outcome of their flirtation would soon be laid in the clubs of St. James's. It amused her, but it also annoyed her. It made her feel like some prize specimen at a county fair. She didn't think it would amuse Alasdair, either. Not that he was around to be annoyed tonight.

It was close to midnight when Alasdair arrived. He strolled up the great staircase in a crimson domino ten minutes after his hostess had decided there would be no other latecomers and she could at last relinquish her post.

He saw Emma the minute he entered the ballroom.

She was dancing with George Darcy, but as the dance came to an end her hand was immediately claimed by Paul Denis. Alasdair watched, his expression dour. She was laughing at something Denis said. The man's hand was on her arm and he bent and whispered something in her ear. She threw back her head, exposing the long white column of her throat in a gesture that was so achingly familiar he felt once again that jab to his breastbone. Then they walked off together in the direction of the supper room.

Alasdair was detained by his hostess for a few minutes, then, duty done, he made his own way to the supper room. He heard Emma's laugh, deep and melodious and filled with amusement. Her companion was smiling, all complacence at having so amused her. Denis raised a hand in greeting as Alasdair passed close to their table. Emma, in conversation with a young lady at a neighboring table, appeared not to notice him.

Alasdair acknowledged the man's greeting with a slight bow, his expression inscrutable, although his eyes burned behind half-lowered lids. He took a glass of champagne from the tray of a passing waiter and joined a group of his own friends. The conversation was not designed to improve his frame of mind.

"Lady Emma didn't waste time finding herself a favorite," Darcy observed.

"Lucky devil," muttered Lord Everard. "It's that smooth address, you mark my words. Something about a Frenchman, I've noticed it before," he added rather dolefully. "Had my sights set on a young filly two years ago. Twenty thousand pounds. A nice little fortune, nice little girl. But damme if she didn't up and marry a Frenchman."

"Your trouble, Everard, is that you're too slow off

the mark," Alasdair said with an assumption of jocularity. He was not going to let his friends see that he was in the least dismayed by Emma's conquest. "While you're still weighing the pros and cons, someone else has run off with the prize."

"Well, a little caution never did a man any harm," his lordship said.

"Face it, Everard, you're not a marryin' man," Darcy said cheerfully.

Lord Everard shrugged this off. His eyes returned to Emma and her swain. "Dashed fine looking woman, though."

"Who? The one you lost?" Alasdair inquired.

"No, Lady Emma. Dashed fine looking woman. Even without the money," he added.

"Quite so," Alasdair said dryly. He raised his eyeglass and looked across the room at Emma. Immediately, as if she felt his eyes on her, she turned and met his stare. The tawny eyes were lambent framed in the golden mask, and her mouth seemed to Alasdair more than usually rich and wide, her little white teeth gleaming in the smile that remained on her face but was not for him. Then she turned back to her companion and a minute later they walked out of the supper room.

Alasdair had intended to be patient. To plot his intervention in Emma's scheme with subtlety and cunning. But suddenly he knew that he could not endure another minute of it. Could not endure to see the full force of that sensuous personality, that irresistible charm turned upon another man. He was going to put a stop to it right now.

With a word of excuse, he left the table and returned to the ballroom in an angry, whirling maelstrom of determination. The knowledge that he had no conceivable right to interfere, he brushed aside as irrelevant. Ned would not have stood aside and watched her throw herself away on a smooth-mannered fortune-hunting stranger about whom no one knew anything except for some vague supposed connection with the Austrian ambassador.

Emma and her escort left the ballroom and went downstairs. A doorway off the massive entrance hall led into a large glassed conservatory that ran the length of the house.

Alasdair's lips thinned as he guessed this was their destination. He knew the conservatory well. It was an enormous pillared space, dimly lit and filled with orange trees, shrubs, vines, and tubs of fragrant exotic flowers. It was very much a favorite with couples who wished to find seclusion.

He looked around for Maria and saw her sitting on a little chair against the wall, fanning herself, deep in conversation with her hostess.

He went over to her. "Ma'am, may I ask you a favor?"

"A favor? Of me?" Maria looked surprised. "Whatever is it?"

He offered her his arm. "I'll explain in a minute. If the duchess would permit me to take you away for a few minutes."

The duchess signified her assent with a gracious nod, but her eyes were alive with curiosity.

"Oh, dear me, I wonder what it can be." Maria gathered herself together and took his arm. "How intriguing."

Alasdair led her out of the room and down the stairs. "Emma has just walked into the conservatory with Mr. Denis," he said quietly. "I wish you to go and find her and ask her to accompany you to the retiring room for a minute. Only for a minute. I want her to return quickly to Mr. Denis in the conservatory."

"Good heavens! Whatever for?" Maria looked astounded now, her eyes round as saucers.

"I have my reasons."

"But what . . . what shall I say I want her for?"

"To help you make a repair to your gown, perhaps?" Alasdair said vaguely. "There must be some female thing that would require her assistance."

"Oh, goodness me." Maria continued to look startled. "I don't know but what—"

"Oblige me in this, ma'am." Alasdair interrupted her rambling. His voice had a slight edge to it, and his eyes within the mask were both brilliant and stern.

Maria blinked. "Yes, Alasdair," she said meekly.

"And don't mention that I asked you to do this," he said swiftly.

"No, no, of course not, Alasdair." She gave him another startled look and hurried away.

Alasdair followed her after a minute. An ornately carved stone table carrying a bronze statuette of a frolicking nymph stood just within the fragrant green dimness. Alasdair possessed himself of the nymph and then stepped behind a palm tree to wait.

Emma and Maria appeared in a very few minutes. "You poor dear, are you sure you wouldn't rather go home?" Emma was saying solicitously, cupping Maria's elbow with one hand.

"No . . . no, my dear. I shall be all right once I've rested a little. But if you could ask the maid for some hartshorn and water . . . then you must come back to the party. I'm sorry to have disturbed your tête-à-tête with Mr. Denis," she added with a most unusual touch of tartness.

"It was hardly a tête-à-tête, Maria," Emma said, passing out of the conservatory. "We were merely walking a little in the quiet. The air is so pleasant in there."

Maria could believe that if she wished, Alasdair thought grimly. He was not about to. He moved casually out of the shelter of the palm tree and trod softly down an aisle between tubs of oleanders. The air was moist but fresh after the overheated dryness of the ballroom.

Mr. Denis was standing with his back to Alasdair, looking out of the curved glass windows that overlooked the garden at the side of the mansion. He shifted from foot to foot, evidently impatient. Alasdair moved with sudden speed, his lithe body crossing the space that separated them with something akin to a spring. He brought the nymph down at the base of the man's skull with calculated force, and Paul fell backward into his assailant's waiting arms.

"My apologies, Monsieur Denis," Alasdair murmured. "Violence is so ugly but I really had no option."

Alasdair dragged the unconscious body back through a group of orange trees and into the furthest corner of the conservatory. He laid him down and then swiftly although not without some difficulty— Paul Denis was heavier and more muscular than he appeared—removed the black domino. He untied the black mask and examined the dark countenance for a minute. He pressed a finger to the carotid artery. It beat steadily if fast. The man would be out for perhaps an hour. It was the work of a moment to remove his own domino and mask and put on Paul Denis's.

Then he stepped away from the still figure, moved

a pair of orange trees to provide even more conceal-
ment, and went to take Paul's place at the window.

He moved into the shadows of a vigorously leafed
evergreen and waited for Emma.

Emma was reluctant to leave Maria to the care of
the maid in the retiring room. She seemed to have a
rather hectic flush, and her pulse was a trifle tumultuous. But Maria was insistent.

"No, no, my dear. Mr. Denis is waiting for you. It
would be the height of discourtesy to leave him
there," she said, mindful of her instructions. "I shall
lie quietly here and sip this hartshorn and water, and
the maid is burning pastilles in case I should feel faint
again. I am in very good hands." She offered a wan
but gallant smile.

"It seems so heartless," Emma protested. "To be
leaving you here suffering while I racket about enjoying myself."

"Nonsense. Now go at once, my love. It's only
making the headache worse to have to argue with
you," Maria said with a stroke of genius.

Emma still hesitated, nibbling her bottom lip.
"Well, I will go back and tell Paul . . . Mr.
Denis . . ." she amended swiftly, "that I must not
stay. Then I'll order the carriage to be brought around
and we will go home directly. How would that be?"

Maria reflected that if Alasdair had any objections
to that, he could deal with them himself. She'd followed her instructions to the letter. "Very well, my
love," she said faintly, closing her eyes.

Emma paused at the mirror to check her appearance. One of the attendants came forward with a hair-
brush and deftly brushed and twisted the burnished
ringlets clustering around Emma's face. She refas-

tened one of the little ties of silver tissue that fastened the domino down the front and nodded with a smile.

"That'll do, m'lady."

"Thank you." Emma returned the smile, cast one doubtful glance at Maria on the sofa, then hurried out.

The retiring room was also on the ground floor, on the opposite side of the hall to the conservatory. She hurried across the gleaming marble expanse and reentered the dimly lit conservatory.

She wasn't sure quite what Paul had had in mind when he'd suggested a stroll in the quiet seclusion of the orange trees, but it was a reasonable assumption that he hoped to move their flirtation onto more physical lines. A kiss was only to be expected, and Emma found herself in two minds about the prospect. She hadn't been kissed by a man outside her family since her breakup with Alasdair, and she could feel her pulses beating more swiftly, feel that her cheeks had an anticipatory glow to them. But she also sensed deep within herself a certain distaste. Maybe she wanted someone to kiss her, but was that someone Paul Denis?

It was ridiculous to be so contradictory, she told herself sternly. There was no one she preferred to Paul. She had made her plan and she would stick to it. A degree of apprehension was perfectly normal.

The conservatory seemed very quiet, almost like an enchanted garden in its moist green and fragrant dimness. The crunch of gravel beneath her silver kid slippers as she hurried down the aisles sounded very loud, as if echoing in a deserted place.

"Paul?" she whispered, wondering if she was in the right aisle. They all looked the same. There was no immediate answer and she veered to the right. "Paul?"

A whisper came from the far end, sounding muffled. She hurried toward it, at last able to distinguish the dark-clad figure standing against one of the vine-covered windows. "I thought I was lost," she said, sounding a little breathless, although she was not in the least out of breath. "So silly, the aisles all look the same."

Paul reached out an arm and in silence drew her against his side. She allowed him to hold her thus for a minute, without looking at him, just feeling his body so close to her own. Her breathlessness increased; she was holding herself very still, taut with expectation and now unmistakable anxiety. She knew nothing of this man and she was passively putting herself in his power. She could feel the supple strength in the arm at her waist, and there was something intimidating about his silence.

Suddenly he stepped back until he was behind her. His hold moved to her shoulders. Emma seemed unable to move. And then she felt his breath on the side of her face, the lightest kiss on her ear. His tongue darted into the tight shell, and his teeth gently nibbled on her earlobe.

And now Emma knew. That wicked tickling caress belonged to only one man. A man who knew exactly what squirming delight it gave her. She knew but she was frozen . . . frozen in this moment, in this enchanted garden. This was not happening in the real world. In the real world she would not want it. She didn't understand how it could be happening, but she didn't need to understand it. Whatever was happening belonged on some other plane where all was paradox and paradox made sense.

His mouth moved from her ear to her neck. His tongue drew a moist, tantalizing line from the little knob at the top of her spine up the shallow groove to the hollow at the base of her skull.

Emma shivered with delight. A current of lust jolted her belly, sent liquid arousal coursing through her loins. But she didn't move. Moving seemed an impossibility.

He slid his hands around her body, brushing her breasts. His fingers deftly untied the little ribbons of silver tissue that held her domino closed. The domino slipped from her in a whisper of gauze. His hands now reached for her breasts, fingers sliding inside the low décolletage of her ball gown to explore the deep cleft between her breasts. Then his hands cupped the soft mounds within her gown, lifting them, holding them, while a finger rubbed each nipple until they both rose, hard and tight and wanting.

Emma bit her lip. Her belly contracted with every little tug on her nipples. She could feel the moistness of her loins, dampness on her inner thighs. Her blood leaped in her veins and her skin prickled as if with a thousand tiny needles of pleasure.

Then she felt him raising her skirts at the back, slowly inching them up her calves, so very slowly and carefully bundling the elaborate folds of material until she felt the warm moist air on the backs of her thighs, then on her bottom. He held the material against the small of her back and his free hand caressed her bottom, stroking the soft curving cheeks, the swell of her hips.

He used to say with his lazy smile that her rear was the Platonic ideal of a feminine backside. And she had always laughed, thought it funny although wonderfully pleasing. Now Emma remained as immobile as before beneath the caressing, exploring hands. Nothing was required of her except to give herself to this delightful sensual journey in this magical fragrant place.

Then she began to sense an urgency in his caresses. His hands slipped between her thighs, pressing them apart. His fingers moved upward to the wet, hot furrow where her entire being seemed now to be centered. Her legs parted without volition and she moaned. It was a tiny sound, but in the concentrated silence of their two bodies it had the impact of a thunderclap.

His hands moved to her hips, flattened across her belly, pressed against the bones of her pelvis. The pressure gave clear instruction and she bent forward. There was a wide stone sill at waist height, and she rested her own flat palms there, her backside jutting, the small of her back hollowed, a red mist of passionate need engulfing her.

He held her hips and penetrated her open aching body with one deep thrust. She moved backward against him, her bottom pressed into his belly, her forehead resting against the vine-laced window.

He drove into her again and she felt his breath sigh against her bent neck, and the deep throbbing of his flesh against her womb. Then she was lost in the maelstrom of ecstasy, flooded with her own juices, drowning in joy.

From far away came the strains of music, the sounds of voices, of footsteps, but such sounds, although heard, meant nothing. She was barely aware of the moment when he withdrew from her. Barely aware when her skirts fell back, once more covering her. She rested, feeling the window glass against her forehead, the stone under her hands.

She knew that she was alone. Alasdair had gone. Slowly she straightened. Her head cleared. The music was stronger now, penetrating the closed world of passion. Voices, footsteps, footmen calling for carriages.

Emma stood up. Her domino was at her feet. It was the work of a moment to put it on, tie the ribbons. A smoothing touch to her skirts and all was concealed. Only she was aware of the residue of lovemaking—the scent, the soft pulse, the dew of a shared climax.

She walked out of the conservatory and ordered her carriage. She was behaving exactly the way she would have done in ordinary circumstances. She went to the retiring room.

Maria was still prostrate on the sofa, rather anxiously awaiting Emma's return, which seemed to be taking longer than she'd expected. She had decided that Alasdair had wanted to have a word with Mr. Denis alone. It seemed natural to assume that the word had concerned Emma. Alasdair would not like to see Emma in the émigré's pocket any more than Maria did.

Unable to conceal her curiosity, she asked, "I trust Mr. Denis was not offended at your leaving him so suddenly?"

"No," Emma said. "Not in the least."

Maria was disappointed. Surely a man who'd just been warned off would have shown some reaction. But she sensed something different about Emma. She was looking unusually distracted and seemed rather tense in her abstraction.

"Is everything all right, my love?"

Emma smiled quickly. "Of course, Maria. I own I'm a little tired though. The carriage will be here in a few minutes. Are you able to move now?"

"I feel much better." Maria rose gracefully from the
sofa, gathering up her shawl and fan. "But I'll be glad
to reach my bed, too. So fatiguing, these balls. Of
course, I'm always happy to chaperone you, my dear,
but sometimes I think I'd sooner stay quietly at
home," she added mendaciously.

Emma forbore to smile. She gave Maria her arm
and escorted her to the street.

છ

Paul Denis came to in the dark, deserted conservatory
when the sounds of merriment had been extin-
guished, the last guest departed. He sat up and gingerly felt the base of his skull. The skin didn't appear
broken but the swelling was large and throbbed. His
head ached unmercifully.

Who? And why?

He could come up with no answer to either question. Then he became aware that his domino and
mask were lying on the floor beside him. They'd been
taken off him . . . but why? Who could possibly
have wanted them?

He could find no answers and in his present groggy
condition was unlikely to. He was aware of a deep
upswelling of rage both at his assailant and at himself
for allowing such a thing to happen. It didn't matter
that he'd been unaware of any possibility of danger. It
was his business to be alert to the possibility in even
the most unlikely of circumstances.

Emma had presumably returned and found him
gone. She'd wonder why. He'd have to come up with
some plausible excuse.

He got to his knees, stifling a groan at the fierce
stabbing pain in his head. He gathered the domino

and mask to his chest and slowly dragged himself to his feet. He stood swaying slightly, taking stock.

There were still sounds of life in the house beyond the conservatory. Servants putting things to rights after the ball, he assumed. They would be astonished at the appearance of this forgotten guest, emerging disheveled and pale from the conservatory. Paul had lived as long as he had in his chosen profession by never drawing unwanted attention to himself, not even that of the lowliest menial.

Reasoning that there would be a way out of the conservatory into the garden, he walked unsteadily around the perimeter and was rewarded with a small door at the rear. He unlocked it and found himself out in the crisp chill of early morning. The cold air revived him and cleared his head. An iron gate at the front of the garden gave onto the street. It was padlocked but the street was empty and he was able to climb over it undetected.

He walked to Half Moon Street through the deserted streets. Even linkboys had gone to their beds at this hour, and there were no hackneys plying their trade.

But it was not a long walk and he was letting himself into the house within half an hour.

Luiz was dragged out of sleep by a rough hand on his shoulder. He sat up blearily. "Eh, Paolo, what are you doing at this hour?" He examined his surprise visitor and said, "You look sick as a dog. What happened?"

Paolo told him.

"You think someone's onto you?" Luiz shook his head in puzzlement.

"I don't see how they can be," Paolo said curtly. "And if they are, why not do away with me altogether? Why just knock me cold? What could it achieve?"

"A warning perhaps?" Luiz suggested.

Paolo snorted with disgust. "What kind of amateur would give the game away like that?"

"Perhaps these English *are* amateurs."

"Or perhaps this particular agent is," Paolo mused. "But I still don't understand how they could know. I've made no mistakes. *None.*"

"Perhaps someone else made the mistake." Luiz sounded hesitant, knowing he was propounding heresy.

"The governor, you mean?" Paolo shook his head and then winced at the sharply renewed pain.

"Perhaps there's a spy in our own ranks."

"Possibly." Paolo stood at the window, glaring out at the dawn sky across the jumbled rooftops. A cart laden with produce rumbled along the street below, heading for the market in a neighboring street. The city was coming to life.

"I think it's time to move," he said eventually, more to himself than to Luiz. "If my cover's blown, then there's no time to lose. I shall have to take the woman and persuade her to talk." His mouth took an ugly twist. "It's so unsubtle, so clumsy, but I don't see any alternative."

"We could try a search of her rooms first," Luiz suggested.

"They're at the front of the house. There's no way to enter them from the street undetected."

"No, but there are glass doors opening onto the garden at the back of the house. It's secluded. Easy to access over the wall. I did it myself."

"We stage a break-in," Paolo mused. "Once in, it will be simple to find her chamber at the front."

"And if you find nothing, then you take the woman. We go prepared with ropes and a gag. We bring her here and you can get what you want out of her where no one can hear." He shrugged as if to indicate how simple the whole process would be.

Paolo frowned. Absently he touched the swelling at the base of his skull. The ugly twist to his mouth became more pronounced. He would not be defeated. They'd shown their hand. Always a mistake. He turned to Luiz and gave a curt nod of agreement.

Chapter Eight

Emma closed the door of her bedchamber and gave a sigh of relief. Thank God she'd sent Tilda to bed. The fire still glowed in the grate, and there was a tray with milk and a plate of macaroons on the dresser with a little oil lamp over which she could heat the milk if she chose.

There was something so wonderfully ordinary and comforting about the idea of hot milk. It carried all the reassurance of the nursery.

She threw off her clothes, casting them onto the chaise longue beneath the window, and poured water into the ewer. It was still hot, so she guessed that Tilda had only recently gone to bed. She washed herself carefully, aware of the slight soreness, the stretched feeling in her groin. It had been so long since she'd last made love, her body had become tight, almost virginal again.

Had Alasdair noticed?

Emma dropped her nightgown over her head and lit the little oil lamp. She set the pan of milk over it and watched it dreamily until the first bubble appeared. She poured it into the cup, put a macaroon into the saucer, and climbed into bed. A wonderful feeling of lethargy flooded her limbs as the deep feather bed nestled around her. She sat up against the pillows, the cup of milk resting on her stomach, and at last allowed herself to consider what had happened.

But all the consideration in the world couldn't make sense out of it. Alasdair had been waiting for her. He'd taken Paul's place, dressed in Paul's domino. He hadn't spoken, hadn't looked directly at her. And yet he could not have imagined that she wouldn't know him. Surely he couldn't have believed he could deceive her with his body? Had he thought she was going to make good her promise to take a lover and substituted himself?

Or had it been some kind of revenge? Some way of proving to her that she couldn't do anything without his approval?

But Emma knew that revenge had not been in Alasdair's mind. He had made love to her, not assailed her with vengeance or malice. And she? She had let it happen. Had reveled in it. It had been so right. So absolutely right.

She dipped the macaroon into the milk and carried the soggy morsel carefully to her mouth. She savored the milky almond sweetness. Every sensation seemed heightened. The warmth and softness of the bed, the brush of lawn against her skin, the honeyed taste in her mouth.

What had happened to Paul Denis? Had he given up his domino and mask at Alasdair's request? Ridiculous! Why would he do such a thing? She was *his* prize. And there was no vanity attached to that acknowledgment. He wanted her money, and if he enjoyed her company and found her attractive, then that was merely a bonus. Emma had no illusions. But he wouldn't step out of the lists at the request of another man. Not Paul Denis. He was too strong, too determined, too self-assured to stand aside tamely.

So what had Alasdair done with Paul Denis?

Interesting though that question was, it was nowhere near as vital as the issue of what was to happen now between herself and Alasdair. Would he acknowledge that explosion of passion? Could he possibly fail to? And if he didn't, should she?

And once again she wondered, what in the name of Satan had been his motive? If he had intended to show her that they remained somehow inextricably connected, then . . . then he'd succeeded.

There was no point denying it. But she didn't have to like it. Didn't have to accept it meekly. Had anything changed?

Everything.

Emma lay back, gazing up at the ceiling, watching the flickering shadows thrown by the candle on her bedside table. She'd sworn to have a lover by the feast of Saint Valentine. Alasdair had made sure she was not forsworn.

But it had completely defeated her own purposes. Instead of freeing her from Alasdair, it had tied her to him with a Gordian knot.

She set her empty cup on the bedside table and leaned over to blow out the candle. Then she lay, still wide awake, listening to the hiss and pop of the fire, enjoying the soft golden light it threw.

She would have to wait and see what Alasdair did. And she would have to follow his cue.

He was the most infuriating, damnably unpredictable, totally controlling man! He'd engineered the whole situation so that she was somehow hopelessly entwined in his coils, forced to dance to his tune. And his damned tune was the most irresistible music.

Plus ça change, plus c'est la même chose.

Her eyes closed beneath an inexorable wave of sleep.

❦

Alasdair rode up to Mount Street the next morning, at the correct hour for visiting. The elation that had followed loving Emma was still with him. He couldn't wait to see her. To see how she was. Of course, she had known it was him. His little game of an incognito lover had never been intended to deceive her, only to heighten the experience for both of them. He knew Emma so well, knew that the risk of discovery, the exotic situation, the aura of mystery, the silence of the encounter, would have fueled her passion and given her the excitement she craved. And he had no intention as yet of bringing the game to a close.

He dismounted and handed the reins to Jemmy, who was riding the pretty roan mare Alasdair had bought for Emma. Without haste, he mounted the steps to the front door and pleasantly greeted the butler who opened it for him.

"Good morning, Harris. Are the ladies at home?"

"Lady Emma and Mrs. Witherspoon are in the salon, sir. They are at home to callers this morning." He took Alasdair's hat and whip.

"Who's here?" Alasdair inquired, drawing off his gloves.

"The duke of Clarence, the Misses Gordon, Lady Dalrymple, Lord Everard, and Mr. Darcy, sir." Harris reeled off the names of society's elite with distinct relish.

Alasdair nodded. It rather suited him to find her in the midst of visitors. There would be less temptation to drop the pretence. After the first meeting, the facade would be easier to maintain. "I'll announce myself, Harris." He went to the stairs.

Emma was standing at the far end of the salon, talking with the duke of Clarence. She had her back to the door, but as Alasdair entered she felt the fine hairs on the nape of her neck lift, and a current of electric excitement brought goose bumps to life along her arms. She raised her head to the mirror above the fireplace, and her eyes met Alasdair's. Immediately he turned his eyes away as if he wasn't aware of her gaze and went to greet Maria.

So that was how he wanted to play it, Emma thought grimly. It had never happened. Well, she could play that game as well as he could. She turned the full force of her attention on the duke, who was so unnerved by the suddenly fixed golden gaze that he lost his thread for a minute and stared blankly at her, wheezing slightly in his creaking corset.

"Newmarket, duke?" Emma prompted politely.

"Oh, yes . . . yes, indeed. My horse, Needlepoint. You're a horsewoman, ma'am, you'd have enjoyed watching him win. He flew . . . flew on wings. Like . . . like . . ." A frown crossed his amiable if somewhat red and mottled countenance. "That Greek horse . . . can't remember the name."

"Pegasus," Emma supplied helpfully.

"That's the ticket!" he said. "I wouldn't have put you down for a bluestocking, ma'am." He beamed at this pleasantry and managed to bend his stout frame in the semblance of a courtly bow. His corset creaked even more noticeably.

"Emma a bluestocking, sir!" Alasdair exclaimed from just behind them. "I assure you she was never overly fond of her books." He bowed to the royal personage before giving Emma a pleasant smile. "Isn't that so, Emma?"

"Perhaps," Emma said with a cool smile of her own.

"Ah, well, you would know, Chase, lucky dog," the duke boomed. "Known the lady from the schoolroom . . . trustee too, I gather. Yes, lucky dog!"

"The role of trustee gives me few privileges, sir," Alasdair responded blandly. He glanced sideways at Emma, a wicked gleam in his green eyes, a tiny quirk to his straight mouth. "Isn't that so, ma'am?"

"Since I don't know what privileges a trustee might expect to have, I can't really answer you," Emma replied. She turned back to the duke. "If you'll excuse me, sir, I see that Mrs. Dawson has just come in. I must greet her."

"Yes, yes . . . play the hostess . . . of course," the duke said heartily. "Do the pretty with your guests . . . don't mind me. No need to stand on ceremony, y'know."

Emma bowed, smiled, and withdrew. She had the feeling that the duke was going to propose marriage one day soon, as he did invariably whenever a new heiress appeared on the social scene. It occurred to her that when she'd compared Alasdair and his liaison with his opera dancer to Clarence's situation with Mrs. Jordan, she had been unfair. But the provocation had been great; it was no wonder she had struck to hurt.

The image of Lady Melrose came to mind. Had he kept his engagement with her the evening after their visit to Tattersalls? Oh, it was madness to torment herself in this way. What had happened between them last night had been a dream . . . an aberrant dream. And she would forget it and continue exactly as she'd been intending. Alasdair Chase was not the lover she wanted for Valentine's feast.

As if on cue, Harris announced Paul Denis. Emma froze. Now what? Something had happened between Paul and Alasdair last evening. She glanced quickly at Alasdair, who was still talking to the duke and appeared not to have noticed Paul's arrival.

She went swiftly to greet the newcomer, inspiration coming to her. Last night had never happened. None of the participants wished to acknowledge it, so neither should Paul have to explain his own part in a situation engineered by the Machiavellian Alasdair.

She spoke in a low voice before he had a chance to open his mouth. "Oh, Mr. Denis, can you forgive my bad manners? I do beg your pardon for not returning to the conservatory last evening, but poor Maria was suffering so badly, I couldn't leave her." She smiled brilliantly. "Do say you forgive me."

Paul bowed over her hand. "Madame, you could never be at fault," he murmured. "Of course you had to attend to your companion. My own claims were insignificant."

"I trust you didn't wait long for me." She waited curiously for his response. Did he know what was going on? Did he believe that she hadn't returned after he'd been induced or persuaded to leave?

Paul believed it. But he couldn't believe his good fortune. There was no need now to produce an excuse for his own hasty departure. "An eternity, madame," he said jocularly. "Every minute out of your sight is an eternity."

"Now you're being absurd again," Emma accused. "Oh, I believe the duke is leaving. I must make my farewells."

"Mr. Denis, I haven't run into you for a couple of days." Alasdair greeted him with a smile. "Not since we met at Tattersalls. I trust you found a horse to your liking."

Emma, while seeing the duke to the door of the salon, strained her ears to catch their exchange. They were both behaving perfectly normally. Chatting like old acquaintances who hadn't had seen each other for a while. And there was no constraint between them. But they must have met last night. And how could it have been a pleasant encounter? Her head was beginning to ache with the puzzle. They must both be supreme actors, carrying their parts without a misstep. But *why*? Were they in some kind of partnership? Was *she* a factor in that partnership?

Oh, she wanted to scream with the frustration of it all.

Instead she went to talk to Lady Dalrymple and listened to a minute account of that lady's latest ailment and the revolutionary treatment of her new physician.

"Yes, only think, Emma," Maria said in awe. "Two days ago, Lady Dalrymple was laid upon her bed, unable to lift her head. And now see how well she is. And it's all thanks to sheep's blood and vinegar. Isn't that truly amazing."

"Truly amazing," Emma concurred faintly.

"I trust you're feeling more the thing, Maria." Alasdair spoke amiably from behind Emma's shoulder.

"Oh, yes, thank you, Alasdair. Just the headache,

you know. But it soon passed." Maria looked a trifle flustered.

Alasdair nodded, exchanged a word with Lady Dalrymple, and turned to Emma. "I understand you've purchased a racing curricle, Emma."

She looked startled. "How could you know that?"

"I received the bill," he said dryly. "You'll cut quite a dash."

"That was my intention," she returned coolly.

Alasdair met and matched her tone. "Your horses were delivered this morning. Jemmy has set up stabling for them in a mews off Park Street. Perhaps you would like to take a look at the mare. I don't believe you saw her at Tattersalls."

"She's here?" Emma dropped the cool facade.

"In the street with Jemmy." A smile lit his eyes at her eagerness. Until three years ago, she had always been so enthusiastic about everything, so utterly open in her responses. It was good to see the wariness that seemed to have replaced those qualities no longer uppermost.

"Do you care to come down and make her acquaintance?"

"Oh, yes, immediately!" Emma was halfway to the door even as she spoke.

Alasdair followed, that enigmatic smile still alight in his eyes. She was ahead of him on the stairs, her floating muslin skirts gathered in one hand as she almost jumped down the last steps. She hurried across the hall. A footman, looking a trifle startled at this inelegant haste, jumped to open the door for her.

Emma ran down the steps to the street. "Good morning, Jemmy. Oh, isn't she pretty?" She took the mare's face between her hands and stroked the velvety nose, before walking around her, examining her carefully. "Lovely lines," she murmured appreciatively.

"Aye, Lady Emma. See those sloping shoulders." Jemmy sounded as proud as if the mare was his own possession. "She'll have rare speed, I'll lay odds."

"Mmmm." Emma rested a hand on the horse's hindquarters, letting her know she was behind her, as she ran a hand down her flanks. "She's beautiful, Alasdair."

"Did you expect me to buy you a jobbing hack?" he protested, teasing her.

She looked over at him. He was smiling, a warm smile certainly, but even with the greatest self-deception and the best will in the world, one could see no particular significance in his expression. Emma returned the smile with a fleeting one of her own.

A northeasterly wind gusted suddenly from around the corner of Audley Street. Emma shivered and the mare lowered her head.

"You'll catch your death in that flimsy muslin," Alasdair said swiftly. "Get back inside. If you wish to try her paces, then change your dress and we'll go to Richmond."

His hand closed over the back of her neck. The clasp was warm and firm and brought back a host of memories. It was one of his favorite ways of touching her, and it dated from their earliest acquaintance. When she'd been a small girl, he'd often held her in this way. Sometimes to propel her along his desired path, other times just because she was standing close to him and his hand had seemed to find its way to her nape with a possessive familiarity that had always seemed quite natural.

Emma's mouth was suddenly dry. The pit of her stomach seemed to drop and her loins tensed, the muscles of her thighs clenching in involuntary response. She resisted the pressure for a second and he moved his other hand to the small of her back.

"Inside, Emma! It's freezing out here and that gown, height of fashion though it is, offers little more protection than a nightgown."

He urged her back to the house, his hands firm on her back and neck. There was nothing overtly sensual about his touch, and yet Emma found its easy familiarity, its casual possessiveness arousing.

Her response infuriated her. There was no indication that Alasdair was similarly affected. He seemed merely impatient to get her out of the cold.

She shook his hand off her neck and stepped away from the warm pressure on her back, hurrying up the steps and into the house, distancing herself from him.

Alasdair followed at his own pace. In the hall, he said casually, "So, do you care to try her out?"

Emma paused. She could say that she would ride the mare in Hyde Park at five o'clock, during the fashionable hour of the promenade. Or she could do what she really wished to do and ride to Richmond, where she could give the horse her head and really see what she could do. But she could not go to Richmond without an escort.

"I need a groom," she said, instead of answering the question directly. "Does Jemmy have any friends?"

"You have a groom," Alasdair informed her. "One of Jemmy's many contacts. Probably of rather dubious origins, but Jemmy vouches for him, and I interviewed him early this morning. He struck me as ideally suited to the position. Not too polished in his manner, but I'm sure you won't mind that. His way with horses is unimpeachable. And Jemmy assures me he's handy with his fives and can use a pistol should the need arise. So you should be safe enough in his company."

"Oh," Emma said, taken aback by Alasdair's sweeping arrangements, and yet knowing that she should have expected it. "Where is he to live?"

"In the mews. You may send a footman to him with your orders whenever you wish to drive or ride out." Alasdair raised an eyebrow inquiringly, clearly waiting for further questions that he was also so clearly willing and able to answer.

"You appear to have arranged everything," Emma said finally.

"Only with your satisfaction in mind," he responded politely. "You must tell me if any of my arrangements don't meet with your approval."

Emma was betrayed into a laugh. "Impossible! As well you know, sir."

"So I hope," he said, and his eyes suddenly narrowed. "I like to think that I know both your needs and what pleases you."

There was a tiny silence. A silence laden with the unspoken. Emma fought the urge to speak out, to challenge him, to force the truth. She fought the urge and won. Whatever game Alasdair was playing, she was prepared to play it too. She would not be the first to crack. If this was one of his competitions, then she would meet and match him.

"What's this paragon's name?" she inquired placidly.

"Sam," he replied. "He's an ex-jockey too. But I suspect he augmented his earnings as a jockey with a little pickpocketing. But Jemmy assures me he's a reformed character."

"And Jemmy is always to be trusted," Emma said

with perfect truth. "I'm expecting my curricle to be delivered this afternoon."

"Sam has taken delivery already."

Emma could manage this absurdly polite exchange no longer. She went into a peal of laughter. "Alasdair, if you weren't so damnably efficient, I could shoot you for being so managing. I'm quite capable of handling these arrangements myself."

"But it pleases me to see to them for you," he said simply.

"So you're not merely taking care of a simple-minded woman who can't be trusted to manage her finances alone?" she said with a touch of asperity now.

"You almost deserve that I should say yes, that is precisely what I'm doing," he returned. "Now, are you going to change and come riding? Or would you rather stand here and exchange pointless banter for the rest of the morning?"

That was not a realistic choice. "Richmond?" she queried.

"That's what I said. Will it take you more than twenty minutes to change?"

"Make my excuses to Maria." Emma ran up the stairs.

Alasdair stood for a moment, poised to follow her, one hand on the newel post, his foot on the bottom step. How the hell long was he going to be able to keep this up? He could barely keep his hands off her. He realized that he'd been hoping she'd have shown some sign of that explosion of passion. That she had been marked in some way that only he could detect. He'd been looking for the special glow in her eye, the increased translucence of her skin, the softness that had always lingered on her after their lovemaking.

But the wretched, uncooperative creature had been as cool and composed as he. Except that *his* cool composure was entirely feigned. But was Emma's?

He shook his head with a gesture of impatience and was about to mount the stairs when Paul Denis appeared at their head. Alasdair waited for him to descend. "You seem to be finding your way around society, Mr. Denis," he observed with a bland smile.

"Yes, I thank you. Princess Esterhazy has been most charming and helpful," Paul replied. "She has provided me with vouchers for Almack's. I intend to be at the subscription ball this evening."

Alasdair's meaningless smile remained on his face, although his eyes were sharply assessing. His neighbor didn't look to be in the pink of health. There were dark shadows under his eyes and a grayish cast to his countenance. Alasdair wondered whether Mr. Denis had called for the watch when he'd recovered his senses in the conservatory. If he had, the tale of his assault amid the orange trees at the duchess of Devizes's masked ball had not yet circulated. But to call for help and demand justice would surely be the most natural action. Indeed, it would be very strange if he had not.

"I was hoping to discover if Lady Emma planned to be there, and if so to solicit her hand for the waltz," Paul said. "But she disappeared before I had the chance to speak to her." He gave a small, self-deprecating smile that nonetheless spoke of disgruntlement.

"Well, it wouldn't have helped even if you had spoken to her," Alasdair replied bluntly. "Even if Emma is willing to waltz, which I doubt, Almack's rules would prevent her standing up with you before you were offered to her as a suitable partner."

"Oh, I didn't realize." Paul gave a despairing shrug. "So many rules . . . so many unspoken conventions. London society is very difficult for a newcomer."

Alasdair smiled his agreement and prepared to move on up the stairs, but was arrested before he'd taken the first step.

"Lord Alasdair?"

He turned at once. "Mr. Denis?"

"This is a trifle awkward." Paul touched his mouth with his fingertips. "But, I trust you would have no objections if I made a push to press my suit with Lady Emma."

Over my dead body!

But that Alasdair didn't say. Instead, he said evenly, "I suggest you discover if Emma has any objection, Mr. Denis. Legally, she has been her own mistress for two years. In practice, for much longer than that; since her father's death, in fact. Her brother was no heavy-handed guardian. You will discover, if you have not already done so, that Emma has a very definite mind of her own." He nodded in farewell and continued up the stairs.

Paul went out into the street, his brow furrowed. It had occurred to him, as a sudden flash of inspiration, that perhaps Alasdair Chase objected to his pursuit of the lady. They had a shared past; they had been betrothed; he was her trustee; and the tension between them was unmistakable. But then so too were the moments when they were so obviously at ease. When they seemed to relapse into a mode of communication that could exist only between old friends . . . or erstwhile lovers.

He had recognized that the lady was no inexperienced chit. Had she and Lord Alasdair anticipated the conjugal bed?

If the jilted lover still carried a torch for the lady, he might well object to new suitors. Even to the extent of knocking the aspiring lover on the head to break up a tête-à-tête.

And yet Paul couldn't see the calm, debonair Lord Alasdair doing anything so crude. And he had given not the slightest indication of discomfort in his victim's presence. Not a flicker of an eyelid had rewarded Paul's question. No, it wasn't possible. It would have been satisfying to have found such a simple reason as male jealousy for the attack, but Paul knew in his gut that it wasn't that. Someone was on to him.

❧

Emma returned to the salon within twenty minutes. Her appearance brought gleams of admiration to the eyes of the men gathered there, looks of envy from the young ladies, and pursed lips from their mamas.

"Lady Emma, that is the most modish habit," George Darcy said with wholehearted approval.

"Indeed, ma'am, you will have all the young ladies eating their hearts out," Lord Everard agreed. "Epaulets, are they?"

"Yes, aren't they dashing?" Emma said with a merry laugh. "But I most particularly liked the shako. I fell quite in love with it at first sight and knew I had to have it."

"Not every woman could wear it," said George seriously. Like his friend Lord Alasdair, he was accounted something of an arbiter on matters of female dress.

"Not every woman would wish to wear it," Lady

Dalrymple was heard to mutter as she rose to take her leave.

Maria's eyes sparkled. "No, indeed, Lady Dalrymple, one would hope not," she stated. "One would need Emma's flair to carry it off."

Emma caught Alasdair's amused eye and grinned. Maria, sweet nature notwithstanding, could always be relied upon to stand up for her chick. Alasdair responded with a lazy wink that brought back memories of so many occasions in the past when that conspiratorial little gesture had comforted her through some childhood trouble or scolding, or had invited her to share privately in his own wicked amusement at some individual or situation he considered comical.

She offered Lady Dalrymple her most charming smile as the lady took her leave, soon followed by the rest of the company.

"I'm going to Richmond with Alasdair, Maria. You don't mind my deserting you?"

"No, indeed not, my dear. If we should have other visitors, I daresay I can entertain them on my own," Maria said placidly, adding with a degree of satisfaction, "although it's not me they come to see. I'm not so deceived as to think that." She laughed.

"What nonsense, Maria!" Emma protested. "You know perfectly well that Lady Dalrymple and her like don't come to see me. They disapprove of me heartily for the most part."

"Old cats," Maria stated.

Emma hugged her. "You are a true friend. You always know just what to say to make me comfortable . . . even if it isn't true."

"Goodness, Emma, I never tell a lie." Maria was

shocked. "I dare swear I've never knowingly spoken anything but the truth."

"Your partiality for Emma, ma'am, leads you to see truth where perhaps others do not," Alasdair said with a smile that was a touch sardonic.

"Well, of course I can find no fault in Emma," Maria said stoutly. "It isn't to be wondered at."

"Oh, Alasdair would wonder at it," Emma said, glaring at him. "Alasdair has never failed to see all my flaws of character. And never failed to point them out to me at every opportunity. Alasdair's notion of honesty doesn't admit of the kindly falsehood. Isn't that so, sir?"

Alasdair gave her an ironic bow. "I don't believe in lying to my friends," he said. "The truth, while it might hurt a little, can only do good if it's offered in the right spirit. Shall we go now, ma'am?" He held open the door for her.

Emma yielded the field, although it went against the grain to do so. She kissed Maria goodbye and went past Alasdair, saying over her shoulder, "Why must you always put me out of charity with you?"

"It was not my intention," he said seriously. Then a smile glinted in his eyes and he said, "Stand still for a minute and let me take a proper look at you."

Emma stood still on the landing, regarding him with a challenging tilt to her chin. "Well, sir?" she demanded. "Do you find fault with my riding habit?"

Alasdair did not immediately reply. Emma's riding habit of emerald green broadcloth was cut to accentuate the rich curves of bosom and hip. It was styled like a hussar's uniform, with epaulets on the shoulders, gold braid on the tight buttoned sleeves, and frogged buttons marching down the front of the jacket. The whole was surmounted with a tall plumed shako. Darcy had been correct, Alasdair reflected with quiet enjoyment. Only a woman with such a body and undeniable sense of style could wear such a daring costume and not be called fast.

"Well, sir?" Emma demanded again. "Will you be embarrassed to be seen with me?"

"I can fault you in only one instance," Alasdair said solemnly.

Emma's eyes flashed. "And what, pray, might that be?"

"Turn around," he said.

Emma obeyed, although she didn't know why she should.

Alasdair grinned appreciatively. "If your intention is to inflame the passions of every man you encounter, my sweet, then you have succeeded. If such is not your intention, therein lies the fault. One should always ensure that one's dress creates the desired impression."

Emma turned back to him, unsure whether she'd received a compliment or not. Then she saw his grin. "Odious man!" she declared, and flounced down the stairs ahead of him.

Alasdair followed, enjoying the view.

Chapter Nine

❧

The roan was spirited, fidgeting and sidling beneath her rider. "She's testing me," Emma declared with satisfaction, relishing the challenge. It took all her concentration to hold the horse to a steady pace through the noisy traffic of Piccadilly.

"Does she have a name?" Emma inquired finally, once she was sure she had the mare well in hand.

"Not that I know of," Alasdair replied. He held his own black close beside the roan, prepared to assist if Emma needed it. He knew she'd be furious at his intervention, but he also knew that his hands were stronger than hers and the roan was clearly not a typical lady's horse. She had a definite temperament of her own. Not unlike her rider's, he reflected with a private smile. They were going to be well suited, these two.

"Then I shall call her Swallow," Emma said, drawing back on the reins as a rambunctious stallion be-

tween the shafts of a tilbury showed an interest in the
roan.

The gentleman driving the tilbury hauled back on
the reins, cursing vigorously, and his horse shied and
rose up in the shafts with a panicked whinny.

Alasdair reached instinctively to take the roan's bridle at the bit, but Emma shot him such a fierce and
outraged look that he refrained with a half gesture of
apology. Emma steadied her mount with a hand on
the neck and a soft word, and the mare trotted past
the rearing gelding with what in a human would have
been a distinctly lofty air of contempt.

The driver of the tilbury, a gentleman in a bright
yellow waistcoat and a cravat so impossibly high that
he could barely turn his head, ogled Emma as she
passed him and went so far as to raise his eyeglass for
a better look.

"Vulgar cit," Emma declared in a carrying voice.
The ogling gentleman flushed and dropped his glass.

"Your horse . . . if you please," Alasdair said in a
pained voice as he drew Phoenix aside from the now
prancing gelding.

The gentleman yanked back on the bit and his
horse reared again in the shafts. Alasdair, without a
backward glance, encouraged Phoenix to trot past.

"Your Swallow, for all her spirit, has been well
schooled," he observed, coming alongside Emma.

"She has lovely manners," Emma agreed with enthusiasm. "Such a soft mouth."

"I'm delighted my choice gives satisfaction," Alasdair responded solemnly.

Emma only chuckled. The crisp January day was
too exhilarating, the pleasure of riding such a perfect
horse too heady for anything but wholehearted enjoyment of the excursion.

When they reached Richmond Park, Alasdair immediately directed Phoenix toward one of the smaller grassy rides that meandered through the trees alongside the major thoroughfares where horse and carriage traffic abounded.

Emma followed him and they trotted in companionable silence until they reached a glade from whence stretched a broad grassy path disappearing into the distant trees.

"So," Alasdair invited. "Try her out."

Emma looked along the ride. The roan raised her head and sniffed the wind. She shifted eagerly on the soft ground.

"*Ventre à terre?*" Emma murmured.

"Go, Emma."

She threw him a glance of pure mischief and gave the mare her head. They flew down the broad ride.

Alasdair waited, watching her critically. Then he shook his head in admiration. "By God, she can ride!" he muttered aloud. He nudged Phoenix in pursuit, and the black galloped flat out after the roan.

Emma heard Phoenix pounding the turf behind her. She leaned low over Swallow's neck and whispered encouragement. The roan increased her speed. Emma laughed and glanced sideways at Alasdair. Phoenix had pulled up with them and his stride now matched the mare's.

Alasdair grinned at her, his teeth flashing white, his eyes alight with his own exhilaration. They galloped side by side until Emma felt the mare beginning to tire. She drew rein and eased the horse into a canter and then a trot.

Alasdair reined in Phoenix immediately and they trotted together beneath the bare branches of oak and beech tree, enjoying the quiet, the sense of privacy, after London's noisy bustle. One couldn't set foot outside one's house without drawing remark.

Although it had been three years since she'd last been at Richmond, Emma recognized the ride Alasdair had chosen. It had always been one of their favorites in the old days because it was so rarely used. When Ned was around, the three of them would spend all day under these trees, sometimes without seeing another soul.

As she understood how very alone they were, their seclusion undisturbed by even the faint sounds of distant voices, she became aware of a slight tension building in the pit of her stomach. It was anticipation, she realized, a warm flush creeping over her face. She allowed Swallow to break into a canter, hoping the fresh wind would cool her cheeks and do something to tamp down the unbidden swirl of arousal that seemed to be taking charge of her body.

But the horse's motion did nothing to help, quite the opposite.

"Hey, where to in such a hurry?" Alasdair rode up beside her.

"I think it's going to come on to rain." Emma offered the first thing that came into her head as excuse for that burst of speed. She kept her eyes on the track ahead.

Alasdair glanced up at the sky. "I believe you're right," he said, indicating the growing mass of black clouds. "It's looking quite ominous up there. We'd better find shelter before the heavens open." He turned his horse off the ride and into the trees.

Emma followed, glad of the diversion. Swallow didn't seem to like trees. She edged through them with every expression of disgust, and it needed all Emma's soft reassurances and firm hands on the reins to coax her along the narrow aisle between two lines of poplars.

They broke from the trees just as the first drops of rain fell. A small grassy knoll lay ahead of them, crowned with a replica of a Greek temple.

Alasdair gestured with his whip. "We'll shelter in there until it blows over."

"If it blows over," Emma said with a shiver as a gust of very cold wind pierced her jacket. "I didn't think to bring a cloak."

"It'll be better out of the wind," he said and cantered Phoenix up the hill.

The cold had certainly dampened her ardor, Emma reflected with a degree of grim relief as she followed.

Alasdair rode Phoenix around the temple to the shelter of a grove of trees. He dismounted and turned to Emma. "Dismount here and run into the temple. I'll take care of the horses." He raised his hands to grasp her waist, steadying her as she slid from the saddle.

Emma's skin prickled anew and for a second their eyes met. There was no mistaking the pure flame of desire in Alasdair's hooded green gaze, and Emma was flooded with a heady sense of relief that she was not suffering this disquieting arousal alone.

"Get inside," Alasdair said, and there was a catch in his throat.

"I'll take care of Swallow first."

"No, you won't." He turned her around, his hands light on her shoulders. "Get out of the wind." He attempted to sound jocular but that husky catch remained in his voice. He gave her a little push and lightly swung his riding whip against her rear. "Run along, Emma."

Ordinarily Emma would have vigorously protested

this paternalistic dismissal, but she understood what
Alasdair was trying to mask . . . understood it all
too well. She left him without a word and hurried
into the temple.

Alasdair blew out his breath in a noisy exhalation.
It wasn't going to be possible to keep up the game. He
was hard as a rock, and all he'd done was brush her
waist with his hands.

He turned to his horse, fervently hoping that the
practical business of loosening the girths, knotting the
reins, and tethering the animals would quieten his
rampant flesh. It was an effort to keep his mind a
blank while he performed these automatic tasks, but
he was rather more comfortable by the time he was
ready to join Emma in the temple.

He unstrapped a cylindrical leather box from the
rear of his saddle, hoisted it over his shoulder, and
raced for the shelter of the temple as the rain began in
earnest.

Emma was standing between two pillars, looking
out at the view, at the rain scudding across the flatter
expanse of land beneath the knoll. She turned as Alasdair came in, her eyebrows lifting at the box. "What
have you got?"

"Provisions," he said, setting the leather box on a
stone bench well within the portico and away from
the driving rain. "I thought we might feel the need of
fortification, so I have wine . . . cheese . . . cold
chicken . . . bread." He set each of these items on
the bench as he named them.

Emma, who was distinctly hungry, came forward
eagerly. This domestic little feast had somehow managed to sever the cord of sexual tension. "You brought
glasses too," she said in mock awe.

"And napkins, ma'am." He flourished a white

damask square. "Pray be seated." He gestured to the bench beside the food, and when she sat he arranged the napkin on her lap with all the courtly expertise of a waiter at the Pantheon.

Emma couldn't help but laugh. The rain was drumming on the roof now and slicing inward between the pillars, but they were far enough inside to be dry, even though it was cold and cheerless. At least, she thought, it ought to have been cheerless, but with a glass of wine in one hand and a chicken leg in the other, she felt far from miserable.

Alasdair sat at the far end of the bench with the picnic arrayed between them and helped himself to bread and cheese. "So, what do you think of our French émigré, Monsieur Denis?" he inquired casually.

"What should I think of him?" Emma asked, wiping her fingers on her napkin, every nerve stretched, every muscle taut. Was his abrupt question a prelude to the truth?

"I don't know. But you seem to enjoy his company." Alasdair sipped his wine and regarded her over the lip of the glass.

"Is that a crime?"

"No. But he's a fortune hunter."

"I am aware," she said dryly. "You needn't fear, Alasdair, that I have an overly high view of my own personal attractions."

"Fishing, Emma?" he asked softly, his eyes resting on her face with a good deal of amusement . . . and something else, much more disquieting.

She flushed. "No, of course I'm not. I know a great deal better than to fish for compliments with *you*."

"Oh, I don't know," he said lazily. "I could provide a few." He reached out a hand and caught her chin on a fingertip. His eyes held hers and a little smile played over his mouth. "For instance, you have the most beautiful eyes. And your mouth has such a wonderful way of turning up at the corners. And the hollows under your cheekbones always seem to hold shadows, so that often you look—"

"Oh, stop!" Emma interrupted, jerking her face away from his hand. "Don't be so odious!"

"Now, that, my sweet, is no way to receive a compliment," he said with mock severity. "You should smile, and blush, and maybe lower your eyes in confusion; but flying at me as if I've insulted you definitely will not do."

Emma tried not to smile but the corners of her mouth wouldn't stay still.

"That's better," he approved. "Laugh at me by all means. I won't take offense."

"Oh, you're too absurd," Emma declared roundly, taking up her wineglass again. "Is the rain stopping? The horses will be miserable."

Alasdair ignored this. He reached for her glass and took it from her suddenly nerveless fingers. All amusement had left his expression. Leaning over, he cupped her face in his hands. His eyes were utterly serious, utterly intent as they looked deep into her own.

There was an eternity of silence. Emma could hear her own heart beating in her ears; she could feel the whisper of his breath on her face. She felt as if her body were suspended in crystal, poised, liable at any minute to shatter.

Alasdair broke the silence. "So, Emma?" he said softly, his fingertips lightly caressing her cheekbones.

What was he asking? But she knew. She made no

reply, merely gazed steadily into his eyes, waiting to see what he would do next.

He smiled a little ruefully. "What must I say, Emma?"

The game was over, she realized with a surge of relief and a tremor of apprehension. She responded obliquely. "What did you do with Paul Denis?"

"Oh." His smile grew even more rueful. "Must I tell you?"

"Yes."

"Well, if you must know, I hit him over the head with a brass nymph."

"You did what?" Emma exclaimed in shock. "What a dreadful thing to do to the poor man."

"Well, he was in my way, you see," Alasdair explained apologetically. "And there wasn't time for more subtle measures." The tips of his fingers moved to her mouth, lightly brushing over her lips, making them tingle.

"Does he know you hit him?"

"Good God, I hope not. He'd be bound to call me out." Alasdair sounded genuinely horrified at the prospect. "Pistols or small swords at dawn has never sounded like an appealing prospect."

Since Alasdair was a superb marksman and an excellent fencer, Emma gave little weight to this protestation. "It was a barbaric thing to do," she declared.

"Perhaps," Alasdair agreed. "But I really cannot like the fellow. And I'm afraid, my sweet, that I was not . . . am not . . . prepared to stand aside while you take Paul Denis as your lover. Nor am I prepared to see you throw yourself away in marriage to an acknowledged fortune hunter. So . . ." He shrugged. "What could I do?"

"You have no right," Emma said in a stifled voice.

"You cannot manage my life the way you choose, Alasdair."

"You are mistaken," he replied with a glint of mischief in his eyes now. "I only intend to manage your life the way *you* choose." His mouth hovered over hers, and Emma with a violent exclamation jumped up from the bench.

She stepped away from him, almost as if she would ward him off. She stood with her back against a pillar, looking remarkably like a hunted animal, Alasdair thought, a frown now in his eye.

He didn't move for a minute, watching her closely. When he did rise from the bench, it was so swiftly that Emma didn't have time to react before he stood in front of her. She was backed up against the pillar, unable to move as he placed his hands on the pillar on either side of her head.

"Don't run from me, Emma," he said softly. "After last night, we both know that nothing's changed between us."

"Don't you understand?" she cried. "That's the problem. We're doomed, Alasdair. We are so very bad for each other and yet we do things so well together. Everything . . . music . . . singing . . . loving . . . quarreling . . . *everything*. And yet we destroy each other at the same time."

"How are we bad for each other?" he murmured. "Like this, perhaps . . . or like this . . . or this . . ." His mouth moved to her ear, his teeth nibbled her earlobe, his tongue traced a moist path over her cheekbones, darted into the corners of her mouth even as his teasing whisper rustled against her ear.

He moved his arms around her body so that he was holding her tightly against him, his hands sliding over her backside, gripping the rounded flesh beneath her habit with urgent fingers, lifting her so that involuntarily she rose on tiptoe. His erection pressed hard against her lower belly, and her loins were filled with a liquid weakness that made her thighs quiver.

Now there was no caution, no wariness, only this wild, urgent need. At this moment, Emma couldn't have cared if Alasdair was the devil incarnate. He was what she wanted. What she had always wanted. Her hand went to the hard bulge of his penis beneath his britches, cupping its shape, feeling it move and harden yet more under her hand. She sighed with pleasure, shifting her body against him.

"God, how I've missed you," Alasdair whispered. He felt for her breasts where they were outlined beneath the tight-fitting jacket. He pressed the soft mounds into his palms and Emma sighed again, but with increased urgency.

"Jesus, Mary, and Joseph! We can't do this here." Alasdair wrenched himself away from her. "For God's sake, look where we are!" A short laugh escaped him at the ludicrousness of their situation. "A drafty Greek temple in the pouring rain!"

"Yes, but what can we do? Where can we go?" Emma demanded, her arms crossed over her breasts, her teeth chattering as much with frustration as cold.

"I know somewhere," Alasdair said with brisk decision. "Stay here and I'll bring up the horses."

"You'll get soaked."

"In my present state, that can only be to the good," he responded with a wry grin. "Pack up the picnic. I'll be back in five minutes."

Emma threw the remains of their picnic higgledy-piggledy into the leather box. Her hands were shaking, whether with cold or frustrated passion she didn't know. Her skin was cold, but her blood was

hot as molten lava, racing through her veins. She was
incapable of coherent thought; her brain seemed to
have take up residence in her loins, and it was the
only part of her anatomy of which she seemed fully
aware.

Alasdair brought the horses up. They were wet and
doleful, hanging their heads in misery. "You're going
to get soaked," Alasdair said, tossing Emma into the
saddle with a hand beneath her foot. "But it'll only
take us about fifteen minutes."

"Where are we going?" She gathered the reins, feeling the water dripping coldly down the back of her
neck.

"Richmond." Alasdair fastened the leather picnic
box to his saddle and sprang up. "Follow me." He set
off into the rain, urging Phoenix to a gallop. Swallow
was more than ready to follow suit, and they
pounded through the rain at a breakneck speed more
suited to a chase across a hunting field.

They turned out of the park and instead of taking
the London road, Alasdair turned his horse toward
the village of Richmond nestling at the gates of the
park. He drew rein outside a thatched inn in the center of the village. He handed his reins to Emma with
the instruction to stay where she was for a minute,
then jumped down and ran into the inn.

Now what? Emma thought, shivering. The inn sign
showed a green goose. As an establishment it seemed
well maintained from the outside, if rather small.

A lad ran out from around the back, tugging on a
jacket. "I'm to take the 'osses, ma'am," he said.
"You're to go on inside."

Emma with relief dismounted, yielded the reins to
the lad, and hurried to the inn. The door opened before she could reach it, and Alasdair grabbed her

hands and pulled her inside. "My poor sweet, come into the snug. It's private and there's a good fire there. Eliza is making sure the fire's lit in the bedchamber."

Emma's mind whirled. She allowed herself to be pushed into the snug, a small wainscotted room off the taproom. She could hear the rumble of voices through the hatchway leading into the taproom and smell the pipe smoke that hung in a blue cloud beneath the blackened rafters.

"Where are we? What is this place?" She bent to warm her frozen hands at the fire.

"It's the Green Goose; didn't you see the sign?" Alasdair took Emma's hands and dragged off her sodden gloves. "Eliza will lend you a dressing gown while your clothes dry."

"Who's Eliza?"

"The landlady." Alasdair looked a trifle puzzled. "Why all the questions, Emma?"

She shrugged. "I suppose I'm just surprised you should know this place so well. It's rather off the beaten track, isn't it?"

Alasdair's mouth thinned. It was clear where these questions were taking her. But he wouldn't allow anything to spoil this reunion. If he was to rebuild what they'd once had, they had to start somewhere. He didn't answer her but turned instead to a gate-legged table where a punch bowl and the necessary ingredients stood.

He said cheerfully, "Eliza shall take the makings for a brandy punch abovestairs and I'll make us a bowl . . . Ah, Eliza, is all ready?"

"Aye, Lord Alasdair. It's warm and cozy up there." The gray-haired woman who had entered the snug nodded to Emma but avoided looking at her closely. "There's a wrapper on the bed for the young lady. If she'll leave her clothes outside the door, I'll have them dried and pressed for her. Yours too, Lord Alasdair."

"Thank you, Eliza. And we'll take a punch bowl with us." Alasdair moved to the door. "Come, Emma."

How many other women had he brought to this little love nest? Did he bring only his lightskirts, his pieces of muslin, or did he bring the likes of Lady Melrose too? Was she herself merely just another in a long succession of women who had gone up those stairs with Alasdair? Emma stood, unable to move either forward or back.

Then Alasdair repeated, "Come, Emma." He reached for her hand. "Trust me," he said softly.

That she could never do again. Trust was such a frail thing; once shattered it was well nigh impossible to repair it. She could never again trust Alasdair with her heart.

But she could enjoy herself with him, Emma told herself. She could be like Alasdair. Enjoy the passion while keeping her heart and soul intact. Last night, and again in the Greek temple, she had been swept with lust. She had known then all there was to know about Alasdair. So why should it now trouble her? She had come here for passion. And that was what she would have.

She took his hand and went with him up the stairs.

The chamber at the head of the stairs was small, but clean and bright, with wax candles, polished brass, and a blazing log fire in the grate. The rain drummed against the mullioned window, making it seem even cozier.

Emma glanced at the bed. There was a patchwork quilt and the hangings were a cheerful chintz. How many other women had shared that bed with Alasdair? *No! She* would not admit such thoughts again.

"Come to the fire." Alasdair drew her to the warmth. He took off her hat with its dripping, drooping plume and placed it on a chair. Then he unpinned her hair. It cascaded to her shoulders and he took a handful on either side of her head and held her thus. "Don't let bad thoughts spoil this, love," he said in soft plea. "I know you're having them. But let them go." He kissed her mouth. "I want you so much. I have missed you so much."

And Emma let the bad thoughts go beneath the sweetness of his mouth.

He began to unbutton her jacket, his fingers slipping on the frog buttons where the loops had tightened with the rain. "What a damnable garment this is," he complained, when he realized that in order to remove it he would have to unfasten the row of tiny pearl buttons on the sleeve.

Emma, shivering with her own impatience, said, "Why don't you undress yourself and I'll undress myself."

Alasdair shook his head. "No, I wish to make you naked myself. I must learn patience; it'll be good for me." He tackled the sleeves and with a grunt of satisfaction drew the garment away from her. He untied the starched linen stock at her neck, throwing it aside, then unbuttoned her shirt.

"Did you always wear so many clothes? I don't seem to remember this taking so long before."

"Neither do I," Emma murmured. "Perhaps we were in less of a hurry . . . or perhaps," she added mischievously, "you were more skillful."

"God, you're as provoking as you're exciting, woman," Alasdair declared, pushing her shirt off her shoulders. He inhaled with a deep breath of satisfaction as her breasts were revealed. Blue veined and creamy white, they jutted proudly, their rosy crowns erect within their smooth dark circles.

He lightly brushed each soft mound with his fingertips. "I had forgotten quite how magnificent your breasts are," he murmured, cupping them on his palms, holding them, feeling their weight, their velvet richness. He lowered his head and kissed each in turn, his teeth grazing her nipples, so she moaned with pleasure, throwing her head back, exposing the long white column of her throat.

Alasdair kissed the fast-beating pulse in her throat; he licked upward beneath her chin, then he nipped the point of her chin, making her laugh, releasing the tension for a minute.

It was a habit he had, Emma remembered. He would bring her to fever pitch with his caresses and then do something funny or absurd in the context so that she couldn't help but laugh and the spiral of arousal would be slowed . . . only to be started up again with renewed fervor.

Smiling, he stood back from her, running his eyes over her bared flesh. "Where to now?" he murmured, taking her waist between his hands, moving his warm clasp up her rib cage, teasing them both with the delay.

Slowly he reached for the hooks of her skirt at the back. They sprang free and the garment slid to the ground.

"Hell and the devil!" he exclaimed. "I'd forgotten about the damn riding britches."

"And the boots," Emma pointed out helpfully. She was wearing leather pantaloons strapped beneath her riding boots.

Alasdair ignored this. He stood back from her, his eyes hungrily drinking in her form in the tight-fitting garment. "Perhaps I'm not in so much of a hurry after all," he said. "Would you put your hands on your hips and turn around, please."

Emma did so, the sensual demand sending a current of lust jolting her belly, dampening her loins.

Alasdair placed his hands on her hips, tracing their curve with his palms; then slowly, lingeringly, he caressed her bottom. Emma knew her backside was as clearly outlined in the pantaloons as if it were bare, and she felt somehow more exposed than if she were naked beneath his hands.

"Such a treasure trove," Alasdair murmured. "But now I think I have to see you properly." The button at her waist came undone, and with the same slow, lingering movement he peeled the pantaloons over her hips and down to her knees.

He knelt behind her, holding her hips. He kissed each rounded cheek, before running his hands down the backs of her thighs. He kissed the hollows of her knees, and Emma quivered, waiting for the next touch, the next brush of his lips, wishing he would finish undressing her and yet aware on some sensual level that this feeling of being half naked was making every sensation even more acute. It would take but a well-placed touch to send her over the edge, and she knew Alasdair was aware of it.

He turned her with his hands on her hips as he remained on his knees. He kissed the smooth white plane of her belly, stabbed at her hipbones with little darts of his tongue, then moved his fingers through the dark muff at the apex of her thighs, playfully tugging at the damp curls.

Emma clasped his bent head, her own fingers curling convulsively into his glossy dark locks. His gently exploring touch had slipped between her thighs now, and she was one taut line of tension, poised on the outermost edge of bliss as the great wave of joy held itself at the crest. He parted the soft petaled lips of her sex, and the wave crashed over her. His fingers moved deep inside her while his thumb played on the little nub that was hard and swollen beneath his touch. The wave receded and crashed yet again and Emma cried out, leaning forward to bury her face in his head, smothering the wild sounds of her joy.

Alasdair held her tightly until it was over, then he stood up. His expression was taut, lined with the effort of his own restraint, and Emma could only guess at how difficult it must have been for him to have kept himself in check.

She kissed him gratefully, and with a little laugh, he pushed her back onto the bed. "Let's finish this now." He snapped the strap of her pantaloons away from her boots and yanked off the boots, throwing them carelessly over his shoulder. With the same rough haste, he pulled off her last remaining garment and finally she was naked.

"Now let me undress you," Emma murmured from the languid depths of afterglow.

"No time." Alasdair shook his head, his own hands busy with his clothes. "Can't wait, my sweet."

Emma chuckled and spread her legs invitingly on the quilt. "I am ready for you."

"You always were," he said, pushing off his britches and drawers in one movement, hopping on one leg and then the other to drag off his stockings.

He was beautiful. Emma's gaze roamed over his spare, sinewy body. His sex jutted powerfully from the dark curling bush of pubic hair, and her own body rose in anticipation. As he came down on the bed beside her, she reached out to clasp him in her palm, wanting to give back some of the pleasure he'd given her.

"No," he whispered hoarsely, drawing back from her. "Touch me, Emma, and I shall be lost." He leaned over her, resting on his elbows, gazing down at her face. "I'm very much afraid, my sweet, that I'm going to leave you behind." He kissed her brow with a regretful little smile that nonetheless contained his own urgency.

"I very much doubt it," she murmured, sliding her hands to his waist as he held himself above her. "Hurry now."

Alasdair gave a low laugh. He slid a hand beneath her bottom, lifting her as he slid within her eagerly opened body. He closed his eyes for a minute as the soft velvety sheath closed around him. "Don't move," he whispered. "One wriggle and I shall lose what little control I have left."

Emma lay still, feeling him deep inside her, the throbbing pulse of his flesh filling her, becoming a part of her. She looked up into his face, saw the rigid lines of control etched around his mouth as he fought to hold back the coming hurricane. The muscles in his forearms were corded; the tendons stood out in his neck. He opened his eyes and met her gaze, his eyes deep and glowing as emeralds.

Emma reached around his body. Her hands slid along his thighs, before with precise intent her fingers dug into the taut muscles of his backside, pulling him down to her. In the same instant, she lifted her hips to meet the deep thrust of his body.

Her own body convulsed around him and Alasdair threw back his head on a low, throbbing cry. He pulled himself out of her body, and his hot seed spurted over her thighs and belly as he fell on top of her, his limbs tangled with hers.

Only their deep, gasping breaths could be heard for a long time. Then Alasdair slowly rolled off her. A possessive hand rested heavily on the damp curls covering her swollen pubic mound. He turned sideways, propping himself on his free elbow, and gazed down into her face. Slowly he smiled.

"You were right about one thing, my Emma. We are very, very good together." He bent to kiss her brow, moving his mouth up into her hairline, licking away the salty dew of exertion.

"Can we try to put things together again, sweet?"

Emma was silent, but she raised a hand to his face, stroking his cheek.

"Is that a maybe?" Alasdair tried to hide his disappointment, but it was there in his voice.

"It's not no," Emma said.

Chapter Ten

❦

"Emma love, I've been so worried. Wherever have you been?" Maria, dressed for the evening in lavender silk and a ruched butterfly cap, hurried out of the salon as Emma came into the house. It was already dark and the rain had not abated. Alasdair had hired a chaise in Richmond to bring Emma home, himself riding back, leading Swallow.

"We were caught in the rain," Emma explained. "We had to take shelter in Richmond."

"Look at your habit!" Maria flung up her hands in distress. "It's so creased!"

The attentions of Eliza had been less than skilled, Emma reflected ruefully. Her riding habit was certainly bedraggled. "I was soaked. But Tilda will be able to retrieve it," she said. "Did you put dinner back? It'll only take me half an hour to dress." She moved toward the stairs, for some reason finding it difficult to meet Maria's eye.

"Perhaps we should stay in this evening," Maria suggested doubtfully. "After such an ordeal, you mustn't put yourself in the way of catching cold."

"Since when does getting caught in a shower qualify as an ordeal?" Emma scoffed, running up the stairs. She called over her shoulder, "But I think I shall take a bath to warm me up. Half an hour and I'll be down."

Maria shook her head over this, but Emma could be a whirlwind when the need arose. However, to be on the safe side, she told Harris to set back dinner an hour. It would still give them ample time to arrive at Almack's well before the witching hour of eleven o'clock, when the doors were firmly barred to all late-comers.

Not even the Prince of Wales would dare to challenge such an inflexible rule. Not that he was likely to appear at Almack's under any circumstances, Maria reflected, returning to the drawing room. Dancing, not cards, was the entertainment offered at Almack's, and the refreshments were not of the kind to appeal to a robust and bibulous appetite.

Tilda exclaimed and lamented over the condition of the riding habit as footmen toiled up the stairs with jugs of steaming water for Emma's bath.

Emma stripped off her clothes with a sigh of relief and stepped into the copper tub. The hot water laved her skin and eased the slight soreness engendered by a long afternoon's play.

She smiled rather dreamily as she rubbed verbena-scented soap between her hands. How she had missed this wonderful feeling of languid fulfillment, the sense that every part of her body had been touched with passion. She felt soft and open and aglow. And she would not yet spoil the feeling by allowing herself to think about where it was going to lead.

"The green crepe gown, Tilda," she said. "The one with the white half-slip." She rose dripping from the bath and took the towel Tilda handed her. She could smell the faint fragrance of the soap on her skin, and she could still feel Alasdair's body against her own. She'd noticed in the past how her skin and muscles seemed to have memories of their own.

"I think the paisley shawl, Lady Emma," Tilda said positively as she rubbed pomade into her mistress's side curls until they shone a rich, burnished tawny gold. "The green and gold will complement the gown."

Emma acceded to this with a nod. She slipped her silk-stockinged feet into green kid slippers and fastened three strings of matchless pearls at her throat. They had been a twenty-first birthday present from Ned. The matching pearl drops that she clipped to her ears had been Alasdair's present.

There was a knock at the bedchamber door, and Tilda went to answer it. "Oh, such a pretty posy, madam," she said, taking it from the footman outside. "White roses. They'll go beautifully with your gown. We should pin them to your glove at the wrist."

She brought the posy to Emma. Three perfect white roses bound with silver ribbon. Tasteful and delicate. But what else would one expect from Alasdair? Emma thought with a smile, removing the little engraved card.

Ma belle, wear these for me and make me the happiest man. Your most devoted servant, Paul.

"Oh," Emma said, her nose wrinkling unconsciously. The posy was delicate, the message presumptuous. Surely she hadn't given the man that much encouragement? But honesty obliged her to acknowledge that he could have read enough into her flirtatious manner to justify encouragement. She had, after all, intended to encourage him. And now she'd have to withdraw—depress his pretensions. A most unpleasant business that would make her appear to be a flirtatious tease, unless she could think of a gracious way to handle the situation.

"No, I won't wear them, Tilda," she said as the maid was about to pin the posy to her long silk gloves.

"Oh, but Lady Emma!" Tilda protested.

"They're pretty enough," Emma responded. "But I'm going to wear the gold bracelets that belonged to my mother." She opened her jewel case.

Tilda looked curious, but she set the posy down on the dresser and fetched the paisley shawl. She draped it over Emma's elbows and stood back to judge the effect. "Very modish, Lady Emma," she pronounced with satisfaction, adjusting the tasseled cord that confined the gown beneath the bosom.

Emma's own smile was a trifle distracted. The rich patina of the evening had worn a little thin at the prospect of disillusioning Paul Denis, particularly under Alasdair's eye. Alasdair had said he would be at Almack's, and she was going to find it very difficult to be in the company of both men without thinking of the brass nymph.

It was probable that the story of the attack on the émigré was all over town by now. Paul would surely have mentioned the assault to the duke of Devizes, since it had occurred in his house. And then she remembered that when she'd produced her own fabrication that morning, pretending she hadn't returned to the conservatory, he had said only that he had waited for her, "for an eternity." Why hadn't he told her then of the attack? It would have been natural enough.

Pride perhaps? He couldn't bear to admit such an ignominious assault. It seemed the only answer, and it seemed a likely one. Paul Denis would not willingly expose himself to the sniggers of society. And he would be the target of malicious jokes . . . anyone would have been. Society loved to poke fun at any scandal-brewing misfortune.

Thoughtfully she went downstairs. Maria fluttered around her, anxious that she shouldn't have suffered from her exposure to the elements. "Are you sure, my dear, that you shouldn't take one of Dr. Bennet's powders . . . just to ward off a quinsy? I do so dread a quinsy, my love. A putrid sore throat is the worst thing."

"Smallpox and typhoid I could do without as well," Emma teased.

"Oh, yes, to be sure . . . but you know what I mean."

"You're a mother hen," Emma said with an affectionate smile. "Come, let's go into dinner. I'm famished." The picnic in the Greek temple seemed a long time ago, and the brandy punch that Alasdair had made before they left the Green Goose had done little to appease hunger, although it had given her a pleasant glow on the cold drive home.

Maria's anxieties were somewhat allayed by this. A hearty appetite bespoke good health.

They were about to sit down to table when Emma

heard a voice in the hall. She stood still, her hand resting on her chairback.

"Why, it's Alasdair," Maria said in surprise. "Has he come for dinner, I wonder?"

"If he's invited," Alasdair said cheerfully from the door. "I've just delivered Swallow to her stable. Sam seems to think a bran mash will take care of any possible ill effects of the rain. I thought you'd like to know, Emma."

He smiled with the complacent air of one who knows he has done noble service, and ran an eye over the table. "If those are Aylesbury ducklings, I am definitely staying for dinner. And after I will escort you both to King Street."

He was dressed in the regulation attire for Almack's. Emma had always considered that the black satin knee britches, white waistcoat, striped stockings, and waisted coat with long tails were particularly suited to his slender frame. And she didn't revise that opinion now. He looked like a particularly elegant, supple panther, she thought. Understated and yet emanating a certain restrained power.

"I'll lay a cover, sir." Harris snapped his fingers at a footman, who hurried to set another place at the table.

Alasdair moved behind Emma's chair, holding it for her. His hands brushed her shoulders as he pushed it in beneath her. He felt the little quiver run over her skin and lightly clasped the back of her neck for a second before moving around the table to take his place.

He raised his eyebrows at the wine bottle on the sideboard. "Claret, Emma? With dinner?"

"Should I bring up the burgundy, sir?" Harris inquired.

"Do you have any of the '99 left? The consignment

that was given to Lord Edward for his coming-of-age?" Alasdair asked.

"There are six bottles, sir. I will fetch one up from the cellar." Harris moved to the door.

Emma frowned. This was *her* household, and Harris should have deferred to her. But old memories stuck fast and the butler had obviously slipped back into the old habit of regarding Alasdair as one of the family, on a footing with Ned.

Alasdair glanced across the table and caught her expression. "Oh," he said with a rueful grin. "Did I just overstep myself?"

"Gentlemen know much more about wine than ladies," Maria said comfortably. "Emma wouldn't object in the slightest to your giving order about the wine."

"Maria, that is such nonsense," Emma protested. "You have such antiquated notions. I know as much about wine as Alasdair does."

"So you should," Alasdair said promptly. "Since everything you know Ned and I taught you. Although you seem to have forgotten one or two of the essentials," he added, shaking his head in reproof.

Before Emma could protest this injustice, Maria spoke. "Well, to be sure, Emma, you're rather out of the common way of young ladies," she conceded. "But in general, I find it best to leave such matters in the capable hands of the gentlemen. Alasdair, do take some of the duckling. And I think you'll find the broiled mushrooms to your liking."

Alasdair helped himself. Harris reappeared with two crusted bottles of Ned's burgundy and solemnly began to pour.

"Oh, just a very little for me, I thank you," Maria said. "I find burgundy a trifle heavy."

"Pour Mrs. Witherspoon a glass of claret, Harris," Emma instructed, shooting Alasdair a pointed look. "Mrs. Witherspoon is liable to get the headache with burgundy."

"Ah, so that explains such a solecism," Alasdair said, sounding relieved. "I was afraid, Emma, that you'd lost your palate. Claret is all very well for drinking before dinner, but not with food." He smiled benignly at her over the rim of his glass.

He was so infuriating. One could never put Alasdair out of countenance, and he had such an air of being at home, of such complete relaxation, that it was impossible to maintain an offended dignity without looking silly. Emma helped herself to the raised mutton pie, reflecting with a sudden stab of loss that all it needed was Ned at the table for time to roll back. She could hear his voice, gently teasing in counterpoint to Alasdair's rather more caustic wit. She could hear his laugh, its rich timbre against Alasdair's lighter, more mellow laugh.

She looked up and met Alasdair's steady gaze. He knew what she was thinking. His eyes were filled with compassion and his own loss . . . their shared loss. Ned would have been overjoyed at what had happened between them. He would be congratulating himself on a very sound strategy. But would he understand that she was no nearer to marrying Alasdair now than she had been when she'd left him at the altar three years ago?

Maria, seemingly oblivious of the sudden cloud that had fallen over the table, was relating some piece of gossip, her voice serenely rippling forth into her companions' silence. After a minute, Alasdair made some casual comment and the two chatted, leaving

Emma to her own thoughts until she was able to gather herself together and join in.

She was not sorry to be spending the evening in a large crowd. Her thoughts could follow their own course while she kept up the inane chatter that passed for conversation at such social gatherings. She and Alasdair would stand up for a couple of dances, but more would be frowned upon as breaking one of the club's unspoken conventions, and if Paul Denis chose to take umbrage at her for not wearing his flowers, he wouldn't be able to express it.

"Why so preoccupied?" Alasdair asked quietly as he held her cloak for her in the hall after dinner.

She gave him a quick smile and answered as quietly, "Don't you think I have reason?"

"Then I trust it's a pleasant preoccupation," he responded, with a little frown in his eye. He didn't think Emma's reflections were of unqualified rapture.

She shrugged slightly and went ahead of him to the street, where the carriage awaited. The rain had stopped and a fitful moon played with the scudding clouds.

❦

Paul Denis had arrived unfashionably early at the assembly rooms. He had been greeted pleasantly by the patronesses and presented to several damsels sitting patiently along the wall, waiting for a partner. But his eyes were on the door, watching for Emma Beaumont's arrival. In his pocket was a small vial containing enough laudanum to put someone twice the Lady Emma's height and weight into a very deep sleep. He intended to administer the sleeping draft at the very end of the evening.

The refreshments were meager to say the least: tea,

orgeat, and lemonade. But he reasoned that a night's dancing would make the lady thirsty. It would be perfectly natural for him to procure her a drink toward the end of the evening, and the matter of a twist of his wrist to add the draft.

She would go home in her carriage. Her maid would put her to bed. And she would sleep through any possible disturbances—through an abduction even, should it prove necessary. He hoped it would not. It was such a messy business and even if she survived interrogation, she could not be allowed to live. Paul was not averse to murder, or assassination as he preferred to consider it, but in general he favored a tidier solution.

He was engaged in desultory conversation with a tongue-tied and extremely young lady when Emma entered the room. He saw immediately that she was not wearing his roses, and a surge of cold anger rose into his throat. It was a calculated insult. There was no other way to interpret it. He'd chosen white roses because they would complement any color she chose to wear, giving her no reason not to carry them. And, indeed, he hadn't expected her to wish for an excuse. The posy was a courtier's gesture. He was courting her and she had not shown herself averse to the courtship, quite the reverse.

His anger grew colder when he saw that she was escorted by Lord Alasdair. But there was no sign of his inner turmoil when he excused himself from the very young lady and made his way across the now crowded room. He was smiling a melancholy smile as he bowed before the ladies.

"Madame, I am desolated," he murmured, raising Emma's hand to his lips. "I had so hoped my little gift would find favor."

"It was very pretty, sir." Emma smiled and took back her hand when it seemed he intended to keep it. "So delicate, in fact, that I couldn't bear to see the roses wither and die in this heat. They have pride of place on my dresser."

She turned to Maria, explaining, "Mr. Denis sent me the prettiest posy of white roses, Maria. You must see them when we are at home."

Alasdair was for a moment unaware that he was frowning fiercely. When he realized, he smoothed his expression to its customary bland neutrality and drawled, "You put us to shame, Denis. Such elegant gestures."

Paul smiled, a cold flicker of his lips. His eyes were hard. Alasdair's sardonic tone was impossible to miss. "Lady Emma, will you do me the honor?" He gestured to the dance floor, where a set was forming for the cotillion. "Or must I first be presented to you as a partner?" He gave a rueful little laugh. "I become so confused with these unspoken rules."

Emma put her hand on his arm. "Only for the waltz, sir. And I shall not waltz tonight." She smiled up at him, but her eyes were grave. She must make matters clear between them as soon as possible. Alasdair was not looking at all friendly. It was to be hoped there were no brass nymphs handy!

Paul led her into the set. Alasdair glowered.

"Lord Alasdair, allow me to present you to a most charming partner." Lady Jersey bustled over to him before he could make good his escape. "Bedford's granddaughter. New on the town, but she conducts herself prettily."

"Insipidly is what you mean," Alasdair declared, with perfect truth. "You fill me with dismay, Sally."

Sally Jersey regarded him with a gleam in her eye.

Alasdair was one of her favorites. "If you don't like milk and water, sir, I suggest you press your advantage elsewhere." Her gaze went deliberately to where Emma was dancing with Paul.

"Believe me, I'm trying, Sally," Alasdair said before he could stop himself. He sighed. "Don't breathe a word! She'll run from me like a hart before the hounds if there's a whisper of it about town."

"Oh, you know me, Alasdair. Silent as the grave." Sally smiled with blithe assurance. Alasdair contented himself with a raised eyebrow. Sally Jersey was generally known as "Silence," because of her inability to keep her mouth shut.

"To which of these debutantes are you intending to sacrifice me?" he asked, raising his eyeglass to survey the room.

"The girl in pink tulle."

Alasdair shuddered slightly. "I was afraid of that. Why would a redhead wear pink?"

"She's clearly not lucky enough to be advised by such a one as you," Sally responded with a touch of acerbity. "Now, don't be disagreeable. Just because your Emma is engaged with that charming Frenchman." She put her hand on Alasdair's arm and led him across to where the pink lady was sitting with her mama.

The movements of the cotillion were sufficiently complicated to prevent too intense or intimate a conversation, and Emma contented herself with small talk with her partner when the dance permitted it, but as the musicians laid down their instruments, she said, "Perhaps you could procure me a glass of lemonade, sir? I own I would prefer to sit out the next dance."

"Allow me to escort you to a chair." Paul moved

swiftly, leading her to a secluded corner close to a potted palm. "I'll be back in a minute, madame."

Emma sat down on a low gilt chair and opened her fan. The interview was going to be uncomfortable, but she was not one to shirk discomfort when duty lay clear.

Paul returned within a very few minutes, bearing a glass of lemonade. He gave it to her and drew up another chair. He'd changed his plans. Emma should drink her sleeping draft now. She would become ill and have to be taken home. There would be more fuss, it would be messier than he liked, but he wasn't prepared to let this opportunity slip in the light of what he sensed was about to happen.

Emma held the glass in her lap. "Mr. Denis, I am afraid I may have given you the wrong impression." She twisted the stem between her fingers. "I . . . I am not looking for a husband," she said directly. "My brother's death is still too recent a memory for me to . . . to . . ." She took a sip of lemonade. "I had thought I could put it behind me, but I find that I cannot."

"Your confidence does me honor, madame," he said gravely. "But you will allow me to be your friend?"

"I have many friends, sir." She smiled up at him. This was much less unpleasant than she had expected. He was behaving impeccably, more so than she deserved. "I should be honored to include you among them." She raised the glass to her lips again.

Paul smiled and watched her drink.

"Mr. Denis." Princess Esterhazy hove into view, a vision in bright yellow silk with turquoise ribbon knots. "Ah, Lady Emma." She bestowed a chilly smile on Emma. "You must allow me to take Mr. Denis away for a minute. There's someone I wish him to meet. A niece of my husband's great-aunt. You will know of her, Mr. Denis, since you are distantly connected." She swept the gentleman away before he could demur.

Emma took another sip of lemonade. She saw the duke of Clarence wending his way toward her with a very purposeful air, his eyes rather bloodshot, his nose rather red. He'd presumably wined and dined well. Emma set down her glass, wondering if she could evade the coming encounter. She rose from her chair, intending to slip away to the retiring room, but the duke hailed her in booming tones.

"Ah, Lady Emma. Don't run away. I most particularly wish to talk with you." He came up to her, beaming. He bowed his stiff and creaking bow. "Sit down, sit down, dear lady." He gestured expansively to the chair Emma had vacated. "I'll sit beside you."

He eased himself into the chair next to Emma's. "Not much of a dancer, I'm afraid." He nodded, beating time with one hand against his plump, satin-clad thigh. "But I enjoy music. Runs in the family, y'know. M'brother Wales is very fond of all kinds. Quite the patron, he is. Don't know how many composers and such he's taken under his wing."

Emma murmured something suitable and picked up her lemonade again.

"You're counted something of a musician, I understand, Lady Emma," the duke declared. "You'd be wantin' your own music room and teachers and suchlike, I'll be bound. Finest instruments too." He nodded again. "No need to fear we couldn't manage it . . . no, no need to fear that."

Emma was at a loss. The duke appeared to be talking as if they were betrothed and on their way to the altar. She didn't think he'd made a formal proposal, unless she'd been unconscious at the time. She set down her glass and said firmly, "I have an excellent music room in my house on Mount Street, sir. It does me very well, and I have no need of another."

"Ah . . . ah . . ." The duke looked a little nonplussed. "Thought we might come to an understanding, you and I, dear lady."

Emma unfurled her fan. "Sir, forgive me, but I'm at a loss to understand you." She rose from her chair. "I beg your pardon, but I must retire for a few minutes. Would you excuse me?" She bowed and hastened away, leaving the royal personage to scratch his head, wondering if he hadn't made himself quite clear. It was marriage, not a liaison, that he'd been proposing.

Emma fled to the retiring room, much inclined to hide in there until she could reasonably go home. She felt beset on all sides. The room was empty except for the attendants, and she went behind the screen to use the commode, thankful for the moment of peace and quiet.

It didn't last long.

Voices soon came from beyond the screen. Emma recognized Lady Melrose's voice immediately. Her tone was pitched a little high and sharp, as if she were annoyed about something.

"Alasdair tells me she intends to lionize in a racing curricle," she declared. "He says she's as vulgar as Letty Lade. She creates a scandal to beat all scandals, and then returns to society flaunting her wealth, expecting every man to fall at her feet."

"Clarence is dangling after her," Lady Bellingham declared. "But that's only to be expected."

"Well, if she wants a royal title, she couldn't do

better," Lady Melrose trilled maliciously. "Unless, of course, she's set her sights on the prince of Wales."

Emma sat seething behind the screen.

"Lord Alasdair seems to be dancing attendance on her these days," spoke a woman whose voice Emma didn't recognize. "You'd think once bitten twice shy!" She dropped her voice a little and added spitefully, "You don't fear a rival there, I trust, my dear Julia."

Julia Melrose said sharply, "Alasdair's opinion of Emma Beaumont has to be heard to be believed. He's forced into this odious position as her trustee." Her trilling laugh sounded again, but at a distance as if she was moving away. "Believe me, my friends, he can't wait until she finds herself a husband and he's free of her."

There was a short silence, then Lady Bellingham said, "I think our dear Julia expected Lord Alasdair to come up to scratch well before now."

"Oh, that one will never marry Julia," the other woman said. "Why should he indeed, when she's so anxious to give him what he wants without a ring?" Both women laughed uproariously, as only the privacy of the retiring room allowed them. Their laughter and voices faded as they followed in Lady Melrose's wake.

Emma emerged from the screen, white with hurt and anger. So Alasdair discussed her with Lady Melrose. He'd told his mistress about her racing curricle. Told her he couldn't wait to be rid of his responsibilities to her. What else did he tell her? Did he discuss how she made love? Did he compare her with his mistress? *With all his other mistresses?*

She felt dizzy and sat down on a thimble-footed stool before the mirror. Her face was very pale. Her head spun.

"Are you all right, ma'am?" a hovering attendant asked anxiously.

"Could you bring me a glass of water, please?" The retiring room seemed very hot and a strange heaviness was creeping up the back of her neck.

Emma took the glass the attendant brought her and pressed its coolness against her forehead. She began to feel a little better in body if not in spirit. How could Alasdair have discussed her with his mistress? It was the ultimate insult. She'd accepted the fact of the other women in his life. She would never trust him again, but she'd made some kind of mental and emotional accommodation whereby she could take advantage of the good things in their relationship and not risk hurt. Or so she'd thought.

But just the thought of him talking her over with another woman made her burn with fury. She drank the water and tentatively stood up, smoothing down her skirts. All her pleasure in the day was gone; every scrap of the delicious languor of fulfillment was banished. She felt drained, emptied of all emotions except anger and disillusion.

She left the retiring room and was immediately assailed by the heavy odors of perfume, of overheated bodies. Even the music seemed unnaturally loud. She put a hand on the wall to steady herself.

"Emma, what is it? You're pale as a ghost." Alasdair appeared out of the mist that was clouding her eyes.

She rubbed at her eyes, trying to clear away the mist, but it didn't help. "I feel sick," she said, hearing how plaintive and almost childlike she sounded. She didn't want Alasdair anywhere near her, but suddenly she hadn't the strength to tell him so.

He had fetched Maria, summoned the carriage,

wrapped her in her cloak, and supported her to the carriage in what seemed a very short time. She lay back against the squabs, closing her eyes, drifting in and out of sleep.

"I knew she should never have gone out this evening," Maria said to Alasdair as he handed her into the carriage after Emma. "After getting caught in the storm. I do so hope it isn't a quinsy."

"Emma's barely had a day's illness in her life," Alasdair said, but he was unable to hide his own unease, and the guilty feeling that he had in some way been responsible for Emma's drenching that afternoon. It was ridiculous to feel so, of course; he hadn't had control over the weather. But he felt it nevertheless.

"Send me word how she is in the morning," he directed Maria, leaning into the carriage as she sat down opposite Emma. "And don't hesitate to send for Dr. Baillie."

"No, indeed not. I shall send for him in the night if necessary." Maria leaned over and touched Emma's forehead. "She doesn't seem feverish. I think she's asleep."

Alasdair closed the door and stepped back to the flagway, signaling to the coachman to drive on. He frowned as the carriage bowled away. *Asleep.* Why in the world would she fall asleep in the middle of a ball? Unless, of course, it was a symptom of some illness. He thought of typhoid and shuddered.

He had no interest in returning to Almack's and strode off to St. James's Street, hoping that a few games of macao at Watiers would distract him. There was nothing he could do for Emma at this point, and fretting himself into a frenzy was futility itself.

Chapter Eleven

Paul Denis stepped back into the ballroom as Emma and her companions disappeared down the stairs to the street. A grim smile curled his lips. She should sleep now for upward of twelve hours. He would wait until the early hours of the morning before he and Luiz effected entrance. The servants would be well asleep by then, the streets deserted.

By midday tomorrow, he would have the information he sought—one way or another.

When the clocks struck one, he left Almack's and walked quickly to Half Moon Street. The streets were wet, glistening in the moonlight, and where the pavement ended thick mud began.

Luiz was waiting for him. "You made good time, Paolo. I've rope and a gag . . . and a crowbar. If we can't force the lock on the French door, we'll have to break the glass. There's treacle and paper." He indicated the small valise on the table.

"Good. I've given the woman a powerful dose of laudanum. Enough to knock out a horse. I doubt she'll wake before midmorning." Paul began to throw off his evening clothes.

"She took it all right, then?"

Paul gave a scornful laugh as he stepped into a pair of dark britches. "She was asleep before she left that absurd establishment. Of all the insipid amusements. No drink, no cards, except for sixpenny points, and a host of starched matrons enforcing ludicrous rules. I tell you, Luiz, I shall be glad to leave this godforsaken country. Its inhabitants are either mad or double-dyed rogues."

He thrust his arms into a dark jacket, buttoning it right up to the neck so that not a glimmer of white from his shirt was visible. He drew on thin black kid gloves, smoothing them over his long fingers.

There was something ineffably sinister about the way he flexed his fingers. Luiz felt his scalp crawl. He'd seen Paolo strangle a man with those gloved hands. And he'd seen his face as he'd done so. Utterly impassive, without a twitch of emotion as he steadily squeezed the life out of his victim.

A wise man would ensure he never got on the wrong side of Paolo. It would be well for the woman if the document they sought was readily to be found.

They left the house, moving swiftly through the night-dark streets, blending with the shadows. Paul carried a swordstick. Pistols were thrust into his belt beneath his coat. In his pocket he carried a weighted garotte.

A member of the watch, his lantern held high on a pole, emerged from a dark alley, his boots thick with mud. He glanced at the two men and shifted his heavy bludgeon in his free hand. God-fearing citizens on legitimate business did not walk the streets in the dark of the night. Carriages were one thing, foot traffic quite another.

He demanded belligerently, "Where're you gents off to at this time o' night?"

Paul was in a vicious mood. He had been humiliated twice in two days. First by his assailant of the previous night, and then again by Emma Beaumont. Even though her rejection didn't affect his plans adversely, his pride was badly damaged.

The watchman took a step toward him. It was a mistake. The wicked strip of weighted leather curled through the air and snapped around the man's neck. In the same movement, Paul had stepped behind him, catching the free end, drawing it tight.

It was over in a matter of seconds. The man slid heavily to the ground, his lamp crashing in a flare of flaming oil.

"Get rid of him, Luiz." Paul gestured disdainfully toward the dark alley from whence the watchman had emerged. He stamped on the flame and kicked the still-sputtering lamp into the mud of the kennel.

Luiz dragged the body into the lane, rolling it up against a wall, where it blended with the black mud beneath it. It would be discovered sometime in the next day or two, just one of the many unsolved crimes that littered the city's back alleys. It would draw no more than a shrug from the ineffective watch.

"Eh, Paolo, was that necessary?" he muttered when he returned.

Paul coiled the garotte and dropped it into his pocket. "He annoyed me. I felt like it," he said with a dismissive shrug. He started off again, Luiz hurrying at his side.

A wise man did not get on the wrong side of Paolo. Oh, no, most definitely not.

They met no other challenge and turned onto Mount Street just as the clouds most conveniently rolled over the moon. "The gods smile on our little enterprise," Paul remarked. He was feeling lighter, as if relieved of some weight.

"This way." Luiz led the way into the passage that ran between Emma's house and its neighbor. The bare branches of the beech tree hung over the top of the wall. Luiz put down the valise, shinned up the wall with surprising agility, and swung himself into the branches of the tree.

"Are there lights?" Paul called softly.

"No, house is dark as the grave," Luiz replied, then reflected that that was an unfortunate simile in the light of their recent encounter. "Throw the valise up."

Paul tossed it up and Luiz caught it easily and dropped it to the ground. Then he jumped from the branches of the tree to the soft earth beneath.

Paul was up and over the wall before Luiz had straightened from picking up the valise. Paul looked at the dark bulk of the house, getting a sense of it. "The woman's chamber is at the front. She will have a boudoir or dressing room. We'll look there first."

He darted at a crouch across the lawn to the glass doors to the music room, then stepped aside to give Luiz room. Luiz was the expert at breaking and entering.

"There's a bolt," Luiz said with a grunt. "I'll have to break the top pane and reach it from there."

"Well, get on with it, then." Paul glanced impatiently up at the top-floor windows. It was close to three in the morning. No one would be awake.

Luiz spread treacle on the paper and plastered it

against the windowpane. He raised the crowbar and drove it against the paper-covered glass. It shattered with barely a sound as the broken glass stuck to the treacle. Carefully Luiz peeled away the paper, dropping it to the grass. Then he reached in and drew back the bolt. It took him a minute to break the rather fragile latch, and the door swung open onto the darkened music room.

Now Paul moved ahead. He crossed the room to where a door stood open onto the passage leading to the central hall. A candle burned low in its sconce, casting sufficient light for him to see into the hall with its curving staircase.

He nodded to Luiz, who was beside him now, and moved out. He clung to the wall, sidling soundlessly. The house was in dead silence. He trod up the stairs, testing each one for a creak before stepping on it, tiptoeing along the edge closest to the banister. Luiz faithfully stepped into his footsteps.

At the head of the stairs, Paul stopped to get his bearings, ears straining to catch the slightest sound. The landing stretched to right and left. A corridor ran off it to the chambers at the rear of the house. Those held no interest for him.

A pair of handsome double doors faced the head of the stairs, centered on the landing. He pictured the windows she had pointed out to him from the street and knew that she lay asleep behind those doors.

Once behind those doors, he would have all the time he needed for a thorough search. She was not going to wake up, and the household wouldn't stir before five-thirty at the earliest.

He stepped across the landing and laid a hand on the gilded doorknob. Luiz was behind him; he could hear his rapid breathing. The knob turned without a squeak and the door swung open.

The chamber was softly lit by the well-banked fire. Paul slipped inside, pressing himself against the wall as Luiz followed him, closing the door soundlessly at his back. They both stood motionless until any disturbance in the air caused by their entrance had dissipated. Now they could hear the regular breathing from the poster bed, the creak of the bedropes as the woman stirred in her sleep.

The curtains were not drawn around the bed, but it didn't matter, Paul reflected. There was no danger of her opening her eyes.

There was a door leading off the chamber from the right-hand wall. The boudoir or dressing room. He moved forward, on tiptoe across the thick carpet, glancing once toward the bed. She lay on her back, her arms flung above her head, the covers disarrayed over the long sprawl of her limbs.

Paul felt the first stirring of arousal. For all his acting, he had not once felt the slightest desire for the woman. She was merely a means to an end. But now, seeing her so vulnerable, so available, that quickness of wit and movement slowed, that clever tongue silenced, his blood heated, his flesh hardened.

But now was not the moment for distraction. Maybe he could have her later. After the business was done. She owed him some recompense. He trod swiftly to the door, opened it, and found himself in a small dressing room.

Luiz closed the door and they stood there in the dark room. There was no firelight to aid them.

"Light a candle," Paul instructed softly.

Luiz found flint and tinder on the mantelpiece and lit a wax taper that stood on the dresser. The light flickered and then burned strong, throwing their shadows, huge and distorted, against the papered walls.

Now they didn't speak. Paul rolled back the cylinder front of the secretaire and examined the contents. There were twelve little drawers, for monthly accounts, and two larger ones in the main body of the piece.

On the writing shelf was a leather writing case. It had a gold lock. The key was not immediately apparent. He began to go through the little drawers. They were filled with pieces of paper. Behind him, Luiz, silently methodical, was searching the armoire.

In the adjoining room, Emma sat bolt upright. Her head felt thick and achy, her throat was dry, and there was a nasty taste in her mouth. But she barely noticed these discomforts.

What had awakened her?

She blinked into the firelit gloom of her chamber. She couldn't remember going to bed. The last thing she remembered was getting into the carriage outside Almack's on King Street. And even that memory was somewhat blurred.

But something had awoken her. And then she saw it. The tiny flicker of gold beneath the door to her dressing room. She sat motionless, holding her breath. No servant would be in there at this time of night. Could it be Maria? No, of course not. What would Maria want in there?

She listened, straining her ears, and heard the faintest sounds of movement. The slight scrape of a drawer, the creak of a cupboard door.

Her heart began to pound. There was some indefinable menace in the air. Whoever was in there was up to no good. Thieves? Had to be. Should she confront them?

No.

Emma didn't lack courage, but neither was she stupid. A lone unarmed woman confronting an unquantifiable danger was a fool. She reached for the bellpull beside her bed, took a deep breath, and yanked on it . . . again and again and again. It would ring in the servants' quarters—an urgent peal that would bring Tilda running.

Then she slid soundlessly to the floor and went to the door leading to the corridor. She flung it wide and yelled for help at the top of her voice.

Paul dropped the leather writing case with a vile oath. Luiz stood frozen for a second. They both stared at the door leading to the bedchamber. Then Luiz raced to the window of the dressing room and flung up the sash. It looked down onto the side passage. A copper drainpipe ran alongside the narrow sill. Luiz swung himself through the window and onto the drainpipe with all the agility of a monkey.

Racing feet sounded on the stairs; shouting voices. Paul bent to snatch up the writing case and raced for the window just as the door to the bedchamber was flung open.

Harris in his nightshirt stood there with a blunderbuss. He fired at the window as the dark-clad figure disappeared over the sill. "Missed him!" he said furiously, running to the window. The blunderbuss had only one shot and he stared in helpless frustration at the wiry figure scrambling down the copper drainpipe.

Emma ran to his side. "Get people to give chase, Harris! Try and trap them in the passage."

Harris ran from the room, bellowing orders to the excited crowd of servants thronging the corridor.

Emma leaned out of the window as far as she could, trying to keep the figure in view. But he was already blending with the shadows. The side door opened, sending a shaft of light to pierce those shadows. The figure ducked expertly away from the light. But in the fleeting moment of illumination, she had seen another figure farther down the passage. An accomplice, presumably.

"My dear . . . oh, my dear, whatever is happening?" Maria appeared in the dressing room, her nightcap askew over neat rows of curling papers, feet bare, her wrapper hanging open over her nightgown. "Is it a fire?" Her eyes were wide with shock.

"No. Thieves," Emma informed her, surprised at how calm she now was. She continued to hang out of the window as her own servants poured into the passage. "They've gone toward the mews," she called down.

"Oh, my lord. You could have been murdered in your bed." Maria collapsed on the chaise longue, patting her palpitating chest with one hand. "I think I shall faint away."

"They've gone," Emma said, disappointed. She withdrew from the window. "Once they reach the mews, our men will never catch them."

She looked around the dressing room. "I wonder if they took anything."

"We must send for Lord Alasdair," Maria stated with unusual firmness. "We must send for him at once. He will know what to do."

"There isn't anything that can be done," Emma said

somewhat absently. She was examining the opened drawers in her secretaire.

"Oh, madam, have they taken your jewels?" Tilda hurried into the room.

"It doesn't appear so," Emma said. Her jewel case was lying in open sight on the dresser. "It doesn't look as if they went anywhere near it."

She stared down at the writing shelf of her secretaire, frowning, wondering what was wrong. "They've taken my writing case!" she exclaimed. "Why would they do that? What could they possibly want with it? It's old and shabby, apart from anything else."

"I shall tell Harris to send someone to fetch Lord Alasdair." Maria stood up, drawing her wrapper more tightly around her.

"No, don't be ridiculous, Maria!" Emma said sharply. "There's no need to drag him from his bed. There's nothing anyone can do now except shut the stable door after the horse has bolted."

"They broke in through the music room, Lady Emma," Tilda volunteered. "Must have come in over the side wall, Mr. Harris reckons."

"I don't care what you say, Emma, this situation requires a man to deal with it," Maria declared. "I am going to send for Alasdair at once. He's your trustee. Who better to call upon?" On which statement she marched from the room.

There were times when Maria's confident reliance on the superior skills of the male ceased to be amusing, Emma thought crossly. She didn't want Alasdair here.

She was remembering now what she had overheard in the retiring room at Almack's, and the mingled anger and hurt was as strong as it had ever been. Although she couldn't understand why it had made her feel so ill.

She brushed a hand over her forehead, rubbing her temples. She still felt muzzy, as if her thoughts were coming at her from a long distance, and her mouth was as dry as the desert. She massaged her throat, frowning fiercely. Something was wrong . . . well, everything was wrong. Being invaded by thieves in the dead of night was hardly a matter for congratulation. But something didn't ring true about any of it.

"Nothing seems to have been disturbed belowstairs, Lady Emma." Harris, a dressing gown now over his nightshirt, entered the dressing room. "Just the broken pane in the music room. But none of the silver's gone." He frowned in puzzlement. "There's plenty of things they could have pocketed, but I can't find anything missing."

"Why did they come in here?" Emma shook her head. "And why did they take my writing case?"

"I've sent a footman to Lord Alasdair," Harris said in a tone that, like Maria's, seemed to imply that all would then be explained and put right.

"I fail to see what Lord Alasdair can do. Or what light he can throw on anything," Emma snapped. "The thieves are long gone, and we'd all do best to go back to bed and send for the Bow Street runners in the morning."

"Shall I bring you some tea, Lady Emma?" Tilda suggested solicitously.

"Might I suggest a drop of brandy," Harris put in. "For the shock."

"I'm not suffering from shock," Emma said, then sighed. They were only trying to help. "Tea, Tilda, please. I would love a cup of tea."

Alasdair's first thought when Cranham awakened him with the news that a footman had come from Mount Street was that Emma's earlier indisposition had turned into something desperately serious. He was out of bed before he was truly awake, heading for the salon, where the messenger awaited.

"What is it? What's the matter with Lady Emma?" he demanded, throwing off his nightshirt. "Where's my shirt, Cranham? Quickly, man!"

"Nothin', I don't believe, sir." The footman shifted his feet.

Alasdair grabbed his shirt from Cranham. Naked, he held it for a minute, staring at the messenger as if the man had taken leave of his senses. "Then just what, pray, are you doing here?" he inquired, pulling the shirt on over his head.

"Mr. Harris sent me, sir. Mrs. Witherspoon said he was to," the footman said with scrupulous adherence to the facts.

Alasdair's head emerged from the collar of his shirt, his hair disheveled, his green gaze snapping. In a voice of patient courtesy that made Cranham shudder, he asked, "Maybe it wouldn't be asking too much for you to tell me exactly *why* I should be dragged from my bed at . . ." He glanced at the long-case clock against the wall. "Four o'clock in the morning."

"There's been a robbery, sir."

"*What?*" Alasdair paused on one leg in the act of putting on his drawers. The mask of ironical forbearance was wiped clean away. His eyes, brilliant and sharp, rested on the footman with unnerving penetration.

"That's what I come to tell you, sir," the footman said with a slightly injured air. "Thieves . . . they broke into the 'ouse through the music room."

"What did they take . . . no, never mind, how could you know. . . . Cranham, send Jemmy for my horse . . . no, that'll take too long. I'll walk." He sat down to pull on his stockings and his boots. "Did anyone see these thieves?"

"Harris and Lady Emma, sir. We run after 'em, but they got clean away through the mews."

"They didn't hurt anyone?" Alasdair shrugged into the coat that Cranham held for him, reflecting dryly that if Emma was chasing off thieves, there couldn't be much the matter with her.

"No, sir. Harris fired on one of 'em, when 'e was on the drainpipe, but he got away."

"Drainpipe . . . ? Oh, never mind. I'll hear the details when I get to Mount Street." Alasdair was striding from the room as he spoke. "Cranham, send Jemmy round to Mount Street, and tell him to bring Sam, Lady Emma's new groom."

He reached Mount Street in ten minutes and ran up the steps to the front door, hand lifted to the knocker. It was opened on the instant.

Harris, dressed now in his formal black uniform, greeted him with serene dignity. "Lord Alasdair. Quite a to-do we've been having."

"So I hear." Alasdair strode into the hall. "What was stolen?"

"Nothing that we can see, sir. That's the puzzle."

"Oh, Alasdair, I'm so glad you came. Emma would have it that we weren't to disturb you . . . that there was nothing you could do." Maria came hurrying down the stairs, straightening her nightcap that she still wore over her curling papers. "But I'm so afraid.

My heart's beating like a drum. A household without men, you know, is so vulnerable."

"For heaven's sake, Maria, this house is swarming with men." Emma's impatient voice came from the head of the stairs. "There's Harris and half a dozen able-bodied footmen."

She came halfway down the stairs, her gaze skimming over Alasdair as she said distantly, "There was not the slightest need to send for you, sir. You may as well return home and go back to bed."

Now what was going on? It had been several days since she'd used that tone to him, Alasdair reflected. Or looked at him with that cold indifference. But he didn't have time for that puzzle at present.

"Where were the thieves?" he inquired calmly.

"In Emma's dressing room," Maria supplied. "Only think. There was Emma sound asleep next door. Anything could have happened."

"But it didn't," Emma pointed out waspishly. "I woke up, sounded the alarm, they ran off, and the only thing that's missing is my old writing case." She turned to go back upstairs. "If you'll excuse me, I'm going back to bed with my tea."

"Just a minute, Emma." Alasdair put a foot on the bottom step. "Did you say they took your writing case?"

"Yes. Now, I'm very tired, so if you'll excuse me . . ." she repeated.

"Your pardon, Emma, but unfortunately it's not that simple." Alasdair ran up the stairs. "Come, I wish to take a look at your dressing room." He caught her around the waist and swept her up the last three stairs.

Emma was immediately aware of the current of tension running through him. It was apparent in the hard arm at her waist. There was an intensity in his eyes that hadn't been there before, and his mouth and jaw were set. It had the effect of stifling her protests, and she allowed him to impel her back to her dressing room.

Maria, hurrying up the stairs after them, found the door to the dressing room firmly closed as she reached it a few paces behind them. She opened the door somewhat hesitantly. "My dear . . ."

"Not now, Maria," Alasdair said. The curt tone was not one Maria was used to hearing when he spoke to her. She realized that something had happened in the last minutes to banish his usual urbanity.

"Very well," she said meekly, and backed out, closing the door.

"What is it?" Emma forgot the retiring room at Almack's for the moment.

Alasdair didn't immediately answer her. He walked around the dressing room. "Is everything just as they left it?"

"Yes. I don't think Tilda's had time to tidy up." She poured tea and took a sip, watching him curiously.

Alasdair went to the window. "They escaped this way?"

"Mmm." She continued to sip her tea, waiting.

"Your writing case was on the writing shelf in the secretaire?" He ran a hand over the flat glossy surface of the shelf. It was where he'd seen the writing case on his own investigation.

"Mmm."

"What was in it?" He turned to face her, resting his flat palms on the shelf at his back. His lean, angular countenance was very intense, his eyes beneath half-lowered lids as sharply penetrating as dagger tips.

Emma shrugged. "Only what you'd expect. Writing materials. Pens. Paper. Sealing wax."

"Letters?" The one-word question cracked with the force of a musket ball.

Emma stared in surprise. "I don't know."

"Think!" Again a pistol shot of an instruction.

Emma regarded him with a touch of resentment. "Why? What could it matter?"

"More than you know. Now, *think!*"

"I can't think when you're bellowing at me as if I were a recalcitrant spaniel!"

Alasdair ran a hand distractedly through his already disordered locks. He sighed and consigned Charles Lester and his instructions to the devil. Charles Lester didn't know Emma Beaumont.

"Was there any correspondence from Ned in that writing case?" he asked, quietly now.

"No," Emma said decisively. "I kept his last letter in there for a while . . . except that it wasn't a letter. It was the strangest poem . . . a very bad poem." She bit her lip suddenly and was silent.

"Where is it now?" Alasdair didn't move a muscle.

Emma frowned. "What's all this about?"

"Just tell me where the poem is."

She rose and went into her bedchamber. Alasdair followed her. "I keep it in my copy of *Ode on Intimations of Mortality,*" she said, a tiny catch in her voice. She took the slender volume of Wordsworth from the bedside table and handed it to Alasdair.

He opened it and let the rust-stained parchment flutter into his open palm. He stood looking at it in silence.

"For God's sake, Alasdair, what's going on?" Emma demanded in frustration.

He looked up. "This," he said softly, raising the

parchment. "This is an encoded outline of Wellington's intended spring campaign in Portugal."

Emma stared in disbelief. "But why do I have it?"

"That's a good question." Alasdair raised an almost amused eyebrow as he tucked the parchment into his breast pocket.

"Ned entrusted this, and a letter to you, to the man he was with when he was killed. It seems that Hugh Melton mixed up the two. Ned's letter to you arrived at Horseguards just before Christmas. They assumed, of course, that it was the real thing, and it took them longer than it should have done to realize at last that it was actually only what it appeared to be. An innocent letter from a brother to a sister . . . no more, no less.

"Of course, by that time, Napoleon's conscripted Portuguese and Spanish allies were chasing after the document too. They'd known Ned was carrying it at the time of his death. They gave up when they thought it had been transported safely to England. However, it appears that they have a mole at Horseguards. He was able to inform them that in fact it had gone missing. It didn't take a genius to work out what had happened."

His smile was sardonic as he continued, "Then, you see, my sweet, it was a matter of who could get it first. It's been a regular hunt-the-thimble. Time is of the essence, as you can imagine. The information will be no good to Napoleon once Wellington begins his campaign in March. They need to know what troop movements he's planning before he makes them."

Emma nodded. It made sense. "But why didn't Ned's masters just ask me for it?" she said with customary pragmatism.

Alasdair sighed. "Another very good question.

There was a feeling that if you knew what it was you had, you might let it slip to the wrong person."

"I can keep a secret!" She was indignant.

"There was a feeling that in certain circumstances you might not be able to," Alasdair said carefully, regarding her closely now.

Emma stared at him in dawning comprehension. "You mean someone might try to . . . to *compel* me to tell them?"

"Uh-huh." He folded his arms, his eyes still on her face. "Do you know the poem by heart?"

Emma nodded. "Yes, of course I do. I've read it countless times. Trying to make sense of it, if you must know."

"Recite it to me," he commanded.

Emma frowned, then recited Ned's strange and meaningless poem without hesitation.

Alasdair listened in silence. When she'd finished, he said, "You see the point, Emma. You have Ned's communication in your head. If the enemy have you, they have no need of the parchment."

"How very nasty," she said in classic understatement. "But it's all right now. Now you have the paper, you can give it to the right people, and then everything will be fine."

"One would like to think so."

"But you don't?"

"No." He shook his head. "Which is why, my dear Emma, I am going to be sticking closer than your shadow for the next few weeks. Once the campaign begins, then there'll be no further danger. If the weather is favorable, Wellington intends to begin campaigning at the beginning of March. Until then, you may consider yourself at risk . . . and you may consider me as a species of bodyguard."

He crossed the room and yanked on the bellpull. "We'll leave by midmorning. Jemmy and Sam will ride as outriders."

"Leave for where?" Emma said faintly.

"Lincolnshire. I have that little hunting box, if you recall. Left me in my uncle's will. It's in some degree of disrepair, but I daresay we can make it habitable."

"But I don't wish to go into Lincolnshire," Emma protested, gathering her dissipated forces around her as if they were tattered rags blown about by a storm. "I have engagements here."

Alasdair looked at her. "Don't set yourself against me in this, Emma. You won't win. And your own common sense must tell you that it's the only sensible course of action."

Emma glanced toward the still-open window. They had been so close to her. If she hadn't woken up, what would they have done to her?

She crossed her arms over her breasts and shivered.

Alasdair nodded grimly and turned to give brusque instructions to Tilda, who had appeared in answer to the bell.

૭

"Enough to knock out a horse, you said." Luiz flung his hat and cloak across the table in the drafty room in Half Moon Street. "Some horse!" For once, he felt superior to his companion. Paolo had bungled the job. It was almost unheard of, and Luiz couldn't help a certain perverse satisfaction in the contemplation of it.

Paul let loose a stream of Portuguese obscenities. He pulled a knife from his belt and attacked the lock of the writing case. "She must not have finished it!" he declared savagely. "If that Esterhazy bitch had not interrupted, I would have watched the woman drain it to the dregs. She must have set it down when I left."

The lock broke open and he began to search the case, tossing the contents aside. When it was empty, he held it up by the spine and shook it. He swore again with ever more powerful obscenities.

Luiz listened with some admiration to this fluency. "So what now?" he inquired.

Paul picked up a flagon of brandy and tipped it to his lips. His throat worked as he gulped thirstily at the fiery spirit.

"So?" Luiz prompted, when his companion came up for air.

Paul wiped his mouth with the back of his hand. His expression was now utterly impassive, his voice cold and clipped. "We take the woman. We take her off the street if necessary. And we take her today!"

Paul stared into the grate, where the ashy embers of the fire offered a meager glow. His mission had taken on another dimension, he realized. A personal one. He wanted vengeance on the woman who had led him on, rejected him, and outsmarted him. It was always dangerous to mix personal motives with business, but in this case he was going to do it.

He began to pace the small room. "We need two other men . . . you can find them?"

"Aye." Luiz nodded. "Compatriots."

"Good. Then fetch them here."

Luiz picked up his cloak and hat again and went out into the brightening dawn.

Chapter Twelve

"No, Maria, I'm not traveling in the chaise," Emma said firmly, slicing the top off a boiled egg. "You and Tilda will be more comfortable with just the two of you. I shall drive my curricle and my new chestnuts."

"But you can't drive in the open all the way into Lincolnshire," Maria demurred, dipping a finger of toast in her tea.

"Yes, I can. But I might also ride. We shall tie Swallow to the rear of the chaise."

"But what of Alasdair?"

"What indeed?" Emma said with a dangerous glint in her eye. "If he wishes to travel in the chaise, that's his business."

"Oh dear," sighed Maria, seeking fortification in tea. "You and Alasdair seemed to be getting on so amicably together, and now . . ." She shook her head in dismay.

Emma offered no comment. She sprinkled salt on her egg and contemplated the coming journey. Being cooped up in a chaise for the three days it would take to get to Doddington was not an appealing prospect. Even if they changed horses regularly, they couldn't hope to accomplish more than ten miles an hour. But she could make a virtue of necessity by getting to know her chestnuts. And when they needed to be rested, then she could ride Swallow and Sam could bring the chestnuts along by easy stages. It might be possible to derive some satisfaction from this enforced journey.

But however hard she tried, she could derive not a glimmer of satisfaction or pleasure from the thought of Alasdair's company. Julia Melrose's voice trilled in her ear, a constant nag like the dripping of rain from a clogged gutter. It was the worst humiliation—to think that he freely discussed her with his other women. It made her sick to think about it.

"Emma dearest," Maria ventured. "You're looking very fierce. Don't you wish to go into Lincolnshire? Perhaps if you told Alasdair that you really didn't wish it, he would—"

"For pity's sake, Maria, Alasdair is not controlling what I do!" Emma cried, at last stung beyond patience by her companion's blithe assumptions that as a woman she must be directed by a man. That without such direction, no woman could be trusted to make a decision, let alone a correct one.

"I am not going into Lincolnshire because he says so. I'm going because *I* have decided I must."

"Yes, dear," Maria murmured. "I didn't mean to upset you. It's been such an upsetting time, one way and another." She reached over and patted Emma's hand. "Such a dreadful business. But I'm sure Alasdair knows what's best."

Emma ground her teeth in silence.

෧

Alasdair returned to Mount Street just before midmorning. He was driving his curricle, a valise strapped to the box at the back, Jemmy on his perch, a pair of pistols primed and ready at his feet. A groom rode Phoenix, who trotted placidly along at the rear of the curricle.

Alasdair had delivered the missing communication to Charles Lester and described the events of the night. Lester had been all in favor of putting Emma securely out of harm's way. If and when they managed to locate the men responsible for the attempted robbery, or if, as was more likely, they were able to uncover the mole among their own ranks, she would be safe. But not until then.

He had offered Alasdair some men of his own as further protection, but Alasdair was not comfortable with the idea of strangers who might feel the need to act for themselves following the orders of another master. He would employ the usual postilions and outriders. John-coachman was loyal and could use a pistol. But his main reliance would be on Jemmy and Sam.

The luggage was being stowed on the roof of the chaise as Alasdair drove up to the front door. Emma's racing curricle, with the chestnuts in the traces, was being walked up and down by the redoubtable Sam, who had the crumpled, rearranged face of an exprizefighter, and an air of one who relished a dust-up. He tugged a forelock and opined that Lady Emma's horses were a fine pair of blood cattle.

"So they are," said Alasdair, alighting from the curricle, handing his reins and whip to Jemmy. "But what are you doing with them this morning?"

"Lady Emma, sir." Sam nodded. "Said as 'ow she was agoin' to drive 'em to Lincolnshire."

"Oh, did she, indeed," Alasdair muttered. "That's a fine procession we're going to make. A post chaise, postilions, two riding horses, two curricles, two outriders, and two pairs of driving horses."

So much for a discreet departure from the city.

He went into the house, where Harris informed him that Lady Emma was in the breakfast parlor.

"Emma, you can't be intending to drive all the way to Lincolnshire," he said as he walked in, drawing off his gloves, thrusting them into the pocket of his caped driving coat.

"Yes, I can," she said, taking a piece of bread and butter.

Alasdair pulled out a chair and sat down. He tried for a reasonable tone. "Just think for a minute, Emma. We'll be so spread out along the road, with such a damned ridiculous procession, that anyone could stage an attack."

"An attack!" squawked Maria. "Oh, my goodness, who's going to attack us?"

Maria had not been let in on the ramifications of the situation. She had simply accepted that after the unpleasantness of the night, they all needed a spell of rustication in the countryside. Indeed, as she had said, her own nerves were shot to pieces. Of course, dear Emma must be similarly suffering.

"Highwaymen," said Emma with some relish. "Footpads. Men with blunderbusses and—"

Maria looked about to swoon away and Emma said

in quick remorse, "Oh, I'm only teasing you, Maria. Alasdair is just being an alarmist."

"No," Alasdair said. "No, I am not."

"Well," said Emma, reaching for a silver pot of raspberry jam. "Maybe we could cut down the size of this procession if you didn't bring your own curricle." She slathered jam on her bread and butter. "I will have mine. Why would you need yours?"

Alasdair recognized that he'd been neatly finessed. He propped an elbow on the table and, resting his chin in his palm, regarded her with a gleam of appreciation. "And will you permit me to drive your horses once in a while, ma'am?"

"If you can prove to me that you can handle them," she returned, picking up her coffee cup. "They're quite spirited, you should know."

Alasdair pushed back his chair, observing affably, "I cannot understand why no one ever managed to break you to bridle, Emma. But I suppose we must all live with the consequences."

He went to the door, continuing, "You and I will start out in your curricle in half an hour. We'll take a turn around Hyde Park to give the impression that we're just going for a drive. We'll make the first change at Potters Bar, so we'll wait there for the chaise."

"Why must it look as if you're going for a drive?" asked poor bewildered Maria.

"It's a little complicated," Emma replied. "When we're at Doddington, then I'll tell you about it. But there's no need for you to worry."

"Well, I own I'm thankful that Alasdair is with us," Maria said, giving him a grateful smile.

Alasdair bowed low. "I could wish you were in company, Maria." He left the breakfast parlor.

But the minute he was outside the door, his expression darkened. Something had happened to change Emma's attitude since yesterday at Richmond. But he couldn't for the life of him think what. He hadn't done anything to upset her. He always knew when he had, and he knew categorically that he had done and said absolutely nothing.

So what in the name of Beelzebub was going on?

He went back to the street and told Jemmy to take his curricle and horses back to the mews. "Give order that they're to be exercised every day, then ride Phoenix to Potters Bar and lead Lady Emma's Swallow. We'll meet you at the Black Gull."

"You're not takin' them bays with you?" Jemmy was stunned, his eyes wide in his wizened face.

"Apparently not," Alasdair replied wryly. "Put my valise in Lady Emma's curricle and stow the pistols under the seat."

Jemmy, muttering, obeyed and sprang into his master's curricle, taking up the reins and whip.

Alasdair watched his favorite equipage disappear around the corner onto Audley Street with glum resignation. Emma was going to have to make the next round of concessions, he decided.

However, it was not to be.

Emma appeared fifteen minutes later in a severely cut driving dress of a brilliant flaming orange broadcloth edged with black braid. She looked like a bird of paradise, Alasdair thought with something akin to despair.

"If I was hoping to smuggle you out of the city, I can forget it," he said as she came down the steps to the street. "That flagrant display of color is going to attract attention for miles around."

"Oh, but I have my veil," Emma responded with an

innocent smile. She adjusted the little black hat that was perched upon the stripey braids encircling her head.

The veil was a mere ornamental wisp, any potential for discretion completely counteracted by the flourishing black plume that curled onto her shoulder. The effect was striking; in fact, Alasdair reflected, it was magnificent. Once seen, not easily forgotten.

"Anyway," Emma continued in the same innocence as she took the reins and whip from Sam and prepared to climb into her curricle. "I understood we wanted everyone to see us taking a drive through the park. While the chaise leaves unnoticed from Mount Street, I shall be *lionizing* in my curricle."

She cast him a sharp look as she quoted Julia Melrose in less than dulcet tones. But Alasdair showed no reaction. It was almost as if he hadn't heard her.

"Making a vulgar exhibition of myself, even," she elaborated pointedly.

A frown crossed Alasdair's expression. "Why would you do that?" he said, and then, without waiting for an answer, turned to give John-coachman instructions for the first stage of the journey.

Emma reflected with derision that he'd probably forgotten what he'd said to his mistress. He probably chattered on without regard for his words in the full flood of lust. . . .

Sour bile rose in her throat and she swallowed bitterly, turning her head away from Alasdair, contemplating the street as if it seethed with interesting sights. Not that she'd have been able to take them in if there had been any. Her eyes were clouded with angry tears.

"Right. Let's get moving." Alasdair sprang into the curricle beside her. "Sam, let go their heads."

The chestnuts, as if released from a trap, sprang forward. Emma checked them, feeling their mouths with a delicate tug on the reins. They responded immediately.

"Nice," Alasdair said.

"Very," Emma agreed and was about to launch into an enthusiastic commentary on the chestnuts' responses when she realized that once again that infuriating amnesia had overcome her anger at Alasdair. One minute she could be hating him with the most profound and hurtful detestation, and the next she'd find herself completely absorbed in a discussion about one of the many experiences and enthusiasms that they shared with such passion.

She compressed her lips tightly and gave all her concentration to her horses.

Alasdair shot her a puzzled glance. Something was definitely amiss. Maybe it was a nervous reaction to the robbery. He'd first noticed her distance when he'd walked into the house after Maria had sent for him. He understood that she'd been annoyed that Maria had sent for him. But her companion's somewhat foolish insistence on the necessity of a male pilot through life always annoyed her, although usually she laughed it off.

In normal circumstances, Alasdair would have looked to his own behavior to find the cause of Emma's coldness, but he knew he had nothing for which to reproach himself. There was no possible way he could have angered or distressed her between yesterday at Richmond and now.

She could reasonably be upset and maybe even frightened about being pursued by spies with distinctly evil intent, but her distance had been there before she'd understood the real situation.

So what in hell was it?

"I'm glad to see that you've recovered from whatever ailed you last evening," he said, as they turned into Hyde Park. "I've never seen you so sleepy. And it was so sudden."

Emma said nothing. The only explanation she could produce for that strange turn was her shocked misery at what she'd overheard in the retiring room. She wouldn't have expected herself to react in such a missish fashion, but the body could play strange tricks on occasion.

"But then, we did have a somewhat energetic afternoon," Alasdair murmured with a smile. His hand for a second rested on her thigh. She went rigid beside him, her eyes fixed on the path ahead. He let his hand fall away, his puzzlement turning to a familiar frustration.

If there was something the matter, why didn't she just tell him?

❦

Paul Denis, from the seclusion of a shrubbery just a little off the path, watched the curricle bowl past along the tan. That damned Alasdair Chase seemed to stick to her like a fly to honey. It wouldn't be possible to take her here in the middle of the park, but a carriage accident, a diversion of some kind, in the busy streets outside the park, would give them the opportunity.

He and the two useful men Luiz had found for him would be an easy match for the ugly looking tiger on his perch at the back. But adding Alasdair Chase to the equation changed the numbers.

Paul had been waiting for her to enter the park. Luiz had stationed a boy at the mews where her horses were kept. As soon as the curricle had been sent for, the urchin had delivered his message, received his sixpence, and gone whistling on his merry way.

The plan was beautiful in its simplicity. Once he saw Emma, Paul had intended to waylay her. He would ask her to take him up for a turn around the park. An utterly ordinary request and one she could not refuse without grave discourtesy. They'd parted amicably the previous evening at Almack's. She would have no reason to be rude to him.

He would ask her to drop him off at Fribourg and Treyer's, where he wished to freshen his snuff. Again he didn't think she could refuse such an innocent request. And his men would be waiting in the street outside the shop to create the accident.

His fingers curled over the small piece of lead piping in his pocket. A blow to the base of the skull would render her insensible. It would appear she'd been injured in the accident. In the diversion and the inevitable milling crowd, it would be simplicity itself to hand her up to Luiz, who would be waiting in a gig.

A foolproof plan—except that it didn't take into account Lord Alasdair. However, it would not be unusual either for Paul to ask Chase to yield his place in the carriage. Lady Emma was still on the marriage mart as far as society was concerned. She still had her choice of suitors. Sharing her attentions was part of the game they all played.

Paul stepped out of the shrubbery and resumed his casual stroll along the path, watching for the curricle's return circuit. But he watched in vain. The curricle did not return.

It took him the better part of fifteen minutes before

he was certain he was now on a fool's errand. Swearing under his breath, he left the park and hailed a hackney.

He turned onto Mount Street just in time to see Maria Witherspoon climb into a laden post chaise. A maidservant followed with a jewel case. Of Emma there was no sign.

Paul rapped on the wall behind the jarvey, and the man pulled in his horse. He leaned back to shout through the window. "You want out 'ere, gov?"

"No, just wait here until I tell you to move on."

The jarvey shrugged and leaned back on his seat, shaking out an old copy of the *Gazette*. Paul rested his arm on the window and watched the scene outside Emma's house.

Postilions, outriders, a mountain of luggage—all the signs that a long journey was contemplated.

But there was no Emma, only her companion and the maid.

Emma was driving her curricle in the park with Alasdair Chase.

Paul pulled at his sharp chin. If she was going on a journey, why would she go for a drive in the park first?

To throw anyone interested in her movements off the scent, of course.

He had shown his hand by taking the writing case last night. They would reason now that while she was riding in the park, no one would be interested in the house. If they managed to leave London undetected, then they'd be well nigh impossible to trace. The roads out of London were numerous at all points of the compass. Possible destinations were as varied as the colors of a rainbow.

The post chaise started to move. Paul leaned farther
out of the window. "Follow the chaise."

"Where to?" The jarvey folded his newspaper
again.

"If I knew that," Paul snapped, "I wouldn't need
you to follow it."

☙

Emma took the curricle through Cumberland Gate at
the northern end of Park Street and headed north to
the Holloway road. At the toll gate before Islington
Spa, Sam sprang down to get the tickets that would
open the next three tolls for them.

Alasdair had finally had enough. "Is this silence
going to continue until we reach Potters Bar, Emma?"

"I don't have anything to say."

"Yes, you do," he asserted. "You are bursting with
something to say. Something is eating you alive, and I
think you'd better get rid of it before it consumes you
completely."

Sam jumped back on his perch and Emma started
her horses again. On the one hand, she wanted to
accuse him. She wanted to see his confusion and em-
barrassment. She wanted to hear him stumble over an
explanation, or a denial that he couldn't possibly
make convincing.

But on the other hand, she couldn't bear to risk
hearing him shrug it off . . . laugh at her for being a
naive chit for caring a harlot's curse what he said to
anyone. She had almost persuaded herself now that
that was how he would react. He would chastise her
for such an unrealistic, unsophisticated concern. They
were all grown men and women with no illusions. It
was the way of the world.

And she couldn't endure to hear that.

Alasdair waited for an answer. He waited through the pretty village of Islington Spa, up the hill into Highgate and down the northern side. He waited until they were on Finchley Common, where the lonely track stretched ahead of them across the heath under a steely gray sky.

He waited as they passed the gibbet at Fallow Corner. The rotting corpse of an erstwhile highwayman swung in its chains, creaking as the wind blew off the flat heath. The silence in the curricle was profound until Sam, holding pistols at the ready in expectation of an extant highwayman, began to whistle half under his breath as if to dispel his own discomfort.

They came off the heath without encountering sight or sound of danger and stopped for the toll in the village of Whetstone. Alasdair by now had lost his far from limitless patience, but nothing could be done while Sam was sitting behind them. They might quarrel in front of Jemmy, but Sam was a newcomer.

"Stop at the Red Lion," he instructed curtly as they drove into the busy town of Barnet two miles after Whetstone.

"I thought we were stopping at Potters Bar."

"I need a drink, and the horses need watering."

Emma pulled into the courtyard of the Red Lion. Ostlers were racing to change horses for a trio of post chaises heading out on the Great North road.

Alasdair sprang down to the cobbles. "Come." He held up a hand to assist Emma to alight.

She hesitated for an instant, then took the hand and stepped down herself. She knew Alasdair was now angry and she knew that in her typically perverse fashion she had engineered the scene that was about to unfold. Despite her dread of his reaction, she needed the confrontation. They had never been able to conceal their emotions from each other, rocketing from one tempestuous peak to another. Maybe it wasn't the most mature way of going on, but neither of them seemed able to help it.

Alasdair released her wrist the instant she had touched ground. "Go into the inn and bespeak a private parlor," he said, adding with frozen courtesy, "And a jug of ale for me, if you please."

Emma did as he asked. The landlord, bowing in the doorway, assured her that he had a private parlor overlooking the street. He would send refreshments immediately. He snapped his fingers at a maidservant, instructing her to show the lady up.

Emma followed the girl upstairs and into a square, wainscotted apartment. She was standing at the mullioned window overlooking the street when Alasdair came in.

"The landlord is sending up ale and coffee," she said tonelessly, drawing off her gloves. "Also some cold chicken and a game pie. I didn't know if you were hungry."

"Not particularly," Alasdair said. He stood with his back to the fire, lifting the tail of his driving coat to warm his backside.

"I suppose Maria must be well on her way by now," Emma observed, not turning from the window.

"All right, Emma, that's enough!" Alasdair declared. "What the hell's going on here! You've been sulking ever since I arrived in Mount Street this morning and—"

"I have not been sulking!" Emma cried, swinging round on him. "I *never* sulk."

"Until this morning, I might have agreed with you," he retorted. "Just why am I getting the cold shoulder?"

Emma dropped her gloves onto a gate-legged table. "As it happens, I don't care to hear . . ." she began, then broke off as the maidservant returned with food and drink. Emma turned back to the window.

The girl looked curiously at the two occupants of the parlor. The tension between them was so thick you could cut it with a knife. She laid out the contents of her tray, making more of a bustle than the simple task warranted, but the silence in the room was so noisy that she felt an overpowering need to fill it.

"Will that be all, sir?" She bobbed a curtsy in Alasdair's direction, since Emma still had her back to the room.

"Yes . . . yes," he waved her away with a brusque gesture. She curtsied again and hastened from the room with her empty tray.

"Let's begin again." Alasdair poured himself ale. "What is it that you don't care to hear?" He took a deep draft from his tankard and regarded her through narrowed eyes. He was conscious of his own anxiety, the apprehension flickering beneath his annoyance, and it didn't do anything to make his demeanor more conciliatory.

"I do not care to hear myself discussed by the likes of Lady Melrose," Emma said, her color now rather high, the faintest tremor in her voice. "Discussed in disparaging terms that are attributed to *you*!"

Alasdair stared at her for a moment in complete bewilderment. He set his tankard back on the table. "I don't understand you."

"Don't you?" Her voice shook with anger now. "Perhaps you don't remember giving your opinion of me to Lady Melrose, in terms that I understand had to be heard to be believed. Vulgar as Letty Lade, I believe was one of them. Perhaps you don't recall say-

ing to her that you couldn't wait until I found a
husband and you could be free of your *odious* responsibilities as trustee."

She caught her breath on an angry little sob and
pressed her fingers to her mouth, fighting for control.
She would not give way in front of him.

"What else did you discuss with her?" she continued, taking advantage of his momentarily stunned silence. "My skills at bedsport, perhaps? Do you enjoy
comparing your mistresses, Alasdair?"

Alasdair paled. "That's enough!" he declared, his
eyes ablaze in his white face, a muscle twitching in
the corner of his rigidly set mouth. "Let me just get
this right. You are accusing me of discussing you with
other women?"

"Not just discussing," she fired back. "Disparaging
me to your other women, so that they can repeat what
you've said to their friends and acquaintances and
anyone else in society who cares to hear . . . so that
your words are on the tongue of every old cat and
gossip in the entire town!"

She whirled away from him, unable to look at him,
swept away on the hot crimson tide of her hurt and
her anger, and unsure which emotion was now uppermost.

"How dare you!" Alasdair spoke with a quiet ferocity that was merely intensified by the softness of his
voice. "How *dare* you, Emma!"

"How dare I what?" she flung over her shoulder. "I
am merely repeating what I heard. And heard in the
most public place."

"You *dare* to believe I would do such a thing? That I
would be so blind to decency, to propriety, that I
would discuss *you* in personal terms with *anyone*?"

"I heard it," she said flatly. "I believe what I heard."

Alasdair crossed the room in two strides. He caught her shoulders and spun her around to face him. "By God, Emma, I have never been so close to striking a woman as I am now."

"Oh, go on, then!" she cried. "Violence is only what one would expect of a man who would belittle one mistress to curry favor with another." She flinched from the look in his eyes. His fingers curled bruisingly on her shoulders, and she waited in a kind of dreadful expectancy for him to do as he'd threatened. It would make her despise him even more. It would finally, absolutely kill all other emotions.

Alasdair's hands dropped from her shoulders. He stepped away from her. He sighed a long, deep, shuddering breath, then rubbed his eyes and his mouth with his fingertips, ran his flat palms across his face in a gesture of utter weariness.

Emma saw that his hands shook.

"Instead of hurling accusations at me, why don't you simply tell me what occurred?" he said, his voice now as calm as a millpond. "Clearly you have some reason for this insult. And, by God, Emma, it had better be a good one."

The first faint possibility came to her that maybe it was all a mistake, a hideous mistake. She felt the first stirring of hope. She knew Alasdair and she knew he could not have been feigning his anger. He gave not the slightest sign of guilty awareness, of even the remotest hint of conscience.

She took a deep breath and told him exactly what she'd overheard in the retiring room at Almack's.

Alasdair listened, his expression growing livid as she spoke. Emma's voice faltered once or twice as she saw the bright rage sparking in his eyes, but she continued steadily with her tale, careful not to embellish what she'd heard.

When she'd finished, Alasdair said, "Listen to me, and listen to me very carefully. I have never, I would never, discuss you with anyone in any personal terms whatsoever. Julia Melrose has a mischievous tongue. And she may consider she has an ax to grind. Whatever she attributed to me did not come from me."

Emma rubbed her hands together as if they were cold. "But can you deny that she could have received such an impression from you that would make her feel justified in saying those things?"

"I cannot say what impression she might have received from me," he said with curt dismissal. "I have no idea what she might have twisted to suit her own purposes."

"So you would never talk about me with another woman?"

"Have I not just said so?" he demanded angrily.

Emma swallowed and for the first time ever mentioned the taboo subject. "Not even with the mother of your child?"

Alasdair's face closed. He said with icy finality, "We will leave Lucy out of this, if you please. I will no more discuss her with you than I would discuss you with her."

"So you really do think it's possible to keep all your women in separate compartments?" Emma observed.

They'd started on this road and she was now determined to go down it to the very end. It was way past time, and if it led to the final irrevocable break between them, then so be it. She knew now she couldn't live like Alasdair. The ephemeral pleasures of passion and amusing and enthusiastic companionship were not enough for her. And they never would be.

Alasdair turned away from her. He picked up his tankard and took another drink. He walked to the hearth and stood, one foot on the bright copper fender, his left arm stretched along the mantelpiece, his eyes on the fire. He raised his head and drank again.

Emma waited, her chest suddenly tight, her breath suspended.

"How many mistresses do you think I have, Emma?" he asked conversationally.

"I don't know. There's Lady Melrose, there's me, if I can be called one, there's the mother of your child," she said doggedly.

"There's you." The simple statement was spoken so quietly that for a minute she wasn't sure she had heard him aright.

"That is," he continued, "assuming you consider yourself to be my mistress."

"Only me?" she said.

"Only you."

"Oh." It was on the tip of her tongue to ask what had happened to the others. Was this the ax Julia Melrose was grinding? But then she reflected that it wasn't her business. She could hardly accuse him of talking about her in one breath and then ask him to talk about other women in the next.

"Just me . . . *at the moment*?" It was important to get this absolutely clear.

"Until you decide otherwise."

"Oh," she said again. There was silence, into which drifted the sounds from the street below: the rattle of iron wheels on cobbles, a hawker crying his wares, the squeal of a kicked dog.

"Come here," Alasdair said, setting his tankard on the mantelpiece.

Emma hung back for a minute. He had a certain look in his eye that she wasn't sure about.

"Emma, come here," he repeated quietly, crooking a finger at her.

She went over to him, reflecting crossly that it was absurd to feel this defiant bravado, as if she was somehow in the wrong. She had had every right to confront him.

Alasdair clasped her face between his hands. "You, my sweet, are the most suspicious, crosspatch of a termagant it was ever any man's misfortune to adore."

Emma's eyes glowed gold. "Adore?" she queried.

"Yes, damn you! For my sins." He kissed her roughly, his hands hard on her face. "You are not in the least adorable, and yet I've adored you from the moment I first saw you with your stripey pigtails and torn petticoat."

"Did I have?" she asked, in genuine surprise at such a recollection.

"You always had a torn petticoat."

"That has to be an exaggeration," she protested.

"Quite possibly." His arms slid around her back until he was cupping her shoulder blades in his palms, holding her tight against him. He gazed steadily down into her eyes.

"I don't know what else to say, Emma. I want you. I need you. I love you as I have never loved another woman. If that's not enough for you, I don't know what else I can do or say."

There was such plea in his voice. It was so uncharacteristic of Alasdair, Emma was silenced. She stood in the circle of his arms, just looking at him.

"Do you love me?" he asked when the silence became intolerable.

"Yes," she said in a low voice. "I have always loved you. Even when I loathe you, I love you."

Alasdair laughed softly and kissed the corner of her mouth. "Well, maybe that's as much as I can expect . . . for now."

She would learn to trust him again. He told himself that the battle was almost won as her body softened in his arms and her mouth yielded to his kiss. They were made to be together, inextricably entwined. Emma could not hold out against this truth forever.

Chapter Thirteen

They reached the Black Gull at Potters Bar soon after noon. Sam led the horses off to bait them and Emma went into the inn to order a nuncheon for when Maria arrived in the chaise. They should arrive soon after one o'clock, Alasdair reckoned. The journey from Potters Bar to Stevenage, where they would stop for the night, would take the chaise another two hours this afternoon. An easy enough journey that wouldn't tire Maria unduly.

Emma gave her orders in the inn and then went back to the stableyard. Alasdair was standing under the arched carriage entrance to the yard, looking down the street.

"Can you see them?" She came up beside him.

"Not yet."

"Let's take a stroll. I could do with stretching my legs."

He nodded agreeably and gave her his arm.

"I've been thinking," Emma said.

Alasdair groaned. "Not again. That always seems to lead to trouble."

"Be serious."

"Believe me, I am being."

Emma treated this with the disdain it deserved. "Don't you think it would have been much more convenient for those men last night if I hadn't woken up when I did?"

Alasdair's step slowed. "Meaning?"

She shrugged. "I'm not sure what I'm getting at, but I don't normally fall asleep in the middle of a ball. I thought . . ." she hesitated, then continued, "I thought I just felt ill because of what I'd overheard. But I wasn't ill. I was asleep."

Alasdair stopped at a low wall running alongside the narrow village street. He leaned against it, looking out over the rolling countryside, considering this. "What did you eat or drink at Almack's?"

"Nothing. It's hardly inviting fare." She turned and hitched herself up on the wall beside him, swinging her long legs.

"True." He frowned. "You and I drank the same wine at dinner. We ate from the same dishes."

"Yes." She shook her head. "Never mind, it was just something that occurred to me . . . that if they weren't ordinary burglars, then maybe they could have arranged to put me to sleep."

"I don't know why I didn't think of it myself." He stared out across the wall. "But I don't see how it could have been done."

Then he turned and put his hands at her waist, scolding, "Such an indecorous creature you are, sitting on walls like a little girl! It's a wonder you don't still have torn petticoats." He lifted her down, shaking his head. "The wall's covered in moss. Turn around."

He twisted her and dusted off the back of her orange skirt with a degree of vigor, then his hand paused, traced the curve of her backside, kneaded the firm flesh beneath her skirt.

"Alasdair, we're in the middle of the village!" she hissed, pulling away. "Don't do that!"

"But I like to," he said simply.

"Satyr!" Emma accused. Then her attention was caught by the sound of carriage wheels. "Here's the chaise! For pity's sake, *behave*."

Alasdair merely chuckled.

Maria descended from the carriage in a breathless sweep of chatter. "Such a well-sprung vehicle, I do declare. I've never had such a smooth journey. And not the slightest moment of alarm crossing Finchley Common, although I do so dread highwaymen. Did you enjoy your drive, Emma love?" She beamed upon Emma and Alasdair.

"Yes, it was lovely," Emma said, lying through her teeth. It had been one of the most uncomfortable drives of her life. "My horses have the softest mouths."

Maria's nod conveyed knowledgeable understanding of this important issue, although she had never held a pair of driving reins in her life.

"This afternoon we're going to ride to Stevenage," Emma continued cheerfully. "To rest the chestnuts. But come into the inn, now. Nuncheon is waiting for you. And there's a bedchamber where you may refresh yourself first."

"Oh, how pleasant. What a pretty village this is." Maria entered the inn, as always prepared to be pleased. "I own I would like to wash my hands and comb my hair. Come up with me, love."

Alasdair remained behind in the stableyard. "Everything all right, Jemmy?"

"Aye." Jemmy dismounted from Phoenix. "Traffic's summat chronic, though. Couldn't 'ardly get through Barnet, it was such a press."

"It should be quieter now we're out of London. You'll find Sam in the kitchen when you've stabled Phoenix and Swallow. Make sure they give us a good team for the next stage."

"They'll not fob anythin' but prime-goers on me, guv," Jemmy declared, spitting into the straw at his feet.

"No," Alasdair agreed with a half smile. He went into the inn.

❦

The four horsemen were at this point passing the gibbet at Fallow Corner. "You're certain they're heading north, Paolo?" Luiz slouched in his saddle like a sack of potatoes. He was a dreadful rider and disliked the exercise intensely.

"I followed them to the Islington toll. They bought tickets for the next three stages on the turnpike." Paul sounded as irritable as he felt. He had hoped to have this business over and done with by now, instead of which he was chasing over the open countryside after a procession as long as a Roman triumph.

Luiz grunted and slumped deeper in his saddle. "We make better time than a chaise," he offered. "And they'll be stopping to change horses."

"At Barnet, probably," Paul muttered almost to himself. "We'll pick up their tracks there."

He glanced sideways at the other two men, who rode in silence, with impassive expressions. Their English was sketchy and they were under strict instructions to maintain silence except when they were alone. The minute they opened their mouths, they'd give the game away. But Paul liked the look of them otherwise. He knew the type and they made good servants in business of this kind. They had the solid brute demeanor of those without either imagination or conscience. If they were told to murder, they would do so. If they were told to hurt, they would do so without compunction.

Barnet was a hive of activity as the turnpike traffic from both the Holloway road and the Great North road converged. Paul rode into the stableyard of the Green Man to make inquiries.

A weasel-faced ostler stared at him pityingly. "Nah, we 'avn't 'ad no northbound traffic changin' 'osses 'ere." He sucked on a straw as if considering the issue. " 'Course, we wouldn't expect none neither, seein' as 'ow the Green Man don't do business wi' northern traffic. We only does the southern." He delicately picked a wisp of straw off his tongue, adding with great condescension, "Thought everyone knowed that."

Paul controlled the urge to check the man's insolence with his whip. He turned his horse to ride out of the yard.

"Eh, guvnor . . ." a voice peeped up at him.

He looked down at a scrawny urchin trotting along beside him. "I could tell you where the northerners go." The child held up a grimy hand.

Paul took out a penny. "Well?"

"The Red Lion, guv." The child jumped up, hand outstretched for the penny.

Paul tossed it to the ground and rode back to the street.

At the Red Lion, he struck gold. The inn servants did not recall a chaise with two women passengers, but they did recall a curricle driven by a lady in an orange habit, accompanied by a gentleman. They had stepped into the inn for half an hour to take refreshment before continuing to Potters Bar.

"What now?" Luiz asked, easing his aching back. "We rest a bit here?"

Paul glanced up at the sun. It was beginning its downward slide to the west. "No," he said. "We're in no danger of running into the back of them. We keep going."

Luiz muttered and took the tankard of ale handed up to him by a potboy. He drained the contents in one long gulp. "How long d'you think these beasts can keep going?"

"We'll change them at Potters Bar." Paul was impatient but Luiz was having his tankard refilled and his fellow travelers were doing likewise. He was thirsty himself, but perversely refused to quench his thirst. He had his sights set on his mission, and pride would not permit such trivialities as hunger, thirst, and fatigue to be considered.

"Eh, Paolo, don't be so sour," Luiz chided. "We'll get the woman . . . pick her off easy. Whatever inn they're at tonight, we'll winkle her out of there."

Paul's nostrils flared; his mouth grew small. He knew Luiz spoke the truth. They'd done much harder things in their time. And their quarry and her protector couldn't know they were being pursued.

☙

"Lemonade!" Emma said suddenly. She reined Swallow in to a walk and turned to Alasdair, riding beside her. "Lemonade."

"Lemonade?" he queried. "What about it?"

"I had some . . . last night . . . at Almack's," she said impatiently. "When the duke of Clarence was proposing . . . or at least I think that was what he was doing. He wasn't too clear. He was certainly proposing something."

"I hope you set him right," Alasdair commented dryly.

"Yes, of course I did. I left him . . . but you're not listening to me."

"I am. Lemonade." He raised an inviting eyebrow. "Tell me about it."

"Paul Denis brought me a glass . . . just before I told him that I wasn't going to marry him . . . that I wasn't going to marry anyone, is what I said, so as to let him down gently, you understand."

"I understand," he said rather more aridly than before. "You seem to have had rather a busy evening putting off suitors. Was he brokenhearted?"

"No." Emma glared at him. "Can't you keep to the point?"

"My apologies." He bowed slightly. "Denis brought you a glass of lemonade. You drank it?"

Emma frowned. "I was drinking it and then Princess Esterhazy took him away and the duke arrived. I think I must have lost interest in it at that point. Then, of course, I escaped to the retiring room to avoid the duke and . . . well, you know what happened then."

"Mmm. To my cost."

"Well?" she demanded.

"Well what?"

"Alasdair, how can you tease like this?" she exclaimed, quite out of patience. "There are all these desperados intent on torturing me so that the duke of Wellington won't win his spring campaign, and all you can do is make mock!"

She touched Swallow with her heels and the roan leaped forward, breaking into a gallop.

Alasdair kept Phoenix back. His teasing facade was just that. The puzzle pieces fitted so neatly he couldn't understand why he hadn't picked them up before. Charles Lester had warned him that the enemy had learned Emma had the document. Paul Denis had walked into his life, made a beeline for Emma, and Alasdair had merely seethed with pure masculine jealousy and completely ignored the very real possibility that this plausible, seeming-French gentleman had much more than fortune hunting at stake.

He could have kicked himself for his stupidity. His utter blindness. He'd been so wrapped up in Emma he hadn't looked further than the end of his nose.

Emma, when she realized he hadn't followed her, drew rein and turned Swallow. She rode back to him and saw instantly from his expression what he was thinking. "You're cross with yourself?"

"Mad as fire," he agreed.

"But it doesn't matter now. He didn't succeed last night, and now we're well away."

"That I doubt," Alasdair said softly. "That I doubt."

"You think he might be following us?"

"I think that Monsieur Denis, or whatever his name is, is too clever and too determined to let you go without a fight. Too much is at stake."

"But if we got out of London without detection . . ." she said uncertainly.

Alasdair's expression was grim. "We can always hope."

It was clear he didn't have much faith in hope. They rode in silence for a few minutes, then Emma said with determined cheerfulness, "Well, you'll have to make sure we have adjoining chambers at the inn tonight. My bodyguard will need to stay very close."

"I had it in my mind to suggest that Maria share your bed and Tilda sleep on the truckle bed," he said with seeming seriousness.

Emma looked aghast. "What protection would *they* be? And they wouldn't be any fun either," she added.

Alasdair did not smile. "Do you still remember how to use a pistol?"

"I was almost as good a shot as you and Ned," she averred, her competitive spirit as always coming to the fore.

"I'm not so sure about that . . . however, I'm interested in how good you are now."

"It's been a while," Emma confessed, seeing that there was no hope of lightening his mood.

Alasdair swung Phoenix off the road and into a field. He dismounted and reached under his saddle for the pair of pistols. "All right, let's see what you can do."

Emma dismounted. "Even if I were a dead shot, I don't possess a pistol."

"That can be remedied." He pulled a white handkerchief from his britches pocket and tied it to the low branch of a sycamore tree. It fluttered merrily in the wind.

"Try it at ten paces." He handed her one of the weapons.

Emma regarded the dancing handkerchief with misgiving. "It's a moving target," she protested.

"I doubt Denis will stand still for you," Alasdair pointed out aridly. "Live targets are rather less accommodating than wafers at Manton's shooting gallery."

Emma was obliged to acknowledge the truth of this. She examined the pistol for a minute. It had been a long time since she'd held one. She could hear Ned's voice telling her how to feel the gun's weight, to judge how to distribute it in her hand.

"Feet a little further apart," Alasdair said, behind her. He put his hands on her hips, steadying her. "Now, try."

Emma held up the pistol, squinting along the barrel. The white handkerchief flipped and flopped around the branch. She squeezed the trigger slowly. The report sounded like an explosion and she jumped, the pistol jerking in her hand.

The handkerchief, unscathed, flapped gaily.

"Now, why did you jump?" Alasdair asked with a touch of asperity, taking the smoking pistol from her. "I thought we'd cured you of that years ago."

"I'm out of practice, I told you," she retorted crossly. "And anyway, that target is all over the place. I'd like to see you do better."

"Would you?" He raised a skeptical eyebrow. "I'd be happy to oblige."

"I'm sure you would," Emma muttered. "Let me try again with the other pistol."

Alasdair handed it to her, then stood back, watching critically, arms folded, as she took up her stance. This time, although she missed the target, she didn't jump.

"Well, let's assume that if you need to shoot someone, it'll be at short range and they'll present a large enough target for you not to miss." Alasdair took the pistol from her and began to reload it.

"Always assuming I'm not so feeble that I couldn't bring myself to shoot someone," Emma said with more than a hint of sarcasm.

"I'm relying on the sharp spur of self-preservation," he said. "Fetch the handkerchief." He turned to stow the pistols under his saddle again.

Emma untied the handkerchief and examined it carefully. "Hey, I *did* hit it!" she exclaimed. "Look at this little burned nick in the lace at the corner." She flourished the evidence triumphantly. "See!"

"The wind must have blown it in the path of the bullet," Alasdair observed, utterly straight-faced.

"Why, you . . . you . . . of all the mean-spirited, ungenerous . . . oh, don't laugh at me!" Not for a minute deceived by his apparent solemnity, she glared at him, only with the greatest difficulty resisting the urge to stamp her foot in vigorous punctuation. "There are times, Alasdair Chase, when I could shoot *you* without a flicker of remorse."

"How unsubtle," he murmured, stepping away from Phoenix. Little flickers of fire darted across the bright green surface of his eyes, and Emma caught her breath. The atmosphere was suddenly charged with that electric tension that so often sprang up between them, and so often at the most inconvenient and inappropriate times.

"Keep away from me," she said, taking a step backward, raising her hands as if to ward him off. "We're in the middle of an open field in the middle of winter."

"I want you," he said quietly.

"Now?" She looked at him helplessly, knowing she could never withstand the force of lust when once it caught her.

"Now. Here," he affirmed.

"How?" She looked around as helplessly as before. "I tell you straight, Alasdair, I am not lying on my back on the frozen ground."

"You won't touch the ground, I swear." He reached for her hands, purpose and determination in the line of his fine straight mouth, a firestorm of desire in his eyes.

Emma felt herself melt like butter in the sun. Her will was pure jelly. Sinew, bone, and muscle seemed to dissolve. Without volition, she put her hands in his. His fingers closed warmly over hers and he drew her toward him, inch by inch, until she was standing against him, her eyes almost on a level with his.

Holding her hands, he lifted her arms sideways, away from her body, so that their bodies touched from chest to knee. He kissed her mouth.

Emma became aware of every part of her body where it touched Alasdair's. Her breasts, her nipples, her belly, her hipbones, her thighs, her knees. She felt every part of his body. She was enclosed in the scent of him, the musky male richness of him. She could scent her own arousal, heady and intoxicating. She leaned in closer, felt his erection hard against her pubic mound. A soft moan slipped from her lips.

Without taking his mouth from hers, or releasing her hands, Alasdair moved her backward. They stepped in synchrony, still touching as if engaged in an elaborate pas de deux. Emma felt the sycamore tree at her back, steadying her.

Alasdair raised his head for a second. His expression was strangely stern. He released her hands, letting her arms drop to her sides. "I want you," he said again. "I must have you."

Emma's voice was a husky little throb as she said with an attempt at a chuckle, "That's all very well, but do you intend to have me up against a tree like a waterfront whore?"

A glow of laughter banished the sternness from his expression. "That's the general idea. But what, pray, do you know of waterfront whores?"

"Only what I learned from my brother and his friends," she answered. The badinage had loosened the taut line of sexual tension, but only to retie it, tighter than ever.

The deep expectant recesses of her body were damp and aching. Her hands were at the waist of his britches, unbuttoning him. She reached for his penis with her own hungry need, stroking and squeezing the hard, pulsing flesh. He had pulled up her orange skirts and pulled down the doeskin pantaloons beneath in one unbroken sweep.

She parted her legs, lifting herself slightly on tiptoe as she guided him into her eager welcoming body.

Alasdair cupped her buttocks. "Wrap your legs around my waist, sweet."

She did so, her arms around his neck as he supported her bottom. He pressed deep within her as she moved herself against him, taking his full length until she felt him against her womb. Her inner muscles quivered and tightened in response; the muscles of her belly contracted in expectation.

Alasdair released his breath in a shuddering sigh of

joy. "Oh, to be inside you is to be buried in honey," he whispered. "Almost intolerably sweet."

Emma brought her mouth to his, her arms tightening around his neck. Her tongue dived into the warm, moist cavern of his mouth as if only thus could she possess him as he possessed her. She clung to him now as if to a piece of driftwood as the maelstrom caught her, tossed her hither and thither, until it receded, leaving her beached on the shore, sobbing for breath.

Alasdair let her slide down his body until her feet were on the ground. He stroked her cheek as it rested against his shoulder. "Dear God," he murmured. "You are miraculous."

"It's my day for compliments," she returned with a weak smile. "First adorable and now miraculous. When will it ever end?"

"You also have the devil's own ability to shatter a mood," he retorted, stepping away from her to adjust his dress. But there was a laugh in his voice, ready amusement in his eye.

Emma mopped herself with the handkerchief before setting herself to rights. "The chaise has probably overtaken us by now. They'll be wondering what happened to us." The prosaic comment served to restore practical concerns.

"Well, let's be on our way," Alasdair said briskly. "In Stevenage, I'll purchase a small pistol for you. One you can carry easily in your pocket." He offered his cupped palm for her foot.

"You really think I might need it?" She mounted Swallow with a spring from Alasdair's hand. In truth she hadn't been at all sure how seriously to take Alasdair's concern. It seemed almost fanciful to imagine she was being pursued across the English countryside all because of some ridiculously bad poem of Ned's. It seemed even more fanciful to imagine Ned encoding something so vital to his country's concerns in a bad poem.

"I wouldn't be going to all this trouble if I didn't," Alasdair said evenly. He swung into the saddle and turned Phoenix back to the lane. "I have no particular desire to spend the next weeks in an ill-appointed hunting box in not very good hunt country. I had some extremely important business on hand in town, as it happens."

"What kind of business?" Emma regarded him curiously.

"Financial. Your trust and my own affairs," he told her. "There are some interesting government stocks being floated on the Exchange this week. I had intended to do some dealing."

"Is that how you manage to live so well?" she inquired, fascinated now. "I've always wondered how, without a feather to fly with, you always seem to live like a wealthy man." She gave a half laugh, confessing, "I just assumed you were in debt. I was always expecting to hear you'd been thrown into some sponging house."

"I'm flattered you should have found my affairs so interesting," he said in a voice as dry as sere leaves. "Had you asked, I would have told you. Ned was always well aware of my interest in the financial markets."

"Don't snub me, Alasdair. It was only natural I should wonder . . . and, no," she added, "I didn't ever think you wanted to marry me for my money. I know I said that once, but the provocation was insufferable. I just struck out with whatever came into my head."

Alasdair remembered the quarrel all too well. However, that particular accusation had not concerned him. He had understood perfectly that Emma had simply wanted to hurt him, but the weapon she'd grabbed in her anger had been so ridiculous it hadn't troubled him in the least.

"Well, we'll not reopen old wounds," he said. "Let's make up some lost time." He touched Phoenix with his heels and the horse broke into a gallop.

Emma hesitated, considering old wounds. Then she shrugged and set Swallow to follow.

They reached the Swan inn at Stevenage just after four o'clock. The post chaise had not yet arrived, but turned into the courtyard within half an hour.

Maria was heartily glad to be finished with the day's journey. "My bones are jangling," she complained, adding in case she hurt anyone's feelings with her complaint, "Not but that it isn't a very well-sprung chaise. But I own I'll be glad to lie down upon my bed for half an hour before dinner."

The Swan was a large posting-house, the yard a constant bustle of ostlers and postboys, busy with a constant stream of vehicles changing horses.

"I don't know how quiet it'll be overnight." Emma gestured to the noisy bustle around them. "We've taken a room for you at the back, away from the taproom. If you don't mind, Tilda shall sleep on the truckle bed in there with you."

"Oh, but she should sleep with you," Maria said, taking Emma's arm as they went into the inn. "In case you have need of her in the night."

"I shall not have need of her in the night," Emma said firmly and with perfect truth. "I don't care to sleep with anyone, anyway. So if you don't mind, Maria . . ."

"Oh, not at all. I own it'll be a comfort," Maria said instantly. "I don't like sleeping in inns, you know, my love. The sheets are so often damp, and one never knows who it is who's tramping around outside."

"The sheets have been thoroughly aired," Emma reassured her. "I discussed it with the housekeeper, who insisted that you would have nothing to fear. She's instructed a maid to air the sheets with a warming pan again, just to be on the safe side."

"Oh, you think of everything." Maria looked much happier.

"Well, why don't you and Tilda go up to your chamber now, and Tilda can help you undress so that you can rest before dinner. Alasdair's hired a private parlor and they'll serve dinner at six. Country hours, I know, but it's been a long day."

"Oh, goodness me, yes . . . and after last night!" Maria threw up her hands in horror. "Hardly a wink of sleep we had then. An early dinner and bed is just the thing we all need."

Chattering thus, she accompanied Emma to the handsome apartment at the back of the inn on the third floor where her portmanteau had already been carried by one of the inn servants.

"Oh, yes, this will do nicely." She took off her bonnet with a sigh of relief and sank down onto the bed. "Where are you to sleep, Emma dear? Close by, I trust."

"Uh . . . well, not exactly," Emma said. "They had no other chambers on this floor. I shall be on the floor below."

"Oh, goodness me, no! On a separate floor . . . on your own! No . . . no, my dear, that will never do!"

"Alasdair has a chamber on the same floor," Emma said. "In fact, right next door."

"Oh." Maria considered this as she unbuttoned her pelisse. "I think you should have Tilda with you, my love."

"No," Emma said firmly. "I shall not have Tilda."

Maria looked at her in silence for a second, her eyes unusually shrewd, then she said, "I suppose you know what's best, dear."

Emma smiled. "Yes, Maria, I do."

"I don't think it's quite proper, mind you," Maria said. "You and Lord Alasdair alone in adjoining rooms. I wouldn't be doing my duty, my love, if I didn't say so."

"No one is to know," Emma pointed out. She was not going to pretend if Maria chose not to. "Who are we likely to meet in Stevenage?"

"Very true." Maria nodded, then added diffidently, "It would make my heart glad if you and Lord Alasdair could . . . well, could come to an arrangement again. I always felt that you and he were so perfectly suited. I never did understand what happened."

Emma gave a rueful laugh. "We quarrel all the time, Maria. You know that. How could we be perfectly suited?"

"I don't know." Maria shook her head. "It is a puzzle, I agree. But I still think it's true."

Tilda came in at that moment and Emma, not sure whether she was glad or sorry to bring the subject to a close, left them together.

☙

The four horsemen passed the Swan soon after six o'clock. They didn't stop there, but rode instead to a smaller establishment on Danestrete.

"You know what to do, Luiz." Paul dismounted in the yard of the Hare and Hounds.

Luiz grunted in acknowledgment. He half fell from his nag and swore under his breath as he massaged his aching back and shook out his legs. "Godforsaken way of getting about," he muttered.

"We'll be here, waiting," Paul said, ignoring this complaint. "We'll take her after midnight, so you need to find a way to get at her without noise. You can do that?"

"Don't know till I see what's what," Luiz returned. He pulled down his hat, turned up the collar of his greatcoat, and slouched out of the yard, making his way to the Swan.

Paul gestured to his two remaining companions. "Take yourselves away . . . anywhere in the town. Just don't make yourselves noticeable. Come back here at midnight."

They took themselves off without a word, and Paul went off to do his own work. He hired a chaise and six fast horses from the Hare and Hounds with the instruction that they were to be ready and waiting in the church square at midnight. He had his own coachman, so would need no inn servants. The chaise and horses would be returned to the Hare and Hounds within the week. He paid well for the privilege. Then he went for his dinner.

Luiz slouched into the Swan's taproom and took up residence in a secluded corner. He ordered ale and did what he did best. Looked and listened.

He noted the preparations for a dinner for an aristocratic party in a private parlor abovestairs. He heard the discussions about the members of the party, about their insistence on having the sheets aired anew with warming pans. About the quality of the wine the gentleman had ordered to accompany their dinner.

He partook of dinner at the inn's ordinary table in

the company of a voluble group of travelers who, once they'd realized he wasn't of an outgoing nature, left him to his mutton and ale.

After dinner he took a stroll around the inn, a dark-clad figure who blended with the shadows, with the comings and goings of servants and customers alike. At the end of the evening, anyone would have been hard pressed to have offered a description of the nondescript and taciturn customer.

Chapter Fourteen

❦

Alasdair awoke with a start. A dreadful sense of foreboding filled his head like tangled cobwebs. He was lying on his belly, one arm flung across Emma's still form curled against him, the bedcovers tangled around their thighs. Her head was close to his on the pillow. He could hear her deep, regular breathing, feel her breath rustling against his cheek.

He knew someone was in the room before he felt the sharp, deadly prick of the knife on his back. The knowledge came with his first waking breath, while his limbs were still locked in sleep. Then came the knife. He lay rigid as a sharp line was drawn slowly down his spinal column, not breaking the skin . . . not yet.

"Get up slowly, Lord Alasdair."

It was the voice of Paul Denis. But that now came as no surprise.

Alasdair pushed himself upright, turning to look at

the intruders. In the gray-darkness of night, he could make out three men other than Denis. They had encircled the bed and they all regarded him without expression. Four pistols were aimed at his chest.

There was something familiar about one of the men. Something about the round-shouldered slouch. Of course . . . the man who'd been watching outside the house on Mount Street . . . who had climbed into the garden over the side wall.

Emma stirred and muttered, "What's the matter?" She rolled onto her back, opening her eyes. She gazed, disbelieving, at the figures around the bed, then with an instinctive movement reached down to cover herself with the tangled sheets.

Alasdair laid a hand on her shoulder in what little reassurance he could offer. He was consumed with rage at himself. He had locked the door but now that seemed the most pathetic precaution. A locked door would not keep out these predators. His mind worked furiously. He was one man, and a naked one at that, facing four assassins. His hand slid backward, feeling for the pistol beneath his pillow.

A gun barrel slammed into the side of his head. Emma cried out, a short, sharp sound that was instantly silenced by a pillow pressed against her face.

"For God's sake, leave her alone," Alasdair gasped, wiping the blood that trickled into his eye.

"Unfortunately, my business lies with Lady Emma . . . as well you know, Lord Alasdair," Denis said smoothly. He nodded to the man who held the pillow over Emma's face.

Emma gulped in air as the suffocating pressure was removed. She sat up, holding the covers to her throat. "You brute!" she declared, her fear for the moment subsumed in anger at what they'd done to Alasdair. "You unmitigated bastard!"

Paul offered a mocking bow. "Forgive me, but Lord Alasdair made it necessary." He turned back to Alasdair. "Would you be good enough to get up, please?"

Alasdair stood up, conscious of his nakedness, of his absolute vulnerability. Conscious now of the utterly pitiless eyes of the men he faced.

Paul Denis stepped to Emma's side of the bed. He bent and in one swift movement picked up the pillow and pressed her back into the mattress with the pillow against her face again. She flailed, fighting for breath, and then realized that she was not being suffocated, she was being silenced. If she lay still, she could breathe.

The dreadful sounds filled the room. They were soft and vile. The sounds of flesh slamming into flesh. From Alasdair came strange, ugly, animal sounds of protest and pain . . . not loud, more like sighs than cries.

Now Emma kicked and fought, biting the pillow that silenced her and kept her in darkness. She didn't know what they were doing to Alasdair . . . but she knew they were hurting him.

And then the sounds stopped.

When they stopped, Luiz, who held Alasdair's arms at his back, released him. The beaten body slid unconscious to the floor.

Paul raised the pillow from Emma's face. He held a scarf wadded in his hand and as she opened her mouth on a shriek of outrage, he crammed the wadded material into her mouth.

"Get dressed," he said quietly. "Unless you want us to take you from here as you stand."

Emma's shocked eyes found Alasdair's crumpled

figure on the floor. He was bleeding, his face swollen, his torso darkening with contusions. She retched, her chest and stomach heaving. She gagged violently on the scarf in her mouth. Tears streamed down her face. She made a move to pull out the gag and reeled as Paul hit her hard on the side of the head.

"Get dressed," he commanded again in the same quiet tones. She was aware now of the eyes of the men on her naked body. They were standing silently around the almost formless shape on the floor, two of them reflectively massaging their knuckles.

Emma stumbled to obey. Under the steady, interested gaze of her audience, she found her riding habit. She scrambled into it, desperate to cover herself, trying not to look at Alasdair because to do so would bring the dreadful nausea again and she couldn't vomit. She didn't dare touch the gag again, or even put her hands to her face to wipe away the tears that blocked her nose, poured down her cheeks.

Why did no one hear this horror? How could it be that in an inn full of guests and servants, no one was aware of what was going on in this chamber? But it had all been so quiet, so swift, so mercilessly efficient.

When she was dressed, Paul bound her wrists behind her with a thin leather strap. He bound them tightly and the strap bit into the tender flesh, chafing her wrist bones immediately. He moved her toward the door with a hand in the small of her back.

He bent his head to her ear and said almost pleasantly, "Lord Alasdair is still alive, I believe. He will not remain so if you do anything other than put one foot in front of you until I tell you otherwise. Is that clear?"

Emma nodded her head. She didn't believe Paul Denis would tell her the truth, but if there was the faintest possibility that Alasdair had not died beneath those savage fists, then she could do nothing but obey her abductor.

They passed along the corridor and down the stairs like spirits through a house of dreamers. There was no sound beyond the ordinary creaking and settling of the old building. Luiz opened a side door that let them out into the street, well away from the stables, where a restless horse or a prowling dog might give the alarm.

They progressed, as silently as before, through the dark streets of the sleeping town. In front of the church, the post chaise with its six horses stood in the charge of a sleepy postilion from the Hare and Hounds.

As if following a rehearsed and well-orchestrated movement, Luiz stepped in front of Emma as Paul stepped forward to speak to the postilion. One of the other men was behind her, and she found herself bundled upward between them into the chaise, thrust into the far corner. The postilion would never have seen her.

Paul paid the postilion, who loped off to his bed, only mildly curious as to why the gent should choose to travel at dead of night. Luiz jumped from the chaise and onto the box. His two assistants sprang into the saddles of the two leading horses. Paul in leisurely fashion entered the chaise.

He sat opposite Emma, regarding her thoughtfully. She returned his stare with a baleful one of her own. Her head was clearing, her terror receding somewhat if she didn't allow herself to think of Alasdair. She knew what Paul Denis wanted of her. She knew that he would go to any lengths to get it. But could she perhaps persuade him that she didn't have it? As an option, it didn't seem promising. But it was the only one she had.

The chaise rattled at breakneck speed out of Stevenage on the London road. Emma had no way of telling which direction they were taking. The blinds were drawn over the windows and she was conscious only of the speed of their progress. The strap binding her wrists was biting deep now, and her hands were beginning to tingle. She tried to spit out the gag, but her mouth was so dry she couldn't manage to work her tongue loose.

"Don't worry, Lady Emma," Paul said, as he saw her struggles. "When it's time for you to talk, you'll be able to. And you'll talk to good purpose. Until then, if you'll take my advice, you'll save your breath until you need it." He smiled, a flicker of his mouth in the gloom, folded his arms, and closed his eyes.

☙

Jemmy threw down the dice with an exclamation of disgust. "Lord, but you was always a devil wi' the dice, Sam."

Sam grinned and reached for his ale pot. "Anyone else?" he invited.

The other men shook their heads. "Nah, I'm about done fer the night." An ostler got up from the upturned barrel where he was sitting and stretched. "You see that chaise goin' 'ell fer leather down the main street?"

"No." Jemmy stood up and followed him to the door of the tack room. "Goin' which way?"

"Lunnon. Six 'osses kickin' up some dust."

"When?"

"Oh, abaht 'alf an 'our ago. When I went out for a piss." He scratched his groin in comfortable recollection. "Not many folks take to the 'ighway at this time o' night."

"No," Jemmy agreed thoughtfully. He turned back to the fusty warmth of the tack room, which smelled of leather, horseflesh, sweat, and ale. "Sam, you reckon the master'd be interested in a chaise goin' 'ell fer leather to London?"

"At this hour?" Sam drained his ale and swept the handful of coins off the upturned box they'd been using as a table, dropping them into the deep pocket of his britches. "You know 'im better'n me, old lad."

"Said as 'ow we've to keep our ears an' eyes on the lookout fer anythin' unusual," Jemmy said in the same reflective tone. "Reckon we'd best tell 'im."

Sam shrugged agreeably. "Don't take both of us."

"He might 'ave orders fer us both," Jemmy said. "Best you come too." He tugged at the bottom of his jerkin as if preparing himself for the interview. "Come on, then."

Sam followed him, yawning prodigiously.

They entered the inn by the back door that opened onto the inner courtyard, and crossed the somnolent kitchen. "You know where Lord Alasdair's lodged?" Sam inquired through another vast yawn.

"Aye," Jemmy said shortly. He led the way up the back stairs and turned unerringly down the corridor leading to the front of the inn. At Alasdair's door, he paused, his hand on the latch. Then tentatively he knocked. There was no reply. He knocked again. Still no answer.

"Reckon you'll be disturbin' 'is beauty sleep," Sam offered helpfully.

Jemmy didn't respond to this obvious fact. He raised the latch and pushed the door open. The chamber was empty, the bed unslept in. Jemmy scratched his head. "I'd swear it was this'un. I was in 'ere this evenin' when the master was dressin' fer dinner. He give me me orders fer the mornin'."

"Well, he ain't 'ere now," Sam declared with another yawn. "I'm fer me bed." He turned to leave, then stopped. "Eh, what was that, then?"

Jemmy had heard it too. A faint moan from the other side of the wall. He stood stock-still, head cocked toward the wall. It came again.

The two men exchanged a look, then with one mind raced from the room to the door to the neighboring chamber. The door was not properly closed and swung open with a slight push.

"Lord-a-mercy!" Jemmy exclaimed, dropping to his knees beside the crumpled figure. "Lord-a-mercy."

Sam bent over Alasdair, pressing his finger to the carotid artery. " 'E's alive," he said. "Saints alive! Whoever did this knew what they were adoin'." He examined Alasdair's body with a degree almost of respect as one who had had experience of the finer points of beating a man to a pulp.

Jemmy gave a grunt of disgust. He stood up and fetched the jug of water from the washstand. "I 'ates to do it," he muttered, "but 'e needs to come back." He dashed the contents of the jug into Alasdair's face.

Alasdair came to. He turned his head sideways and vomited in agonizing misery, waves of nausea coursing through him as his excruciated body returned to full awareness.

"Eh, sir, easy now." Jemmy held his head until the sickness receded. "Lie still while we see what the damage is." He laid his head gently down again.

Alasdair closed his eyes. His mind was a blank; he was aware of nothing but pain. And then gradually memory returned. He groaned in a horror of despair. They had Emma.

"Coupla broken ribs, I'd say." Sam's knowledgeable hands were moving over Alasdair's body. "Collarbone's all right, though." He sat back on his heels and pronounced, "Could be worse . . . aye, could be a lot worse."

Alasdair tried to find some comfort in this, but looked in vain. For a moment of pure self-indulgence, he wished he were dead, out of this pain, and out of the dread that consumed him.

"We'll strap up the ribs, sir," Jemmy offered. "Not much else you can do wi' 'em." He spoke with the authority of one who had broken a good few in his career as a jockey. "The bruisin's summat chronic. Must 'urt like the devil."

"An understatement, my friend." Alasdair was astonished that he could produce such a dry response. He tried to sit up and immediately blacked out again.

When he came to, Jemmy was efficiently strapping his ribs with strips of linen torn from the bedsheets. "Sam's gone to fetch arnica and witch 'azel, sir. 'E says a poultice of mallows'd be best, but he ain't got any to 'and. We'll get some from the apothecary when it's daylight."

He sat back and examined his handiwork, then slid an arm behind Alasdair's shoulders. "Let's see if you can sit up now, sir."

Alasdair tried to help himself but the strain on his abused stomach muscles made him cry out, and Jemmy took his full weight, heaving him into a sitting position.

The effort exhausted Alasdair and he leaned back against the wall, eyes closed, his breath coming in ragged, labored gasps.

"There's laudanum too," Sam announced as he came hurrying back into the room with an old leather kit bag. "A good dose o' that, sir, an' a good long sleep." He set the bag down and took out vials of arnica, witch hazel, and laudanum.

"Sam's somethin' of an 'orse doctor," Jemmy informed Alasdair, stepping aside so Sam could go to work.

"Then do what you can," Alasdair said. "But the laudanum'll have to wait. Saddle Phoenix and two others from the stables here. They need to be strong and fast."

"Eh, sir, you'll not be ridin'!" Jemmy was aghast.

"You seem remarkably uncurious as to why you find me in this miserable condition," Alasdair observed with a gallant effort at his customary sardonic humor, hoping thus to keep the threatening panic at bay.

"Eh, sir, I 'aven't 'ad a chance." Jemmy defended his lack of curiosity with a hurt air. "We was too busy."

"Yes . . . yes." Alasdair raised a placatory hand. "Lady Emma has been abducted." He closed his eyes again, trying to force away the pain and the dread. If he allowed his desperation to take over, he would lose what little strength and will he had remaining.

"We have very little time to get her back before . . ." He shook his head. He *must* not think about what they could be doing to her.

"Eh, mebbe she was in that post chaise, then," Jemmy said.

Alasdair's head seemed to clear. His eyes focused properly for the first time. "What post chaise?"

"That's what we come to tell you, sir." Jemmy gave his news.

Alasdair listened, feeling the first faint glimmer of hope. If they knew what they were following and which direction to take, they had a chance. Denis would not have expected the beaten man to recover consciousness until the morning. Probably not until he was discovered by an inn servant much later. By which time Denis would be well away, plunged into the dark chaos of London's underbelly, where Emma could be hidden and disposed of without remark.

"There, sir, that's the best I can do." Sam stood up, regarding his patient with concern. "I doubt you'll be able to sit an 'orse, though."

"I must. Help me stand up." Alasdair took a deep breath and gathered his forces. The deep breath sent an agonizing shaft of pain stabbing into his chest.

Jemmy and Sam took his arms and heaved him upright. His head spun and the blackness threatened to engulf him again. But he fought it off. Breathing was an agony and he tried to take shallow breaths.

"Sam, go and see to the horses. Jemmy, help me dress."

"Take a small dose of laudanum, sir," Jemmy suggested. "Just enough to take the edge off, but not enough to put you out."

"Aye. Riders do it all the time." Sam produced his vial. "It'll 'elp."

Alasdair decided that the combined advice of an ex-jockey and a man whose face was as battered as a prizefighter's was worth taking. He swallowed the measured dose Sam handed him.

Even with Jemmy's assistance, dressing was so painful and such an effort that he wondered how it had ever been so simple and automatic a procedure he had never given it a thought. His head was clearing fast though, the pain becoming a part of him so that it no longer encompassed him and blocked all else from his mind.

"Did you say six horses, Jemmy?" Barely breathing, he eased his jacket over his shoulders.

"Aye, sir. Goin' like bats outta hell." Gently, Jemmy drew the sides of the jacket closed over Alasdair's strapped-up chest.

Alasdair glanced at the clock on the mantelpiece. It said three o'clock. He calculated rapidly. The chaise had maybe a two-hour start. But they would have to change horses somewhere. Or at least rest them. They certainly couldn't drive them at racing speed for any length of time. Fast-riding horses would have a chance to overtake them on the turnpike.

Unless they took the byways. But Alasdair dismissed that possibility. A chaise and six would have a hard time on the narrow, rutted lanes across country.

He sat down gingerly on the end of the bed, and Jemmy put his boots on for him. Bending was an impossibility. His eye caught his image in the mirror on the dresser. He was surprised to see that his face was less marked than he'd expected. They had concentrated most of their blows on his ribs, abdomen, and kidneys. Presumably it was where they could do the most damage in the shortest space of time, he reflected grimly. The attack had been utterly without the personal malice that would have led his assailants to disfigure him.

And these men with the same chilling efficiency would soon be working on Emma.

He stood up again. "Bring my pistols, Jemmy. They're under the pillow." He walked to the door, every step a supreme effort of will. But now he was infused with a terror-fueled determination that transcended his body's weakness.

Sam was waiting for them in front of the inn. He led Phoenix to the mounting block used by ladies, and overweight squires after an indulgent evening in the inn's taproom.

Alasdair managed to heave himself into the saddle, where he slumped for a minute, getting his breath back. It was so hard when he could take only these short, shallow breaths. Then he straightened in the saddle, taking up the reins.

Jemmy fastened the pair of pistols to the saddle. "You and Sam have your own?" Alasdair asked, adding grimly, "You'll be needing them."

"Oh, aye," Sam said. "Pistols and this." He grinned, and the moonlight caught the flourish of a curved cutlass. "Prefer knives. They're quieter."

"Oh, there's nothin' like a blunderbuss for creatin' mayhem," Jemmy said with his own grin, patting the weapon that was strapped to his own saddle.

Alasdair felt his optimism grow a little at his companions' apparent enthusiasm for a scrap. He had little doubt that their skill and courage matched their enthusiasm.

"Let's go."

They took the London road at a gallop.

❦

Emma had lost the feeling in her hands after the first interminable hour. Her head pounded remorselessly. Her fear grew with every passing moment. Paul Denis sat opposite her, his arms folded, his eyes sometimes closed, but mostly they watched her with all the cold interest of a snake watching the approach of a prey.

He had no reason to keep her in this acute physical discomfort except to soften her up for what was to come. To increase her dreadful anticipation. And it was working. By degrees her determination to resist his questions, to deny all knowledge of Ned's poem, was being eaten away.

She was not prepared for the moment when Paul leaned forward suddenly and pulled the gag from her mouth. The relief was astounding. But for a moment she still couldn't speak. It was as if her tongue had lost the power or the memory of movement.

"So, let us talk a little of your brother."

She stared blankly at him, trying to moisten her parched mouth.

"Would you like water?" he inquired almost solicitously.

Emma nodded.

He bent and brought a leather flask from beneath the seat. He opened it and held it to her lips. She drank greedily, heedless of the water spilling down her chin. He took away the flask long before she'd slaked her thirst, but at least it was better than nothing.

"So?" he said, replacing the stopper. "Your brother. Let us talk a little of Lord Edward Beaumont."

Emma thought of Alasdair, lying unconscious, beaten and broken. She faced Paul Denis, her eyes flaring in her pale face. "My brother is dead," she said. "Why would you be interested in him?"

"Oh, I believe you know," Paul said, leaning back and folding his arms again. "I'm quite certain your lover has told you all there is to know. Why else would you be trying to escape me?"

"Why indeed?" Emma said with scorn. "Whatever makes you think we were trying to escape anyone? We were going into Lincolnshire for the hunting."

"Oh, come now, don't try my patience." He shook

his head almost regretfully. "It's really not in your interests to do so."

Emma closed her mouth firmly, although her belly was quivering with dread. She didn't think she'd ever met anyone as intrinsically terrifying as Paul Denis. She couldn't understand why she hadn't noticed it before. But she had, deep down. She'd been aware of that predatory aspect to his nature. She'd been aware of his air of being perpetually poised to strike. And God help her, there had been a time when she'd found it attractive.

"I can't feel my hands," she said.

"A pity." He shrugged. Then he moved abruptly, leaning forward, seizing her jacket at the throat, jerking her upright so that her face was very close to his. "You received a communication from your brother after his death. What did it say?"

His breath was hot and slightly sour. His black eyes were pinpricks of menace. Emma tried to pull away. His hand tightened and his knuckles pressed against the pulse in her throat.

"His last letter was full of instructions about the estate," she said, trying to turn her head aside. "I can't remember all the details. Why would they interest you?"

"Your brother was a spy, and a courier, and a master encoder," Paul stated, articulating each word so that they were spat at her.

"Was he?" She made her voice careless. "I didn't know."

He pushed her from him with a vicious movement, and she fell back onto the seat in a heap, unable to help herself with her hands.

He leaned forward, grabbing her face, pressing his fingers into her cheeks so that tears started in her eyes. He forced open her mouth and shoved the wadded scarf inside. Then, his face wiped clear of all expression, he lifted the blind at the window and leaned out.

"Luiz!"

"Aye, Paolo?" Luiz slowed his horses and leaned down from the box.

"Find a place to turn off. I want a secluded field. No houses in sight. Nothing within earshot," he said in a short staccato burst of instruction.

Emma began to tremble deep inside. Her skin was cold and clammy. She looked at him fearfully.

"We might as well start our little discourse now," he said in conversational tones. "I had hoped you'd prove to be a little more sensible. A little more accommodating. But, no matter." He shrugged. "It's all the same to me how I get what I want."

The carriage swung abruptly to the right. The iron wheels thudded along a deeply rutted track. He had left the blind up at the window, and Emma saw the dark bulk of the hedge, so close to the side of the carriage that it brushed the varnish with a lonely scraping sound. They must be on a very narrow cart track.

"This'll do," Luiz called down, as he reined in the horses. "No one for miles around that I can see."

Paul opened the door and jumped down. It was bright moonlight, a crisp, cold night. He looked along the dark track, then jumped over a narrow ditch into a stubble field where a stand of poplars served as a windbreak. There was no sign of habitation.

"Bring the woman."

Luiz hauled Emma out of the chaise. She stumbled to her knees as she half fell from the high step. He yanked her up and propelled her across the ditch and into the field.

"I'll be taking care of the horses," he said to Paolo. "You don't need me for this business."

His discomfort was apparent and Emma had a faint flicker of hope that maybe he would come to her aid. But it died immediately when he turned and stomped out of the field, and the two thugs who'd been riding the horses crossed the ditch and came over to them.

"Light a fire," Paul instructed. "Over by those trees."

No one seemed to be taking any notice of her. Emma looked around. Could she make a run for it? But even as she assessed the hopeless prospect, Paul swung back to her. "Get over by the trees." He prodded her in the small of her back, pushing her forward.

She stumbled over the hard-packed stubble to the stand of trees, where the two men were busy gathering kindling and bigger branches. Why was he lighting a fire? Because he was cold? Because he liked to be comfortable when interrogating his victims?

Numbly she watched the kindling catch, and then the bigger branches. Smoke curled, a flame shot up.

"Put her down." Paul's instruction came out of the night like a pistol shot. The two men caught Emma and forced her to the ground beside the fire; one of them held her shoulders against the ground; the other unlaced her boots.

And then she understood. She could feel the heat of the fire on her bare feet. Horror filled her.

"Your brother's last letter to you," Paul said kneeling beside her. "Let's see how much you can remember, shall we?"

Chapter Fifteen

"Looks like they were goin' quite a clip," Jemmy observed, examining the tracks of the chaise and its six horses. "Them 'osses are beginin' to tire about 'ere. What d'ye think, Sam?"

Sam dismounted for a closer look. "Aye," he agreed. "The leaders're pullin' to the left."

"Well, let's get on." Alasdair was impatient with this and yet he knew it was necessary. If the chaise left the turnpike at any point and they weren't watching for it, they could overshoot it. Neither did he want to come thundering down upon them. They were outnumbered already, and he'd be no good in his present condition in hand-to-hand combat. Stealth and surprise were his only advantage.

They rode on under the moonlight. Jemmy and Sam knew how to get the best out of their mounts, and their horses fairly skimmed the ground. Phoenix matched them easily. But Alasdair knew that they had to make up a two-hour start.

The laudanum had dulled his pain and it existed now on the periphery of his awareness, waiting in the wings. His mind was clear, examining and discarding options. Should they spring their attack on the road or wait until they reached London? An ambush would be the best chance, but they'd have to get ahead of the chaise for that. Once it was daylight, opportunities would be fewer.

Finchley Common. An ambush on the heath. There were any number of suitable places there. If they could get there first, they could lie in wait.

"Eh, they've gone off 'ere."

Sam's hissing whisper snapped against his absorption, and he looked up.

"See." Sam gestured to the ground with his whip. "They've turned the chaise right 'ere. Gone off down that cart track."

"Bleedin' stupid thing to do," Jemmy opined. "It ain't 'ardly wide enough for a gig."

"Why?" Alasdair said, staring around. He thought he could detect the faintest lightening of the eastern sky. The false dawn. Did Denis have a hideout somewhere around? Was he not taking Emma to London after all?

But the questions were pointless. He swung Phoenix onto the path. "No sound now," he murmured. "They may be close."

They followed the tracks in the mud until the lane curved around. Alasdair drew rein and beckoned to Sam to come up beside him on the narrow path. "Dismount and take a look," he mouthed, the words little more than a soft rustle in the cold air.

Sam swung down and moved into the deep shadows of the overgrown hedge. He crept around the corner.

Alasdair waited, his heart in his mouth, hideous dread clutching at his soul. Was he too late?

Sam was gone for what seemed an eternity, during which Alasdair became aware of every bruise on his body. The laudanum was wearing off and the effects of his two hours on horseback became screamingly evident.

When Sam materialized out of the shadows of the hedge, Alasdair controlled the impulse to yell at him. "Well?" he whispered.

"They've stopped about a hundred yards down the track. One man's left in charge of the 'osses. T'others are in a field. They've lit a fire." He looked up at Alasdair, still on his horse. "Reckon they're attendin' to Lady Emma by the fire," he said steadily.

Alasdair's already white face was ghastly, the moonlight giving it a greenish, waxen tinge. But his brain was now as cold and deadly as a rapier. If they were working on her, they hadn't killed her. That was all he needed to think about.

"Sam, can you take the man with the horses? Silently!"

"Aye, reckon so." Sam fingered the cutlass at his belt.

Alasdair dismounted stiffly, but he no longer felt pain. His body moved as his brain directed, ignoring every other signal.

Jemmy dismounted beside him and swiftly tethered the three horses.

"Go now, then. Take the man and release the horses from the traces," Alasdair instructed Sam. "We'll give you ten minutes before we make our own move."

Ten minutes! He would not think what they could

do to Emma in ten minutes. "Jemmy and I will approach across the field here. We need to make it seem that we're many more than we are. When you hear Jemmy's blunderbuss, you drive the horses at the men in the field. I want chaos. You understand me?"

Both men nodded immediately. Jemmy reached up for his blunderbuss. It was primed with lead shot that would spew forth in a wide scattering arc of destruction.

Alasdair took his pistols. He would have one shot with each. They would have to count. And Paul Denis would have one of them.

Emma was sweating. The ground she lay on was hard, frozen mud, but her body was bathed in sweat. The fire's heat was intense and the soles of her feet, although not yet burned, seemed to curl and shrivel in dreadful anticipation.

Paul Denis had pulled the gag from her mouth and now he was talking quietly to her. She could feel hands banding her ankles. As he spoke they pulled her shrinking feet closer to the heat. She wanted to tell him what he wanted, but something, some deep, stubborn cell of pride, would not let her.

She thought of Ned. She thought of Alasdair. She let her mind drift back to childhood. To all the things they had done together. She thought she could hear Ned's rich laugh, Alasdair's teasing voice. They were in the summer fields, following the haymakers. She could hear the steady swing of the scythes, the swish of the flails. She could taste strawberries on her tongue.

She screamed.

Alasdair heard the scream. He heard it on some distant plane. He continued to move around the field,
clinging to the hedge, Jemmy just behind him. The
flames of the fire lit the scene. The three crouched
figures around one on the ground. He judged the distance carefully. They would have to be close enough
for the blunderbuss to do damage as they charged,
but not so close that they would be detected before
they were ready.

His pistols were in his hands. His body was moving
as fluidly as water now. It didn't seem to belong to
him, but that didn't matter. He backed up against the
hedge when he could see the outline of the chaise on
the track through the bare branches. Then he nodded
to Jemmy.

Jemmy leaped from the shadows with a great
skirling yell of triumph. He ran forward a few paces
before he fired the blunderbuss. Alasdair was just behind him, his pistols ready as he searched for his target.

Sam fired a pistol from beyond the hedge, and the
entire team of horses plunged across the ditch and
into the field, driven by Sam, cracking his whip. The
horses raced toward the fire before they realized what
it was, then they reared back, nostrils flaring at the
smell of smoke, the heat of the flames. Sam whipped
at them and they careened forward again, rearing,
hooves flailing.

The men at the fire leaped to their feet, trying to get
out of the way of the flailing hooves. The shot from
Jemmy's blunderbuss swept through them.

Alasdair raised his pistol and sighted. Paul Denis
stood outlined against the flames. Alasdair squeezed

the trigger. Paul fell to his knees, clutching his shoulder.

Sam's pistol sounded as he waded into the fray. He cast aside the gun and his cutlass flashed. He was grinning with the sheer joy of the fight as he slashed to left and right.

Paul's men struggled to recover themselves but it was too late. One of them managed to get off a shot from his pistol, but it flew harmlessly across the field to bury itself in the trunk of a poplar. Sam's cutlass slashed across his arm, immobilizing him. The other fell beneath a blow from Jemmy's cudgel, kept in reserve.

Emma had tried to roll herself clear of both the fire and the rampaging horses. But with her hands still bound at her back, pressed to the ground beneath her body, she could get no leverage. She curled herself into a ball and held her breath.

Then suddenly there was silence. A great calm seemed to settle over them. Emma wrists were suddenly freed. She still couldn't feel her hands, but a great wash of relief flooded her.

Alasdair bent over her. He tried to lift her but couldn't, and it was Sam who hoisted her into his arms. "Eh, you all right, lass?" he asked, his voice thick with concern.

"Just about," she said, looking at Alasdair in wonder and disbelief. "I was so afraid they'd killed you."

He shook his head in swift dismissal and took her feet in his hands. He swore a vile oath as he saw the blisters. He turned to Paul Denis, who had staggered to his feet, his hand pressed to his shoulder. Blood welled from between his fingers.

"I owe you a few minutes of my time," Alasdair

said quietly. Without taking his eyes off Denis, he gestured to Jemmy.

Jemmy, in immediate comprehension, without a word handed him the long coachman's whip.

Alasdair curled his fingers around the smooth wooden handle. Still without looking away from Denis, he instructed evenly, "Sam, take Emma to the chaise, and Jemmy, get the horses back in the traces. Give me five minutes with this scum and then both come back and help me secure them."

"Right y'are." Sam nodded cheerfully and set off with his burden back to the lane.

Jemmy looked a little doubtful. Lord Alasdair was still in bad shape, and he didn't like the idea of leaving him with three men, even though they were all handicapped. But Lord Alasdair's expression was such that the tiger could almost find it in him to feel sorry for the three men. With a short nod, he went off to round up the horses.

It seemed to take Emma a long time to realize that the nightmare was over. Sam carried her with as much ease as if she were a featherweight, his brawny arms cradling her with comforting strength. She was as cold now as she'd been hot before, shivers coursing through her, her teeth chattering.

"It's the shock, lass," Sam said as he lifted her into the chaise. " 'As that effect on a body. I'll fetch ye summat for it."

He disappeared for a minute or two, during which she could hear Jemmy talking to the horses, calming them as he put them back in the traces. Emma thought she ought to get out and help him. But when she set her feet to the floor of the chaise, the pain was so intense she fell back with an involuntary cry. Vaguely she wondered what had happened to the fourth man, the one called Luiz who had been driving the chaise.

Sam returned with a leather kit bag and flask. He unstoppered the flask and held it to her lips. " 'Ere, take a good swig o' this."

It was rough brandy that scorched her throat and jolted her belly. But the fumes alone seemed to bring her out of her strange trance. She sat up and shook her head as if to dispel the lingering tendrils of the nightmare.

She held her hands in her lap. They were a curious dead white and she couldn't seem to make them move . . . not even her fingers. "They won't work," she said to Sam in a plaintive little voice.

He took each hand in turn and chafed it between his rough, callused palms. "They'll come back in a minute, lass."

Emma decided to believe him. Sam had transferred his attention to her feet. The burned flesh stung dreadfully, but the upper part of each foot was numb with cold.

Sam rummaged in his medicine bag and brought out a foul-smelling ointment that he slathered on the soles of her feet. It had an immediate soothing effect.

"I'll be off to 'elp the master now. Sit tight 'ere, an' we'll be back in a minute or two." He jumped from the chaise and bent to examine the figure of the coachman, lying motionless in the ditch where Sam had rolled him after hitting him over the head with a stout stick. "Eh," Sam muttered. "Best take you along, fellow-me-lad." He hoisted Luiz over his shoulder and carried him back to the field.

Alasdair was standing over Paul Denis, the lash of the long carriage whip trailing on the ground at his side. Paul Denis lay on the ground in a fetal curl, barely conscious.

Sam dumped Luiz on the ground beside the other two men, who, no longer a pair of expressionless instruments of violence, stared fearfully at the avenging devil with the whip.

"Tie them up," Alasdair instructed curtly. "Gag them, then put them in the trees, out of sight. I want them left here to be picked up later."

Charles Lester would be very glad to get his hands on Paul Denis.

Sam and Jemmy went about their work with cheerful enthusiasm. Alasdair, once more back in his abused and pain-filled body, couldn't help them. He turned and made his way to the chaise, every step an agony now.

He hauled himself into the chaise and fell back onto the seat opposite Emma, closing his eyes, his breathing shallow and ragged.

"Alasdair!" Emma leaned over and tried to take his hands. Then she gasped as the circulation began to return to her own hands and they came to agonizing life. "God in heaven!" She clasped them between her knees, pressing tightly in an effort to contain the pain.

Alasdair opened his eyes immediately. "What is it, sweet?"

"Just my hands. They're starting to work again." She offered him a tremulous smile, saying with a supreme effort at humor, "What a pathetic pair of casualties we are. I was trying to touch you but I can't seem to manage it."

"I want to hold you but I can't seem to manage it," he responded, trying to match her tone.

"That was one adventure I'd rather not have again, if I can possibly help it," Emma said with another valiant smile. As a child she had always been yearning for adventure, following Ned and Alasdair, dogging their footsteps because she was convinced they would have an adventure and she wouldn't be there to share it.

An answering smile flickered over Alasdair's set mouth as he caught the reference. "That, my sweet, was the kind of experience that gives adventures a bad name. Even Ned would agree."

"Are you going to be all right?" Her smile vanished now. He looked dreadful. Gray and green and waxy, his eyes pain-filled hollows.

"I feel as if I've been trampled by a team of shire horses," he confessed ruefully. "But Jemmy assures me it's nothing worse than bruises and a couple of broken ribs." He took a few shallow breaths, then said, "How are your feet?"

"Sam put something on them. I don't feel them anymore." She looked at him with a worried frown, then said, "Did you kill Denis?"

"Not quite," he said in a flat voice. "I might have done so, except that there are a few people who are *really* going to want to talk to him."

"Then I hope they talk to him in the way he talked to me," Emma said savagely.

"We're ready to go, sir." Jemmy stuck his head through the open door. "We've tethered t'other 'osses to the carriage. We goin' back to Stevenage, or on to London?"

"What of Maria?" Emma exclaimed suddenly. "She'll be out of her head with worry. We have to go back to Stevenage."

"No, we have to go straight to London," Alasdair said. "I have to arrange for those animals to be collected before I do anything else. We'll change horses at Barnet and hire postilions and a coachman to take you and me on from there. Sam and Jemmy will ride back to Stevenage with a note for Maria. They can arrange for her immediate return to Mount Street."

"Right y'are, sir." Jemmy closed the door of the chaise and vaulted onto the back of one of the leaders. Sam flicked his whip and the team started forward along the narrow track.

"There's brandy in that bag of Sam's." Emma indicated the kit bag on the seat beside Alasdair.

He found the flask and drank deeply, then leaned forward and held it to Emma's mouth. "This is damnable!" he swore. "I need to hold you so badly, but I can't move a muscle. And if it weren't for my own godforsaken stupidity, none of this would have happened!"

"How was it your fault?"

"I should have taken more precautions at the inn," he said bitterly, taking another swallow of brandy. "I should have had Sam or Jemmy posted outside the door . . . I should have moved your chamber at the last minute to throw them off the scent . . . I should have stayed awake. . . . Oh, the list is endless."

Emma frowned. "You talk like someone who does this kind of thing all the time. First I discover that my brother is some kind of spy and . . . and . . ." She frowned, trying to remember what Denis had said. "A master encoder, that was it. And now it seems you're a professional bodyguard or some such."

Alasdair shook his head. "No, I'm afraid not. I'm a hopeless amateur. I was dragged into this business because Ned's masters at Horseguards thought that as an old friend and now your trustee, I'd be able to get close enough to you to find the document. In the best of all possible worlds, I would have searched your rooms and discovered the poem without your being any the wiser."

Emma was silent. She was too tired and drained to think clearly, but she didn't like the feeling that for weeks she'd been discussed and manipulated by faceless men who knew nothing about her. And she didn't like the idea that Alasdair had had more than one motive for involving himself in her life again.

"Why did you agree to do it?" she asked after a minute.

"For Ned," he replied simply. "Ned died for the information in that poem. He wasn't to have died in vain."

Emma nodded. She could find no fault with that. And yet she was still dismayed at the realization that Alasdair had in some sort been spying on her. He hadn't confided in her until his hand had been forced. He was still as secretive as ever.

She closed her eyes and tried not to think of anything at all. Her feet had begun to sting again, and she didn't know why, instead of feeling joy and relief that the nightmare was over, she simply wanted to cry like a baby.

Alasdair gave his body up to the rocking motion of the chaise. Every jolt hurt him as if he were on the rack, but his guilt and self-directed anger were much the harder things to bear. He could feel Emma's distress, but he didn't know how to alleviate it. He lifted her feet onto his lap, cradling them in his palms. It was the only thing he could do . . . the only way he could touch her in his present state of disrepair.

Chapter Sixteen

꧁

Maria fairly hurled herself up the steps of the house on Mount Street. Harris opened the door for her and she almost tumbled into the hall, untying the ribbons of her bonnet.

"Where is Lady Emma? Has Dr. Baillie been sent for? Oh, my goodness, what a terrible thing. Cook must make some calves' foot jelly at once. And some gruel . . . oh, my heart! My heart! The palpitations!" She ran up the stairs, discarded shawls, bonnet, reticule, and gloves falling around her as the words poured forth upon the stolid Harris, who followed her, picking up the scattered belongings.

"Dr. Baillie is with Lady Emma now, madam. Cook would have already prepared the jelly," he assured her, a touch defensively, "but Lady Emma, as we all know, doesn't care for calves' foot jelly."

"Oh, but she must . . . she must. Tell cook at

once." Maria flew along the corridor to Emma's chamber.

"Oh, dearest, dearest girl!" She burst in. "Alasdair's note . . . I didn't know what to make of it. An accident, he said. Oh, my heart!" She patted her chest with a trembling hand. "An accident in the middle of the night! What could you have been doing, my love? Oh, doctor, the case is not desperate, I trust."

She flew to the bed and bent to kiss Emma before collapsing on the chaise longue, fanning herself with her hand.

"No, indeed not desperate, Mrs. Witherspoon," the doctor reassured her. "Lady Emma has some burns on her feet. I have dressed them with salve."

"Burns!" Maria's round eyes opened like saucers. "On your feet! However could that have happened, my dearest love?"

"I fell asleep with my feet on the fender," Emma said. "Very foolish of me." She was sitting up on the bed, fully dressed except for stockings and shoes. "Pray calm yourself, Maria. This is no great matter."

"Oh, why aren't you in bed? You must be undressed and put between the sheets at once. Must she not, doctor?" Maria flew up from her perch. "I'll fetch Tilda to you. And there must be calves' foot jelly."

"Maria, I loathe calves' foot jelly," Emma protested. It was Maria's answer to all ills. "And I have no need to go to bed. It's barely noon."

But she spoke to empty air. Maria had run off, calling for Tilda.

"You'll not want to go walking about on those feet for a day or two," Baillie said, finishing his bandaging. "Fell asleep with your feet on the fender?" He raised a disbelieving eyebrow.

"Yes," Emma said firmly. "Wasn't it foolish of me?"

"Must have been a very heavy sleep," Baillie said pointedly. "For you not to wake up with the pain."

"I sleep very heavily, doctor."

"Oh, is that so?" He began to repack his bag. "I've another patient to see. Very busy morning, this. Seems Lord Alasdair Chase had a bit of an accident too."

"Oh, really," Emma said with an air of shocked curiosity. "What an astonishing coincidence. It must have occurred after we returned to town. Was it a riding accident perhaps?"

"A driving accident, I understand. He overturned his curricle and the wheels ran over him. Very nasty, his man says."

"How unfortunate." Emma shook her head and tutted. "And Lord Alasdair is a veritable nonpareil, too."

"I daresay even a nonpareil can misjudge his horses," the doctor observed dryly. "Now, if you'll take my advice, Lady Emma, you'll swallow a dose of laudanum and get some rest." He cast her a shrewdly assessing look. "You've had something of a shock, I'd say. Over and above the burns. Not looking too chipper at all."

Emma was feeling far from chipper. Indeed the prospect of a period of unconsciousness was very appealing. But she was anxious about Alasdair and knew she wouldn't be able to rest until she'd had a report from Jemmy about the doctor's visit.

Maria came bustling in with a silver porringer. "Here's some barley broth for you, my love. Very strengthening. And if you won't take the jelly, I've instructed cook to make up a tisane to my own special recipe."

She set the porringer on the bedside table, continuing in almost the same breath, "I'll send for you immediately if there's the slightest cause for concern, Dr. Baillie."

"There won't be," Emma said, wondering what Maria was going to make of the news that Alasdair also had suffered an accident . . . an unrelated accident, of course. But nonetheless the coincidence would pique anyone's curiosity.

"Dr. Baillie has to attend to his other patients, Maria," she declared firmly. "I shall go on very well now."

Maria accompanied the doctor to the door. "You must give me your instructions, doctor. I'm a competent nurse, you should know."

Emma grimaced, listening to Maria's busy chatter receding down the corridor. She sniffed at the contents of the porringer and shook her head. Maria was a darling, but she was a dreadful fusspot. And she was going to want a great deal more explanation than she'd been given so far.

"Dr. Baillie says you should take laudanum and get a good rest, my love." Maria hurried back into the chamber. "Now, I'll feed you some of this broth. It will help you get your strength back."

Emma declined the offer of being fed, but took some of the broth to satisfy Maria.

"But how did it happen?" Maria asked, hovering anxiously as the invalid spooned up the broth. "Why did you leave without a word? And in the middle of the night?" She was genuinely bewildered.

"I fell asleep and burned my feet. Alasdair thought we should return to London at once to consult Dr. Baillie . . . I was in some pain, you understand." Emma was amazed at how glibly the lies, unconvincing though they were, fell from her tongue. "Alasdair was very worried. So worried that I don't think he thought of anything but getting on the road. But when we were changing horses at Barnet, he remembered to send you word. It should have reached you before you awoke. I hope it did." She looked innocently at Maria.

Maria shook her head. "Well, yes, it did, thank heavens for that. Indeed I don't know what I would have done if I'd found you gone from your bed without a word. Such a shock it would have been, I doubt I'd have recovered."

"I really do beg your pardon, Maria," Emma said, reaching out for the other woman's hand. "It was an infamous thing to do, but I was in such pain and Alasdair was so worried, that I'm afraid all else went out of our heads."

"Well, I can see how it must have been," Maria said, still sounding doubtful. "So easy to forget, of course."

She sat on the end of the bed, still looking very bewildered and rather hurt. "But I do so wish you had woken me. I could have been dressed in a trice."

"I think Alasdair may have thought the burns to be worse than they are," Emma offered. It didn't really matter whether Maria believed this cock-and-bull story or not. All that mattered was that she tacitly agree to accept it.

"Well, to be sure, I don't know." Maria shook her head again. "But here's Tilda to help you into bed."

Emma decided that meek acquiescence in the role of invalid was probably wise. It would appease Maria and she owed her some appeasement. Maria would enjoy fussing over her, and if left to do what she wanted, would probably soon stop asking questions. Of course, once she heard of Alasdair's "accident," she was bound to be intrigued. But that bridge had yet to be crossed.

ᛆ

Alasdair endured the doctor's ministrations with tightly clamped lips. He refused to be bled, however, maintaining that he had enough bruises already without adding gratuitously to the sum.

Dr. Baillie humphed a bit but didn't press it. "A driving accident, your man said, sir." He wound fresh strips of linen around the broken ribs.

"Yes," Alasdair agreed through clenched teeth. "Damn fool thing to do. Overreached myself."

"Racing were you, sir?"

"In a manner of speaking," Alasdair replied. "Ouch! For God's sake, man, be a bit more careful."

"The strapping has to be tight, sir, otherwise the bones won't knit," Baillie said, stolidly unaffected by the flow of curses cascading on his head. "There's danger of a punctured lung from one of these ribs if you move around too much for a day or two. You'll need to lie flat to give them time to knit."

Alasdair swore with increased vigor, but he knew the man was right. The stabbing pain he felt every time he breathed was evidence enough.

"I've just come from Lady Emma," Baillie continued placidly. "You were with her when she burned her feet, I gather?"

"If I'd been with her, she wouldn't have burned them," Alasdair snapped with perfect truth.

"Quite so, sir. On the fender," Baillie mused. "Fell asleep with her feet on the fender." He shook his head. "Most odd thing to do . . . almost impossible, I would have thought."

Alasdair didn't offer a response. Baillie was a notorious gossip. He would have a wonderful time regaling his many society patients with the strangeness of these two accidents. The story would be all over town within the week. A dignified silence seemed the only possible response. His own friends would tease him unmercifully at the idea that he of all people had overturned himself in a curricle. But he'd have to endure it.

"A letter has just come for you, Lord Alasdair." Cranham entered the bedchamber with a silver salver. "The messenger said there was no answer."

The insignia of Horseguards sealed the missive. Alasdair broke the wafer. Charles Lester informed him that the four parcels had been safely collected and would be unwrapped within the next few hours.

Alasdair nodded grimly. He had little doubt that the men of Horseguards were as skilled and impersonal at interrogation as Paul Denis and his cohorts. It was a satisfying case of the biter bit.

It seemed the business that had begun with Ned's death was finally finished. Now he could concentrate on Emma without distraction. Or at least, he amended, he could when he stopped hurting so damnably.

It was three days, however, before he was able to get out of bed. He was as weak as an infant, and even without Baillie's strict instructions to lie flat and give his ribs a chance to knit, he wouldn't have been able to move around with anything approaching comfort.

His doorknocker hadn't stopped banging as news of his accident reached his friends, and he'd perfected the rueful shrug and self-deprecating admission of clumsiness, enduring the heavy-handed mockery with as good a grace as he could muster.

Of Emma he heard very little. A message produced

the information that she was feeling much better but still had difficulty walking, so was remaining in seclusion. She and Maria were not receiving visitors. He sent flowers, masses of roses and sweet violets, and received a polite thank-you. He fretted, wondering why this apparent distance. It seemed that every time he thought that they had reached some kind of an understanding, she withdrew from him again.

He wondered if she blamed him for what had happened to her. God knew, she had the right to. He blamed himself every minute of the day. He wondered if the ordeal had so terrified her that she still had not recovered her customary bright spirits, the vibrant energy and sense of humor that were her essence.

For three days he lay flat on his back and fretted and fumed. His breathing gradually grew a little easier, and the sharp stabbing pain lessened. On the fourth day, he got up, managed to walk as far as the armchair in the salon, and collapsed, sweating profusely, cursing and swearing at such ridiculous weakness.

"Give it time, sir." Cranham hovered over him.

"I don't have the time to give it," Alasdair snapped. He didn't know why he had this feeling that all the while he was immobilized he was losing precious time. That something was going on with Emma and he wasn't there to stop whatever it was.

હ

Emma was as confused as Alasdair. She didn't know what was the matter with her. There was a gray patina over everything. She told herself it was the weather, constant dreary English weather at its worst, a weeping drizzle from leaden skies. She told herself it was just reaction to the ordeal.

But it wasn't. She knew that she'd come to some kind of watershed. She'd been approaching it for weeks now, and their confrontation in the Red Lion at Barnet had brought matters to a head. But it had still not resolved the only issue that mattered. Now the horror of that night at Paul Denis's hands had somehow cleared away all the emotional debris so that she could see the one clear truth. Either she agreed to marry Alasdair, or she never saw him again. She could not live on lust and passion alone.

She loved him. She'd told him so and it was the truth. When she was with him, she felt she was wholly alive, living life to its utmost, draining every vestige of emotion and experience from every minute. Whether she was loving him or loathing him, it was the same. And they were after all but two sides of the same coin.

But could she live with a man who kept so many secrets? For whom it was simply natural to keep secrets. A man who resented questions, responded with unmerciful sarcasm to anything that he considered had the faintest suspicion of prying.

On the one hand, she knew him. She knew him very well. But there were also great reaches of his soul that remained closed to her. He had always held himself aloof. Even as a boy, he would on occasion withdraw completely, refusing to talk to anyone, not even to Ned. Then he'd played his music, gone for solitary walks, snubbed with almost vicious pleasure anyone who tried to penetrate his withdrawal.

Ned had always said it was because of Alasdair's family. Because he never felt he belonged to them. He had cut himself off from them and chosen another family. But the wounds of a hurt child healed slowly if at all. Emma had understood this even as a small girl herself. And she and Ned had closed around Alasdair, allowing him his withdrawal and his frequently hurtful responses to their efforts to reach out to him in his loneliness.

But could she live with him . . . be his wife . . . knowing that he would turn on her if she overstepped the bounds by accident or intent? Could she endure to live with someone who had his own private life that he would share with no one? He said he loved her, and she believed he did. But did he love her enough to share himself with her? Could Alasdair ever share himself with anyone?

She lay awake, staring up at the ceiling, where the firelight flickered and the night crept on. He had promised her she was the only woman in his life now. She was willing to believe that, because Alasdair didn't lie. He despised lies. If he didn't want to talk about something, he simply refused to do so.

And he would not talk about the mother of his child.

Lucy. She hadn't even heard the name before he'd spoken it in the inn at Barnet. She didn't know whether he had a son or a daughter. How could she marry him if she didn't know these things and didn't dare to ask? He would say it didn't affect her. But of course it did.

He was a wonderful lover. He was obviously a wonderful manager of fortunes. But Alasdair would never make a husband. Not for someone like herself, who needed everything to be aboveboard, transparent, straightforward. She couldn't abide secrets. She couldn't bear to think that someone was deceiving her. Maybe it was a character flaw, but Emma knew herself. She knew that to commit herself to a man who didn't see the need for total honesty in a relationship would bring her only utter wretchedness. Better to make the clean break now, while the pain would be manageable.

And yet every time she thought she'd made the decision, she found herself rethinking it. Each night as she lay looking up at the firelight on the ceiling, she went over it again and again. Looking for a way to change her mind.

After five nights of this, she could bear it no longer. She rose in the morning and hobbled down to the breakfast parlor, where Maria was at her customary repast. She looked up from her tea with an expression of concerned surprise.

"My dear, why aren't you breakfasting in bed?"

"I've had enough of bed," Emma said, sitting down at the table. "I'm going out as soon as I'm dressed."

"But you can't go out!" Maria exclaimed. "Indeed you can't! What about your poor feet, my dear?"

"My feet are almost better." Emma buttered a piece of toast. "I shall wear silk slippers. They won't pinch."

"Well, I'm sure if you wish to take an airing, then that's what we shall do," Maria said, amenably changing tack. "A little drive in the barouche won't do any harm, I daresay."

"This morning I have an errand I must do alone," Emma said. "But this afternoon we shall drive in the park at five o'clock and show the world that we're back in circulation."

"Alone?" Maria was clearly hurt. "What could you possibly need to do alone, my love?"

Emma frowned. If she told Maria she was going to do something as outrageous as visiting Alasdair at his lodgings, the poor woman would throw a fit of hysterics. Young women did not visit gentlemen's lodgings, even when the gentleman was an old friend and a trustee.

"That I can't tell you," she said after a minute. "Indeed, you really don't wish to know." She smiled at Maria. "Trust me, Maria. You really don't wish to know."

"Oh dear, is it something scandalous?" Maria was clearly very distressed.

"I shall do my best to ensure that no one sees me." Emma attempted reassurance.

"Oh, mercy," sighed Maria, obviously unreassured, and when Emma told Harris to fetch a hackney to the front door, she threw up her hands in horror and retreated to her boudoir.

Emma directed the jarvey to Albermarle Street. An anonymous hackney was her best chance of avoiding remark. They turned onto Albermarle Street and she leaned out of the window, trying to read the numbers on the houses. She was looking for number sixteen.

"It's the next one on the right, jarvey," she called, and the driver pulled in to the side of the road. Emma as she alighted looked up at the bow windows on either side of the front door. Then she froze, one foot on the street, the other still on the footstep.

She was staring straight into what was clearly Alasdair's drawing room. And she was staring at what was clearly Alasdair. He was holding a woman in his arms. A small woman whose head reached only to his chest. His arms were wrapped around her, his hand palming the back of her head as he held her.

Emma felt sick. She climbed back into the hackney. "Driver, go to the end of the street. Stop on the corner."

The jarvey shrugged and obliged. He drew in at the corner of Stafford Street. His passenger stared out of the window, down the street to number sixteen.

Had she really seen it? Seen Alasdair embracing a woman in his own drawing room? Her mind whirled as the frenzied questions chased each other. He'd promised her she was the only woman in his life. He'd *promised* her.

As she continued to stare at the house in a numbed trance, the door opened. Alasdair came out onto the step. His arm was around the woman, who was gazing up at him with what to Emma looked like naked adoration. As Emma watched, Alasdair took the woman's shoulders and kissed her, before hugging her tightly, so tightly her feet almost left the ground.

Alasdair was supposed to be nursing his wounds . . . too battered as yet to leave his house to visit Mount Street. And yet he was not too battered for a little love play! He was smiling and he gave the woman's cheek a little caressing pat.

Emma was filled with a pure red tide of anger. How *dared* he lie to her? He was the same shameless tomcatting rake he'd ever been. He professed love and marriage out of one side of his mouth and played pretty little love games out of the other with anyone who took his fancy.

She watched as the woman went off down the street while Alasdair stood on the top step waving to her. When he went back inside, Emma fumbled in her purse for a shilling for the jarvey, then she jumped down, disdaining the footstep, gathered up her skirts and ran back down the street to number sixteen.

She hammered on the knocker, so wild with fury now she could hardly see straight, let alone think.

Cranham stared in astonishment at the tall young woman whose eyes blazed in a face white with rage.

"Lord Alasdair is within, I believe," she said and pushed past the manservant, marching immediately to the door to the left of the front door.

Cranham closed the front door and hastened to open the drawing room door, but she forestalled him, flinging it wide as she stalked in. It banged shut in Cranham's nose.

"Emma!" Alasdair turned in astonishment from the table where he was pouring himself a glass of sherry. "To what do I owe this pleasure, my sweet?" He came toward her, hands outstretched, then he saw her face. His hands dropped to his sides again and his delighted smile faded. His eyes grew wary.

"Oh, don't tell me you're not accustomed to having female visitors," Emma said scornfully. "Don't expect me to believe *that*, sir. I imagine they come in droves . . . positively lining up for the privilege of—"

"Emma, for Christ's sake, stop it!" Alasdair exclaimed. "I don't know what the *hell* you're talking about. Which, now I come to think of it, is frequently the case when you're flinging accusations at me," he added with a bite now to his voice. "What in the devil's name have I done this time?"

"You don't *know*?" She stared at him incredulously. "You are beyond belief, Alasdair!" She took a turn around the room, her step agitated, the embroidered flounce of her pale crepe gown swinging with her stride.

Alasdair watched her in confusion, but his own ready anger was rising in response to hers, even though he was as yet quite in the dark about its cause.

Emma came to a halt in front of him. Speaking very slowly, articulating every word as if she were trying to educate a dunce, she said, "You told me I'm the only woman in your life. Do you remember saying that, Alasdair? Do you?" She jabbed at his shoulder with a finger. "You tell me that and then I see you locked in the embrace of some—"

"Be very careful what you say, Emma!" he interrupted, grabbing the wrist of her still-jabbing hand. His voice was very soft. "Be *very* careful."

Emma decided that it wasn't necessary to cast aspersions on the woman she'd seen him with. It didn't matter whether she was a whore or a woman of impeccable birth.

"So, who is she?" she demanded with sardonic curiosity. "The woman you were embracing in this very room ten minutes ago? The woman you kissed on your front door step? Not a stranger, I would have said. Someone you know very well. Someone with whom you are on the closest, most intimate terms."

She turned from him with a gesture of disgust. "Not that it matters. Why should I care? I could never trust you. You lied to me. You have always lied to me."

"I have *never* lied to you," Alasdair stated quietly. "Don't turn your back on me!" He reached for her shoulder and spun her around to face him again.

"You talk of trust, Emma. Well, have you considered that I can't trust *you* to trust me? Have you thought of that? Why do you have to put the worst construction on what you saw? What possible justification do you have for that? Do you know how wearing it is to be constantly under suspicion? To feel you're always watching me, jumping to conclusions, waiting to catch me out?"

"But it's not like that," Emma cried. "I am not like that. But you're so secretive. There are great areas of your life that you won't even discuss. How can I trust you when I don't know what's going on in your life, even what you're thinking half the time. When you refuse to share things, of course it looks as if you have something to hide. After the last time . . . after what you hid from me before . . . how can I trust you?"

She dashed a hand across her eyes, where angry tears were gathering. "You won't tell me who that woman was. So what *am* I to think?"

"No," Alasdair said with sudden icy finality. "I'd thought we could put things together, but obviously we can't. This is just not going to work. I cannot and I will not live under suspicion the entire time, watching my every step."

"No, you're right," Emma fired back. "It is *not* going to work. That was what I came to tell you anyway." She turned to the door in a swirl of crepe. "Goodbye, Alasdair." The door banged shut behind her.

He walked to the window, his mouth set, his eyes hard, and watched her walk swiftly away down the street without so much as a backward glance.

"Of all the obstinate, ill-tempered, mistrustful *vixens!*" Alasdair exclaimed to the velvet curtains. No man worth his salt would put up with it. Was he to account for every minute of his day, every conversation he had, every acquaintance he met?

He had not expected Lucy's visit that morning. Indeed, she had never done such a thing before. But Tim had decided unilaterally that he was not going to school anymore. Mike had refused to get involved, and Lucy, whose dearest wish was that her son should grow up to be a gentleman just like his father, had come to appeal to Alasdair to intervene.

Alasdair didn't know whether he would have explained all this to Emma if she'd asked him about his visitor in a reasonable tone of voice instead of jumping to ridiculous conclusions.

He eased himself into a chair, his ribs aching, his bruises once more throbbing as if in sympathy with his mood. In all honesty, he didn't think he would have told Emma. He would have frozen her questions in his usual fashion, resenting them as always.

But was she entitled to an explanation? He reached for his sherry glass and sipped reflectively, as his temper cooled down and his aches and pains eased off again.

Damn the woman! Was there ever such a shrew and a virago! And just what had she meant about coming to tell him that it wouldn't work? Had she finally decided not to marry him?

He drained his glass and set it down again. A cold finger seemed to be pressing against his spine. Was this more significant than their usual quarrels? Surely she hadn't meant it. He certainly hadn't. They both said things in the heat of the moment that were never intended to be taken seriously. It was the way they were.

But if she had been coming to tell him that, before that explosion of wrath, then it was a very different matter. He knew the strength of her will. If Emma had made up her mind, it could not easily be changed.

But change it he must. He could not live without her. Suspicious, impossible, hot-tempered creature that she was.

He rose from his chair and went to the piano. Sitting down, he played a series of chords before settling on Haydn's *The Seasons*.

If it was true that music had charms to soothe a savage beast, he was in dire need of such soothing, Alasdair thought with an ironical quirk of his mouth. He was preparing to break the defensive habits of a lifetime.

Chapter Seventeen

Maria listened to the sounds from the music room. At first there had been a great tumultuous cascade of music, but now the music was in a minor key, soft as weeping, and it wrung Maria's heart. It would have taken someone a lot less sensitive than she to fail to recognize that Emma had not been herself since the return from Stevenage. She had been tense and jumpy, and her face in repose had an expression that seemed to Maria to be both sad and confused. But there had been nothing as powerfully depressed as the music pouring from her now. Maria was not given to fanciful rhetoric, but she thought she was listening to the expression of a soul in pain.

Maria had no idea where Emma had gone that morning, but she'd come back like a whirlwind, slamming into the house and into the music room without a word to anyone. And now the music filled the house with its hopeless sadness. And Maria was helpless.

The music room was sacrosanct. Only Alasdair ever went in there when Emma was playing.

Emma played to banish all thought from her mind. She had not gone to see Alasdair to break off their relationship irrevocably, for all that she'd said so. She had gone to talk to him, to ask him to understand her anxiety. She had gone hoping that he would give her something that would make it possible for her to love him without condition.

Now she had no hope. And only now that she understood that everything was finally and irretrievably over between them did she understand how much she had lost. It had been bad the first time, but the second time was almost unbearable. She had been tormented by the possibility of happiness, only to have it snatched away.

ॐ

Alasdair drove up to the house in his curricle in the middle of the afternoon. He tossed the reins to Jemmy and went up to the front door, his step somewhat less light and agile than usual.

Harris let him in. "I trust you're recovered from your spill, Lord Alasdair."

Alasdair grimaced. Even the servants had the gossip. "Pretty well, thank you, Harris."

He stood in the hall listening to the message in Emma's music pouring from the back of the house. His mouth was stern, his eyes grave. So she really had given up. But only the greatest unhappiness could have fueled her playing, and he must take what encouragement he could from that.

He strode past Harris with a brief nod. At the door to the music room, he hesitated for a moment. Then he opened the door and stepped inside. The latch clicked as the door closed.

"Go away," Emma commanded over the music, furious that someone should break her unspoken rule and disturb her when she was playing.

"No," Alasdair replied.

Her hands came down in a crashing chord on the keyboard.

"Put on your pelisse." He came up behind her, putting his hands under her arms and lifting her upward off the bench. He forestalled her protest with a flat, "Don't argue with me, I'm all out of patience."

She turned and stared up at him dumbfounded. "What are you doing?"

"You're coming with me," he responded steadily. He turned and picked up the pelisse she'd been wearing that afternoon and had carelessly discarded over a chair. "Put this on. It's quite a long drive and it'll be cold when it gets dark."

Emma shook her head. "I'm not going anywhere with you. It's over, Alasdair, don't you understand?"

"No," he said, holding out the pelisse. "I neither understand it nor accept it. Now put this on, please."

Emma didn't think she'd ever seen him like this. He was calm, his voice even, but there was a taut severity to his expression, in the set of his mouth and the gravity of his eyes. It was not anger, but it was absolute determination. The kind of last-ditch determination that would keep a drowning man clinging to a piece of driftwood.

She found herself putting on her pelisse. He handed her her gloves and stood waiting patiently with her hat until she'd drawn on her gloves. Then he set the dark blue chip hat on her head and tied its pale blue velvet ribbons beneath her chin.

Emma tried again, a note of desperation in her voice. "Alasdair, this is ridiculous. It's a waste of time. Nothing's going to change. You can't compel me to go with you in this way."

"Come," he said, moving to open the door for her.

It was as if he held her on some kind of invisible leash, Emma thought, unable to believe that she was going with him utterly against her will and yet without the slightest overt force on Alasdair's part. She walked past him into the hall.

"Oh, are you going out again? Alasdair, I saw you from the window." Maria came hurrying down the stairs, her relief that the music had stopped ringing clear in her voice. "Are you taking Emma for a drive? Have you recovered yourself? Such a terrible thing to happen. And just after Emma's accident . . . such a peculiar coincidence."

"Don't wait dinner for Emma," Alasdair said, not troubling to answer Maria's ramble of questions.

"Good heavens, why not? Where are you going?" Maria stared at him, suddenly taking in his expression, Emma's white, strained countenance, and the almost palpable tension between them. "Is something wrong?" she asked fearfully.

"No," Alasdair said quietly. "Nothing at all. Come, Emma." He put a hand in the small of her back and urged her to the front door.

Emma, feeling like a marionette on a string, obeyed the pressure wordlessly. In the same silence, she allowed him to hand her up into the curricle.

Jemmy greeted her cheerfully, but then he too realized that things were not as they should be. He sprang onto his perch as the horses started forward, and held his tongue.

"Where are you taking me?" Emma found her voice at last.

"Somewhere I should have taken you long ago," Alasdair replied in the same even tones. "But you'll have to forgive me if tell you that I am not at all in the mood for conversation."

It was such a supremely arrogant remark in the circumstances, and so absolutely typical of Alasdair, that Emma almost gathered up her skirts and jumped from the curricle.

As if reading her mind, Alasdair put out a hand and laid it firmly on her thigh. Emma stared over the horses' heads and closed her lips tightly.

By the time they were trotting through the sleepy village of Kensington, she was intrigued despite herself.

Jemmy sat up abruptly on his box and muttered, "Well, now, 'ere's a turn-up." He nodded sagely, now well aware of their destination.

They went through Hammersmith and crossed the river at Chiswick. Emma glanced at Alasdair. He seemed to have relaxed at last, his mouth less rigid. But then, he wouldn't allow his tension to communicate itself to his horses, she reminded herself. He was probably not in the least relaxed.

They turned under the archway of a coaching inn that bore the sign of the Red Lion. Alasdair alighted and held up a hand to assist Emma. She descended and looked around. One Red Lion was very like another. What were they doing here?

"I'll be waitin' 'ere, then, guv?" Jemmy took the reins from Alasdair. "Jest as usual."

Alasdair nodded and took Emma's arm. "We have a short walk."

"How fortunate my blisters aren't troubling me," she said acidly.

"It was fairly clear they weren't this morning," he responded. "Judging by the way you were running down Albermarle Street."

Emma's glare threw daggers at him and for a moment his expression lightened, the old glint of amusement sparking in his eye, then it was gone and his countenance was once again set.

They left the inn yard and walked down a narrow lane of small cottages until they reached the end. The last cottage was larger than the others, and Emma saw the outbuildings of a small farm clustered in the surrounding field.

Alasdair opened the garden gate and gestured to Emma that she should precede him up the path to the front door. He knocked. It was opened immediately by a gangling lad who regarded Emma with curiosity.

"Emma, I'd like you to meet my son," Alasdair said calmly. "This is Tim. Tim, this is Lady Emma Beaumont."

Her mind reeled. *Why hadn't he warned her?* But of course he wouldn't have done. It was typical of Alasdair. This was his way of punishing her just a little for forcing this upon him. Well, she could meet his challenge. But oh, how the boy reminded her physically of the young Alasdair!

Emma held out her hand to the boy and said with a frank smile, "Tim, I'm very happy to meet you."

The lad bowed but his mind was clearly elsewhere. He cast his father an anxious look. "Mama came to see you."

"This morning, yes," Alasdair agreed. "Is she in?"

"She's in the kitchen with Sally. They're making mincemeat."

"Well, would you ask her if she'd—"

"Alasdair!" The glad cry came from within the house. "I heard your voice. It's so good of you to come so quickly."

The woman Emma had seen that morning appeared at the door. She was wreathed in smiles. An apron covered her round gown of sprig muslin, and she held a large wooden spoon in her hand.

"Oh, goodness me," she said when she saw Emma. She wiped her free hand on her apron, looking flustered. "You didn't say you were bringing visitors, Alasdair."

"No, he's very secretive that way," Emma said, stepping forward, taking charge of this encounter. She held out her hand. "You must be Lucy . . . oh, I beg your pardon, that's very forward of me. Mrs . . . ?"

"Hodgkins," Lucy said, taking the hand. She looked inquiringly at Alasdair.

"Allow me to present Lady Emma Beaumont," Alasdair said. "I intend to marry her."

Emma's jaw dropped at this barefaced effrontery. The man was impossible. Lucy beamed. Tim shuffled his feet with an air of unease.

"Why, I'm so happy . . . bless me, but that's wonderful news," Lucy said. "Come in, come in. We must have a glass of elderflower wine to celebrate. Mike's still in the fields. Timmy, go and fetch him . . . right away. Come in, Lady Emma. Do excuse the mess. I wasn't expecting company."

Lucy, like most people, was clearly not inclined to question Alasdair's stated intentions, Emma reflected, stepping into the small hall. It hadn't occurred to her to wonder if Emma intended to be made Alasdair's wife.

But it would have been churlish to spoil this meeting. Everyone seemed so genuinely delighted and pleased with Alasdair's news, and interestingly didn't seem to think there was anything strange about his bringing her to meet them. Did they know a different Alasdair? A less secretive Alasdair? The urbane, sardonic man society knew would certainly not have fitted so comfortably into this cozy domestic setting.

Mike Hodgkins, who soon arrived with Tim, was as happy as his wife. He shook hands, congratulated her and then Alasdair with scrupulous formality, then gave a great guffaw of laughter, kissed his wife, and tossed back several glasses of wine in quick succession.

Emma noticed that Tim seemed to cling to his stepfather's side. He hung on Mike's words, laughed when he did, hurried to fill his glass when it was empty. And yet Tim wasn't at all uncomfortable with Alasdair, she thought. And Alasdair treated him with the affectionate friendliness that outsiders so rarely saw. It was the side of him that she loved. That Ned had loved.

But Tim was obviously Mike Hodgkins's son in all but blood. Did this trouble Alasdair? He knew what it was to be estranged from his parents . . . to feel no emotional ties to his family. How was it with this son of his?

And as she watched and listened and played her part, Emma thought of how much time she and Alasdair had lost because he wouldn't open this side of his life to her. These questions were ones that she needed answered. She loved him. How could anyone who loved someone not want to understand, to know about such vital issues in a loved one's life? And how could he possibly not have realized that?

She caught herself looking at him with an almost

frustrated impatience that he would be so stubborn. And then he glanced across at her and what she saw in his eyes took her breath away. It was both question and plea. And then she understood how much of himself he had risked this afternoon.

She smiled and held out her hand to him. He rose and crossed the small parlor. He took her hand and brought it to his lips. There was silence in the room, but it was a silence that seemed to enfold them.

Then Alasdair gave her back her hand and said in a voice that was utterly normal, "Tim and Mike and I have some business to discuss. Will you and Lucy excuse us for a few minutes?"

Emma inclined her head in acknowledgment. She thought Tim looked anxious as he went out with the two men who fathered him. And she thought he probably had not the slightest reason for his anxiety.

Lucy moved to the window seat to sit beside Emma. "I don't know what's for the best," she confided, settling the baby on her lap. "Alasdair wanted to send Tim to his old school, and it would be such a wonderful thing for Tim. But he doesn't want to go."

"Eton?" Emma wrinkled her nose. "My brother and Alasdair never had a good thing to say about the place."

"But it would turn Tim into a gentleman," Lucy said.

"Not if he doesn't want it to," Emma said. "It'll just make him miserable."

"But he *must* go to school," Lucy insisted. "He's saying now that he won't even go to the dame school . . . or to the rector, who teaches him Latin and Greek. I went to ask Alasdair what to do about it this morning."

Emma nodded. This morning seemed a lifetime

ago. A whole mistaken, confused, topsy-turvy life-time ago. "What does Tim want to do?"

"He wants to be a farmer like Mike." Lucy played with the baby's fingers. "Mike's a good farmer . . . he's a good provider. I couldn't ask for a better husband. But Tim could be something else. He could have chances."

"But maybe Alasdair could ensure he has chances that suit him better," Emma said hesitantly. She didn't want to interfere. And this whole situation was so new that speaking for Alasdair seemed a very dangerous business, and yet at the same time quite right.

"If he wants to farm, then he'll be a better farmer if he can read and understand things. There are new things to learn about farming all the time these days. Crop rotation and enclosures . . ." She stopped, realizing that she was being carried away by her own enthusiasm. She was talking about big estate management. Lucy and Mike had a smallholding.

But Lucy seemed unperturbed. She was nodding thoughtfully.

"Mama, I don't have to go to the rector *ever* again!" Tim bounded into the parlor, his face flushed, his eyes bright. "And I don't have to go away to school after I'm too old for Dame Baldock's. I'm to go and learn how to manage a big farm as soon as Mike says I'm old enough."

Nicely done, Alasdair. Emma nodded her silent approval. Both men seemed at ease with a decision that had clearly been a joint one.

Alasdair bent to kiss Lucy. "Be happy with it, Lucy. It's for the best."

"Yes," she said, smiling now. "So Lady Emma was saying."

Alasdair cast Emma a slightly startled look, then he

said, "Well, I don't think we want to intrude on you any longer. Come, Emma." He offered her his arm.

Emma took it, made her farewells, and accompanied him outside. As they walked down the path, Alasdair observed reflectively, "I'm glad we see eye to eye on Tim. But then, my bride-to-be, you've always shared my opinions on most things."

"I haven't yet shared my opinion on the matter of marriage," Emma pointed out with some asperity.

"Then share it now, my sweet."

Emma took a deep breath. "You are an arrogant, opinionated, cozening, insinuating minister of hell!"

Alasdair grinned. "Never have I heard you speak sweeter words, my honey-tongued angel."

"Oh, I haven't even begun," Emma declared. "I shall fill your ears with insults every day of the rest of your miserable existence."

"Darling girl, you will make me the happiest man on earth," he declared airily, then added, "and besides, if I ever grow tired of hearing myself abused, I have a very simple way of stopping it."

"Oh, yes?"

He stopped in the shadows of the lane. His eyes glowed bright as emeralds in the dusk as slowly he sealed her mouth with his. "Do you doubt it, Emma mine?" he murmured, moving his mouth to the soft curve of her cheek.

"No," Emma whispered. "I have no doubts . . . none of any kind." She traced the line of his mouth with her thumb. "Not a doubt in the world."

Epilogue

❧

"I thought we were going to Vauxhall." Emma looked in puzzlement as the two oarsmen sculled past the water entrance of Vauxhall Gardens. The myriad lights from the garden illuminated the river, and strains of music from the rotunda drifted across the water on the cold night air.

"I changed my mind," Alasdair said with a lazy smile. He was sitting opposite her in the boat, his arms folded, his gleaming eyes resting on her countenance. She was looking particularly enchanting this evening in an opera cloak of white velvet trimmed in silver fox fur. The collar stood up at the back, framing her face beneath the high-piled crown of stripey hair. Her eyes looked pure gold under the light of the cresset in the stern, her full mouth eminently kissable.

"I didn't change mine," Emma retorted, still very puzzled. "Besides, we were engaged with a big party, you said."

"I may have exaggerated a little."

"Just what's going on, Alasdair?"

"A little surprise," he replied. "But I don't intend to spoil it, so you may as well save your breath."

Emma sat back. She'd noticed something strange about him when he'd arrived in Mount Street to escort her to this party at Vauxhall Gardens—a secretive air; one almost of suppressed excitement, except that Alasdair didn't really get excited about things.

She regarded him with narrowed eyes, perfectly willing to be surprised. A little thrill of anticipation rippled down her spine. She tucked the fur rug more closely around her knees and watched the riverbank slide past. Soon they left the lights of London behind, and the only sounds were the soft, rhythmic plash of the oars in the dark water.

They turned into a broad reach, where the river stretched wide and long. A light glimmered ahead from the south bank. The oarsmen swung the scull into the bank, to bump gently against a flight of water steps.

"Where are we?" Emma asked, looking up at the bank. At the top oil lamps, hung in the branches of a bare oak tree, flickered and glowed, illuminating the steps and the river, but she could see nothing of what was behind them.

Alasdair merely smiled his lazy smile and stepped out of the scull. He held out his hand to her and she stood up, the little boat rocking slightly on the tide. A waterman handed her up to Alasdair.

Asking where they were wasn't getting any results, so she went up the short flight and stepped onto the riverbank. A tree-lined gravel path wound away from the river, lit by lanterns in sconces planted at intervals. At the end, she could make out a low-roofed, whitewashed building, lamplight pouring from every window, throwing golden arcs across a smooth green lawn.

"Oh, how pretty!" she exclaimed involuntarily. "What an entrancing place."

Alasdair paid off the oarsmen and came up to her. "I'm glad it pleases you, ma'am." He smiled at her and caressed her cheek with a gloved fingertip. "Come, let's go inside. It's getting chilly."

He caught her hand, twining his fingers with hers, as they walked up the path.

A maidservant stood in the open doorway. She curtsied and smiled. "Everything's as you ordered it, sir. If you need anything, you have only to ring."

"Thank you." Alasdair took Emma's hand again and led her to the flight of stairs at the rear of the stone-flagged entrance hall. They climbed one flight and Alasdair turned down a corridor.

Emma was intrigued. She had decided that they must be in the village of Chelsea. But why had Alasdair paid off the watermen? Perhaps they were to return by road. He may have considered that it would be too cold later to return by water.

Alasdair opened a door at the end of the corridor and stood aside to let her pass through. She stepped into a large corner apartment, heavy velvet curtains drawn over the windows on two sides. A log fire blazed in the grate, crocheted rugs were scattered over the luminous polished floor. A four-poster bed dominated the room.

She glanced up at Alasdair with an inquiring eyebrow.

"That's for later," he said, reaching over her shoulders to unclasp her cloak. "First we have supper." He indicated a gate-legged table and two carved wooden armchairs drawn up before the fire.

The table was set with silverware and platters, crystal glasses and two pewter candlesticks. There was a scent in the warmed air, of lavender, rose petals, and apple blossom. Emma looked for the source and found it in a small pan of potpourri simmering on a trivet over the fire.

Everything about the chamber was soft and sensual. A fragrant, languorous room that seemed to exist in its own space and time. There were no sounds from the building around them, no sense that there was anyone in the world besides themselves.

She turned to look up at Alasdair, who was watching her, smiling, her cloak still hung over his arm. Then he tossed her cloak onto the window seat, sent his own after it, and strode to a sideboard set against the far wall.

Emma's eyes followed him. There was food on the sideboard. A great silver platter of oysters, opalescent in their craggy gray shells, mounded on lemon-strewn ice. There were quails in aspic, bright pink lobsters with a saffron sauce, a delicate puree of green peas. A feast for the eyes as much as the taste buds.

Alasdair was opening a bottle of champagne, easing off the cork with his thumbs. He poured the straw-colored foaming liquid into a cup.

Emma hadn't noticed the cup before but as he brought it over to her she gasped with delight. It was a two-handled chalice of engraved silver, studded with emeralds and sapphires.

"A loving cup," he said, smiling with pleasure at her reaction.

"Where did it come from?"

"Norway, I believe, sometime in the twelfth century. It's been in my family for generations." He held it to her lips.

She drank the champagne, feeling its effervescence on her tongue, the bubbles exploding against her palate like ripe berries. This was no ordinary champagne. Alasdair drank from the other side, his eyes holding hers over the cup.

"The loving cup is only used on certain occasions," he said gravely, tipping it to her lips again. "We must drink to the bottom."

Emma drank again. They drank alternately until Alasdair said softly, "Hold it yourself now. See how beautiful it is on the inside."

Emma did so. She looked into the cup. The reverse facets of the jewels had a dull glow like a stained glass window on a cloudy day. A small amount of champagne lay in the bottom of the cup, and something winked up at her through the pale liquid. She tilted the cup and there was a tiny little clink.

Delicately she reached into the cup, dipping her fingers into the champagne, and drew out a circlet of chased gold. Sapphires of the deepest, darkest blue were embedded in the gold.

She looked up at Alasdair in wonder, unsure what to say or do.

He took the ring from her. "Do you know what day it is, Emma?"

"Tuesday," she answered, confused by the question.

He took her left hand and held it for a minute. He shook his head at her in mock reproof. "It's the feast of Saint Valentine. There was a time not so long ago when you decided it would be a very important day for you. Have you forgotten so soon?"

Emma said, "It seems to me that I've already achieved what I said I would."

Alasdair slipped the ring on her third finger. "A lover, and a future husband. Was that right?"

"You know it was." She held up her hand to the light. Sapphires were her favorite stones and these were heart-stoppingly beautiful. "I didn't expect a betrothal ring this time," she said with a rueful little smile. "Having thrown the last one in your teeth."

"Well, I'm going to make certain you don't have the chance to do that again." He reached inside his waistcoat and drew out a paper and a small twist of tissue.

"I have here a special license and a wedding ring. The local vicar will be ready for us in the morning, and until then . . ."

He caught her chin on his palm, his expression a curious mixture of gravity and amusement. "Until then, my sweet, you and I shall stay in this chamber. I intend to ensure that come morning you will be too exhausted to do anything but stagger up to the altar and stammer your responses. There'll be no flight to Italy this time."

"There'll be no need for one," she said, meeting his gaze steadily.

Alasdair nodded slowly. "The feast of Saint Valentine," he mused. "It seemed to me that there was a curious resonance to the idea of spending our prenuptial night in the arms of the patron saint of star-crossed lovers."

"His blessing might forestall further star-crossing, you mean?"

"Sometimes a little extra help can't go amiss." He reached behind him to the sideboard and took an oyster from the salver. "Open."

Emma opened her mouth and he fed her the oyster.

The cold, fishy, sea-tasting morsel slithered down her throat, and she closed her eyes involuntarily. "I'm not sure I need aphrodisiacs," she murmured.

Alasdair took the loving cup from her. "I think supper will have to wait." He reached for her hands and pulled her against him. Holding her tightly, he fell back with her onto the bed, rolling her beneath him. Leaning on his elbows, he looked down at her. "God, but you're so beautiful, Emma. I want you so fiercely."

"Then have me," she said with a wicked little grin. "I am yours, sir." She flung her arms wide on the coverlet in a gesture of mock surrender. "But don't tear my gown, or else I'll have to stand at the altar in my shift."

"An irresistible invitation," he murmured, his eyes alive with passion. He kissed her with the savage desire she was inciting, biting her bottom lip so that she could taste a little bead of salty blood. His hands were at the neck of her gown of delicate spider-gauze. He ripped it from neck to hem, and Emma laughed exultantly.

She reached for his shirt and tugged, heedless of the buttons flying loose, lifting her body on the mattress so that he could free her hips and thighs of the half-slip of blue silk she wore beneath the gauze. Her silk stockings tore under a raking fingernail as he felt for her. She tore at the buttons of his waistband, freeing the hard jut of his erection.

He lifted her legs onto his shoulders and in the same movement drove deep inside her. His gaze, as exultant as Emma's, scanned her. He reached down to touch her face with his palm, then he began to move within her, ever deeper, ever more probing, so that she felt more truly possessed than she had felt before.

She turned her face and bit his palm as the great fierce joy grew and grew until it could no longer be contained. And then just as she knew she was lost, he withdrew to the very edge of her body, holding himself there. Her eyes, drowning in need, lost themselves in his.

Slowly, very slowly, he smiled, then inch by inch sheathed himself within her again.

And they both cried out in savage triumph as the hot juices of their loving flowed and they clung to each other, jubilant in ecstasy.

And Emma thought, as weakly she drew Alasdair down into her embrace, that Ned had been a very powerful deus ex machina. She kissed Alasdair's damp shoulder and felt his lips on her breast. And she knew that he too was thinking of the man who had insisted that against all appearances, against all the odds, they belonged together.

About the Author

JANE FEATHER is the nationally bestselling, award-winning author of *The Hostage Bride*, *The Emerald Swan*, *The Silver Rose*, *The Diamond Slipper*, *Vanity*, *Vice*, *Violet*, and many more historical romances. She was born in Cairo, Egypt, and grew up in the New Forest, in the south of England. She began her writing career after she and her family moved to Washington, D.C., in 1981. She now has over two million books in print.

Coming next . . .

The Brides' Trilogy, which started with *The Hostage Bride*, continues with . . .

The Accidental Bride
by Jane Feather

Three unconventional young women vow never to get married, only to be overtaken by destiny. In *The Accidental Bride*, Phoebe—the "awkward" one—stumbles into passion, intrigue, and the romance of a lifetime.

Read on for an excerpt of this captivating new love story from the nationally bestselling Jane Feather . . .

Lady Phoebe Carlton lay very still listening to her
bedmate's even breathing. Olivia was a very light
sleeper and woke at the slightest sound. And tonight,
Olivia mustn't know what Phoebe was about. They
never had secrets from each other and were as close if
not closer than sisters. But Phoebe couldn't afford for
her dearest friend to know about her present enterprise.

Phoebe pushed aside the coverlet and slipped to
the floor. Olivia stirred and turned over. Phoebe
froze. The fire in the grate was almost out and it was
so cold in the chamber that her breath formed a pale
fog in the dim light from the guttering candle on the
mantel. Olivia was afraid of the dark and they always
kept a candle burning until she was asleep.

Olivia's even breathing resumed and Phoebe tiptoed across the chamber to the armoire. She had left it
partly open so it wouldn't squeak. She took out the

bundle of clothes and the small cloakbag and crept on her freezing bare feet to the door. She lifted the latch and opened it just wide enough for her to slide sideways through and into the dark passage beyond.

Shivering, she scrambled into her clothes over her nightshift. There were no candles in the sconces in the passage and it was pitchdark, but Phoebe found the darkness comforting. If she could see no one, then no one could see her.

The house was silent but for the usual nighttime creaks of old wood settling. She dragged on her woolen stockings, and carrying her boots and the cloakbag, crept down the corridor toward the wide staircase leading down to the great hall.

The hall was in shadow, lit only by the still glowing embers in the vast fireplace at the far end. The great roofbeams were a dark and heavy presence above her head as she tiptoed in her stockinged feet down the stairs. It was a mad, crazy thing she was doing, but Phoebe could see no alternative. She would not be sold into marriage, sold like a prize pig at the fair, to a man who had no real interest in her, except as a breeding cow.

Phoebe grimaced at her mixed metaphors, but they both nevertheless struck her as accurate descriptions of her situation. She wasn't living in the middle ages. It should not be possible to compel someone into a distasteful marriage, and yet, if she didn't take drastic action, that was exactly what was going to happen. Her father refused to listen to reason; he saw only his own advantage and had every intention of disposing of his only remaining daughter to suit himself.

Phoebe muttered under her breath as she crossed the hall, the cold from the flagstones striking up through her stockings. Reminding herself of her father's intractable selfishness buoyed her up. She was terrified of what she was about to do. It was absolute madness to attempt such a flight, but she would not marry a man who barely noticed her existence.

The great oak door was bolted and barred. She set down her boots and cloakbag and lifted the iron bar. It was heavy but she managed to set it back into the brackets at the side of the door. She reached up and drew the first bolt, then bent to draw the second at the base of the door. She was breathing quickly and, despite the cold, beads of sweat gathered between her breasts. She was aware of nothing but the door, its massive solidity in front of her filling her vision, both interior and exterior.

Slowly, she pulled the door open. A blast of frigid air struck her like a blow. She took a deep breath . . .

And then the door was suddenly banged closed again. An arm had reached over her shoulder, a flat hand rested against the door jamb. Phoebe stared at the hand . . . at the arm . . . in total stupefaction. Where had it come from? She felt the warmth of the body at her back, a large presence that was blocking her retreat just as the now closed door prevented her advance.

She turned her head, raised her eyes, and met the puzzled and distinctly irritated gaze of her intended bridegroom.

Cato, Marquis of Granville, regarded her in silence for a minute. When he spoke it was an almost shocking sound after the dark silence. "What in God's name are you doing, Phoebe?"

His voice, rich and tawny, as always these days sent a little shiver down her spine. For a moment she was at a loss for words and stood staring, slack-jawed and dumb as any village idiot—not even acute dismay could prevent the cross comparison.

"I was going for a walk, sir," she said finally and absurdly.

Cato looked at her incredulously. "At three o'clock in the morning. Don't be ridiculous." His gaze sharpened, the brown eyes, so dark as to be almost black in the shadowy dimness of the hall, narrowed. He glanced down at the cloakbag and her boots, standing neatly side by side.

"A walk, eh?" he queried with undisguised sarcasm. "In your stockinged feet, no less." He put his hands on her shoulders and moved her aside, then shot the bolts on the door again and dropped the bar back in place. It fell with a heavy clang that sounded to Phoebe in her present melodramatic mood like a veritable death knell.

He bent to pick up the cloakbag and with a curt, "Come," moved away toward the door at the rear of the hall that opened onto his study.

Phoebe glanced at her boots, then shrugged with dull resignation and left them where they were. She followed the marquis's broad back, noticing despite herself how the rich velvet of his nightrobe caressed his wide powerful shoulders, fell to his booted ankles in elegant black folds. Had he been about to go up to bed? How could she possibly have been so stupid as not to have noticed the yellow line of candlelight beneath his door. But it hadn't occurred to her that anyone would still be up and about at this ungodly hour.

Cato stalked into his study and dropped the cloakbag on the table with a gesture that struck Phoebe as contemptuous. Then he turned back to her, the fur-trimmed robe swinging around his ankles. "Close the door. There's no reason why anyone else should be forced into this vigil."

Phoebe closed the door and stood with her back against it. Cato's study was warm, the fire well built and blazing, but there was little warmth in the marquis's gaze as he regarded her in frowning silence. Then he turned back to the bag on the table.

"So," he began in a conversational tone, "you were going for a walk, were you?" He unclasped the bag and drew out Phoebe's best cloak. He laid it over a chair and continued to remove the contents of the bag one by one. His eyes beneath sardonically raised brows never left her face as he shook out her clean linen, her shifts and stockings and chemises, laying them with exaggerated care over the chair. Lastly he placed her hairbrushes on the table with the little packet of hair pins and ribbons.

"Strange baggage to accompany a walk," he observed. "But then anyone choosing to go for a walk at three in the morning in the middle of January is probably capable of any oddity, wouldn't you think?"

Phoebe wanted to throw something at him. Instead she went over to the table and began stolidly to replace the pathetic assortment of her worldly goods in the bag. "I'll go back to bed now," she said colorlessly.

"Not quite yet." Cato put a hand on her arm. "I'm afraid you owe me an explanation. For the last two years you've been living, I assume contentedly, under my roof. And now it appears you're intending to flit away by moonlight without a word to anyone . . . Or is Olivia a part of this?" His voice had sharpened.

"Olivia doesn't know anything, my lord," Phoebe stated. "This is not her fault."

Olivia's father merely nodded. "So, an explanation, if you please."

How could he not know? How could she possibly be so drawn to this man . . . find him so impossibly attractive . . . when as far as he was concerned she was of no more importance than an ant . . . merely a convenient means to an end. He hadn't looked at her properly once in the two years she'd been living under his roof. She was certain the idea for this marriage had come from her father, and Cato had simply seen the advantages.

His wife, Diana, Phoebe's sister, had died eight months earlier. It was common practice for a widower to marry his sister-in-law. It kept dowries in the family and maintained the original alliance between the two families. Of course it was to Cato's advantage. Of course he'd agreed.

No one had consulted Phoebe. They hadn't thought it necessary. There had been not even the semblance of courtship . . .

Cato continued to frown at her. Absently he noticed that the buttons of her jacket were done up wrongly, as if she'd dressed in haste and in the dark. Her thick, light brown hair, incompetently dragged into a knot on top of her head, was flying loose in every direction. The clasp of her cloak was hanging by a thread. She was very untidy, he caught himself thinking. He realized that he'd noticed it often before. He remembered now that Diana had complained about it constantly.

"Phoebe . . ." he prompted with an edge of impatience.

Phoebe took a deep breath and said in a rush, "I do not wish to be married, sir. I've never wished to be married. I won't be married."

It seemed that she had silenced the marquis. His frown deepened. He ran a hand through his close-cropped thatch of dark brown hair back from the pronounced widow's peak to his nape. It was a gesture with which Phoebe was achingly familiar. It was something he did whenever he was deep in thought, distracted by some detail or contemplating some plan of action. And these days it never failed to turn her knees to water.

Cato turned and went over to a massive mahogany sideboard. He poured wine from a silver decanter into a pewter cup, took a thoughtful sip, and then turned back to Phoebe.

"Let me understand this. Do you not wish to marry *me* in particular . . . or do you have a generalized dislike of the marital state?" His voice had lost its edge and sounded merely curious.

If I thought there was the slightest chance you might pay me as much attention as you pay your horses, or find me as interesting as politics and this godforsaken war, I would marry you like a shot, Phoebe thought bitterly.

She said, "I'm not interested in marrying anyone, Lord Granville. I don't see the advantages in it . . . or at least not for me."

It was such an extraordinary, ridiculous, statement that Cato laughed. "My dear girl, you cannot live without a husband. Who's to put a roof over your head? Food in your belly? Clothes on your back?"

The laughter faded from his eyes as he saw her wide generous mouth take a stubborn turn. He said brusquely, "I doubt your father will continue to support an undutiful and ungrateful daughter."

"Would you refuse to support Olivia in such a situation?" Phoebe demanded.

Cato responded curtly, "That is not to the point."

It was to the point since Olivia had even less intention than Phoebe of submitting to the dictates of a husband but Phoebe held her tongue. It was not for her to say.

"So rather than find yourself the Marchioness of Granville, living in comfort and security, you choose to fly off into the night, into a war-torn countryside infested with roaming soldiers who would rape and murder you as soon as look at you?" The sardonic note was back in his voice. He took another sip of wine and regarded her over the lip of his cup.

Phoebe, never one to beat about the bush, asked bluntly, "Lord Granville, would you please tell my father that you don't wish to marry me after all?"

"*No!*" Cato declared with a degree of force. "I will tell him no such thing. If you held me in distaste, then I would do so, but since your reasons for disliking this marriage are utterly without merit . . . the mere whims of a foolish girl . . . I will do no such thing."

"I am not foolish," Phoebe said in a low voice. "I am surely entitled to my opinions, sir."

"Sensible opinions, yes," he snapped. Then his expression softened somewhat. Although she was the same age as her sister Diana had been at her marriage, Phoebe was somehow less protected, he thought. She had fewer defenses. Diana had never exhibited the slightest vulnerability. She had moved through life, beautiful and perhaps as brittle as the finest porcelain. Graceful and regal as any swan. Cato didn't think she had ever questioned herself, or her entitlement. She knew who she was and what she was.

Diana's rounded, tangled little sister was a bird of a rather different feather, he thought. A rather ragged robin. The comparison surprised him into a fleeting smile.

Phoebe caught the flicker of the smile. It was surprising coming after that uncompromising statement. But then it had disappeared and she thought she'd been mistaken. Why would he smile in this horrible situation? Why would anybody smile?

"Go back to bed," Cato said. He handed her the cloakbag. "I'll not mention this to your father."

That was a concession. Phoebe understood that he

was in duty bound to tell Lord Carlton of his daughter's outrageous conduct. And with another father, it might have been no bad thing. But Lord Carlton would not consider that desperation could have fueled his daughter's actions. He would see only intolerable disrespect and would act accordingly.

But she couldn't quite bring herself to thank the marquis. The fact that he had the power to make her life miserable and chose not to exercise it didn't strike her as a matter for congratulation. She sketched a curtsy and left his study, making her way back to bed.

She undressed in the passage again, as anxious not to awaken Olivia as she'd been before. But for different reasons. Before, Olivia's ignorance would have protected her from any accusations of implication in Phoebe's flight. But now, the flight in ruins, if Olivia awoke Phoebe would have to tell her everything. And she had no idea how to explain this bolt from the blue that had felled her just before Christmas.

She'd been sitting in the apple loft, overlooking the stableyard, wrestling with a recalcitrant stanza of a poem she was writing, when Cato had ridden in with a troop of Roundhead cavalry. For two years Phoebe had seen the marquis of Granville go about his daily business and he'd barely impinged on her consciousness. And she'd known she hadn't impinged on his. But that crisp December day something very strange had happened.

Once more in her shift, Phoebe crept into bed beside Olivia. Her side of the bed was cold now and she inched closer to Olivia. She was wide-awake and lay looking up at the dark shape of the tapestry tester, idly picturing the bucolic scene of a May Day celebration that was depicted above her.

But her mind wouldn't let go of the memory of that moment before Christmas when she'd fallen in love . . . or lust . . . or whatever this hideous inconvenience was . . . with Cato, Marquis of Granville.

She'd watched him ride into the yard on his bay charger—something she'd seen many times. He'd been at the head of the troop, but when he'd drawn rein, Giles Crampton, his lieutenant, had come up beside him. Cato had leaned sideways to talk to him.

He was bareheaded and Phoebe had noticed how in the sunlight his dark brown hair had a flicker of gold running through it. He'd moved a gauntletted hand in a gesture to Giles, and Phoebe's heart had seemed to turn over. This kind of thing happened in poetry all the time. But, poet though she was, Phoebe was rarely plagued by an excess of sentiment and she had never imagined that verse was a veritable expression of reality.

And yet she'd sat in the apple loft, her quill dripping ink on her precious vellum, her apple halfway to her mouth, while the entire surface of her skin had grown hotter and hotter.

He'd dismounted and she'd gazed, transfixed, at the power behind his agile movements. She'd gazed at his profile, noticing for the first time the slight bump at the bridge of his long nose, the square jut of his chin, the fine, straight line of his mouth.

Phoebe grimaced fiercely in the darkness. It should have gone away . . . should have been a moment of angelic lunacy. But it hadn't gone away. She heard his voice, his foot on the stair, and she was rendered weak as a kitten. When he walked into a room, she had to leave or sit down before her knees betrayed her.

It was absurd. Yet she could do nothing about it. For a rational being, it was the ultimate injustice. And then two days ago her father had informed her that she was to replace her dead sister as Lord Granville's wife. For a moment the world had spun on its axis. The glorious prospect of achieving her heart's desire lay before her. Love and lust with the man whose simple presence was enough to set her heart beating like a drum.

The marquis had been standing beside her father. He had nodded to her.

Lord Granville had said nothing to her. Not one single word. He had simply nodded to her when her father had completed his announcement. After the announcement had come a brief catalogue of details relating to her dowry and the marriage settlements. And Cato had listened impassively. It was clear he'd heard it all before. Indeed, Phoebe had had the impression that he was either bored or pressed for time. But then he was always pressed for time. If he wasn't conducting some siege of a royalist stronghold somewhere in the Thames valley, he was meeting with Cromwell and the other generals of the New Model Army, planning strategy in their headquarters outside Oxford.

Phoebe and Olivia rarely saw him. They lived their own lives in the comfortable manor house that Cato had acquired in Woodstock, eight miles from Oxford, when the theatre of war had moved from the north of England to the south and west. He had not wanted to leave his family unprotected in Yorkshire so had brought them with him. Diana's death had made little or no difference to his life, it seemed to Phoebe.

It had, however, made a significant difference to Phoebe's and Olivia's. Freed of Diana's tyranny, they'd been able to pursue their own interests without hindrance, and until two days ago . . . or rather until just before Christmas, Phoebe amended . . . nothing had occurred to disturb their peace.

Now she was condemned to marry a man who would as soon marry a healthy sow if she came with the right dowry and the right breeding potential. Not even Dante's inferno had created such a fiendish torment. She was to be compelled to spend the rest of her life with a man whom she loved and lusted after to the point of obsession, and who barely acknowledged her existence.

And the unkindest cut of all — there was no one in whom she could confide. It was impossible to explain any of it to Olivia. There were no words . . . or at least none that Phoebe could think of.

Portia would understand, but Portia was in Yorkshire. Ecstatically happy with Rufus Decatur. And if Cato Granville hadn't been up and about at three in the morning, Phoebe would be on her way to Yorkshire.

With something resembling a groan, Phoebe flung herself onto her side and closed her eyes.